"Joanna Elm's insider knowledge of TV tabloids takes the reader on a breathless tour of the scandal business, kidnapping, chills, and murder. A tightly written debut novel that will have readers shivering in their jammies as they stay up till 3:00 A.M. to finish every page."
—Julia Grice, author of *Suspicion*

"Joanna Elm's debut is twisty, topical, and terrific. She's a born storyteller who has a great sense of people and place. SCANDAL has got all the elements of a major bestseller."
—E.J. Gorman, author of *The First Lady*

The glare of the headlights suddenly hit Kitty's rearview mirror again and, instinctively, she hit the brake.

It's the same car . . .

It can't be the same car . . .

Her heart thudded   one thought: someone   had spotted a woman dr   And, if that were the c   ning onto Island Road.   n Everglades Island runn   he other. If she crossed the   . . .ould, quite simply, be trapped.

She eased to a stop, conscious of her hands trembling on the wheel, willing the car behind her to pull out and drive over the bridge first.

Instead, the bright glare of high beams flooded her Blazer. She tried to focus on the driver behind her but all she could see was a silhouette.

The high beams flashed again.

He wanted her to move. Forward. Across that bridge.

Scandal

Joanna Elm

A TOM DOHERTY ASSOCIATES BOOK
NEW YORK

NOTE: If you purchased this book without a cover you should be aware that this book is stolen property. It was reported as "unsold and destroyed" to the publisher, and neither the author nor the publisher has received any payment for this "stripped book."

This is a work of fiction. All the characters and events portrayed in this book are fictitious, and any resemblance to real people or events is purely coincidental.

SCANDAL

Copyright © 1996 by Joanna Elm

All rights reserved, including the right to reproduce this book, or portions thereof, in any form.

Cover art by Tim Jacobus

A Forge Book
Published by Tom Doherty Associates, Inc.
175 Fifth Avenue
New York, N.Y. 10010

Forge® is a registered trademark of Tom Doherty Associates, Inc.

ISBN: 0-812-54471-4

First edition: February 1996

Printed in the United States of America

0 9 8 7 6 5 4 3 2 1

Acknowledgments

I am indebted to my agent and dear friend, Robert Diforio, for his tenacity on my behalf, and to my editor, Camille Cline, whose input was sensitive, creative, intelligent, and invaluable.

For clarifying facts and figures, I thank: Detective-Sergeant Michael Mason of the Palm Beach Police Department; Linda Foglia of the N.Y. State Department of Correctional Services, David Ernst of the N.Y. State Division of Parole, and Sharri Berg of *A Current Affair*.

Thank-yous, also, to Shirley and Phil Bunton for bringing relief on those hot Florida Friday nights; to my dear friend and colleague, Judy Calixto, who bolstered not only my insights into tabloid TV but also my ego, and to her husband, Michael Goldman, whose photographic skills, and patience, produced the author portrait.

I save my biggest thanks for the two most important men in my life: my son, Daniel, who was, and is, my inspiration—and my husband, Joe, who cracked the whip. Without his enduring support, encouragement, patience, critiquing skills, and unique talents there would be no *Scandal*.

❧ Chapter 1 ❧

Wednesday, August 30

*H*e could do it here. He could snatch Jamie Fitzgerald right out of the schoolyard.

He'd cased the neighborhood already. The school was on a quiet, residential street with no parking restrictions. A neatly trimmed ficus hedge ran around the perimeter of the yard. It was low—sparse enough for a good view of the play area but high enough to provide him with some cover.

He stared hard at the little ones in the yard. The kindergarten class had just been let out for their last break of the day. A young blonde stood by the side gate, her eyes scanning the yard. But she did not bother looking beyond the hedge. Nothing untoward there had caught her attention. Why should it? His car was unobtrusive. White Cadillacs were a dime a dozen in Boca Raton.

He reached behind the car seat for the pellet gun and cracked the window open. Resting the barrel on the top of the pane, tilting it upward, he fixed his sight on the jungle gym. Gingerly, he let his index finger curl but did not allow it to tighten around the trigger.

"Pow!" He mouthed the word silently and grinned. Then he placed the gun back behind the seat and once again played out the rest of the scene in his head: The sting of the pellet would make the boy lose his grip on the bars and fall to the ground ... maybe with a cry or a scream ... everybody would turn to look. ... The young blonde would scurry over to the boy, and nobody would notice the man getting out of a car, walking down the path and in through the schoolyard gate.

Excuse me, ma'am. I was just driving by. I saw what happened. The name's Doctor Stroud. Can I help?

Then she would notice him in his green hospital smock top. He'd lean over the boy, taking a few seconds to check his pulse and feel for fractured bones.

I think he'll be okay but I'm not sure. We should get him checked out in ER. A pause. *As a matter of fact, I'm on my way to work. I can have him there in five minutes. ...*

The plan was simple, carried out quickly—and it had worked before.

It could work here too, if Jamie Fitzgerald decided to climb the jungle gym; if the shot caught him in the right spot and caused him enough pain to stop him from bouncing right back up again; if the blonde bimbo, who watched the kids at playtime, got flustered enough. ...

Mothers in city playgrounds and parks got flustered. But would a teacher or a teacher's aide or whoever she was react the same way? Or would she tell him: *Thank you, but we'll wait for the paramedics?*

He leaned back against the leather headrest, sweat trickling down the side of his face. He would have liked to get a little cool air through the air conditioner vents but he dared not draw attention to himself with the noise of a running engine.

Cracking the window had only made it worse. The heat had seeped in and enveloped him instantly, choking his nostrils, his throat and even his eyes.

The image of an open beer can, droplets of condensation running down its icy sides, filled his mind but he blinked to erase its tempting image and looked instead across to the passenger seat where a copy of *Boca Raton* magazine lay open at a one-page profile on Kitty Fitzgerald. The headline read: "Top Tabloid TV Reporter Loves Boca." Underneath it a large color picture of Kitty Fitzgerald and her son, Jamie, dominated the page. The words were sparse but helpful. He had learned that Kitty Fitzgerald, Florida-based reporter for the top-rated tabloid TV show *Inside Copy*, worked out of a rented office on the premises of a Spanish-language TV station on Dixie Highway in Fort Lauderdale, while her son attended the Learning Academy in Boca Raton.

Lucky for him that the school year started before Labor Day in Palm Beach County, and he could get on with the job, pronto.

The article also reported that Kitty Fitzgerald's love of South Florida did not extend to its wildlife. The caption under the picture read: "I would rather run into a panhandler outside my front door than a Bufo toad," says resident Kitty Fitzgerald, who moved here from New York City three years ago. He had filed that little tidbit of information in the back of his mind.

The article, however, gave no clue to where she lived. And he had not been able to find her address in any of the local newspaper articles about her. (There had been three in the last year.) Nor was she listed in the telephone book. Nor in the tax rolls.

He had done his research well. Of course. No one had ever accused him of being stupid. The first shrink who had ever examined him had estimated his IQ around 140.

He stared into the yard again, his eyes scanning the little heads as he chewed on the soft, fleshy skin around his thumbnail. It took him a couple of minutes to pick out Jamie Fitzgerald, running across the yard with another boy. They were running toward him, to the ficus hedge.

They stopped, their arms and legs shooting out in wild, angled karate chops.

"A—i-aaa!"

"A—i-aaa!"

He stared at his target's little face and took note of the dancing, mischievous eyes, the sweet little mouth that opened to reveal white, even baby teeth, and the strawberry-blonde hair falling across his forehead in straight, neat bangs. Jamie Fitzgerald was a handsome little boy, all right. So was his friend. He studied the two: Both were blonde and about the same size and build. They could have been twins.

He looked at the magazine picture and then again at Jamie Fitzgerald. He wiped the sweat off his face with the back of his hand as he concentrated on finding some distinguishing characteristics. Something he could focus on, at a distance . . .

That was the big problem with the schoolyard. There were so many damn kids running around, milling and darting, here and there, all over the damn place.

Take it easy. There's no rush, he warned himself. Not yet. He had time to get it right. And he would get it right. He was thorough and smart and patient. At least, he always had been until the unfortunate accident with Billy Wright. But there was no point in thinking about that now. That was past and gone. Jamie Fitzgerald was his future.

In about an hour, school would be over for the day and little Jamie would have to head for home. And where Jamie went, he would follow. He would get his chance to check out the house and the street. Maybe it was one of those streets where kids played outside alone. Maybe Jamie rode a bike or, better still, a skateboard. Everyone knew that small boys on skateboards were accidents waiting to happen . . . especially if something caused them to lose their balance.

And if he could snatch the boy from outside his own home, all the better. The Fitzgerald bitch would never forgive herself. Oh, the anguish, heartbreak, and guilt. Oh, the beauty of it.

He checked his watch and ran his tongue over his dry, thick lips. He would have to sweat it out for another hour.

But the boy was worth it. Jamie Fitzgerald was a double whammy—a $100,000 ticket to the future, and an old score settled. All in one.

It had never been this good.

❧ *Chapter 2* ❧

*K*itty Fitzgerald hurried across the parking lot. Her car was parked less than two hundred feet from the office door, but before she'd covered half the distance she felt the familiar prickling sensation of perspiration breaking out around her neck and hairline. There would be no relief from the heat for at least another month. And maybe not even then.

She dabbed irritably at her upper lip and rummaged in her skirt pocket for her car keys. As she inserted her key into the lock she sensed a sudden movement behind her.

"Miss Fitzgerald?"

She spun around, dropping the keys. "Yes?"

She did not stoop to pick up the keyring even though, eyeing the stranger in his neatly pressed tan slacks and striped, long-sleeved shirt with French cuffs, she felt the thumping of her heart subside a little.

"I'm sorry, I didn't mean to startle you." He held out a business card. "Benjamin Fearon. I'm an associate with

Singer, Lamb, and Mellen." A pause. "Do you have a moment?"

Kitty recognized the name of the law firm. Singer stood for David Singer, a Fort Lauderdale attorney who, five weeks before, had been found dead—stabbed fifty-eight times—in a sleazy Dixie Highway motel.

Police had initially put out the story that he had been lured to the motel on false pretenses. But one of Kitty's police contacts in the Fort Lauderdale PD had tipped her off to a very different saga of a tormented double life: Singer, respected citizen, and beloved husband and father-of-two, apparently had spent his nights looking for a little side action in gay bars and hangouts.

Sex, scandal, and murder with a bizarre twist. The tragedy had contained all the elements of a perfect *Inside Copy* story. Until Kitty had discovered, to her dismay, that Singer's children were two little boys, just five and seven years of age.

"What can I do for you, Mr. Fearon?"

"I'm here to do something for you, Miss Fitzgerald." His jaw tightened. "I'm giving you fair warning that there will be very serious repercussions if you air your story about David Singer."

"Really!" Kitty sighed inwardly. She didn't much care for the lawyer's threatening tone, nor did she want to get involved in defending a story that she had soon regretted pitching.

Benjamin Fearon removed his dark glasses and stared intently at her. "First of all, Miss Fitzgerald, let's start with your harassment of Mrs. Singer. You and your cameraman intruded on her privacy and the children's privacy and trespassed on her property to videotape her home."

Kitty shook her head. If nothing else, she could, at least, defend herself on the legalities. "We didn't trespass, Mr. Fearon. We were on a public street. And we most certainly did not videotape the children."

She recalled the footage Bernie, her cameraman, had produced after his stakeout of the Singer home: shots of the sprawling, pastel-yellow stucco mansion on a corner lot on the Intracoastal, and of a swingset and jungle gym in the backyard where it sloped down to the water. She had intercut that footage with the shabby, peeling, pink facade of the Heavenly Hour Motel where Singer had gone looking for a good time but instead had been slashed to death. For good measure she had included shots of the room where dark stains of blood were still visible on the yellow shag carpet.

The next day the local paper had run a picture of Singer's children at his memorial service. The caption mentioned that Darren, the younger son, had turned five the previous month. Just like Jamie.

She had found herself staring at the sweet, somber little faces and her heart had gone out to the two little boys. Responding to what she could only explain as some sort of maternal attack of conscience, she had immediately returned to the editing room to recut the tape, taking out the shots of the bloody carpet.

Benjamin Fearon made some sort of noise that sounded like a snort of disgust. "You harassed and badgered Mrs. Singer for an interview—"

Kitty interrupted. "One letter and one phone call is not exactly badgering."

"A severely distressing phone call," Fearon erupted, "asking her to talk about her husband's *bizarre* lifestyle! I'm talking about inflicting grave emotional distress on a widow and two babies. . . . Sandra Singer is my sister so I know exactly what she's going through."

Kitty silently noted that Fearon wasn't making any attempt to deny the actual story of David Singer's "bizarre lifestyle" and momentary resentment flared inside her. She considered slamming right back at him with the obvious comment that she was merely reporting the facts and any distress felt by Mrs. Singer was surely of her husband's own making. *You play. You pay.*

But she bit back the retort. David Singer was dead. He

wasn't the one who was going to be paying for anything anymore.

She became aware that her silk tank-top was damp and clinging to her back and the strap of her tote was digging painfully into her shoulder. She had emptied her overflowing, neglected office in-tray into the bag and thrown in a bundle of local, week-old newspapers, planning to catch up on her mail and reading at home. It would all have to wait until Jamie was in bed, of course, so that she could work without the threat of a Batmobile scattering her paperwork or a Power Ranger teleporting through the newspapers in the eternal quest to vanquish Rita Repulsa and Lord Zed. But it had to get done tonight.

The paperwork had piled up over a busy week. Unusually busy for this time of year. Summer was generally a slow season and most of the other tabloid TV shows went into reruns. But not *Inside Copy*. As Todd, her executive producer, had so profoundly pointed out, "Crime and scandal never take a vacation, my dear."

Especially not in South Florida, thought Kitty. On Monday, a Boca Raton accountant had filed for bankruptcy, and two hours later he had gunned down his wife as she exited Bloomingdale's in the Town Center Mall.

On Tuesday, a Pompano councilman who had campaigned on an antiporn platform had been arrested with his mistress for performing lewd and lascivious acts in their backyard hot tub (home video available for $500 from the neighbor and irate father-of-three who had filed the complaint).

This morning, Wednesday, police in Jupiter had arrested a modern-day Robin Hood, a computer hacker who had gained access to the accounts of a local bank and disbursed their profits to selected local charities.

In between there had been follow-up calls on a half-dozen leads including a worthless tip from *Inside Copy*'s anchorwoman, Dana Lewis, who had heard from one of her equally worthless sources that Madonna was getting married at her Miami palazzo.

Sex, crime, celebrity gossip were all part of the *Inside Copy* mix. Unfortunately, of all the leads she was working on, only the Singer story had been close enough to completion when Todd called this morning badgering her for something, anything, to plug a three-minute hole in tomorrow's show.

She wondered if it was worth explaining herself to Benjamin Fearon. But what was she going to say? That she had tried her best to shelve the story? That she had done a minimum amount of work on it, then put it on the backburner, hoping Todd would forget about it? The story had already died in the local media, and as far as she knew none of the other tabloid TV shows were sniffing around it, either. She had argued about it, in fact, just this morning—before overnighting it to New York. "Come on, Todd, it's not a major exposé. This is not cancer research we're doing here, and there're two little kids involved. Can you imagine them going to school, being taunted by their classmates after that story airs?"

Kitty cleared her throat, aware that Fearon was eyeing her quizzically. "I'm sorry, Mr. Fearon. I understand you're doing this for Mrs. Singer and the children. I sympathize . . . I have a son myself—"

The lawyer interrupted, seizing the new opening she had given him. "So put yourself in that position, Miss Fitzgerald. Suppose it was your husband—"

"I don't have a husband," Kitty cut him off abruptly. "What I'm saying is, that as sorry as I am, there's really nothing I can do about it now. It's out of my hands. The story's already on its way to New York."

Fearon kicked at a small stone on the blacktop with a sudden viciousness. "Why do you have to bring it all up again, now, just when the kids are beginning to adjust?" He paused. "I don't suppose there's any point in calling your boss, is there?"

"You could try," Kitty replied without any enthusiasm. An image of Todd spouting his favorite quote—something he'd read about tabloid journalists having the ethics of tapeworms and the compassion of slot machines—flashed before her eyes. It was the standard by which he judged himself and his staff.

Fearon slammed his fist into his thigh. "You don't give a damn, do you? You don't care who you hurt. It's what you people do all the time. All you care about is titillating your viewers with smut and scandal."

He turned and strode off across the parking lot.

Kitty watched him get into a sleek, silver Lincoln Continental and slam the door shut before she finally stooped to scoop up her keyring from the ground. Then she got into her Chevy Blazer and switched on the engine, waiting for cold air to blast through the vents.

She stabbed at the eject button on her tape deck, feeling shaken and deflated by the confrontation. She was angry with herself. She knew she could have argued more forcefully with Todd. She could have pointed out that the story was already several weeks old or that David Singer was not a celebrity like Nicole Brown Simpson. But her argument had ceased when Todd laughed out loud. "You're going soft, Fitzgerald. The sun's gotten to you. Maybe it's time we brought you home."

His comment had been a sharp, swift reminder of the rumors swirling around the newsroom in New York. There was talk of heavy budget-cutting. Already, the show's Los Angeles bureau had been pruned, and the Dallas bureau was down to a lone freelance cameraperson. She was aware that the closure of the Florida bureau was currently on the agenda in the executive suite.

When Kitty had joined the show, *Inside Copy* had been one of only three tabloid TV shows. Since then six more copycats had been launched, all of them competing for the same stories and audience. The net effect had been lower ratings and a drop in revenues, then the inevitable cost-cutting.

She sighed and retrieved Jamie's tape of Disney tunes and replaced it with her own favorite as she pulled out of the car park. Turning north on Dixie Highway, she reflected how different things had been three years before. Back then, with the show a clear ratings winner, Todd in his most expansive mood had decided that *Inside Copy* had to have permanent reporters and bureaus in the top crime states in the country. He had offered Florida to Kitty.

She had not wanted to move away from the main newsroom to a TV outpost plagued by natural horrors like hurricanes and tornadoes and deadly bugs. The notion of living on reclaimed swampland infested by fire ants, encephalitis-infected mosquitoes, and toxin-spitting Bufo toads had filled her with disgust. But all that had been offset by her need to give herself and Jamie a fresh start. And she had jumped at the opportunity to put twelve hundred miles between herself and Jeff—and his relentless phone calls begging her to come and visit him in Green Haven.

In the last three years she had managed to find things to like about South Florida: living near the beach ... being able to swim in an ocean that was never cold ... playing tennis year-round ... never having to wear pantyhose. More important, for the price of a drafty, one-bedroom Manhattan loft she was able to rent a bright three-bedroom courtyard house with a pool. Jamie loved to step out of his bedroom into a pool, anytime he wanted. Jamie loved Florida. He loved his new school. He loved his new friends. He'd told her he wanted to stay in Boca Raton forever.

Even so, she had never seriously considered making Florida her permanent home until she met Frank Maguire. As she eased into the traffic traveling north on the interstate, she allowed herself a wistful smile, turned up the volume on her tape, and let the disco beat throb through the car as Donna Summer sang about wanting "*hot love, baby.*" She sang with her for a bar or two, Donna's lyrics prompting her to think about the sexy Palm Beach detective.

He had been a part of her life for two years now. Charming, smart, good-humored, and straight-as-an-arrow, he was the kind of guy her sister, Marcy, described as a "keeper." He had been honest with her from the start, making it clear that he wasn't interested in playing games. He had told her three months after their meeting that they belonged together.

It had taken Kitty a while longer to come to the same conclusion. She had hung back, assessing the situation more analytically, not allowing herself to believe that she had found a man who understood her and who didn't feel threatened either by her work or her son.

She had made it clear to Frank that Jamie must come first. That it could not be any other way because she was all that Jamie had. Jamie's father was not and never had been a part of their lives and she bore the sole responsibility for her son's well-being and happiness.

By the time the rumors about the closure of the Florida bureau had started swirling earlier in the summer, she was well beyond the stage of wondering about Frank Maguire. Bureau or no bureau, returning to New York was not a move she thought about anymore. If the bureau closed, she would just look around for other work, she'd told Frank, putting on a brave face.

What she had not spelled out was that a job in local TV news would not give her the independence or flexibility she had in working for a bureau, nor the generous salary that came with appearing on a nationally syndicated show.

Which is why, now, she felt under constant pressure to keep Todd and New York happy. To show Todd that, when others failed him, he could rely on the Florida bureau to deliver. Which is why she had cobbled together the Singer story and sent it to him, pronto. . . .

She eased her foot off the gas pedal, realizing she had hit seventy-five. Stupid. Whether she was five minutes late or fifty, she'd still have to pay the ten dollars for the afterschool program. No point in driving like a demon now. Except that she wanted to see Jamie. See his impish, sweet little face, hear his cheery "Hi, Mom!" and listen to the chatter about his day.

She exited the interstate at Palmetto Park Road, making the left turns automatically. Then the final left, and one right, and she was driving past the schoolyard. As always she slowed to catch a glimpse of her son.

Sometimes it would be a few seconds before she spotted him, playing in the crowd. Sometimes she would forget what he'd been wearing that morning, and it would take a few seconds longer to scan the playground. And she would feel her heart thumping anxiously . . . until she saw him.

ℋChapter 3

ℋe saw the white Chevy Blazer swing into the street and the flash of red curls as she drove past him. But it wasn't until she stepped out of the car that he was sure it was Kitty Fitzgerald.

He glanced across at the picture in the magazine, just to double check. Then back to the real thing: bouncing red curls; no tits; flashy smile. It was Kitty Fitzgerald, all right. In the flesh, though, she looked shorter and skinnier than she did on TV. Her skimpy tank-top revealed delicate arms and wrists and the short skirt showed off slim legs.

He watched her walk to the school gate and wave at the boy who came running toward her. She snatched up his lunchbox from a big redwood picnic table under the awning.

Finally, he could switch on the engine and get some cold air. His green smock top was drenched with sweat. Good thing he had purchased a couple of outfits from the costume store. He put his face up to the vents for a couple of seconds, then immediately turned his attention back to his prey.

They strolled together to the Chevy Blazer, mother and son. She, with her arm around the boy's shoulders. The boy was trying to tell her something and she stooped down to listen to him. She looked as if she had all the time in the world for him. No hurrying him along . . . no impatient tugging at the boy's hand. Throwing back her head, she laughed out loud at something he said. Then they ran to the car.

He pulled out behind her and made the turn at the top of the road with her. Then on Military Trail, dropping back a little, he let a few cars slide in between them but kept his eyes glued to the roof of the Blazer, making all the turns with her. First a left, then a right, and another right. He was about to follow her on another right turn into a long driveway when he realized, just in time, that it led to a gatehouse.

A uniformed security guard sat in the gatehouse and there was a barrier across the road. The barrier lifted to allow Kitty Fitzgerald's car through, then snapped down again.

He drove a couple of hundred yards beyond the driveway before making a U-turn to retrace his route. Pulling to the side of the road, he stopped across from the gatehouse, switched on his hazard lights, got out, and opened the trunk. He stuck his head inside to appear as if he was looking for something but his eyes darted to the entryway of the development.

From where he stood, he could plainly see the big green lettering on the eight-foot-high wall that separated the development from the main street where he was parked. The letters spelled out the name: PALM GLADES.

Of course. He should have known that Kitty Fitzgerald would live in a gated community. Everyone in Boca Raton seemed to live behind gates and walls.

He slammed the trunk shut and got back into the Cadillac, watching as cars pulled up to the gatehouse. Now he noticed there were two entry lanes. One marked for residents, the other for visitors. The residents drove through without stopping, evidently opening the barrier with remote control openers. Visitors checked in with the guard. He saw the guard walking behind the vehicle and noting down the license plate numbers on a notepad.

Beyond the gatehouse the road divided. He'd seen Kitty Fitzgerald turn right at the signpost. A left arrow on the signpost showed the way to a Clubhouse and Rental Office.

He blinked and stared at the Rental Office sign and then leaned back in his seat to think.

He wondered what Kitty and her son were up to. What were they doing right now? She was probably pouring the boy a glass of milk or juice . . . handing him a plate of cookies . . . listening to his chatter about the day in school. Then the boy would shoot off into the backyard or go out for a ride on his bike. He was sure the boy would be allowed to ride and play on the street, in a development like Palm Glades. Maybe there was a playground that he would ride to. . . .

His thoughts focused on his plan. The way he saw it, he had two shots at snatching Jamie Fitzgerald. So tomorrow he would start early. He would be at the school gates when Kitty Fitzgerald dropped off her son. He would get a fix on what the boy was wearing. Then he would wait for the right moment in the schoolyard. And if the moment didn't come—or if the blonde bimbo turned down his offer of help—he would double back to Palm Glades for an appointment at the Rental Office. Then he would "lose" himself in the development until Jamie Fitzgerald came home from school.

Tomorrow, by the end of the day, he would have Jamie Fitzgerald.

On Friday, Kitty Fitzgerald would get the videotape and note.

On Saturday, he'd make the first phone call and demand fifty-thousand dollars.

On Sunday, he'd call again and double the price.

By Monday, Kitty Fitzgerald would be climbing the walls.

He flipped off his hazard lights and pulled out into the roadway, aware that his pulse was racing.

He couldn't wait for tomorrow.

❧ Chapter 4 ❧

Thursday, August 31

The ringing of the phone woke Kitty just before seven, and she reached for the handset without opening her eyes.

"Time to get that sweet little butt out of bed." Frank's cheery voice made her smile sleepily, sending her thoughts back to the previous evening. It had been well after midnight when he'd reluctantly tucked her in and kissed her good night. He had wanted to stay. He always did. But the thought of getting a call in the middle of the night and finding himself more than twenty miles from the incident was enough to drive him back to his own patch in Palm Beach most weeknights.

And so the morning calls had become part of their routine. But this one seemed much too early. Kitty opened one eye, glanced at her alarm clock, and groaned.

Frank's laugh echoed on the line. "Come on, sweets, wake up. It's going to be a busy day."

"For you maybe." Kitty burrowed down in her bed.

"For you too."

Kitty's eyes fluttered open. "Oh?"

There was a pause at the other end. "I'm on my way to the North End . . ." There were sounds of a muffled conversation at Frank's end.

"Frank? Who are you talking to?"

"Don's in the car with me. We're on our way to work."

Kitty propped herself up on one elbow. "You're on your way to work at seven in the morning. . . . Are you trying to tell me something, sweets?"

There was another pause and more muffled conversation. Then Frank laughed. "I guess I wouldn't be if the patrol officer who called in the incident had used something other than his car radio. As it is, I'm sure the news has been picked up on scanners all over Palm Beach. It'll be hitting the wires within the next half-hour."

Kitty sat up abruptly. "What, Frank? What are you talking about?"

"Possible homicide. Female victim in her fifties."

Kitty gripped the phone. A murder in Palm Beach. That would make it only the second one of the year. "Is there a name to go with the victim?" She held her breath.

"Marina Dee Haley."

"Jesus!" Kitty propelled herself out of bed and onto her feet so swiftly that for a second or two everything turned black in front of her eyes. "Frank! Are you serious? What happened?"

"She was found beside the pool this morning by her butler and housekeeper. That's as much as I know right now." He paused again. Then, "Don tells me she used to be big on TV."

Kitty sank back onto her bed, a vivid picture of Marina in her head: Tall, statuesque, with platinum blonde hair swept back into a French bun, Marina Dee Haley had been a familiar sight striding the hallways of WPEN-TV in New York.

"Oh my God!" Kitty shook her head and lapsed into silence again.

"Hey, Kitty, are you okay?" Frank's voice echoed on the line. "Did you know her?"

"Yes." Kitty cleared her throat. "She used to tape her talk show at our TV station in New York."

"You were friends?"

"Not really." Kitty paused. "Marina wasn't the friendly type. I knew Jeff, her son, better. He was her executive producer. We worked on the same floor."

"Is that right?" She heard more muffled conversation between Frank and his partner. Then he was back to her. "Any ideas where we could contact him now?"

Kitty hesitated, realizing that the name hadn't set off any bells clanging in Frank's head. Then she cleared her throat again. "I'd check with the warden of Green Haven, upstate New York."

"The correctional facility?" Frank sounded surprised. "What did he do?"

"Shot Marina's husband."

"Dead?"

Kitty laughed, abruptly. "Yes, quite dead. Jeff Haley's serving five to fifteen for manslaughter."

Before Frank could ask any more questions, she added, "Listen, hon, I can fill you in later but it's a long story and I need to get moving now. Where's the house?"

Frank gave her an address off North Ocean Boulevard. "It's on the beach."

"I'll see you soon."

"I'm sure." Frank laughed and hung up.

The moment he was off the line Kitty speed-dialed Bernie Rutkowski's number. She needed to brief her cameraman on the story and have him pick up a satellite news truck from the rental company they used on occasions when stories demanded live shots. Then showering quickly she wrapped a towel around herself and picked up the phone again, this time to speed-dial the assignment desk in New York.

Ernie Platzer, the assistant assignment editor, picked up

on the first ring and she gave him the scoop as she towel-dried her hair.

"You'll need to get one of the p.a.'s to dig up Marina footage . . . and file footage on the shooting of Larry Davenport, and get someone to check with Green Haven. . . . See if they're going to release Jeff Haley for the funeral. You'll probably need to get a crew up there, just in case—"

"Whoa!" Ernie interrupted. "Run that by me again, would you?"

Nestling her remote between ear and shoulder, Kitty sighed and ran to the kitchen, where she flung a Pop-tart in the toaster for Jamie's breakfast before running to retrieve a pair of pants and a T-shirt for her son from the dryer in the laundry room.

In the meantime, she had to repeat every direction for Ernie, who was enthusiastic but somewhat inexperienced.

"Okay," she spoke slowly, "you know who I'm talking about, right? Marina Dee Haley as in Oprah and Sally Jessy Raphael. She used to tape her talk show at our station, so you should have no problem with her footage."

"I know who Marina Haley is." Ernie sounded peeved. "But I thought she'd died years ago."

Kitty grimaced. "No, Ernie. She retired, five years ago, after Jeff Haley shot her husband. Try our news files for June tenth."

"Wow!" She heard the awe in Ernie's voice. "How do you remember dates like that?"

She deliberately ignored the question. "And Andrea should book the bird so that I can feed my stuff to you . . . and have Todd call me when he gets in, okay? I'll be on the car phone." She was about to hang up when she suddenly remembered her sad run-in with Benjamin Fearon. "Oh, by the way, Ernie, do me a favor. I Fedexed a package to Todd yesterday. When it comes in, grab it and send it straight back to me, will you? It really needs more work and you won't be needing it today."

"You got it, Kitty. Eh, how long do you think your piece will run?"

Kitty rolled her eyes. "Holy shit, Ernie! Think O. J. Simpson. I'm anticipating Todd will want to clear the deck for this one. With my report from the scene and the background on Marina you'll fill twenty-two minutes, trust me."

She hung up just as Jamie walked past her and reached across the counter for his breakfast.

"Oooh, mamma mamma mia," he chanted. "Shit! Shit! Shit! I heard you say that word, Mom. Shit! Shit!" he chanted, wide-eyed and tousle-haired.

Kitty stifled a grin. "C'mon Jamie, we're going to have to hustle this morning."

"But I heard you say it, Mom." He took a bite out of the Pop-Tart.

"That doesn't mean you have to repeat it. And if I hear you repeat it . . ." She stood in the doorway with what she hoped was a menacing look on her face. "Here. When you've finished eating, here's your shorts and T-shirt."

Jamie glanced at the clothes. "Aw, Mom! Not *that* T-shirt. I gotta wear my Power Rangers one today!"

"Jamie, for heaven's sake! I'm asking you to move it." She stopped when she saw his lower lip jut out, a defiant look on his face.

"But Mom, Timmy and Kevin and Alex are going to wear their Power Ranger T-shirts today. If I don't wear mine they won't let me play with them. . . . Mom, I'm *not* going to wear that one."

Kitty gritted her teeth, knowing it would take too long to argue it out. "Okay, okay." She turned and headed back down the hall to the laundry room. If the shirt wasn't in the hamper it had to be in the dryer. Despite her best intentions, clean clothes never quite made it from dryer to dresser drawers unless Sharon was around. On her own she had to cut corners somewhere.

Luckily, she found the desired T-shirt, slightly wrinkled but clean, at the bottom of the dryer. She brought it back into the kitchen, glad she'd made the effort when she saw her son's face light up.

"Okay sport, now let's go." She prodded him and headed back to her bedroom, ignoring the whispered *"Shit! Shit! Shit!"* that followed her down the hallway.

She flung open her closet door and eyed two unopened packages on the floor from Spiegel mail order. She shook her head no. She needed something smart and cool that wouldn't need ironing. She slipped into her comfortable, cotton-knit Jockeys before reaching for a freshly dry-cleaned, linen-weave suit. The tapered jacket hugged her waist and the short skirt revealed, perhaps, too much leg, but the oatmeal color brought out the light tan of her skin and the reddish auburn highlights in her hair. It always looked good on camera—and it was one of Frank's favorites.

A winner, she decided, grabbing for her tote and yelling for Jamie to run for the car.

Despite her son's intrusive, happy chatter her thoughts were already on her work as she drove to the school. She knew she faced a long day. Probably many long, hard days. There would be a lot to cover over the next week—the murder, the investigation, the funeral—and hopefully the arrest of a suspect. Marina's murder was going to be an enormous story. Possibly bigger than O.J. Simpson's.

Marina had had millions of fans. Her show, *Let's Talk,* had been the top-rated talk show for years until eventually Oprah had knocked her out of the No. 1 slot. But then Marina had grabbed back the headlines with her surprise marriage to the much younger Larry Davenport. A marriage that had ended swiftly and shockingly just a few months later.

In the next few weeks, Kitty knew, it would all be regurgitated, the whole story of Marina's stormy life and career. Old friends, acquaintances, colleagues, and rivals would be tracked down and quizzed for their memories and tributes—and even their theories on the murder.

As soon as the news hit the wires hundreds of story co-

ordinators, producers, and research assistants would be put
to work digging up ancient file footage and squinting their
way through hundreds of inches of newspaper microfilm
about Marina.

Kitty's stomach suddenly churned abruptly. Buried
somewhere in those hundreds of inches of microfilm was
her own name. Somewhere among the news reports of
Larry Davenport's killing and the police investigation into
the shooting some enthusiastic researcher would come
across the headline—and the front page story—that had
purported to expose Kitty's relationship with Marina's son.

She blinked as if to erase the memory. She didn't want
to think about it. She didn't want to think about Jeff Haley.
She especially didn't want to think about Jeff showing up
in Palm Beach, in the middle of her big story.

"Mom! We're here. Bye!" Jamie's voice interrupted her
thoughts as they pulled up outside the school doors. He
was already opening the car door and she had to move
quickly to grab him for a big good-bye hug. Then he was
gone and she put her foot down on the gas, harder than
she'd intended so that she shot out of the school driveway,
almost colliding with a white Cadillac parked dangerously
close to the exit gates.

❧ *Chapter 5* ❧

$\mathcal{K}$itty was not the first reporter to arrive on the scene. As she pulled up outside Marina Dee Haley's beachfront mansion, she noticed a Channel Six news van parked right behind the news truck Bernie had rented for the day. She wondered if the Channel Six crew had picked up the information on their police scanner or had been tipped off like herself. Either way, they must have had a truck in the area. There was no way they could have beaten her to the scene if they'd come from their base in Miami.

She had put her foot down hard on the gas on I-95, flying up the interstate at seventy-five, and had faced no major slowdowns until she reached the Flagler Bridge. Waiting for the raised bridge to go down across the Intracoastal, she had applied her mascara. A red light at the top of Royal Poinciana had given her twenty seconds for lipstick. She had ignored the 35-mph-speed limit on the final stretch of North Ocean Boulevard and had taken the curve around the Kennedys' former Palm Beach estate at a speedy but not dangerous forty-five.

In all, a little more than ninety minutes had elapsed between Frank's phone call and her arrival outside the mansion.

She skirted the line of cars and walked toward the three-some outside Marina's wrought-iron gates. She nodded to Bernie and acknowledged the Channel Six reporter, Francesca Rodriguez, and her cameraman, Tony.

Bernie and Tony, their minicams already hoisted on their shoulders, were shooting through the gate railings, although there was no sign of any life except the uniformed police officer who stood guard at the double mahogany front doors. Within an hour or two, Kitty knew, the two cameramen would be swallowed up in the crowd. Satellite news trucks, camera crews, and reporters would swarm into the street jockeying for positions at the crime scene.

Kitty took a minute to glance over the imposing, two-story, salmon-colored stucco house with its terra-cotta roof. Green shutters framed all the windows. A long gravel driveway ran from the gates to the front door and then skirted to the left and along the side of the house to the garage area. Kitty could see a second story above the garage through the branches of an enormous, old, sprawling, banyan tree that dominated the front courtyard.

Kitty estimated the size of the rambling house at around six to seven thousand square feet. It looked beautifully maintained. Kitty had no idea what Marina might have paid for the house, but nowadays oceanfront property in Palm Beach did not leave much change out of a purchase of five million. And then the real expenses kicked in— Palm Beach properties like this one required the services of a little army of household staff, landscapers, exterminators, pool maintainers, and security companies.

She stared at the five vehicles parked in the driveway. She recognized Frank's maroon Thunderbird. There was also an EMS ambulance, two patrol cars, and a dirty white Ford station wagon, which, Kitty surmised, belonged to the household staff. Swankier households in Palm Beach provided their staff with Mercedes station wagons. Marina evidently had not been too concerned about her image.

Kitty turned to Francesca. "Have you been here long?"

The reporter shook her head. "Maybe five minutes ahead of you. We were on our way to cover the Blair trial at the courthouse when we got diverted." She paused and shook her head. "This is bizarre. Did Marina Dee Haley have a live-in lover? Or did she get married again?"

Kitty laughed, grasping Francesca's ready assumption that the murder, surely, had to be a crime of domestic violence. Palm Beach homicides usually were. Residents of Royal Palm Beach did not become victims of random violence, much less random murder. They lived safely and securely in their own little world, insulated not only by money but also by geography.

The spit of sand on which the town sat was bordered by the ocean to the east and was separated from the mainland by the Intracoastal to the west. There were only four access routes into the town, three of them bridges across the Intracoastal that could be automatically raised by the police at the first sign of trouble. Here, at the North End, access was even more restricted. A couple of hundred yards to the north of Marina's mansion the road and the spit of land stopped at the Lake Worth inlet.

"I believe she lived here alone," Kitty finally replied. "But I'm not sure. I never see anything about her in the papers anymore. Last thing I read was she'd gotten a big fat advance for her autobiography." Kitty adjusted her sunglasses and walked over to Bernie, nudging him to follow her down the road to where she had spotted an access path between houses leading to the beach.

From the beach, she figured they would get a view of the crime scene. No use hanging out front waiting for a police spokesperson. *Inside Copy* required an in-your-face approach. They needed graphic footage or, at the very-least, something like the now-famous shots of the bloody walkway where the slain bodies of Nicole Brown Simpson and Ronald Goldman had been found in L.A.

Bernie took the lead when they reached the dunes. At the North End the beach ran wide and the dunes separating the mansions from the sand and ocean were thickly covered with grass and undergrowth.

Kitty grimaced as she stepped through them, feeling sharp little grains of sand in her open-toed sandals. She ran her fingers through her hair. It was dry by now but felt as if it was sticking out at odd angles all over the place.

"How does my hair look, Bern?"

He grinned lazily. "Like you combed it with a hand grenade, chief. Want to borrow my cap?"

She'd have to run her brush through it before going on camera but there was no point in doing anything now. She knew that in about two minutes damp tendrils would be clinging to the back of her neck.

It was overcast but the air felt heavy and humid, unrelieved by any noticeable ocean breeze. There would be a storm later in the morning, for sure. One of those humdinger summer storms with lightning, thunder, and a torrential downpour that would do nothing to relieve the stickiness of the day. She glanced down into the undergrowth beneath her feet, checking for ants.

"C'mon," Bernie egged her on. "There's no bugs out here. Too close to the ocean."

Kitty laughed. "I know. They like it better in my backyard." She clenched her teeth and followed Bernie till they were directly behind Marina's mansion with a clear view across the lawn to the pool area.

The crime scene technicians were already busy at work. Two men were grubbing around the shrubbery that surrounded the pool. Another man was checking around the cabana. Don West, Frank's partner, was taking Polaroids. Kitty noticed an overturned chaise and a white bathrobe lying next to it. Then she saw Frank crouched on his haunches beside Marina.

Her body lay splayed out on the pool deck. Frank, leaning over Marina, obscured some of the view, but she could see long tanned legs, a glimpse of bare buttock, matted dark blonde hair fanning out around her head, and Marina's left hand, already bagged in plastic.

Kitty steadied herself as Bernie started his camera rolling. "Get a wide-angle shot, Bernie. Pull out a bit, don't do a tight shot. Remember, we're on during the dinner hour. Give Todd something he can use."

"I think I got a flash of bare butt, but they can digitize that."

"Okay." Kitty's attention was momentarily distracted as she stared at Frank in conversation with Don. She was not sure if he'd seen her with Bernie. He wasn't looking in their direction so she allowed herself a moment to study her lover in action.

He was a big man, tall and broad-shouldered with a strong face that was not movie-star handsome. Kitty had once teased him that the closest he'd ever come to resembling a movie star was when Kevin Costner had buzzed his hair for *The Bodyguard*.

Now she noticed the animated expression on his face. He looked confident and in control. Of course. Frank had plenty of experience with murder investigations. He had burned out on them as a detective with the Philadelphia Police Department. Reluctant to quit the profession he had opted, instead, for a total change of pace and location, even though Palm Beach PD policy required him to spend a year back on the streets as a uniformed police officer before he could resume working as a detective again.

Kitty nudged her cameraman. "C'mon, let's see if he'll talk before the ME gets here."

"Hey detective, wait up!" She started across the grass toward Frank, who spun around to face her.

"Kitty!" He strode to her, holding his hands with palms out to stop her from moving any closer. "Back up a bit, hon. You're trampling all over the crime scene."

Kitty stopped abruptly and shrugged. "Okay, I'm not going any further." She paused and lowered her voice. "C'mon, sweets. You didn't expect me to wait out front with the rest of the pack, did you?"

Frank shook his head again and grinned, nudging her gently back toward the dunes where Kitty dug her heels in literally and figuratively. "Come on, Frank. We're off the property now. Ten seconds of your time, that's all I need. You're going to have to talk to the press sometime."

Frank glanced around. "What do you need?"

"The usual," Kitty grinned at him. "Who, what, why, when. . . . Start with how."

"I'm not the ME, Kitty, but my guess would be that head injuries were a contributing factor. Possibly fractured skull. Possibly a massive brain hemorrhage." He pointed up a path leading to the house. "That's where it happened. It looks like he attacked her on her way to the pool. There's blood spattered all over that side wall up there. . . ." He paused and lowered his voice. "You can't quote me on this, sweets, but my best guess is he killed her by smashing her head into that wall."

"Then he dragged the body to the pool deck? Why?" Kitty pointed to where the body lay.

Frank shrugged. "Maybe to make it look like she stumbled and hit her head on the concrete accidentally." He laughed out loud at the thought.

"She's not wearing a bathing suit. Was she naked when you found her? Was she raped?"

Frank shook his head. "I can answer one of those. Yes. She was naked when we arrived. But according to the butler she never wore a bathing suit in the pool." He paused and his lips twitched into a smile as he added pointedly, "That should be a lesson to some of us, shouldn't it?"

It was Kitty's turn to laugh out loud. "No, it just proves you should never skinnydip alone, Detective." Then immediately she grew serious again. "You said 'he.' Do you have a suspect?"

Frank shook his head. "I'm assuming it was a he because Marina looks like she was a big woman."

"Do you think he was lying in wait for her by the house? In that shrubbery, perhaps?"

Frank stared at Kitty. "I didn't say he was lying in wait

for her. For all I know, right now, maybe they were on their way to the pool together. Maybe she knew him." His mouth suddenly set in a firm tight line. "Are you going to do one of those graphic reenactments?"

Kitty shook her head. "I don't think we'll have time for it," she replied honestly and with relief, knowing how Frank detested reenactments. The trademark of tabloid TV was the one issue they argued about.

"No reenactments today," she repeated. "But I do need a couple of sound bites. Come on, Detective, you're going to have to talk for the cameras later. Consider this a practice run."

He hesitated, but only for a second longer. "Okay, okay. But just the bare facts, Kitty."

She nodded and smiled sweetly, then turned to Bernie. "Bern, give me a rack focus from the house to Detective Maguire, and then widen out to a two-shot with me." She turned again to Frank. "I'm going to do a stand-up that will precede this so I'll go straight into a Q-and-A with 'Tell us, Detective, what happened here?' Okay?"

Frank nodded resignedly. "Shoot."

With the camera rolling, she and Frank went back and forth, with Frank giving her a sanitized and very abbreviated version of what he'd told her off camera—until Kitty gave Bernie the wrap signal.

"That's it, sweets." Kitty linked her arm through Frank's and gave it a quick squeeze. "See, nothing to it. I'll let you go now."

"Hey, not so fast." He gripped her arm to his side. "How about a little quid pro quo here. A little fair exchange of information. You were right about the son . . . Jeff. He's still inside. In Wallkill as it happens, not Green Haven. They transferred him to a medium security facility about eighteen months ago. And that's where he was last night. But what about the rest of the family? Any other offspring around?"

Kitty shook her head. "Not as far as I know." She paused, swallowing nervously, as she withdrew her arm from Frank's. "Are they releasing him for the funeral?"

"Don't know. Don spoke to the superintendent." Frank brushed off her question, obviously eager to pursue his own line of thought. "So, he could be her sole beneficiary?" A pause. "How did he get on with his mother?"

Kitty shook her head as she picked up Frank's train of thought. "Too well to hire someone to batter her to death just so he could inherit her estate."

"Too well? What does that mean?"

"They were close. Very close. They worked together. They lived together in the same house. Marina relied on Jeff for a lot of things. Before Jeff became her executive producer, she went through about twenty of them. That's just the way she was. Very tough. Very demanding. But Jeff knew how to handle her. He didn't argue with her or lose his temper. He just got out of her way. That's how I got to know him—he used to hide out in our newsroom when she went on one of her rampages."

"You got to know him well?"

"We were friends." Kitty's cheeks flushed. "Anyway, well enough to know he couldn't be responsible for this." She turned away quickly, waving toward Marina's body. "Jeff didn't have any stomach for arguments, much less something like this."

Frank shrugged, his eyes narrowing. "He shot and killed his stepfather, didn't he?"

"That was a little different. He got caught in the middle of a very ugly drunken brawl between Marina and Davenport, and Davenport tried to slit his throat with a piece of broken glass."

"That sounds like self-defense not a manslaughter rap."

"There was more to it."

"Obviously," Frank weighed in dryly and then paused, waiting for her to continue.

Kitty sighed, and checked her watch. It was still early. But she had a lot of ground to cover. On her drive up I-95 she'd spoken with Andrea who'd already scheduled satellite time for one in the afternoon.

At that time Kitty was to feed all her footage, interviews, and sound bites to the New York studio. Although *Inside Copy* aired around dinnertime in most markets around the country, the show was actually taped and fed out to TV stations at four in the afternoon. The three hours in between would be used for editing Kitty's raw footage into a neat, usable segment. Kitty figured that would leave her just enough time, after the first satellite transmission, to speed back to Boca, pick up Jamie, throw some clothes into a bag for him, and drop him off at his friend Alex's house before returning to Palm Beach in time for a live stand-up from the crime scene for the four o'clock taping.

Just as she was about to explain all this to Frank she noticed Bernie hoisting up his minicam, and looking across the lawn she saw that the medical examiner had arrived.

"Well what happened with Jeff Haley . . . ," she positioned herself between the two men to divert Frank's attention from the rolling camera, zooming in on the ME beside the body, "in the first place he lied to the police. Initially, he told them he'd been awakened by his mother's screams and he thought she was being attacked by an intruder. But the police caught him in the lie."

"Why did he lie about it?"

"He thought he was protecting Marina. Davenport was a pig. Young and good-looking maybe, but a real pig who would periodically get drunk and beat up Marina. Jeff thought he could keep that a secret.

"Anyway, then a lot of other stuff came out. The *New York Post* ran a big story quoting some anonymous staff member on Marina's show saying that Jeff and Larry Davenport had had a horrendous argument in the office a week before the shooting. And then a security guard at the TV station came forward and said that he had sold Jeff a .38 two days before the shooting. Bottom line: The cops figured they had premeditation and motive, and enough to charge him with murder. Jeff cut a deal to reduce the charge to manslaughter."

Frank ran his hand over his head. "Not much of a deal. You figure a good defense attorney would have advised him to take his chances—especially with his mother's testimony that hubby had tried to slash her son's throat."

Kitty shrugged. "That was the problem. Jeff wouldn't let her testify. He said he couldn't let her go through the ordeal of a trial or the media circus that would go with it. He said she'd have a nervous breakdown. That's why he made the deal."

"Oh, c'mon!" Frank looked skeptical. "You don't walk into a jail cell because you're afraid your mom's going to go to pieces. Five to fifteen only looks good if you're afraid that Mom's story is going to put you away for life."

Kitty felt the color rush to her cheeks again. Frank's assumption annoyed her—especially since he knew nothing about the case or the people involved.

But just as quickly she checked her anger. Very few people knew the facts like she did. She had been on the scene in the Haley townhouse just hours after the shooting. She had heard Jeff sob out the story to the police in Marina's kitchen. She had seen him shaking with shock and heard him retching in the bathroom.

But explaining this to Frank would only raise more questions and right now neither she nor Frank had the time for her to tell the whole story.

She picked up her tote off the ground, and slung it over her shoulder, then reached for Frank's hand, giving it a little squeeze. "Thanks for the help, sweets."

She looked around for Bernie. Then she glanced back at Frank.

"Oh by the way," his hand snaked into his jacket pocket, "I untangled the damn string on Jamie's yo-yo. Here, you can give it back to him."

Kitty mouthed a kiss to him as she took the small blue yo-yo and dropped it in her tote. Then she walked back toward the dunes, aware that Frank's eyes were following her as she walked away.

Chapter 6

*S*o, what was all that about? Frank's eyes focused absentmindedly on Kitty's legs as she walked back through the dunes. How come the perfect recall of a five-year-old shooting? How come the angry flash in her eyes when he'd questioned Haley's motives for copping a plea?

We were friends, she'd said. And the quick rush of color to her cheeks had not escaped his notice, either. So maybe they'd been more than friends. Maybe. Maybe not.

He hoped not. He'd never heard Kitty mention either Haley or his famous mother and, though neither he nor Kitty were the kind of people who quizzed each other on former loves and lovers, he had to believe that if a convicted felon like Haley had played some significant role in her life, Kitty would have had enough good sense to tell him about it.

He turned and strode back swiftly across the lawn, directing his thoughts onto a more professional level. His questions about Jeff Haley had been a somewhat premature fishing expedition. Greed was always a good motive anywhere and even more so in Palm Beach. But for all he knew, at this point, Marina might have willed her estate away to a Home for Aging TV Talk-Show Hosts.

More relevant was that the former TV star had died as a result of a brutal attack. It suggested a sudden confrontation ... an explosion of rage or fear or even lust in which the killer had used his hands, not a weapon. Perhaps he had not even intended to kill her. Hence the attempt to move her body and disguise the killing as an accident.

Frank had considered the possibility of a botched burglary. The Morettis, the couple who worked for Marina, had told him they'd been out for the evening, and he knew a staff's night off was always a good time for burglary attempts. But he had taken a fast walk-through of the house with Don when they'd arrived and had seen no obvious evidence of ransacking—no emptied drawers, no opened cabinets. Knick-knacks made of crystal, china, and silver, which Frank estimated as valuable, still stood on open display on little antique tables in the front hall and hallways.

He had asked the Morettis to check through the house more thoroughly, only to hear them confirm his initial observation when he walked back into the house to find them waiting in Marina Dee Haley's den.

Roseanna Moretti, a slim, dark-haired woman in her early thirties, sat next to her husband, Vincent. He was also dark-haired and appeared to be the same age but sported a trim beard and mustache.

They sat, sides touching, on an oversized couch that faced a giant-screen TV. Built-in mahogany book shelves framed the TV on either side, and a second entire wall was also filled with shelves from floor to ceiling. Hundreds of clear plastic boxes containing videotapes were arranged neatly on the shelves except for about a half-dozen that had been removed from one of the shelves and now lay scattered on the soft beige carpet. A large, elegant mahogany desk with inlaid leather top stood under the window looking out over the driveway. The desk was neat. Very neat. A stack of yellow legal pads lay on top, to the left.

A Mont Blanc pencil and pen set lay in a little silver tray. To the right stood an antique white telephone.

Frank noticed that both husband and wife looked pale and anxious. He tried to put them at ease. Glancing at the shelves, he asked, "Mrs. Haley was a movie buff?" He threw the question out to neither one in particular, but Vincent Moretti answered.

"They're not movies. They're tapes of all her old shows. Arranged chronologically, from top to bottom."

Chronologically? The butler was an articulate man.

"Okay." Frank paced across the room. "Tell me what happened. You were out last night and you returned at . . . ?"

"Around eleven-thirty. Maybe midnight." Roseanna Moretti nodded.

Frank paced back and forth for a couple of minutes, noting the name of the Cineplex movie theater in West Palm where they had seen *Free Willy II* and the name of a small bar and restaurant where they had stopped for some drinks on the way back.

"Would there be anyone in the bar who would recognize your faces again?"

They looked at each other. Then Vincent replied, "The bartender probably. I gave him a decent tip. I've worked behind a bar myself."

Articulate and *thoughtful!*

He covered the events between their return to the house and the discovery of Marina's body in meticulous detail. Vincent Moretti described how he'd checked the doors and windows before following Roseanna to their apartment above the garage. "The door from the sunroom, off the main veranda, was unlocked but closed," he told Frank. "That was the quickest access to the pool. I realize now why it was still unlocked. . . ."

"You didn't think to check outside to see if Mrs. Haley was out there?"

Moretti shook his head. "Not for a minute. It was dark

out there. The lights were out. It didn't occur to me for a second that Mrs. Haley was out there."

"Are the lights on a timer?"

Moretti shrugged and then nodded. "I believe so. We don't really have anything to do with the exterior. There's a landscaping company and a pool man and so on for that. We just take care of the house."

Before he could ask the next question, Moretti spoke up, "Detective, I'm afraid you may think us unhelpful but there's not a lot we can tell you about the house or about Mrs. Haley. We've only been here two weeks."

"Oh?"

"We're just domestic temps filling in for Mrs. Haley's regular staff."

"Who are due back when?"

Moretti cleared his throat. "In a couple of weeks. I believe there was an illness in the family. Mrs. Haley told us she didn't know exactly how long she would need us."

Frank nodded, disappointed. The Morettis were not going to be as much help as regular staff would have been. Nevertheless he had to go through the motions.

"Is there anything, anything at all, which struck you as unusual in the last couple of weeks? Any strangers hanging around the property? Weird phone calls? Anything unusual said by Mrs. Haley? Anything that suggested trouble?"

Both Morettis shook their heads and then Roseanna added, "Mrs. Haley hardly spoke to us."

"But you would know about visitors, wouldn't you? Did she have many? Any male friends? Female friends? Companions?"

Roseanna shook her head. "Not really. She talked on the phone a lot. Her attorney dropped in a couple of times and Roberta Mallory, her secretary, came by every morning to pick up stuff."

"Stuff?"

"Mail, I guess."

"And pages of her manuscript," Vincent interrupted.

"She was writing a book. Her autobiography. Mrs. Mallory picked up the pages and typed them. Mrs. Haley didn't use a typewriter or word processor. She spent a lot of time in here, working on the book."

Frank walked over to the desk. The pages of the legal pads were clean. He opened the top desk drawer. Nothing in it except a couple of letters. He'd have to come back to those later. He opened the next two drawers but did not see what he was looking for.

"Where did she keep the typed pages?"

The Morettis looked blank.

"The manuscript?" Frank prodded.

Roseanna shook her head. "We didn't come in here except to dust and vacuum once a week. We were not supposed to touch anything else in here."

"Mrs. Haley must have been a very tidy person." Frank scanned the room but not before catching sight of Roseanna rolling her eyes. The legal pads on the desk and the magazines on the coffee table were all neatly stacked. Everything except the half-dozen videotapes on the floor seemed to be in its proper place.

Frank stared at them for a moment. "Would she have left those tapes on the floor like that?"

He walked across the room and picked up the first tape. The label read: May 24, 1987: Wives Who Know Their Husbands Cheat.

Vincent Moretti spoke up. "When we came in here a couple of days ago there were a whole bunch of tapes strewn over the floor. I believe Mrs. Haley used them to jog her memory . . . for her book, I mean."

Frank put the tape down and walked to the window. At the end of the driveway, he saw that the crowd of reporters and camerapeople had grown. TV news vans with satellite antennae sprouting from their roofs were parked along both sides of the street blocking driveways. There was not much he could do about that at the moment. The street wasn't private property. There weren't even any parking regulations that could be enforced.

His gaze wandered from the window across to a corner display cabinet. Framed photographs filled the cabinet. Most of them of Marina. Marina alone. Marina with other celebrities like Johnny Carson, Gregory Peck, a young-looking Barbara Walters. Those were the ones he recognized. He had no idea who the others were. He wondered if any of them included her son.

"So?" He returned to the sofa and the Morettis. "The last time you saw Mrs. Haley alive was around five? Yesterday evening?"

Vincent nodded. "Just before we went out. She was still in here, writing. She did that usually till around seven-thirty, eight o'clock, and then she'd go for her swim."

"Skinnydipping? I understand you told the patrolman she never wore a bathing suit."

Frank thought he detected the sound of a suppressed giggle from Roseanna Moretti. Her husband quickly covered for her. "She didn't wear one while we were here. I ... uh ... mentioned it to her the second day we were here. I mean, I wasn't sure if she realized that the pool was clearly visible from our room."

"And?"

Moretti shrugged. "She didn't seem to care. She told me if I felt a need to watch a naked old lady swimming, then my problem was bigger than hers."

"And the last time you saw her. . . ?"

"She was lying by the pool. We both saw her when we got up in the morning. Spread out there. We thought she'd had a heart attack. Roseanna called the paramedics and I pulled on my pants and ran downstairs."

A uniformed policeman entered the den to tell him that Roberta Mallory was at the front door.

"Let her in," Frank told him, then followed the police officer out into the hall to meet the secretary.

She was standing in the flagstone foyer, tall and straight but looking very comfortable in the midst of all the chaos. Frank estimated her age to be around thirty. She was wearing pink walking shorts with a matching tank-top. The blast of the air-conditioning in the house made it obvious that she was not wearing a bra and Frank made an effort to keep his eyes on her face. For some reason he had not pictured Marina's secretary as a leggy, model-type with big breasts and cascading blonde hair.

He suggested walking out onto the veranda where, he figured, the ceiling fans would have a less dramatic effect on her upper torso. She followed him, her heels clicking on the flagstone.

"So, what happened to Mrs. Haley?" she asked, sitting down on the rattan couch and crossing her long legs.

"Her body was found by the pool this morning. She's dead, Miss? . . . Mrs. ? . . ."

"Mrs. Mallory." She smiled. "Kept the name. Dumped the man. One of those reporters out there said she was murdered. Is that true?"

"Yes, it is." Frank nodded, curious about Roberta Mallory's composure. "That doesn't seem to surprise you, Mrs. Mallory?"

She shrugged. "It's not exactly what you expect in Palm Beach but I guess crime is everywhere nowadays, isn't it, Detective?"

"You weren't particularly close to her, I take it."

Roberta Mallory shook her head. "I drove over every morning to pick up the pages she'd written. That was it. Most mornings she hadn't even come downstairs by the time I was gone."

"She had something for you every morning?"

Roberta nodded. "Absolutely. Even if it was only a page. Although that was rare. Usually it was five or six pages. She wrote every day, even Sundays. Well. . . ," she paused, "it's not as if she had anything else to do, is it? And she got a big advance for the book."

Marina's secretary was not a difficult interview. Frank discovered, very quickly, that she worked from home and freelanced as a typist between bartending and hotel work. "I prefer to be out and about, working with people. But there's more of that sort of work during the season." She smiled at him. "You know, I was working at Au Bar that Easter when that whole Kennedy thing happened." Nodding happily, she added, "I really like Palm Beach and the type of person you meet here, you know what I mean?"

Sure he knew. Rich and famous is what she meant. He'd met dozens of Roberta Mallorys during his five years in Palm Beach. He nodded absently. "Tell me about the book."

"Oh, the book. Well, I type up the pages and then send them off to a ghostwriter in New York."

"A ghostwriter? You mean someone else rewrites the chapters?"

Roberta Mallory shrugged. "I guess. All I know is I type 'em and I send 'em out." She paused. "She was almost finished with the book, you know, so I guess the publisher will be happy about that."

Frank paced along the veranda, then back to where Roberta was sitting, twisting strands of her blonde hair between long, iridescent pink fingernails. He wondered how she typed with such long nails.

"Is it a good book?"

She laughed. "It's gossipy and easy to read. And, there's lots of anecdotes and stories about celebrities."

"What about people who might have a grudge against her? Anyone she'd fired or trashed on her TV show?"

Roberta's laughter pealed out across the veranda. "Take your pick, Detective. Even Marina couldn't make Marina look like a nice person."

"How was she with you?"

She shrugged. "Fine. I wouldn't say she was a friendly or warm woman but she was never mean or spiteful to me, if that's what you're getting at."

Frank allowed himself a smile. "I'm not getting at anything in particular. Why would you think that?"

Roberta seemed to search for an answer but in the end she just shrugged.

Frank let it go, then said, "I'd like to get a copy of the

manuscript, Mrs. Mallory. I'll need the writer's phone number or address."

"You don't need that. I have a copy. What do you think? I couldn't just send off those pages and risk losing them. I have everything on a floppy disk."

"Terrific. Then all I need now is to see if you can find the pages Mrs. Haley worked on last night."

The heels clicked furiously as she followed him across the lobby and into the den. She crossed to the desk. "Usually they're right here. In a blue folder. But I don't see the folder. . . ." She opened the top drawer just like Frank had done and closed it again, then the other two drawers and shook her head. "Maybe she took it to bed with her?"

"Maybe." Frank nodded, not bothering to point out that Marina had not made it to bed. "I'll have someone look for it." He paused, his words prompting another thought. "What do you know about the Morettis?"

She shrugged and shook her head. "Nothing. They're just temps."

"Any idea where I can find the other couple? The Morettis said there was an illness in the family."

"They . . . the Vascos . . ." Roberta paused suddenly and stared at him through long thick lashes. "An illness in the family?"

Frank thought she looked puzzled. Or maybe it was concern? But it lasted no longer than a few seconds.

"I . . . don't know." She smiled again. "I think Mrs. Haley's attorney could probably help you out on that."

"Okay, Mrs. Mallory—"

"Roberta," she corrected him. "You can call me Roberta, or even Bert."

"Okay, Roberta." He smiled. "When can you have the manuscript ready for me? How long will it take to print out?"

"Oooh, that's a toughie, Detective. A while." She paused and flicked her tongue around her lips. "I'll get working on it as soon as I'm finished with another assignment I'm working on, though." She opened her purse and took out a business card, which she handed to him. "Why don't you check with me later? I'm sure by tonight I'll have most of it ready for you to pick up."

As she walked away, Frank wondered about the hint of playfulness in her voice and in the ready assumption that he was the one who'd stop by to pick up the manuscript.

"Oh, by the way," she turned in the open doorway, "do you know who did it? I mean, do you have any idea who murdered Mrs. Haley?"

Oh, by the way! Frank stared at her, then quickly shook his head. "I can't answer that, I'm sorry."

"Oh, don't be." She flashed him a cheery smile. "I knew you'd say that." Then she raised her hand in a little wave, and she was gone.

Oh, by the way? Frank shook his head, bemused. Roberta Mallory had shown more concern over the Vascos and their family emergency than over Marina's death. She hadn't even asked how Marina had died.

He found himself wondering if Roberta Mallory knew more than she'd told him.

❧ *Chapter 7* ❧

*L*unchtime at kindergarten. Feeding time at the zoo. He amused himself with the similarity. They had come running out in a herd, their fat, sturdy little legs carrying them to the tables under the awning. Now their faces were stuck into their lunchboxes, like so many little piggies rooting around in their troughs.

Come on little piggies. Chow down. Let's get on with it. For a few moments he watched the young blonde patroling the feeding area, opening little cartons of juice and milk, fiddling with straws. He leaned back against the headrest and closed his eyes.

He was tired. He'd had a bad night. But he'd made it to the school in time to see Kitty Fitzgerald drop off her little boy. He'd gotten close enough to see her give the boy a cursory hug before speeding out of the driveway. She'd be sorry later that she hadn't taken more time over a longer good-bye kiss. Stupid bitch, she'd been in such a hurry. She hadn't even watched the boy walk in through the school doors.

But he had—and he'd been rewarded for his effort. It was as if Jamie Fitzgerald had dressed for today's special occasion, he'd thought, seeing the boy in his T-shirt with the colorful masked, costumed figures kicking and chopping across his chest.

What a shirt. What luck. He'd felt so good about it he'd treated himself to a big breakfast at the diner on Federal, making it back in time for the first play break and sliding in to the perfect parking spot alongside the ficus hedge, with his driver-side window aligned with a break in the shrubbery.

There had been just one nasty moment after that when he'd thought that, maybe, the third beer had been a mistake. When he'd found himself staring, aghast, at four little chests and four little T-shirts all emblazoned with the same kicking-chopping figures across the front.

But he had recovered quickly. With all four boys in his sight, he could see that two of them were dark-haired and dark-complexioned. And the third one, the blonde one who'd been playing with Jamie the other day, was actually a good two inches taller than his target. When the boys stood next to each other you could tell the difference. Jamie Fitzgerald was a shrimp by comparison. Just a little shrimp.

He opened his eyes and focused on the tables again. Yes, there he was, the little shrimp. Hopping over to the trash can to empty the contents of his lunchbox. All he had to do was keep his eyes glued to that sweet little blonde head and there'd be no problem.

He watched as the children finished up at the lunch tables and began running into the play area. But he kept his eyes firmly on Jamie Fitzgerald.

Stay on him. Stay with him. His eyes followed the boy to the far end of the playground where he watched him horsing around with his friends.

Come on, little Jamie. Over here.

He wanted the boy to be on the jungle gym (he needed a clear shot at him); or on the steps to the slide; or, better yet, swinging across on the monkey bars, his body outstretched. The jungle gym was just on the other side of the hedge—it would not be a difficult shot to make.

He saw the boy breaking away, running—but not in the right direction. He was running back to the lunch tables. A jump onto the redwood bench. A kick, another kick. Arms shooting out to the sides.

But it could happen any moment. The boy was looking around. Go for it, Jamie. There was no real rhyme or rhythm or pattern to the way kids played. One moment they could be chattering by the fence, the next moment, hurtling down a slide.

He took a deep breath, wiped the palms of his hands on his green pants, and turned to reach for the pellet gun stashed behind the car seat.

His eyes were off the boy for less than ten seconds, in which time, he realized, the little shrimp had sprung off the bench, across the sandbox, and onto the bottom rung of the jungle gym. Up he scampered, reaching for the monkey bars . . . legs twisting in the air . . .

Oh, beauty!

His finger tightened round the trigger and he aimed left of the brightly painted figures, right about where the boy's forearm would be the fleshiest.

One hand reached and grasped for the next bar, body hanging loose and long. From fingers to toes, outstretched like that, the boy no longer looked like quite a little shrimp, but the feet still dangled way off the ground. . . .

He took a deep breath and squeezed. . . . He heard the pop. Then the cry, which was more of a yelp as the boy fell to the ground. He thrust the pellet gun under the seat and started his countdown: Ten . . . nine . . . eight . . . seven . . . six . . . five . . . four . . . three . . . two . . . one.

He opened the car door and got out. He walked steadily to the gate and opened it.

The boy was still on the ground surrounded by the other kids. He quickened his stride over to where the blonde woman was crouched, shaking the boy, her long floral skirt spread in an arc around her feet.

"Don't shake him like that. He could be hurt." His voice sounded stern and authoritative—even to himself. It evidently surprised the woman who stared at him with wide eyes. He nodded abruptly at her. "I'm Doctor Stroud. I saw him fall as I was driving by. Here, let me take a look." He dropped down on one knee beside her.

The boy was lying on his belly, whimpering and clutching his leg, which had buckled awkwardly when the boy had hit the ground.

"Easy now." He straightened out the leg cautiously and felt the soft flesh in his fingers. He turned to see the woman staring at him, then at the boy, then back to him again.

"Oh, Doctor, thank God you stopped. Is he okay? Is he going to be all right? Is anything broken?"

As if on cue, the boy groaned. "It hurts. Bad."

He gripped the boy's knee, gently, in both hands, then smiled at the blonde woman. "I think he'll live but we should check out this knee, have it X-rayed in ER. Here, help me lift him."

Then he turned his attention to the boy and, with the woman's help, scooped him up ever so carefully into his arms.

Chapter 8

*K*itty turned down Bernie's suggestion that they grab some lunch at Testa's even though she had not eaten anything since waking. She'd had no time to think about food. All morning she had been on the run trying to get her story together in time for the satellite transmission. The pressure had mounted as the minutes sped by.

After talking with Frank she and Bernie had tried Marina's next-door neighbors who, it turned out, were not home and not expected until the start of the season. Two doors down a perky brunette in running shorts had opened the door, but when Kitty identified herself as an *Inside Copy* reporter the woman's expression had changed abruptly to a look of horror—as if she'd just spotted a couple of big, fat, ugly palmetto bugs crawling around in her Jacuzzi. Then the door was slammed in their faces.

There had been a flurry of activity when a blonde in a red Honda had arrived at the gates of Marina's mansion. Reporters and camera crews had surged to her car window with a cacophony of questions. But she'd kept the window

closed until the uniformed police officer had approached
the car.

". . . secretary . . . she's Marina's secretary . . ." The
buzz had spread through the crowd as the gates had closed
behind her.

A couple of news vans had taken off after her on her
exit but had returned quickly to the scene of the main action.

Kitty had had to think fast. By the time *Inside Copy*
aired that evening most viewers would have heard or seen
news reports that Marina Dee Haley was dead. Thus, Kitty's job was to provide more detail and explanation.

In this case, that would be more on Marina's life in
Palm Beach. When news of Marina's murder hit the air-
ways viewers would sit up and say, much like Ernie had
done this morning, "Wow, I thought she was dead. What
has she been doing all these years?"

What indeed? Kitty had already done a stand-up in front
of the mansion against the backdrop of the gathering and
swelling crowd of TV and print reporters. She had used
the stand-up to expand on Frank's sound bites, to give
viewers a more graphic account of Marina's brutal murder.
The stand-up was a device for relaying all of the information she had gathered indirectly from Frank and all of what
she had seen and heard so far.

She had also spoken with a research assistant in New
York who had culled the news databases for any references
to Marina's life in Palm Beach. There had been very few.
Marina, it seemed, had kept a very low profile. "Now,
Bern, I need someone, anyone, who can talk about Marina
for about thirty seconds."

"When in need, interview another reporter." Bernie had
grinned lazily at her. "What about Suzy Erskine? Isn't that
her over there?"

Bernie had spotted Suzy in the crowd gathered outside
Marina's gate. Kitty had been puzzled by her appearance.
Suzy wrote for the Palm Beach *Daily News*, otherwise
know as the *Shiny Sheet*. A-list Palm Beachers kept a tally

of whose photograph had appeared in the paper. Suzy wrote the captions for the photos that appeared on the society page. She knew every important face in Palm Beach.

But, as Kitty discovered, she was not there to cover the story for the *Shiny Sheet*. She had merely been taking the long way round to the office from her own home on North Lake Way and had stopped to see what had happened.

"On the way in to the office?" Kitty echoed, glancing at her watch. "Nice job, Suzy."

The caption writer had laughed good-naturedly. "Don't forget we're only working at half-speed. Not into daily issues yet. Not till the season starts." She agreed to walk with Kitty and Bernie to the end of the road where they could interview her against the background of the Lake Worth inlet and, while her information was not exactly fact-based, her speculation had the ring of authority.

Marina Dee Haley had, reportedly, snubbed some prominent members of Palm Beach society, including a cousin twice removed of the DuPonts, by turning down a number of invitations to A-list soirees and parties. She had shunned Palm Beach society. How else could you explain her absence at the town's most important fundraiser, the Red Cross Ball? Or at the opening of the Kravis Center? How indeed?

"Marina Dee Haley achieved a distinction all her own," Suzy expounded animatedly, obviously enjoying herself. "Her picture never once appeared in the pages of the *Shiny Sheet*. Which is just extraordinary."

"Yes, just extraordinary," Kitty echoed, barely able to keep a straight face. She turned full-face to the camera and concluded, "But then again . . . maybe not so extraordinary considering that Marina Dee Haley lived all of her working life in the spotlight, and retired here to Palm Beach seeking seclusion and privacy."

Kitty gave Bernie the wrap signal knowing that her conclusion would give Dana Lewis, the anchor, a nice segue into a retrospective on Marina, which would be put together in the New York newsroom.

She and Bernie had waited for the medical examiner to exit with Marina's body before leaving the scene to shoot the route back into the center of town. The route, she had explained on camera, was the one the killer had most likely taken after his brutal battering of the aged talk-show star. She knew it was hokey, but it provided an opportunity for some scenic and glitzy footage of the beachfront mansions and for some name-dropping as Kitty had pointed out, among others, the famous Kennedy compound, recently sold for around seven million dollars.

Now, having made her first satellite feed, Kitty advised Bernie to grab a sandwich before returning to Marina's. Bernie would stay at the scene while she drove back to Boca to take care of Jamie.

"I'll be back," she grinned at her cameraman, using her best Schwarzenegger imitation.

She strode toward the Blazer, deciding that since she'd skipped lunch she had enough time to take the scenic route along A1A. The winding coastal road was pretty and relaxing and would give her a chance to unwind. She pulled out of the street and away from Marina's mansion, turning up the volume on her tape. Donna Summer burst through the speakers with "Bad Girls," and Kitty settled back to feel the beat pulsating through the car seat.

The music was evocative, immediately bringing back happy memories of long-gone days when she and her twin, Marcy, had first arrived in New York with on-air jobs as general assignment reporters. The two of them had been so giddy and so thrilled that they'd made it to the number one TV market in the country.

No matter that they'd had to share a one-bedroom apartment where the room had been no bigger than the walk-in closet in her Palm Glades house. Who had needed a big apartment? She and Marcy had used it only for showering and changing in between pounding the city streets for stories by day and hitting the discos by night.

It had been an exhilarating, exhausting experience with no time to sleep and no time to think of anything except their own pleasures and needs and their dreams of bigger things to come.

The planning and the dreaming had been the fun part. More fun than actually obtaining it all. At least that's what Marcy claimed. And she had some basis for comparison. She was the one who'd gone ahead and done it.

While Kitty had eventually found a niche in the newly emerging phenomenon of tabloid TV and then found herself pregnant, Marcy had plowed her way determinedly into a network newsmagazine job, a Park Avenue penthouse apartment, and marriage to the good-looking, suave network anchor, Daniel Stone.

But Kitty had never envied her twin sister. Not even on the worst days when she had despaired over raising her son alone. There had been tough times though she had never regretted having Jamie. She could not imagine a life without him.

For the first two years of his life she had struggled in New York to keep her career going though her interest in the job waned. Jamie and his activities consumed her and she hated leaving him with the succession of nannies who were constantly coming and going out of their lives.

There had been no time or room, back then, to even think about herself or her needs—or any other relationships. She'd had no interest in dating or making new friends or sharing her life with anyone else. Jamie had been her priority and her main interest.

He still was, of course. Frank had not changed that, but he had made her life fuller and more complete. Even so, the first six months of their relationship had been tough going. They'd been in Florida for a year and Jamie had just turned three when she and Frank had met. In those first six months she'd broken many dates and made many excuses not to see Frank, feeling that she was being stretched in too many different directions. But he had been patient and while she had debated and deliberated and dithered over their future he had simply and quietly become part of their little family. Until Jamie, making a wish on his fifth birthday, had asked them to set a wedding date so that he could finally get to call Frank his "real dad."

So, of course, the date had been set. She had chosen the end of September, just about a month away. Jamie had chosen the place—on Frank's sailboat. And Frank had been left to pick the destination—somewhere in the Keys.

She pictured the three of them anchoring in secluded coves to swim and sunbathe. She saw herself struggling to make dinner in the tiny galley while Frank and Jamie fished off the boat. She saw herself and Frank with cocktails on a moonlit deck while Jamie slept.

Jamie would love sleeping on the boat. . . .

She glanced at her watch as she cruised past the Ritz-Carlton hotel in Manalapan. She would have just enough time to stop in Delray Beach. Somewhere on Atlantic Avenue she would find a store that sold boat stuff. She would buy Jamie something for the trip, maybe a fishing rod or perhaps a snorkel and goggles with some flippers.

❧ Chapter 9 ❧

*T*he tension in Netta Freeman's office was unbearable. Netta felt she was on the verge of losing control. Never in the ten years since she had become principal of the Learning Academy had she faced a situation like this one.

But she could not lose it, must not lose it. That would not help. She took a deep breath and, as calmly as she could, asked the question again, "Think, Janis. Are you sure he said Boca Community?"

It was the third time Netta had prompted the young kindergarten aide, but Janis seemed unable to speak much less answer the question. She sat slumped in the chair across from Netta's desk. Her face was ashen and Netta saw that her hands were clenched in her lap, her fingernails digging into the palms of her hands.

She felt sorry for the girl but she felt even sorrier for herself. She could not begin to think how she was going to explain this: A teacher's aide in *her* school had allowed a total stranger to take a child, unaccompanied, off the premises.

Netta Freeman had felt the hairs on the back of her neck rise when she'd first heard what had happened. "Which emergency room? Where?" She had asked the question through clenched teeth.

"Boca Community," Janis had told her. "He said his name was Stroud. Doctor Stroud."

Netta had immediately dispatched Alice, the school secretary, to follow them to the hospital with instructions to call back the moment she located both doctor and child.

But that had been more than twenty minutes ago.

The principal paced from her desk to the window overlooking the schoolyard, feeling two hot spots of color burning into her cheeks. Why didn't Alice call? What on earth could be taking so long? Boca Community hospital was no more than a five-minute ride from the school. Seven minutes, tops, if there was traffic. . . .

She jumped as the phone rang out and took one stride back to her desk to grab the receiver. At the other end, Alice came straight to the point.

"Mrs. Freeman, they're not here. They're not in the emergency room and I've had the hospital check everywhere." There was a very brief pause. "They also say there's no Doctor Stroud on the staff."

Netta's heart thudded and she sank into her chair, gripping the phone to her ear, her eyes boring into Janis Stern like twin laser beams.

"Thank you, Alice. You'd better come on back," she spoke into the phone softly and then hung up. For a moment she sat perfectly still in her chair and then, as the enormity of the situation hit her, her two balled fists came banging down on her desktop.

Janis Stern burst into tears. "Mrs. Freeman, I'm sorry." The words burst out between choked, strangled sobs. "I'm sorry. I thought I was doing the right thing. . . . The doctor said he was on his way to work . . . that he would be at the ER in two ticks. . . . It would be faster than waiting for an

ambulance . . . and I was going to go with them . . . I followed him to his car . . . then I realized I couldn't leave
the other children in the playground."

The principal rubbed her eyes nervously. Of course, it
would be her mistake from start to finish. She should have
had two aides on duty in the schoolyard. There usually
were two but there were so many things to do and get organized at the start of the school year she'd been using
Eileen for other chores.

She walked around her desk toward Janis and crouched
down beside her, the way she did when she was talking to
one of the children. Her voice was clam and steady when
she spoke, giving no clue to the panic that was rising insider her. "Janis, tell me again what he said. Think hard.
Did he say ER? Or did he say Boca Community? Are you
sure he said his name was Stroud? Janis, you have to tell
me the truth now."

The young aide shook her head, her eyes welling with
tears. "He did say Stroud. He absolutely did, Mrs. Freeman, but maybe he didn't say Boca Community." The
tears spilled over and ran down her cheeks. "I think . . .
maybe I just assumed that . . . maybe I thought that's what
he said . . ."

The principal remained crouched by the chair, ignoring
the tight knot in her stomach. The child could be anywhere. At any one of the half-dozen hospitals in South
County. Finally, she gave Janis's hand a little pat. "Janis,
I'm going to call the police. We can't handle this on our
own. They could have gone to any hospital in the area . . .
but . . ."

She paused. "Look at me, Janis. Wipe your eyes and
pull yourself together. Before they arrive let's do what we
can. I suggest you get the Yellow Pages and start calling
around. Try West Boca Medical Center, and North
Broward . . . okay?"

Netta Freeman stood and walked back to the phone at
her desk as Janis scurried into the outer office. The girl
seemed relieved to be having something to do. And maybe

they would get lucky before the police arrived. *Dear God, please let them get lucky.* Maybe she wouldn't have to get the police involved at all. Maybe this incident could be kept quiet. She shuddered at the thought of police patrol cars in the school driveway when mothers started to arrive for pick-up.

Chapter 10

*H*e'd pulled it off. Had snatched the kid right out of the schoolyard in broad daylight. So, after all these years, he had not lost his touch.

It had really been so easy. He had to laugh at the memory of the blonde gushing all over him, "Oh, thank you, thank you, Doctor."

She had run after him, following him to the Cadillac, and for a couple of seconds, he had feared she was going to jump into the car with Jamie. But then she had apparently remembered the rest of the kindergarten class, left unattended in the schoolyard.

Of course half of it was luck, and the other half was understanding human nature. There weren't too many people who were suspicious of a doctor who stopped to help at the scene of an accident. How many people would say: How strange that a doctor was passing just when the accident happened? No. People expected doctors to come forward on planes or in hotels and restaurants, or in the street, when they were needed.

What was lucky was that the girl had not insisted on coming with him. He had considered the eventuality along with all the other possible glitches. It would have been unfortunate and unpleasant getting rid of her. So, lucky for him . . . and lucky for her, really.

He looked across at his little prize, slumped in the passenger seat. Jamie was sleeping, snoring lightly—the effect of a very mild sedative he'd dropped into the plastic container of tepid Gatorade. Just mild enough to induce a little nap while he left the boy in the car and dropped off the videotape package at the Federal Express office off Yamato Road.

Of course, Kitty Fitzgerald would not be in her office tomorrow when it was delivered. She would most probably be at home, freaking out over her missing son, or cruising the streets of Boca searching for her precious darling. But he would call her office and make sure that her secretary understood the urgency of bringing it to her attention.

Jamie Fitzgerald stirred in the seat beside him, raising a limp hand to wipe away the little beads of perspiration on his brow.

"My arm hurts," the boy whimpered, opening his eyes. "And my knee."

He patted the boy's head reassuringly. "It's going to be okay, Jamie. Just close your eyes and rest."

Damn! He had hoped the sedative would last until he could get into the motel room. He looked to the side of the highway for a sign indicating the next exit. He was only just into Broward County, cruising through Pompano. North Lauderdale was ten or so miles away.

He figured he would motel-hop along Federal Highway in Lauderdale for the next few days, spending only one night in each place.

He had considered checking into something a little grander, getting the two of them comfy in something like a Radisson suite, a place where the rooms had those minibars. He certainly didn't have to be chintzy. But it was a risk, checking into a hotel . . . having to walk across the lobby with the boy . . .

He turned up the volume on the all-news station and the boy stirred again, his eyes wide open. The small hand clutched at the right arm, where the pellet had stung him. "It hurts a lot." There was a whiny note in the little voice. "I think a bee stung me. I felt it sting me, that's why I fell off the monkey bars, you know."

"There, there, Jamie." He tried to sound soothing, as he patted the boy's thigh just above the knee. The skin felt hot and a little clammy. He would run a nice, cool bath for Jamie as soon as they checked in.

No. Don't even think about it. Not with this boy. He removed his hand abruptly and fixed his eyes on the road ahead. There would be time enough for his own pleasures when the deal was done. When he had the money . . . and could take off on his own.

He reached for a cigarette from the pack lying on the console beside him, lit up, and took a deep drag, glancing at the car clock. Less than forty-five minutes had passed since he'd bolted the schoolyard.

"I think my knee is broken. It feels bad."

"We'll be getting it checked out any moment now, Jamie. Just take it easy."

"Am I going to the hospital?"

His hands felt sweaty on the steering wheel as he grunted in reply. He had just sped by a tall brown building on the left with big blue letters spelling out "North Broward Medical Center" across the top floor. Surely the boy had not read all that?

"You're not scared are you, Jamie? A big boy like you . . ."

"No. Of course not." The boy's eyes were staring dully at the road ahead. Then suddenly the little face turned toward him. "Why do you keep saying that?"

"Because I think you are a very brave, big boy."

"No." The little voice sounded very insistent. "I mean, why do you keep saying 'Jamie'? Why do you keep calling me Jamie?"

$\mathscr{C}$ Chapter 11 $\mathscr{C}$

$\mathcal{T}$he executive producer of *Inside Copy* was away from his desk when Kitty checked in with the New York office after her shopping detour in Delray Beach. He would get back to her as soon as he could, she was told.

Kitty didn't know what to make of it. Todd's silence was unsettling. Usually on a big, breaking story like this one, he was on the phone every five seconds driving the reporter crazy with a million questions. Still, there was nothing she could do but wait.

She punched the eject button on her tape and switched on the all-news radio station as she cruised through Highland Beach and Boca Raton. The pristine, white high-rises of the Sea Ranch apartments shimmered on her right. To her left she was treated to an unobstructed view of the ocean. The city fathers had declared this stretch of beachfront to be zoned for the enjoyment of all residents and had forbidden the construction of any residences, high-rise or otherwise.

Boca was a good city to live in. It was clean and pretty

and proud of being both. Lushly landscaped, the wide streets and avenues were lined with Royal palms, banyans, and poincianas. Front yards and grass verges were always freshly mown. Farther south on A1A, white and pink apartment buildings rose along the beach and Mediterranean-style villas sprawled along the Intracoastal. Downtown, almost every building and storefront was painted pink.

Before moving to Florida, Kitty had known next to nothing about Boca Raton except that the name translated, loosely from the Spanish, into "mouth of the rat." It was a total misnomer for the wealthy, upscale community where moms dropped their kids off at school in BMWs and Mercedes and shopped at the local Publix in smart little tennis outfits. Even the McDonald's in the Crocker Center was uptown, boasting of being the only franchise in the country with a marble floor. And when police had picked up a homeless man in Spanish River Park, Kitty, newly arrived from New York, had been astounded to see that it was such a rare occurrence that the story had made the front page of the local paper.

It was a safe city. Or really not so much a city as a cluster of some two-dozen gated communities and country clubs orbiting the Town Center Mall.

Fort Lauderdale had been a good choice for the bureau located, as it was, between Miami and Palm Beach with easy access to airports and the west coast via Alligator Alley. But the Spring Break capital of the world was not, Kitty had felt, a good place to put down roots. Boca, on the other hand, had gated communities with tennis courts, golf courses, little playgrounds, and jogging paths. ·

The phone pealed out as she crossed the bridge over the Boca inlet. She picked up on the first ring, nestling the phone between her chin and shoulder as she reached to turn down the volume on the radio.

"Nice work." Todd's voice boomed down the line. "You earned your pay today, Fitzgerald. Just tell that Polack cameraman of yours that T-and-A refers to living, breathing tits and ass, preferably in hot-pink spandex."

Kitty rolled her eyes but was relieved to hear Todd in a jovial mood. "Sure, Todd. Next time I'll ask the cops to drape a bathrobe over the offensive parts."

The executive producer chuckled. "Okay, point taken. Anyway, sorry I didn't get back to you sooner but we've been checking on young Haley, and I was a little miffed to discover that our superb assignment desk missed the news of his parole board hearing a couple of months back.

"Apparently he was approved and was due out on parole next week, anyway ..." Todd's voice trailed off for a moment, as if his attention had been distracted by someone else in his office.

Then his voice echoed on the line again. "Can you believe that? Not only is he being released for the funeral but he's being released period. Paroled. ASAP. Can you believe that? Goddammit Fitzgerald, this is turning into one helluva story. What poignancy! What timing! Anyway, I've sent a crew up to the jail."

"Good thinking." Kitty cleared her throat. "Do we have any word on who broke the news to him? Or how he took it?"

"According to the superintendent's office he collapsed, overcome with grief." There was a chuckling sound at Todd's end. "I say he was overcome by the thought of inheriting all that loot. Geez, that's the story, Kitty. Haley's the next angle in this story: 'From Jailbird to Palm Beach Playboy,' how's that?"

"Of course." Kitty couldn't help smiling. Todd always thought in promos. If you couldn't describe a story in a one-line promo to Todd, it didn't stand a chance of making it on-air.

"By the way, Fitzgerald. We dug up all the old news footage on the shooting, and we're going to use chunks from the interview you did with Haley the day after he shot Larry Davenport. It was a dynamite scoop, remember?"

How could I forget?

"I seem to recall you and he had a bit of a thing going at the time, right? Let's hope he doesn't forget old friends when he gets to Palm Beach because if Tom screws up and misses him getting out of jail, I'm counting on you to nail him."

He paused, and Kitty wanted to jump in and tell him: *No, please, don't count on me, Todd.*

But Todd was already moving on to other things, without a pause for breath. "Okay toots, gotta run now. Dana's having a shit fit because she's got to track." Todd's voice rose in a perfect imitation of the anchor's: " 'Oh my God! A news story! Why didn't anyone tell me I'd be doing news stories on this show!' "

Then the line went dead and Kitty found herself smiling at Todd's perfect take on Dana, but then the smile disappeared almost immediately. So Jeff was coming to Palm Beach and with him would come more TV newscrews and reporters, and Todd would expect her to be right in there with them.

No, not *with* them—ahead of them.

She knew Todd wouldn't have sounded quite so happy or confident if he had read the last letter that Jeff had sent her.

She shivered, feeling a sudden chill. It was as if a giant hand had suddenly reached out of the sky to yank her out of her comfortable little place in the sun.

The cold feeling stayed with her until she turned into the school driveway. Then the sun seemed to shine again as she looked across the yard and caught sight of her son, his little blonde head bobbing in time to some music in his head.

He saw her and came flying toward her. "Mom! Mom! Guess what?"

She snatched him up into her arms and planted a big kiss on his neck. "What? What?"

"Mom! Timmy fell off the monkey bars. We were play-ing Power Rangers and he had to get across the bars 'cause he was escaping from the Putty Patrol, and he fell and we all thought he was killed."

"Jamie!" Kitty smiled at her son's obvious exaggeration. "But then he was okay, right?"

"Uh-uh." Jamie shook his head, his eyes big and wide. "He was hurt, real bad."

"Really badly, you mean," Kitty corrected her son's grammar.

"Yeah, Mom, really, really badly. He had to go to the hospital. The doctor came and took him."

Kitty took her son's hand and walked toward the teacher standing at the gate. "You mean the paramedics came?"

"Yeah a pam ... pam ... eredic. What's a pam ... ?"

"They come with the ambulance. They're usually the first to get to the scene of an accident." She paused at the gate to talk to Miss Arlene.

"Jamie's telling me that Timmy Myers was taken to the hospital. Is he okay?"

Miss Arlene seemed to stare right through her, then she nodded quickly. "Oh, I believe so."

"What happened?"

Miss Arlene shook her head. "I'm not sure, exactly. I wasn't here. I was on a field trip with the first grade." Then she turned abruptly away to speak to another mother who'd walked up behind Kitty.

"Mom," Jamie tugged at her hand. "Can I call Timmy when we get home?"

"Of course you can call." She squeezed her son's hand. "You can call from Mrs. Baines's apartment. You're going to sleep over with Alex tonight. How does that sound?" Her son started hopping around, his fists punching the air. "Yes! Yes! Great, Mom!" She laughed, catching his little hands in hers. "Come on, let's go pack your bag."

❧ *Chapter 12* ❧

*H*e made an effort to look suitably interested and impressed as Ann-Marie Nevsky, leasing agent for Palm Glades, Boca Raton's premier rental community, beckoned him to follow her up the path. But his thoughts were elsewhere.

He had executed the perfect abduction—of the wrong boy. Not Jamie Fitzgerald. But Timothy fucking Ellis Myers. His sense of loss and frustration threatened to overwhelm him again. How could it have happened? He'd taken his eyes off the Fitzgerald kid for about five seconds to reach for the gun.

Ann-Marie Nevsky stopped abruptly in the middle of the path. "Here it is. This is the little gem, Mr. Stroud. Stroud? Is that the way you pronounce it?"

"Yes, you got it. Bob Stroud." He nodded, searching the rental agent's face for any indication that she had recognized the name. But there was none. It was destined to remain his own private little joke.

Ms. Ann-Marie Nevsky was obviously neither a movie

buff nor a Burt Lancaster fan or she might have cottoned on. But few people ever did recognize the real name of the Birdman of Alcatraz.

She stood beside him in front of wrought-iron double gates. They were set in a six-foot wall that separated the property from the main street. Dramatically, she swung the gates open. "There you are Mr. Stroud, as promised, a little bit of paradise right here in Palm Glades. Our courtyard homes—so called because as you can see they are built around the courtyard—were designed with the utmost seclusion and privacy in mind."

She stood beside him, allowing him to dwell on the scene: A pool sparkled in the center of the courtyard, which was surrounded on three sides by the house. Sliding glass doors from every room opened up onto the pool area and that, together with the pastel stucco and the red barrel-tile roof, gave the effect of a Mediterranean-style villa. Somewhere in this community, Kitty Fitzgerald and her son lived in an identical house.

He stared into the pool, his thoughts churning over the horrible setback he'd suffered. In the moment of realization total blind rage had exploded inside his head. He had thought of opening the car door and just shoving the boy out into the middle of the interstate. But he'd steeled himself against the urge, gripping the steering wheel as if his fingers were welded to it.

There was nothing else he could do but go back to square one, hopefully without arousing too much suspicion. He believed he had achieved that by dropping the boy off at the doors of the emergency room of the medical center.

"Geez kid, this is going to make me late for surgery. Jump out here. I have to park and run. Just go through those doors, tell 'em who you are and that you fell off a jungle gym. I'll stop by later to see how you're doing. Okay, fella?"

That had been it word for word. That's as much as the kid would be able to tell anyone. How much suspicion could it arouse? The boy had been missing for less than an hour. And then, lo and behold, turns up in the hospital. Unhurt, unharmed.

He'd even called the school to ask if someone was on the way to be with the boy. The police might want to find and question a Good Samaritan who'd stopped and just whisked a child out of a schoolyard but let 'em want. How fervently would they pursue it with the kid home, safe and sound?

"Mr. Stroud? Excuse me, would you like to see more?" Ann-Marie Nevsky closed the gates behind them. "A wonderful place to write, wouldn't you say?"

"I beg your pardon?"

"Didn't you say your wife is a writer?"

"Oh, yes, yes she is. I think she'd like this. Very nice. Very nice. I'm just a little concerned . . ." He broke off, hesitating. He had to edge into this carefully.

"About?" Ann-Marie Nevsky frowned and stared at him. He wished he'd stopped to buy a new jacket. All his clothes had been lying in the trunk for a couple of days and, besides, pastel blue was not a good color for him. It made him look pale and pasty and drew attention to the thick black hair that curled on the backs of his hands. He crossed them behind his back.

"Security. I mean, my wife is the nervy one. You know how writers are. And I travel frequently on business."

She nodded quickly. "I understand, Mr. Stroud. But as you probably noticed Palm Glades is a gated community. We have round-the-clock security guards manning the gatehouse. No one can get in to see you or even ring your doorbell without going through the gatehouse. And of course each house has its own state-of-the-art security system. Please follow me and I'll show you."

She skirted the pool, heading for the front door of the house. "As you see," she continued, unlocking the front door, "this is the main entrance into the house. The gates outside are really more of a decorative feature, although you could have bolts put on them." She paused. "But I can tell you most of our residents don't bother. It would be a nuisance for the landscapers and pool people and so on."

Inside the front door she pointed to the left at the alarm pad. "You have four security zones, Mr. Stroud. The first is just for your main doors—front and garage. The second takes care of all the sliding glass doors. The third is for all the other windows and the fourth is an interior motion detector and glass shock sensor."

He stared for a moment at the alarm pad. "The motion detectors don't cover the courtyard, do they?"

Ann-Marie Nevsky shook her head.

"Could they be wired to take in the courtyard?"

The Realtor shook her head. "I've never heard of that. It just wouldn't make that much sense. They're so sensitive that any small lizard or bird could set them off."

"And where is the master control panel?"

She beckoned him to follow her into the kitchen area. "Up here above the cabinets."

"Are the panels in the same location in every house?"

He saw her puzzled look. "As far as I know. But why do you ask, Mr. Stroud? Is it a problem?"

Only for Kitty Fitzgerald, he thought, trying not to let the excitement show on his face. Yesterday he'd watched, frustrated, when they had retreated into their safe little haven. Today it turned out their little haven was not so safe, after all.

He looked around the small foyer that opened into a living room. To the right was the master bedroom, to the left a kitchen area, a family room, and a hallway to the other bedrooms.

He stared out from the living room windows across to the outside wall. Thick lush shrubs and bushes skirted the wall almost to the edge of the pool. It looked like good cover.

"I think this is perfect, Ms. Nevsky. But I would like my wife to see it before I sign the lease. Do you mind if I check out the neighborhood? Drive around, perhaps?"

"No, you go right ahead, Mr. Stroud. I'll be in my office when you're ready."

He walked with her to her car and even opened the door for her. "Oh, one more thing, Ms. Nevsky. Would you be good enough to alert the gatehouse and tell them that I'll be dropping by again to show my wife the neighborhood?"

"My pleasure, Mr. Stroud." She flashed him a wide smile as she pulled away from the curb.

He waited till she'd turned the corner and then got into the Cadillac, grinning. He had time, now, to cruise around the neighborhood and find Kitty Fitzgerald's house. If she hadn't hung her nameplate under the mailbox he would just stop and ask a neighbor. Someone was bound to know where Kitty Fitzgerald, TV star, lived.

Then, he would simply watch and wait. Impatience had caused him to make one mistake, but it was going to be his last. This time he'd get it right.

Maybe he'd have to wait till nightfall. Maybe Kitty Fitzgerald felt safe enough to leave a window open. It would certainly be best if he could make it happen tonight. The package that would be delivered to her office worried him. He had not done anything as crass as demand the money in the note. No. The note had a different, cruder purpose. But it would certainly spook her. . . .

He would not rush things this time, though. The weekend was coming up, opening up fresh possibilities: maybe the supermarket, the mall, the beach, the movies, or a playground. Maybe Jamie would visit a friend.

All he had to do was be there at the right moment. And the right moment would come if he stuck with them. He would not let them out of his sight until he had the boy.

He cruised slowly down the street and then followed the main road through the development observing the 20-mph speed limit. Additional signs warned: Slow Children Playing. It was obviously a community for young families of up-and-coming executive-types. The streets were immaculate, the sidewalks beautifully landscaped. Trees lined the streets and bougainvillea flowered on the walls of the courtyard houses.

Just past the clubhouse, next to the tennis courts, he spotted a small playground. He parked, got out of the car, and headed for a bench near the swings. Way back on the road he had seen two mothers pushing toddlers in strollers, moving toward the playground. They could probably give him the information he needed.

He was about to sit down on the bench to wait for them when he spotted something moving in the grass beside him. With a jump the creature emerged and he found himself staring into the popping eyes of an ugly brown frog. It sat in front of him, unafraid.

He stared back. No, it was not a frog. It was too big. More likely a toad. Maybe even one of those Bufo toads that Kitty Fitzgerald detested.

He grinned to himself, easing off his jacket slowly and carefully. Then he tossed the jacket over the ugly creature in one swift movement before the animal realized what was happening.

"Gotcha! You little bastard," he chuckled, scooping up the squirming bundle.

Chapter 13

*F*rank listened to Kitty's phone ringing. It was the second time he'd tried in fifteen minutes. He'd figured she would be home by now. It had been a long day for her, starting with his early phone call. It had been a long day for him, too, and it would be a while yet before he could leave the stationhouse and turn in.

He was about to hang up to try her car phone when suddenly he heard her breathless voice on the other end.

"Oh, honey! Hi!" Her voice came in short, staccato gasps as if she'd just jogged a marathon.

"Are you all right?"

"Ye-es." She didn't sound it. Then he heard her take a deep breath. "Yes. Yes, I am. Would you hold on a second while I close the doors."

Over the line, he heard the sliding door slamming home before she returned.

"What's going on? I've been trying to reach you."

"I was in the pool." He heard the hesitation in her voice before she laughed. "One of those disgusting toxic toads jumped onto the steps and just sat there." She laughed nervously. "But everything's fine now. What's up? Anything new?"

Frank smiled. "No, but I managed to catch your segment on tonight's show. Pretty good stuff, Kit. I especially appreciate that you didn't attribute all your information to one *police* source."

Kitty laughed happily this time and he felt warmed by the sound. She was obviously satisfied with the day's work. As well she could be, he reflected. She was so good at her job. He thought about her live stand-up in which she'd summarized the latest developments, including information she'd obviously wangled out of a source right in the medical examiner's office. She'd once told him that developing contacts and sources was one of the most important parts of her job.

"So, who gave you the scoop about Marina putting up a fight—and the broken fingernails?" he asked.

"Uh-uh." She laughed again but knew he wouldn't get an answer. Instead she said, "That might make your job easier if they retrieve any fibers or stuff from under the nails, right?"

"Only when we actually pick up a suspect."

"And you don't have one? At all?"

"Not right now," Frank replied and stretched his legs out across his desk. "But the night is young. I'm waiting for a call-back from Marina's attorney. He seems to have been a regular visitor at the house but he's on his way back from Miami."

"I guess that means I won't be seeing you tonight?"

Frank thought he detected a strange edge to Kitty's voice, as if she was peeved that he would not be driving down to Boca. "But that's okay," she added hurriedly. "It's just that . . ."

"Just what?"

"Jamie's sleeping over at a friend's house and I was hoping I'd have a big, strong man spending the night with me." She paused. "But forget it. I can wait." Her voice dropped to a throaty whisper. "I think I'll have a nice relaxing Jacuzzi and pamper myself in some of that bath oil that makes my skin feel so silky and soft."

He groaned. "Come on, babes, don't make it worse for me." He lowered his voice although there was nobody left in the squad room. "I've wanted you since this morning when I saw you in that tight, short little skirt." His voice dropped another notch. "Believe me I intend to make up for it tomorrow night."

Kitty chuckled. "You think you'll have time for dinner, too?"

"You bet. Eight o'clock. Chuck and Harold's."

"Then I'll see if Jamie wants to stay at the Baines's tomorrow night too."

He grinned at the sexy tone of her voice and told her he loved her before hanging up. Then he reached for the two big yellow envelopes on the desk in front of him. They had been delivered earlier in the day after Frank's call to Robert Lacoste, a veteran Palm Beach *Herald* police reporter whom he had met during his first week in Palm Beach and to whom he fed choice tidbits from the police blotter on a regular basis.

This time Frank had asked the favor figuring that while he waited for various calls at the stationhouse he could get a better idea of Marina Dee Haley and her life by going through old press clippings.

Lacoste had offered to reproduce everything from his Nexis database but Frank had said he preferred to see the actual newspaper clippings—if such things were still available.

He chose one of the envelopes and, prying it open, he let the copies slide out onto his desk. There were about two dozen of them, arranged by date. He flicked through the first few, which seemed to be items in gossip columns. The shooting of Marina's husband, however, had made the front page of the *Herald* on June 11, 1990.

TRAGIC FATAL SHOOTING OF
TALK-SHOW HOST'S HUSBAND

New York City—The 42-year-old husband of TV talk-show host Marina Dee Haley was killed last night in a tragic accidental shooting.

According to police, Haley's 35-year-old son Jeff allegedly shot and killed Larry Davenport after mistaking him for an intruder in the family townhouse on E. 68th Street.

The 53-year-old talk-show host is reportedly in seclusion and in shock today. She and Davenport, a struggling stand-up comic, were married just two months ago in a quiet ceremony in New York City's Rainbow Room. Haley's son, who is also said to be in shock, is the executive producer of her top-rated, syndicated talk show, *Let's Talk.*

The headline of the next clipping, dated six weeks later, screamed:

"HALEY THREATENED STEPDAD,"
SAY TV TALK-SHOW STAFFERS

New York City—Police investigating the fatal shooting of Marina Dee Haley's husband have quizzed the TV talk-show host's 35-year-old son, Jeff Haley.

Haley was interviewed at the family townhouse on E. 68th Street. A police spokesperson refused to comment, but a source close to the investigation revealed that Haley was questioned about allegations published by the New York *Post* last week.

In an exclusive front page story, the *Post* quoted talk-show staffers, who work on Marina's show, saying they had overheard "a horrendous screaming argument" between Haley and Marina's husband, Larry Davenport, two days before the shooting. One staffer who was not identified by the *Post* was quoted as saying: "Davenport threatened to have Jeff

fired. Jeff screamed back at him: 'Over your (de-
leted) dead body.' "

Staffers commented that the two men separated by
an age difference of only seven years had argued often since Davenport's marriage to the talk-show
host.

Davenport was killed almost two months ago in a
shooting at the family's Manhattan townhouse.
Haley, who is executive producer of *Let's Talk*, told
police initially that the shooting was an accident—he
thought an intruder had broken into the home. He
later changed his story and told police he was trying
to break up a fight between his mother and her husband. He claimed that Davenport turned on him and
attacked him and that he fired the gun in self-
defense.

The third clipping on the case was dated August 19,
1990.

MARINA'S SON COPS A PLEA

New York City—Jeff Haley, the 35-year-old son
of talk-show host Marina Dee Haley, pleaded guilty
today to manslaughter in the shooting death of his
stepfather, Larry Davenport.

Frank skimmed over the next few paragraphs that re-
capped the story of the shooting and details about the wedding.

In a statement issued to the press, Haley said: "I
am innocent of murder. I am not changing my story.
The shooting was an accident. But the bottom line is
that a man is dead and my mother is on the brink of
a serious mental breakdown. I cannot put her or
those near and dear to me through the added torment
of a trial. I deserve punishment of some kind."

Haley is expecting a sentence of five to fifteen

years. His mother was not available for comment yesterday. She has been staying at her home in Palm Beach since the shooting, and her show is in reruns. Friends close to the family said yesterday they expect an announcement about the future of her show in the next two days.

Frank glanced over the clippings, wishing that he could have read the coverage in the New York papers. Then he picked through the other clippings. There was one gossip column item about Marina's wedding in March of that year. He glanced at the picture of Marina and Larry Davenport, studying the bridegroom's handsome face, shoulder-length hair, and stupid, inebriated smile on his lips.

He was still looking over Davenport when the next clipping on his desk caught his eye—a picture of Kitty. A younger Kitty with longer hair in what looked like a formal studio shot. The clipping had obviously slipped out of the sequence because it was dated August 2, 1990. It belonged right after the story of the New York *Post* allegations. Over it the headline read: "Haley's TV Gal Pal Tells: I Was with Marina's Son on Night of Shooting."

Frank gripped the paper in his hands, and with a deepening sense of foreboding started reading.

Detectives investigating the shooting death of Marina Dee Haley's husband interviewed *Inside Copy* reporter Kitty Fitzgerald at her home in Soho yesterday.

Miss Fitzgerald, who is on maternity leave from the top-rated TV tab, would not comment, but a source close to the investigation explained that Miss Fitzgerald and Marina's son Jeff Haley had spent the evening of the fatal shooting together. "She was the last person to see Haley before he shot Larry Davenport," said the insider. According to some sources at WPEN-TV, where Marina Dee Haley's *Let's Talk*

show is produced, the couple have been constant
companions since the beginning of the year when
Marina's show, *Let's Talk,* moved its production offices into WPEN-TV.

Other sources, however, claim that the relationship
was already ongoing before the move and that Haley,
the executive producer of his mother's show, chose
WPEN-TV because of Miss Fitzgerald's employment at the station.

Miss Fitzgerald, who gave birth to a son on
July 10, has kept mum on the identity of her baby's
father and refused last night to talk about her relationship with Jeff Haley. Asked if Haley is the father
of her child, the popular red-haired TV reporter replied, "No comment."

Frank sat with the clipping in his hand for a few moments, his heart thudding as realization hit him. No wonder Kitty's recollection of the case had been so sharp. She
had been part of the story. She had actually been part of
the police investigation.

His eyes drifted back over the paragraphs and he forced
himself to reread the story. It referred to Haley and Kitty
as constant companions but the innuendo pointed to a
closer relationship. Much closer. . . . The report had only
just stopped short of identifying Haley as Jamie's father.
So, what the hell did Kitty's "No comment" mean?

He rubbed his eyes and face, telling himself to apply
some professional disinterest to the information. All his
training and experience warned him not to jump to conclusions. All the facts—or was it innuendo?—were vastly at
odds with the story that Kitty had told him. He got to his
feet and paced across the office, and then back to his desk,
the memory of his first meeting with Kitty Fitzgerald
flooding back into his mind.

They had met the night Brant Davidson had been ac-
quitted of conspiring to murder his wife. Frank, who had
been the lead investigator on the homicide, had gone to

drown his sorrows in Bradley's Saloon. There he had run into his reporter pal Lacoste and a group of other reporters unwinding after the trial. Sometime during the course of the evening, with different groups milling and intermingling around the bar, he and Kitty had been introduced.

"Too late, now," she had laughed, her big eyes dancing with mischief. "I tried to get through to you during the trial."

He had retorted with something inanely unoriginal like, "Better late than never," and had offered to buy her a drink. Which she had declined, saying she had to get home to tuck her son into bed.

His face had betrayed his disappointment. But then she had thrown him a parting shot and a lifeline, "Single moms don't get to party after work."

He had called her a week later. But the subject of Jamie's father had not come up until their third date. She had been reluctant to discuss him at first but had finally told him that Jamie was the result of a brief fling she'd had with a visiting Australian reporter. The reporter, according to Kitty, had left for his homeland without even knowing she was pregnant and she had not even entered his name on Jamie's birth certificate.

"What was I supposed to do?" she said, dismissing it with a wave of her hand and a smile. "Go through some kangaroo court for child support? Get involved in some transcontinental custody battle? He was married, anyway."

It had made sense at the time. Now, Frank wasn't so sure. He scanned the clipping again and the story of the itinerant Aussie suddenly seemed too convenient. An invention to cover the truth: that her son's father was a convicted felon serving time for killing another man.

Jesus! Frank slumped back into his chair, shaking his head. *No,* he told himself. *No, it wasn't possible.* Kitty had dealt with him honestly in every step of their relationship. She had been straight with him even at the risk of driving him away. He refused to believe that she would have deceived him about something as important as this.

He got to his feet again just as the phone on his desk shattered the quiet of the empty office. The breathless little-girl voice at the other end of the line identified herself as Bert. It took a moment to bring the face to mind.

"Roberta. It's Roberta Mallory, Detective," she prompted. "I just wanted you to know I'm still slaving over the hot printer for you. But it's getting very late and very lonely."

He cleared his throat. "I appreciate it, Roberta. How much do you have left to do?"

"Oh, not that much," she laughed. "Would you like to come and pick it up tonight? I know you're very . . . anxious, Detective."

He hesitated, swiveling around in his chair to turn his back on Kitty's picture and the offensive newspaper clipping. "I'm kinda busy right now, Roberta. I'm waiting for some calls."

"Oh, I won't be done for another hour or two but I've got a comfortable couch and some ice-cold beer in the refrigerator."

He smiled into the receiver, amused by her directness. Then he laughed out loud. "The manuscript and a beer," he repeated, choosing his words carefully. "How can I resist? I'll be there."

Not a smart move, Maguire.

But screw it, he thought, as he hung up. He needed the manuscript—and he needed a beer.

❦ Chapter 14 ❦

Friday, September 1

There were a half-dozen messages waiting for Kitty when she arrived at the bureau just before nine the next morning. All of them marked Urgent. All of them from New York.

"And there's today's mail." Ginny, her assistant and office manger, pointed to a fresh stack of assorted envelopes on the desk as she handed Kitty the sheaf of yellow message slips.

Kitty nodded wearily, dumped her tote on the floor, and slumped in her chair staring at the Federal Express package that lay at the top of the pile. She ripped it open, thinking it had to be the David Singer tape back from the New York office. Instead she saw a padded yellow envelope inside.

It was marked "Personal & Confidential" in thick black marker but she tossed it aside. Eighty percent of her mail—complaints, story ideas, homevideos—arrived marked that way. As if it would make her read it faster. *Fat chance.*

"I've got to get some coffee in me before I deal with any of this," she said. "And I want to call Angela, to check that Jamie behaved himself this morning."

Bernie appeared in the doorway as Ginny left. He looked like he'd slept in the office—which he did, periodically, when Maria, his Cuban live-in girlfriend, kicked him out of their apartment. "I spoke to Ernie a few minutes ago," he told her. "He just got the overnights in. Our ratings went through the roof last night. We blew away the competition.

Kitty nodded. "I would hope so. We were the only ones to devote the full half-hour to Marina. *A Current Affair* and *Inside Edition* had zip compared to us."

Bernie grinned and gave her a thumbs-up. "That's because we're right here. I hope Todd points that out to the suits when they get their beans and pencils out."

Kitty shrugged, although she knew Bernie was as concerned as she was over the rumors about closing the Florida bureau.

He waited while she spoke to Angela. Then he asked: "What's up, boss? You look bad this morning."

"Thanks." She sighed. "I didn't sleep very well. I kept thinking about Marina being battered to death in her own backyard. I thought there was someone in mine last night."

Bernie laughed. "I thought you didn't let these things get to you anymore."

Kitty frowned. "I don't think I was imagining it. When I stepped out to the pool it smelled like someone had been smoking in the yard." She had not mentioned the smell of smoke to Frank or the feeling that she was being watched. She had not wanted him to think she'd been spooked by Marina's murder.

"So, why didn't you get out?"

"I was going to, and then this little fucker leaped out at me from the bushes."

"Who!?" Bernie looked so shocked that Kitty couldn't help laughing out loud.

"Sorry, I meant the toad. This ugly, horrible giant Bufo

leaped right onto the top step of the pool and sat there staring at me with these bulging eyes."

"A Bufo? How could you tell?"

"Oh, Christ, I don't know, Bernie. I just froze in the goddamn water. All I could think of was that if I moved I was going to scare the shit out of it and then it would spray me with that toxic stuff."

"So, what happened?"

Kitty laughed again. "The phone rang, and I thought it was Todd and you know what he's like if he can't get through so I just shoved Flipper at the Bufo and leaped out."

It was Bernie's turn to laugh. " 'Inflatable Toy Dolphin Battles Deadly Bufo and Saves TV Star's Life in Boca Backyard.' You could sell your story to the *Weekly World News*."

"Okay, okay." Kitty rolled her eyes. "It's funny now but it wasn't at the time." She paused and picked up the bundle of message slips. Dana Lewis had called. So had Todd and Ernie Platzer.

"So, Bernie?" She stared at her cameraman as he sprawled on her couch. "What do you think? Shall we do the reenactment tonight? We've got to keep the ball rolling. We can put it together from the info we already have: The killer waited for her in the bushes, attacked her by the house, she fought back, he slammed her into the wall, then dragged her down to the pool, so on and so on."

"Sounds good to me. What about location?"

Kitty thought for a moment. "We can keep the shots tight but we've got to give some idea of a mansion in the background. . . . Something that looks Palm Beachy. I'll give Ann Rensler a call," she added, referring to a Palm Beach Realtor who had allowed *Inside Copy* to use the grounds of a vacant listing on a couple of previous occasions.

She placed the call, leaving a message for Ann at her office.

"Maybe George will play the heavy for us," Bernie suggested, jumping to his feet and cocking his head toward the window. George was a bartender who worked in the sports bar across the parking lot.

"Done." Kitty nodded "And Ginny for Marina?"

Her office manager walked through the door with Kitty's coffee in that same moment. "Ginny for what?" the older woman queried.

Kitty flashed her a broad, mischievous smile. "We'd like to kill you off this afternoon, Ginny, if you don't mind. We think you're a perfect double for Marina."

Ginny took a step back, wrapping her jacket around herself protectively. "Think again, dearie. The way I heard it on the show that poor woman was found starkers. I have to draw the line somewhere."

"Oh, come on, Ginny," Bernie coaxed her. "We'll give you a producer credit on the segment."

"Yeah," Kitty nodded. "Please Ginny, we're going to have to get on this right away and we don't have time to shop around. You're our best bet. Look, run across to Shari's Boutique and get yourself a body stocking and Bernie will shoot shoulders up. I swear . . ."

Ginny stared from one to the other, shaking her head. Then she sighed resignedly, as if knowing from past experience that it was pointless arguing. "All right, I'll do it but I'd like to get a beachrobe as well."

Bernie gave her the thumbs-up sign as she left Kitty's office. "Ooo-kay! We're ready to rock 'n roll."

Kitty breathed a loud sigh of relief just as the phone rang out on her desk.

"Hey, Fitzgerald, don't you ever return phone calls?" The familiar, clipped tones of *Inside Copy*'s anchorwoman sailed down the line without preamble.

Kitty mouthed "Dragon Lady" to Bernie, who threw himself back onto the couch, pulling his baseball cap over his face.

Dragon Lady was the bureau's nickname for Dana Lewis and even staid, proper Ginny referred to her by that name. Kitty pictured Dana sitting at her desk, her mouth set in a thin, angry line. The anchorwoman's natural personality was about one-hundred-and-eighty degrees off the sexy, bubbly image she projected on camera in her little peek-a-boo power suits.

Dana was supposed to be a foil to the content of the show—something pretty to look at after a segment of blood and gore.

"Sorry, Dana." Kitty spoke softly but firmly. "I was about to call you. But I wanted to discuss a follow-up on Marina Dee Haley with Bernie first."

"Yeah, well, I hope you have a good idea because we've got to stay right on top of this story. I worked damn hard to pull everything together last night. You know it's a pain when everything is in bits and pieces. But I did it."

You sat on your butt, Dana. Lindsay's the one who pulled it all together.

"Oh, don't worry about the story," Kitty said, forcing herself to sound pleasant. She didn't want Dana complaining about the bureau. But Dana was not easy to deal with: The last time she'd called Kitty directly it was to demand that Kitty pull some strings at the Fountainbleu Hotel to get her parents a complimentary suite.

"Well, of course I'm worried," the anchorwoman weighed in, enunciating every word. "After all, I'm the one who's going to look stupid if we drop the ball on this. It's my ass on the line every night. . . ."

Kitty's attention drifted as Dana Lewis launched into a monologue on the burdens of anchoring.

Yeah, yeah, yeah . . . Kitty picked up the yellow padded envelope from the top of her pile and ripped it open to find a videotape and a note folded in two. She put the note to one side and inserted the tape into the VCR beside her desk using a remote to turn down the volume on the TV monitor standing on her credenza.

Kitty's attention focused on the screen as Dana babbled on. She found herself staring at a grainy, black-and-white shot of what appeared to be a doctor's examining room. A boy sat on the examining couch with his back to the camera. With a start, Kitty realized the boy was naked.

Then a man stepped into the shot, also with his back to the camera. Kitty stared silently at the screen, her eyes widening. As the man walked toward the boy she realized that she was looking at a naked back. The man was wearing some sort of surgical smock-type top that gaped open to reveal not only his back but—as he moved away from the camera—also exposed naked buttocks and bare legs.

"... Of course, I'm not complaining about last night's scoop. But you've got to admit, more often than not, we're the ones playing catch-up. ..." Dana's voice rose a notch as Kitty watched the doctor come up to the boy, pushing him down on the examining couch as he untied his own smock and let it fall to the ground. Then his hand reached for the boy. ...

"Oh Jeez!" The exclamation tumbled out before she could stop it as she stabbed the Stop button on the VCR.

"Fitzgerald, can you hear me?"

Kitty blinked. "Yes. Yes, Dana, I hear you. But trust me we're right on top of this one." Then she abruptly hung up, cutting off the anchorwoman in midsentence, and reached for the note that had come with the tape.

It was one line, typed neatly across the center of the page.

Little boys like playing doctor. I am sure Jamie will.

Bile rose in her throat. "Bernie! Look at this."

Her cameraman sat up abruptly. "What? What!"

She pushed at the rewind button and let the tape roll again. "Take a look at this. And, this." She tossed the note at him, then got to her feet and walked to the window and took a deep breath as she stared across the parking lot.

Bernie's reaction came quickly. He let out a low whistle under his breath and then about thirty seconds later she heard the click of the Stop button.

"Wow! Sick puppy!" He was shaking his head as Kitty

turned to face him. " 'I'm sure Jamie will.' " He repeated the words in the note. "What's that supposed to mean?"

Kitty shrugged and shivered. "God only knows . . ." She paused, swallowing to stop her stomach from churning. "Do you think it's someone who knows Jamie?"

Bernie shook his head firmly. "Maybe someone who knows *about* him. And that would narrow it down to only one or two million people in South Florida. Heck, remember just after you and Jamie were in *Boca Raton* magazine, you got some really weird calls?" He tossed the note back onto her desk. "I bet McCauley Culkin gets mail like this all the time."

"Oh, Bernie, please. This isn't funny. I can take crackpot mail when it's directed at me. But the thought of some dirty, disgusting pervert drooling over Jamie. . ." She paused again and paced back to her desk, rummaging in the trash can for the Federal Express envelope she had discarded.

She retrieved it and stared hard at the scrawl that filled the space for the sender's name and address. "What's this say, Bernie?"

He took the envelope from her, his eyes narrowing. "B. Strand? Strond? Stroud, maybe. I can't figure the address. But I'm sure it's not his address. I don't think he got Fedex to pick up from his house."

Kitty took a deep breath as she stared at the note on her desk, telling herself it was pointless trying to figure out who had sent it. There were sickos all over the place. She'd had her share of obscene mail and phone calls in her time at *Inside Copy*. But never a porn video like this one. She grit her teeth as all the phones in the office seemed suddenly to ring at the same time. As she grabbed for one of the lines, and Bernie for another, Ginny poked her head around the door to tell her that Todd was holding on the third.

She stabbed the flickering button on her phone, automatically putting him on the speakerphone.

"Toddy," she greeted him with exaggerated joviality. "I

was just dialing your number. I heard we did great in the overnights."

"Not bad, not bad," the executive producer agreed. "But that's yesterday's news. Got anything new for today?"

Kitty took a deep breath. "Bernie and I are going to shoot a reenactment of the murder this morning. We were just on our way."

"Good, good. Excellent stuff. And you can add Jeff Haley to your list. He slipped by us in Wallkill. Superintendent confirmed he was released at eight last night and our latest info is that he's on a plane heading your way, even as we speak. His official release date was sheduled for next week, but they're going to waive the four or five days."

Kitty closed her eyes. The pain in her head that had started as a dull throb during her conversation with Dana Lewis now seemed to be turning into a full-fledged, searing migraine.

She blinked. "I hear you, Todd."

"I want that interview, Kitty." Todd's voice seemed to bounce off the office walls. "We've got footage from Wallkill, interior and exterior, and I want to run that together with Haley roaming through his Palm Beach mansion. I want to see him vowing to get the maniac who robbed him of his mother . . . the maniac who cheated him of their reunion just hours before he became a free man, etcetera, etcetera. . . . Get the picture? I don't want to see Haley on *Inside Edition* or *A Current Affair*."

"Suppose they offer him megabucks?"

"Fuck that!" Todd interrupted. "He doesn't need the money. He's going to be looking for a friendly face down there, someone he can trust. Like someone he once worked with and dated, eh? What do you think?"

"Come on, Todd, I didn't *date* him. You know that." Kitty emphasized the words, aware of Bernie's quizzical expression.

"Oh, that's right. Teenagers *date*." Todd emphasized the word, his voice dripping with sarcasm. "Well, whatever it is you two did ... all those hours you spent together ... that's got to be worth something, Fitzgerald. I have faith in you. In fact, I'm writing the promo for the interview right now." Todd's chuckle filled her office. Then, abruptly, it faded. "Don't let us down, Fitzgerald. The interview is a biggie. Ta-ta."

Kitty depressed the speakerphone button and buried her head in her hands.

"You dated Marina's son?" Bernie's question cut through her thoughts.

"Oh, don't you start, Bernie."

The cameraman surveyed Kitty through narrowed eyes.

"Okay," Kitty sighed loudly. "We were friends. We spent time together ...," she paused, "but, that's all there was to it."

Bernie nodded. "Okay, that's cool, too. So, let's go meet him at the airport. Todd's got a point. Haley might welcome the sight of a friendly face in the crowd."

"Bernie, shut up!"

The cameraman stood up abruptly.

Kitty paced across the room. "Listen Bern, we've got a problem here." She paused, thinking of how best to phrase her next few sentences. "The truth is: Jeff Haley and I are not friends anymore. Okay? Not to put too fine a point on it, I'm probably the last reporter on earth that he would talk to, and if he knew how badly we wanted the interview he'd probably go straight to *A Current Affair* and offer himself to them—for nothing. Get the picture?"

Bernie took a moment to digest everything she had said. Then he threw his cap in the air. "Shit! I thought you were going to tell me the situation is *totally* hopeless."

Despite her dark thoughts, Kitty laughed. Then her face clouded again. "I should level with Todd, you know. Tell him how it is. He could send a reporter down from New York."

"Oh, yeah, good move, Kitty. I can hear him now: 'What's the effing use of an effing bureau in effing Florida if I have to send a reporter from New York every time an effing big story breaks?' "

Kitty paced back to the window. "Okay, okay." She stared again across the parking lot toward Dixie Highway.

"Are you sure the situation is really that hopeless?" Bernie questioned.

Kitty didn't reply immediately. Instead she went to her desk and opened one of the bottom drawers. Rummaging among old file folders buried beneath a layer of plastic sachets of ketchup and soy sauce, she finally found the envelope and handed it to Bernie. "Before you read it," she told him, "you should know that I visited him a few times when he went to jail when I was still living in New York, and I wrote him a few letters. Hell! I was probably the *only* friend who stood by him."

"But ... ?" Bernie prompted.

"But after I moved here ... after I met Frank ... I stopped. I mean I didn't have the time to write, and I didn't really want to be getting calls from a prison with Frank around. So I refused to accept the calls. That's when I got this letter."

Kitty took back the one-page letter from Bernie's hand and read it aloud: "Kitty! I think I've got your message and I'm not going to write or call you again but I do need to let you know how I feel. You must know how much you've hurt me. I feel like someone has severed my life-line. I told you, time and again, what it meant to me to get your letters and to hear your voice, but now you can't be bothered anymore. So be it. It's your choice and there's nothing I can do about it. All I can hope is that with time I'll be able to erase all thoughts of you from my memory. It'll be easier than trying to understand and forgive you— because that's something I don't think I'll ever be able to do. Good-bye. Jeff."

Bernie grimaced as Kitty flung the letter back into the desk drawer. "Well, that's pretty plain and to the point. But I guess somewhat understandable especially if you were *that* close."

Kitty ignored Bernie's pointed remark. "I suppose I could have been kinder. But," she shrugged, "I wasn't."

Bernie punched her gently in the arm. "Hey, maybe he won't feel quite so bitter once he's down here and out in the big wide world again."

Kitty laughed. "Right. But that doesn't mean he's going to do me any favors, either. Would you, in his place?" She sighed and reached for her coffee, then picked up the phone. "Let's see if Ann's found a suitable location for us, and let's get this reenactment in the bag. I'll think about Jeff's interview later."

Bernie nodded and walked out of her office, leaving Kitty with her head still pounding and with the sinking feeling that things were going to get worse over the next few days.

❧ *Chapter 15* ❧

"𝒜s I live and breathe . . . No, it can't be. . . . Yes, it is. *Inside Copy*'s very own star reporter—Kitty Fitzgerald!"

Kitty froze in the doorway of Chuck and Harold's, recognizing the strident, booming voice an instant before her eyes alighted on Rick Tyler's ruddy, well-worn face.

The *Inside Edition* reporter came toward her, pushing his way past a foursome waiting to be seated, and threw his arm around her shoulders, planting a sloppy kiss on her cheek. Kitty figured Rick had come to Chuck and Harold's straight from his New York flight.

She disengaged herself carefully from his grip and stared at him without smiling. "Been here long, Rick?"

"Long enough, doll."

Who didn't know that? She had run into Rick Tyler many times, chasing the same assignments, and she had never known him to make a move on a story without first establishing his "base of operations"—by which he meant finding the most popular bar in town.

She took a step into the restaurant. Looking around she could see that the bar area was unusually crowded. Then she recognized the faces, one by one. The media had arrived.

She felt Rick's hand cupping her elbow and guiding her toward the bar. "C'mon, doll, let me buy you a drink."

She resisted. Scanning the restaurant interior, she spotted Frank sitting at a table by the grand piano in the center of the back room.

"Sorry, Ricky, I'm meeting someone."

"Hey Fitzgerald, don't run away. We hear you've got Haley in the bag. True or false?"

Before she had a chance to say anything a second voice interrupted from within a tight little group, gathered beside the TV screen. "No, we didn't hear that, Tyler. We assumed it. We figured it out. Who's Haley going to talk to, we asked ourselves? And, we said, sure, his old pal from way back when he was in the biz himself."

Kitty freed her elbow from Rick Tyler's grip, pulling away abruptly. It was obvious to her that the whole pack had made their way directly from the airport to the bar. It was also obvious that they'd done some homework. If she said anything at all about Jeff Haley, she'd end up in the headlines herself: "Marina's Convict Son Reunites With Gal Pal in Palm Beach." And she had no intention of becoming part of this story.

"Excuse me, guys." She moved quickly away from the group and headed for the back room.

"Bad choice," she laughed as she approached Frank. "I should have realized they'd all be here." She sat down, attributing Frank's chaste air-kiss to the presence of the reporters in the bar, but a couple of seconds later she noticed he was still looking serious. She remembered that he had sounded a little edgy when she'd called him earlier that afternoon for an update on the investigation.

"Something wrong, hon? Are you pissed because we did a reenactment?" She looked away momentarily. She'd fed several takes of the murder dramatization to New York that afternoon, each one a little more graphic than the last.

"It's not the reenactment, Kitty." Frank's voice sounded weary. "It's this." He paused, reaching into the inside pocket of his navy blazer. "I came across it last night." He handed her a folded piece of paper.

Kitty opened up the Xerox copy of a newspaper clipping and stared in dismay at the old heading: "I Was With Marina's Son on Night of Shooting."

Quickly she folded the sheet of paper. She didn't have to read through the story—it was the one she'd feared would surface. Then she took a deep breath and looked up at Frank, staring directly into his eyes. "Jeff and I were not having a relationship," she said. "We were just friends." She tossed the clipping back to Frank. "And Jeff Haley is not Jamie's father. . . . If that's what you were thinking," she added unnecessarily, because it was obvious that's ex-actly what he was thinking.

Frank raised an eyebrow. "Why the 'No comment'? I thought that's what people said when they didn't want to admit to something."

Kitty shook her head. "I replied 'No comment' to every question they asked. They just chose to quote me directly on that one for the obvious reason: So that people would get the same impression you did."

"So there's a lot of people who think Jeff Haley is Jamie's father?"

She shook her head again. "Not people who matter. Not my real friends. They all knew I didn't even meet Jeff un-til after I got pregnant. That part of the story is true. The rest is just plain innuendo. Surely you can see that, Frank?"

She leaned closer to him and took his fingers in her hand. "Do you honestly think I would have kept it from you if Jeff Haley was Jamie's father? Would it make sense for me to do that knowing he was going to get out of jail someday and perhaps come looking for me and Jamie?"

She stared quizzically at Frank, trying to read what was

going through his mind but she couldn't decipher the look. She waited while a waiter placed their drinks in front of them. A Dewar's on the rocks for Frank and an iced tea for her, which Frank had obviously ordered when he'd seen her come into the restaurant.

"But why didn't you just deny it outright?" Frank persisted, evidently still skeptical. "I mean, surely you must have known that a lot of people were going to jump to the conclusion that he was Jamie's father?"

She waited till the waiter had left. "It didn't seem like such a big deal at the time. It was better than to have them poking around in my personal life to find Jamie's real father."

"Better for people to think that Jamie's father was a convicted felon rather than an Australian reporter?"

"He was not convicted at the time," she replied, hearing the incredulity in Frank's voice. Then she took a long, hard gulp of her drink, aware that she was still on the uphill.

"Frank, listen, I was already three months pregnant when I met Jeff for the first time. That's the part of the story that's true. I never met him till Marina moved to WPEN. I was in the cafeteria having a late lunch one day. I was having skim milk and a bologna sandwich. . . ."

"A memorable meeting, obviously, since you recall the details so well." Frank jumped in as she paused to pick up her glass.

"A memorable *lunch*," Kitty corrected. "It was the day my doctor confirmed I was pregnant and I remember the skim milk because it was in the moment when I picked it up off the counter and put it on my tray that the news really hit me." Kitty paused again. She had not thought about that day for a long time but she was not surprised that she could still recall it so vividly. She began to recount the events to Frank.

She had run through the full gamut of emotions during the lunch: from shock to anger to confusion to fear and back to shock. How could it have happened? How could she have become pregnant on that one night? She had asked the questions like some immature adolescent.

So when Jeff had stopped at her table and said, "We haven't met yet, have we?" she had retorted sharply, "Then consider yourself very fortunate."

As soon as the words were out she had realized how petulant she sounded. But Jeff had not been discouraged.

"I can't imagine you mean that," he told her, sliding into the seat across from her and extending his hand. "I'm Jeff Haley, and I know you're Kitty Fitzgerald. I watch *Inside Copy* every night." He grinned. "Well, every other night."

She'd smiled then, recognizing his name if not his face.

"It's not the worst I've heard today, believe me," he told her as she sipped her skim milk and looked him over.

He was someone she might have passed by in a crowd without noticing. He had a pleasant, not particularly striking face, with dark-blonde hair that he wore a little longer than she liked to see on a man. Wire-rimmed, tinted glasses gave him a slightly intellectual look.

"You're staring," he interrupted her study.

Kitty flushed. "I'm sorry. I guess I was."

His eyes flickered behind the lens of his glasses. "Does it meet with your approval?"

"What?"

"What you see."

Kitty felt uncomfortable for a minute with his directness, then she shrugged. "It really doesn't matter what I think. I have appalling taste in men, believe me."

Jeff had said nothing, letting her words with their tinge of bitterness hang in the air. He just sat there, nodding, staring at her as if trying to figure her out. Maybe expecting her to embellish the statement, which she had no intention of doing.

Finally, she got to her feet and told him she was expected back in the editing room. He had brushed his hand against hers as she reached to pick up her empty milk carton. "I'm a very good listener, Kitty," he'd said.

He had turned out to be more than a good listener. A couple of days later she had emerged from an edit room in the late evening to find a message on her desk from him.

"I was just about to leave," he told her. "But it's pouring outside and I have Marina's limo, so if you need a ride, I'm going your way."

"Oh yeah? Is that a fact?" she'd countered teasingly. "And how do you happen to know which way is my way?"

There had been a brief pause before he'd laughed out loud. "I don't, actually. I just didn't want you to think I'm coming onto you."

She smiled to herself. "Are you?"

"I don't know yet. Maybe I can decide over dinner. How does Chinese sound?"

Kitty was starving. She had not eaten lunch and she knew there would be nothing satisfying in her refrigerator. So they had ended up at the Purple Dragon, just two blocks from the TV station.

Kitty had asked him about his mother. "Is she really as tough to work for as gossip has it?"

"Let's put it this way: If I wasn't there she'd have a new executive producer every month. But I'm used to her moods so it doesn't bother me . . . and it's satisfying because for years I was a pretty useless object as far as she was concerned. Now *she* needs *me* and she knows it."

"A useless object?" Kitty echoed.

Jeff shrugged. "Well, you know what I mean."

She nodded. Marina's early career had been well documented.

Kitty took a break in her recap to sip her iced tea and noticed that Frank had almost finished his Scotch. "Jeff was the first person I told about being pregnant. It was just a relief to share that with someone."

Frank pushed a menu toward her. "Jamie's father was already gone by then? Out of the country?"

"Out of my life." Kitty nodded, aware that she wasn't actually answering Frank's question and wondering if he'd notice. She flicked open her menu, then closed it again, deciding on a Caesar salad without studying the options.

Frank ordered for both of them and then sat back, waiting for her to continue.

"That's all there was to it, really," Kitty continued quickly. "We just became friends. Pals, whatever. I listened to him when he had problems with Marina and he was always there when I needed a shoulder to lean on. Jeff was good at looking after people."

"And you needed looking after? I find that hard to believe." Frank grinned at her and signaled the waiter to bring him another Scotch.

She grinned back. "Believe it. Back then, I was wandering around in a daze, not knowing what I was going to do with a baby, not knowing how I was going to cope. Jeff put some order in my life. . . ." She paused and found herself laughing out loud suddenly. "You should have seen the look on his face the first time he ever looked in my refrigerator."

Jeff had stocked her refrigerator with vegetables, fruit, chicken, and fish. He made a list of the basic food groups and stuck them on her refrigerator door. A couple of evenings a week he'd arrive at her downtown loft and insist on cooking dinner. Sometimes, when she was working late, she'd arrive to find a meal waiting on the table for her. He arranged for a weekly service to come in to clean up and do her laundry. Another evening he had arrived with a list of domestic agencies in the city telling her she'd need plenty of time to interview nannies and check references. He bought her a book of baby names and they had spent an evening reading through it. He had also bought gifts for the baby and gifts for her. One day she had returned home to find an expensive cocktail dress hanging in her closet. It was a dress she'd admired in the Lady Madonna boutique, so she also knew it was way overpriced. But Jeff had insisted she keep it—and wear it to his mother's wedding.

Kitty sighed, and paused while the waiter placed another iced tea in front of her. "I didn't think it was a very good idea for me to show up with him when I was almost six months pregnant, but Jeff said he'd appreciate my support. He hated Davenport from day one. The man really was dreadful. He turned up drunk for his own wedding. Anyway, I figured it was the least I could do for him, when he was always doing things for me."

Kitty sipped her drink. "I know it sounds like a weird relationship but it worked at the time. Jeff was a doer. He liked to get things done while I would have just let them slide."

"A take-charge guy, eh?" Frank eyed her, curiosity written all over his face.

"Very," Kitty agreed, recalling the night she had returned from an out-of-town trip and found that in her absence Jeff had brought in a carpenter and converted a space, next to her bedroom area, into a small nursery. She had mentioned the idea of it to him once but had been surprised that he had just gone ahead and done it.

Just as she was surprised and maybe a little peeved, she admitted to Frank as the waiter placed their food in front of them, that Jeff had also furnished it complete with crib and dresser and changing table. There were certain things she had wanted to pick out herself. But she hadn't said anything. It was done and it was one more item she could cross off her list.

Then about a month before Jamie's birth she had returned home to find Jeff sitting at her makeshift desk in the tiny den off the living room. As she walked over she could see that the mess of mail and clippings and papers that usually littered the desktop was now all sorted into tidy little stacks.

Jeff had turned around to face her, smiling. "I've finally sorted everything out for you. Here, these are bills that need your attention. This is a folder with your clippings on those nanny agencies. . . ."

Kitty had stared, perplexed, as she took the folder from him, noticing that the bottom right-hand drawer in the desk had also been opened. It was the drawer where she kept her important documents and bank statements—and her family pictures. It was where she had placed three photographs that she had taken of herself, as her belly had swelled month by month, posing naked for the camera.

In the next moment she had felt something explode inside her and she had started yelling at Jeff, sweeping all the tidy little stacks of papers off the desktop.

He had stared at her with concern and confusion, had tried to say something but Kitty wouldn't let him.

"That's it, Jeff, you had no right to do this," she had screamed at him. "Those are my things, my papers. I don't want anyone touching them. Get out! Go!"

He had stood there for a few seconds longer, the expression on his face changing from bewilderment to pain. Then without another word he had picked up his jacket and left her apartment.

She had not slept very well that night. Had vacillated between anger at Jeff and anger at herself for flying off the handle at him, feeling that she had overreacted because she was so tired and so fed-up with being pregnant.

Kitty stared wide-eyed at Frank, picking at a crouton as the memories of that awful night stayed with her. "That was the night of the shooting. I was the first person he called after the paramedics and police. . . . At six in the morning."

Frank nodded and reached for his glass, which had stood empty while he picked at his swordfish steak. Under the table he let his hand rest lightly on Kitty's knee.

"And you went?"

She nodded quickly. "Of course I went. I felt terrible about the way I'd thrown him out. And I suppose I felt guilty. After I threw him out he'd apparently stopped in a couple of bars.

"Anyway," she paused, and shrugged, "the day after the shooting, Jeff agreed to an interview with me for *Inside Copy.*"

"You asked him to do an interview?"

"Everybody wanted an interview and Jeff said he had nothing to hide. But he was only going to talk to someone he could trust—and that was me."

Frank nodded, looking pensive. "So you were friends again while he was going through his ordeal?"

Kitty pushed away her plate. "Yes," she replied tersely. "And for a while after that. After he went to Green Haven I wrote to him and we used to talk on the phone."

"Why did you never mention him to me?"

She shrugged. "Because I didn't think it was that important. It wasn't like we'd been involved in any sort of serious relationship. Anyway, I stopped writing and taking his calls after we met—" she broke off, feeling the color rush to her cheeks. "I guess because I felt it wasn't right to be getting serious with a detective while playing pen pals with someone in jail."

Frank laughed. A short, hollow laugh. "Did you tell him about me?"

Kitty shook her head. "No. Of course not. I think that would have been the ultimate kick in the teeth. He took it badly enough. To quote his last letter: 'I hope I'll be able to erase all thoughts of you from my memory because it'll be easier than trying to forgive you. Good-bye.'"

"Obviously left a lasting impression with his words, since you remember them so clearly?"

Kitty laughed out loud. "Not really. I happened to re-read the letter today for Bernie, after Todd told me he expects me to get the big exclusive interview with Jeff when he arrives here."

"What did you say?" Frank signaled their waiter to bring the check.

Kitty laughed again. "What I usually say: Nothing. I just listened while he told me about the promo he's already written for it."

It was Frank's turn to laugh out loud. "How are you going to finagle this one?"

Kitty shivered suddenly. "I don't know, hon. I haven't a clue. I'm afraid Jeff's going to go ballistic if I turn up at the funeral tomorrow. I have this nightmare that he'll have me thrown out."

"He can't have you thrown out of a cemetery. Anyway, Don and I will be there."

"But he could create a scene in front of all those other guys. Wouldn't that be a good story?"

Frank laid his hand over hers and squeezed it gently. "Just don't make yourself crazy over this, okay sweets? It's not worth it. Especially since I take it you're not exactly yearning to meet up with him again. Are you?" He got to his feet and helped Kitty out of her chair, still holding her hand. "Are you?" he repeated.

Kitty squeezed his fingers in return. She was relieved that she'd had the chance to set the record straight on Jeff Haley, relieved that he had asked her about the newspaper report instead of stewing over it in silence like some men might have done.

"No, I'm not crazy about the idea," she finally agreed. "But I've got to try."

❧ *Chapter 16* ❧

*F*rank was preoccupied with his thoughts as they left the restaurant. But he didn't voice them. Linking his arm through Kitty's, as they walked down Royal Poinciana, he told himself enough had been said. He was sure Kitty had told him all there was to tell about her relationship with Haley. He had no reason to doubt her story. With Haley on his way to Palm Beach, it would make no sense for her to continue any kind of charade about him. Still, something niggled at the back of his mind. He couldn't get a focus on Jeff Haley. There was something wrong with the picture.

According to Don the superintendent of Wallkill had extolled Haley's virtues: "Model prisoner. Worked in the library. Kept to himself. Helped my wife edit the family home videos."

According to Kitty he had run his mother's TV show and with Kitty herself he had been caring and supportive. She had described him as a doer and take-charge guy, and as she'd talked about him Frank had pictured a confident, self-reliant individual, perhaps a little on the pushy side.

But there were pieces missing in the puzzle. Pieces that suggested he wasn't getting the total picture. Haley had involved himself in the most intimate details of Kitty's life without, apparently, making any move to become intimate in other ways. And the first time she'd criticized him and thrown him out, he'd fallen apart. Had hit the bars, gotten into the middle of an argument between his mother and stepfather, and had shot the man dead.

That's what bothered Frank the most. He didn't care about the circumstances or how easy TV shows made it look. He knew what it meant—and how it felt—to point a loaded gun at another human being. He also knew how difficult it was to cock the trigger and fire.

He shivered involuntarily and pulled Kitty closer to him to feel the warmth and softness of her breast against his arm as they walked to the bottom of the street and rounded the corner into Bradley Place.

He lived within walking distance of the restaurant, in a townhouse on the Intracoastal, in what he considered the perfect location—just a couple of blocks from Bradley's Saloon. It was not a house he could have afforded on his detective's salary. There was nothing in Royal Palm Beach that he, or any other police officer in the department, could afford, except when they were offered the opportunity of doubling as in-house security.

The owners of Frank's townhouse had bought the home for a winter retreat and, having furnished it lavishly and expensively with art and antiques, they had offered it for rent to a member of the police department for a nominal fee rather than having it sit unoccupied as a magnet for burglars. The only downside was that every season, for a month around the Christmas and New Year holidays, he had to find alternative accommodations, but it was a small inconvenience given the luxury he enjoyed for the remaining eleven months.

He waited for Kitty to retrieve her tote from the Blazer

that she'd parked outside his house. Then he took it from her and led the way up the steps. Inside, kicking the front door shut, he nudged her up against the wall and kissed her fiercely on the mouth.

"Hey Detective, not so fast," she gasped, sliding out of his grasp.

He backed away a step. "I've been waiting to do that all evening . . . all day . . . for two days, to tell the truth."

"So have I," she replied. "But I just need a moment to clear my head." She walked down the hallway and through the spacious, thickly carpeted living room and opened the atrium door onto the brick patio.

He followed her out. "What's on your mind, Kit? You're not still worrying about the story, are you?"

Kitty nodded.

Frank put his arms around her. "Take a break, love. Forget the story for an hour or two."

"You know Todd will have my ass if I don't get the interview."

Frank gripped her hand and playfully pushed her down on the chaise. Then he straddled it, facing her. "You're wrong, Kitty. I'm the only one who's going to have your ass. This ass is mine." He eyed her lazily, reaching for the thin strap of her dress and slipping it off her shoulder.

"Very nice," he murmured fingering the flimsy lace that covered her perfect small breasts.

She laughed throatily. "The best that Victoria's Secret had to offer this month. Delivered just yesterday."

He laughed with her. "The mail-order maven strikes again." He reached behind her to unhook the clasp when suddenly, unbidden and uninvited, the image of Roberta Mallory's full, large breasts flared before his eyes.

Going to Roberta's apartment so late at night had been a stupid move. A sequence of images flashed swiftly in his head: Roberta standing by the printer checking the spewing pages . . . Roberta handing him a glass of beer, telling him to sit down and make himself comfortable . . . Roberta turning to him, smiling, telling him that she was going to change into something more comfortable . . . and then in the next moment pulling off her tight little T-shirt right in front of him, to reveal her thrusting, naked breasts.

Why the hell am I thinking about Roberta Mallory's breasts? He blinked, trying to erase the picture, but he'd wasted the moment.

He realized Kitty was edging out of his grasp and getting to her feet. She paced back across the patio and into the living room.

"Do you think we could have a nightcap?" she asked, glancing across at the liquor cabinet. "I can't seem to relax."

He crossed the room and poured her a Bailey's Irish Cream—the strongest liquor Kitty would touch. Turning around to hand her the glass he noticed that she had spotted Marina Dee Haley's manuscript lying on the coffee table. He groaned inwardly as he saw her eyes light up.

"Marina's autobiography?" she asked, reaching for the pages. "May I?"

He shrugged. "Are you going to put it down and come to bed if I say no?"

He wasn't sure she'd even heard him. She was staring at the first page and giggling. "I love her opening sentence: 'It was the best of times. It was the worst of times.' " Kitty's voice rose on a note of incredulity. "It's certainly an apt description of her wedding day, but do you think she realized that line's already been done?"

Frank laughed too, carrying their drinks over to where Kitty was sitting on the floor and crouching down beside her. "Well, Dickens isn't going to sue, is he? Anyway, it's all being rewritten by a ghostwriter."

"Have you read it all?" Kitty's eyes gleamed.

He shook his head. "I only read as far as baby Jeffie's birth and how she dumped him on her mother."

Kitty nodded. "Yep. That's what she did. Jeff grew up believing his grandmother was his mom, and that Marina was his sister. Of course, she had to keep it a secret. It would have been a big scandal in her day. Would have ended her career. But that's an old story."

"When did he find out the truth?"

Frank's question had Kitty's mouth dropping open in mock horror. "Come on! You're kidding me, aren't you? Everyone knows that story."

Frank shook his head. "Not me. You know I don't read gossip columns or those tabloids." He paused. "Well, are you going to fill me in?"

Kitty smiled teasingly. "Are you going to read the rest of the manuscript?"

"Sure. I've got few other leads at the moment."

"Well then, I'm not going to spoil the story for you. I'm sure it's in there. It was a turning point in Marina Dee Haley's career. Anyway, tell me something I don't know. Does she name Jeff's father?"

Frank shook his head again. "Not in the part I read. Why? Was that a big secret, too?"

Kitty laughed. "The only thing in her life that stayed a secret, as far as I can tell. She refused even to tell Jeff, just glossed over it every time the subject was ever raised."

"Really?" Frank stared at Kitty for a moment. "That sounds an awful lot like another TV star I know." The words were out before he could stop them. And he found himself wondering if that's what had drawn Jeff Haley to Kitty. Seeing her in the same situation as his mother had once been in? Feeling a bond with Kitty's unborn son, who, like himself, was never likely to see or meet his real father?

Suddenly he realized that Kitty was no longer sitting beside him. She'd jumped to her feet and paced over to the wet bar where she was pouring herself another Bailey's, her face set in a grim, unhappy mask.

He crossed the room swiftly and took her in his arms. "I'm sorry," he whispered the words into the hollow of her neck. "That was a stupid thing to say."

She twisted out of his grasp. "No, it wasn't, Frank. It was an obvious thing to say. But you know, I'm sure Marina was doing what she thought best—in everybody's interests."

Kitty backed away a step and stared at him, searching his face, he thought, as if looking for her next cue. Then her eyes seemed to drift over his shoulder, focusing on some distant spot, beyond the patio.

"What is it, Kitty?"

She shook her head. "The whole business this evening . . . your questions about Jeff Haley . . . your suspicions . . ."

"That upset you, didn't it? And I'm sorry, and if it's any consolation I truly didn't believe the newspaper story. I just knew you wouldn't lie about something that important."

She backed away a step. "What if I had lied?"

He shrugged, and held out his hand to her. "I don't know, Kit. I didn't really think about it." He paused and grinned, stepping toward her to lift her into his arms. "Is there a reason for these questions? Or is this some new kind of foreplay?"

She shook her head and buried her face in his shoulder, finally letting her body relax into his as he carried her down the hallway to the bedroom, where he ignored the king-sized bed and instead took her over to the chaise by the window.

Laying her down he deftly slipped her dress off down over her hips. The light reflecting off the waters of the Intracoastal played like a low-wattage spotlight on the chaise, and he stared at her as she stretched out, her arms folded behind her head, waiting for him.

He undid the buttons on his shirt and dropped it on the floor. He unfastened his belt.

"Frank!"

"Yes?"

"I just wanted to tell you . . . I want you to know I would never lie to you about something that—"

"Important . . . I know," he finished the sentence for her

impatiently, kicking off his pants as he lay down beside her.

"Or something that could affect you or me, okay?"

He leaned over and kissed her throat. "Okay," he whispered. He waited, sensing there was more to come. He wondered where the conversation was leading. Kitty seemed so serious and somber he was gripped with a sudden dread. But suddenly, her arms tightened around him as she hugged him fiercely.

"I just wanted you to know that," she whispered. "I would never do anything to hurt us."

In the next moment he felt her fingers tracing a line on the inside of his thigh, moving slowly and teasingly upward till they found their place in the heat of his groin. . . .

Eventually they both dozed off on the chaise. But Kitty woke around three, nudging him to move to the bed where he would be more comfortable.

"Where are you going?" he asked, stifling a yawn as he saw her pick up her dress and slip it on.

She sounded fully awake. "I'd better go, hon. I have to get back. I've got to figure out what to do about Jeff and the funeral. I've got to change, find something suitable to wear. I'm too wound up to sleep, anyway."

He could tell there was no point in arguing with her. He was too sleepy to argue. He watched her gather her things and walked her to the front door.

"Drive carefully, sweets," he said, hugging her. "I'll see you tomorrow. At the funeral."

He watched from the doorway to make sure she was safe in the Blazer before closing the door behind him and walking back to bed.

But when he slid under the sheets he found himself wide awake. He punched the pillows to get more comfortable and lay in the darkness, telling himself that everything would be different after he and Kitty were married. No more driving through the night for either of them. He hated this. He hated sleeping without her.

His thoughts returned momentarily to their lovemaking.

Kitty was so perfect for him in every way. They were perfect together. Partners, soulmates. Friends. They understood each other and supported each other.

He had dreamed about Kitty long before he'd met her. Way back in Philadelphia he had been looking for someone like her. But he'd looked in the wrong places. He'd spent too many hours in too many bars, telling himself that, first, he had to get rid of the frustrations of the day and unwind after the day's grind.

One night, returning to his small, dark, empty apartment on Pine Street, he had realized that he was looking at another twenty years of frustrating days and empty nights. He would not, one night, come home to suddenly find the woman and family of his dreams waiting for him. Nothing was going to change—unless he changed it.

He closed his eyes and for a second the memory of Roberta Mallory's pouting, eager lips and her naked breasts flashed in his head. He had met so many women like her in the old days. She had reminded him of those old days. The depressing, empty memories had come flooding back so forcefully that it had taken no effort at all to pick up the manuscript, thank her for the beer, and walk out of her apartment.

❦ *Chapter 17* ❦

S he could have driven straight across the Flagler Bridge, but Kitty decided against it. She didn't like driving through the quiet, deserted West Palm Beach neighborhood, around the Kravis Center, in the middle of the night.

So she made a left turn around the wide, grassy median on Royal Poinciana and drove slowly to the lights, making a right onto South County Road.

Later, she would remember that the other car was already trailing her along the first stretch of South County that took her past the Breakers Hotel. But she had not, at that point, been paying any particular attention to the road. At that time of morning she expected to have it pretty much to herself and so she had driven, totally preoccupied with her own thoughts and feelings.

She felt edgy and anxious. She had told Frank the truth about Jeff but that was not the same thing as setting the record straight completely. She'd made a pathetic attempt of getting back to the subject after Frank's pointed comment about Marina and her secret lover. But in the end she had not been able to get the words out: *Oh, by the way, Jamie's father isn't an Australian reporter, either.*

Cruising toward the intersection at Royal Palm Way she noted the glare of headlights in her rearview mirror and felt vaguely comforted by the thought that she was not the only driver on the road. The headlights stayed with her as she followed the curve around Worth Avenue, but then the distance between the two cars seemed to narrow, as if the other driver intended to tailgate her, trying to force her to speed up.

She slowed to twenty, instead, and waited for the driver to pass her. But he stayed back as the tall dark hedgerows of the Everglades Golf Links loomed up on her right. Ahead, South County was straight and wide and clear.

Go on, get off my tail.

She touched the brake, wondering why he was making no attempt to pass her. It was as if he was hypnotized by her taillights.

Probably drunk, she thought. Maybe he was using her to guide him along the road.

To hell with that. She had no intention of driving with a drunk on her tail along A1A. Without signaling, she swung right at the end of the Golf Links onto Island Road and checked her rearview mirror to see the other car crawl past the top of the road.

Then she put her foot down. She knew Island Road would eventually take her over a little wooden bridge onto Everglades Island, a narrow spit of land that sat in the middle of Lake Worth. Here, at the top of the road, there were only dark hedgerows on both sides and she didn't want to take a chance on running into the ditch. But she didn't need to go all the way to turn around and come back onto South County. A couple of hundred yards down she would be able to make an easy U-turn where the road widened and branched off to another spit of land known as Tarpon Island.

The glare of headlights suddenly hit Kitty's rearview mirror again and, instinctively, she hit the brake.

It's the same car . . .

It can't be the same car . . .

Well, how many damn different cars can there be on the road . . . on this road . . . at this time of night?

Her heart thudded as her mind seized on one thought: Someone was following her. Someone who had spotted a woman driving alone at three in the morning. And, if that was the case, she'd made a bad mistake turning onto Island Road.

She saw the lights coming up behind her and she took her foot off the brake, then quickly put it back on the gas pedal, building up a little speed.

If he runs into the back bumper, do not get out of the car, Kitty warned herself. Her finger stabbed at the power button that secured the doors, even as she realized that she was moving closer toward the bridge.

No. No way, she told herself. She was not going to cross the bridge. There was only one narrow road on Everglades Island running across from one end to the other. If she crossed the bridge she would, quite simply, be trapped.

She eased to a stop, conscious of her hands trembling on the wheel, willing the car behind her to pull out and drive over the bridge first.

Instead, the bright glare of high beams flooded her Blazer. She tried to focus on the driver behind her but all she could see was a silhouette. Big, broad-shouldered, and hunched over the steering wheel.

The highbeams flashed again.

He wanted her to move. Forward. Across that bridge.

No. I'm not moving, thought Kitty. If she got trapped at either end of the island— If he wanted to get her, if he smashed her windows, if he dragged her out of the car— No one would hear a thing.

She could not see a single light on in any of the mansions across the little bridge. Of course not. Everyone was in bed. Or the houses were still closed for the summer. No

one would hear her car horn or her. No one would call
the . . .

Hey! Talk about dumb, Fitzgerald.

A hysterical giggle bubbled up inside her as she felt
blindly for her tote on the passenger seat. She slipped her
hand inside and rummaged around for her own phone.
Gripping it tightly, she speed-dialed Frank's number first
and let the phone ring out twice. Then, she cleared the line
and punched out 911.

She held the phone up, so that it was in full view, as she
dialed. With her left hand she opened her window, and
stuck her hand out to wave the other driver on.

*Take a good look, buster. I'm calling the cops. So you'd
better move it.*

She heard the operator's voice on the line. In the same
instant she saw the other car ease out and pull ahead of her
with an angry blast on the horn.

"Can I help you? Hello!"

Kitty stared at the car, and the license plate caught in
her headlights. It was a big sedan. Maybe a Lincoln Continental or a Cadillac. She mouthed the numbers and letters
to herself, shaking with relief as the car rolled across the
bridge, turning right before disappearing from view.

"Hello? Is anyone there? Can you hear me?" The dis-
embodied voice came through loud and clear.

"No. Thank you. I'm okay. Sorry."

Kitty threw the cellular back on the passenger seat and
threw the gear into reverse, repeating the license plate
number over and over to herself as she pressed down on
the accelerator. With as much care as she could muster she
maneuvered the Blazer, in reverse, to the top of the road,
aware that her knees were trembling so violently she could
barely keep her foot steady on the accelerator.

❧ Chapter 18 ❧

$\mathcal{H}$e nosed the Cadillac around the circular drive-way of the dark, deserted house and turned left, back onto the road that led to the bridge. He had killed his headlights the moment he'd seen the Fitzgerald bitch reverse like a madwoman all the way back to the main road. But momentary terror had seized him as he had proceeded over the bridge and realized there was only one road to follow.

Pulling into the driveway of the darkest, most secluded house, he felt his pulse hammering with fear. Had she called the cops? Would they be waiting for him when he retraced his route? Waiting at the top of that long road and blocking off his escape?

So he had waited in the darkness, casting his eyes into the rearview mirror every few minutes, just in case they came screeching over the bridge to find him.

He checked the dashboard clock. Twenty minutes had passed since she'd gotten away. Maybe he was safe now. Maybe she hadn't called anybody.

Safe, dammit. But he'd screwed up, for sure. All that

work and effort. It had all turned to shit. Yet he'd been so close at the school, and last night in her backyard. It hurt to even think about it.

Last night she'd taken him by surprise, stepping out to the pool. It had happened so quickly he'd almost choked, inhaling his smoke.

In the small courtyard lights he'd caught a glimpse of the frown on her face. She had smelled the smoke, he was sure. There had been no wind or even a breeze to blow it away.

She had stood for a moment on the top step of the pool and his eyes had taken in her wispy frame. She had worn some kind of striped, flimsy bikini bottom that didn't even cover her behind and he'd had to suppress a momentary tingle of excitement at the sight of the smooth, boyish butt.

Watching her glide across the pool he'd used the sound of the water slurping against the sides to cover the rustling sound as he opened up the brown paper bag to let out the toad.

He groaned at the memory. He had been within seconds of going for her as she stopped dead in the water at the sight of the ugly thing. In another five minutes he would have been in and out of the house with the boy. But the goddamn phone had ruined it all.

He rubbed his face with his hands. He was so tired, he couldn't think straight anymore. He wanted to stretch out on a decent-sized bed, and he badly needed a shower.

He'd lost the boy, for sure. This morning, parked by the clubhouse, he'd watched the Fitzgerald slut drive out of the development, but the boy had not been with her. He thought that maybe someone had picked him up earlier when he was dozing. But he had stayed close to her all day, following her from Lauderdale to Palm Beach, and she had not picked him up after school in the afternoon, either.

Beads of sweat dripped down the side of his face.

Maybe the videotape and note had spooked her, after all. Maybe she had stashed the boy somewhere for safety.

He'd have to rethink the whole plan but he was too tired. He needed sleep. He had to close his eyes and rest. Maybe he could make it out of Palm Beach. The road ahead looked clear . . . no cop cars waiting for him. . . . If he could slide out along A1A he would cruise through to Boynton Beach or even to Delray where there were plenty of small, cheap motels. He had to lie down and recharge his batteries. And he had to do it right now.

❧ *Chapter 19* ❧

$\mathcal{J}$eff Haley walked around to the driver's side of the little gray Toyota and helped the girl out. Her name was Debbie Grant and she was a barmaid at a down-and-dirty pub called O'Leary's in West Palm, which is where he'd headed after losing the reporters who'd tried to follow him from the airport.

He had waited for her to finish work and then she had driven him to another equally slummy bar that stayed open later than O'Leary's. He had bought her a couple of Harvey Wallbangers.

She grabbed his hand willingly, giggling as she slid out beside him, and followed him toward the steps of Marina's mansion.

"Ooh, do you live here alone?" She giggled and hiccuped.

"No. With my wife and the four kids," he replied straight-faced as he tried the door, wondering why it wouldn't budge. He'd told that fellow Morelli (or was it

Moretti?) who'd come to pick him up at the airport to leave the door unlocked.

She gasped and took a step backward, teetering on her heels until he caught her arm and grinned at her.

"Oh, you!" She elbowed him in the ribs. "You're kidding me, aren't you?"

He gave the door another push and then remembered that most doors in Florida opened outward to better withstand hurricane winds. He tugged at the handle and it opened easily, allowing him to usher the girl inside.

He gave her a few seconds to gape at the circular staircase and the vaulted ceiling. The lights had been left on downstairs and he could see her staring through the open doors of the den. She wandered uninvited to the doorway. "Ooh, neato." She stared at the tapes on the shelves. "I bet you've got some good movies, here. I love movies."

"They're not movies. They're dubs of my mother's talk show."

She gave him a puzzled little stare.

"Your mom lives here?"

"She did. She died last week. Maybe you heard. Marina Dee Haley?"

She shook her head. "Nooo. I can't say I did. What did she die of?"

Jeff didn't answer the question. "You don't watch TV news do you, Debbie."

She flashed him a quick smile. "How did you know?" Then her face flushed. "Am I being stupid or something?"

"It's okay," he forced himself to smile at her. "Marina Dee Haley retired about five years ago. There's no reason why you should remember her name. How about a drink?"

He took her by the hand and led her across the foyer down the hallway toward the kitchen and breakfast room. If he remembered correctly his mother had kept the liquor hidden away in a kitchen cabinet.

"Maybe just a teeny weeny one," she giggled again. The giggling grated on him. He wasn't even sure why he'd brought her back to the house except that he'd been left without wheels after the chauffeur had deposited him at O'Leary's. And because she had long red hair, swept off her face, the way Kitty had once worn hers.

Oh, screw Kitty Fitzgerald!

He smiled at Debbie and poured the vodka from a bottle that looked as if it had been around for as long as he'd been in jail, and found fresh orange juice in the huge Sub-Zero refrigerator. "There you go," he handed the glass to Debbie. "A wallbanger without the Galliano."

"That would make it a screwdriver, Jeffie." A giggle with another hiccup. "I may not watch the news but I know my drinks. Anyway, about your Mom ... I'm sorry. ... Was it a horrible shock and everything?"

Jeff took his time, surveying the bottles in the cabinet. He had been drinking champagne at O'Leary's where they had dusted off their only bottle of Moet Chandon for him. But now was a good time to switch. He reached for a bottle of Martell Cordon Bleu.

"Yes, it was a shock," he finally answered.

Debbie put her glass down and came toward him, putting her arms around him. "I knew you were sad about something when you walked into the bar this afternoon. Do you want to talk about it?"

Jeff gently disengaged himself from her awkward hug and sipped his cognac, savoring the slow burn in his throat as the liquid made its way to his stomach.

No. He didn't really want to talk about it. But her mournful expression required some reaction.

"To tell you the truth, Debbie, I can't really explain how I feel. Not yet. It was a shock, yes. But it was more like losing a friend than a mother." He added, "In a way I never thought of her as a mother."

Jeff drained his glass and reached for the bottle to pour himself another. He leaned across the kitchen counter. "I mean I didn't even know she was my mother until I was almost eighteen. Marina wasn't married when I was born so I lived with my grandmother. I grew up being told that Marina was my big sister. And then, when my grandmother died, Marina took me to live with her but she was just getting established in television so she kept up the pretense. Pretty fucked up, eh?" He grinned at the girl whose eyes had widened as he talked.

"Yeah," she nodded. "It must have been really weird when you found out she was your mother." She paused and screwed up her face. "What did you say?"

Jeff laughed suddenly and shortly. "Weird isn't really the right word, Debbie." He paused and stared at her.

"You can tell me, Jeff." She traced the rim of her glass with a short fingernail. "You can share any secrets you want with me. I'd never tell."

This time Jeff laughed out loud. "Oh, it's not a secret, Debbie. At least nothing that a few million other people don't know about—" He broke off, leaning across the counter to bring her face into better focus. "My mother broke the news to me on her TV show. Yep, right in front of the studio audience and millions of viewers watching it live, at home."

"Oh, my God!" Debbie's hand flew to her mouth. "Just like that? Oh, Jeff, how old were you?"

He took a sip of his drink, and then dismissed her question with a wave of his hand. "I was a senior in high school. Old enough to handle it."

· He broke off, his face suddenly flushing at the lie—and the memory that had burned itself into the deepest recesses of his mind: He had been so excited when Marina had told him she wanted him to appear on her TV show, so full of himself, gloating at the thought of what his classmates would say when they saw him on TV.

"Anyway . . . when I got on the set with her, she started by saying the theme of that day's show was Ugly Family Secrets and that she had three guests who were going to reveal their worst, most horrible secret to a member of their family. But first she was going to reveal her own secret. . . ."

Debbie's mouth had dropped open. "That's exactly like

Oprah did when she announced that she'd been raped as a girl."

Jeff sighed. It .wasn't quite the same thing, he felt. But he didn't expect Debbie Grant to grasp the magnitude of his embarrassment and shock that day: He had not realized till the last minute what was happening. He had sat there next to Marina, uncertain and a little perplexed, as she had launched into a story of an out-of-wedlock pregnancy. Big deal, he had thought. So his big sister had let some guy stick it to her. He'd heard all about stuff like that in school. When the words came, he had barely been listening. "But I had the baby . . . and that baby was you, Jeff."

What he had heard was the audible, collective gasp from the audience that turned into a dull, roaring sound in his ears as he had jumped from his chair, trying to back away from Marina.

"What are you saying?" he had screamed at her. "Are you making this up for the show?"

Debbie Grant was shaking her head with a glazed, pained expression on her face. He let his eyes drift down to her breasts. Then, he looked back into her eyes. "Anyway," he grinned suddenly. "It *was* terrific for the ratings. Soon after that, she got to be Number One. And that made Marina happy. And when she was happy, everyone around her was happy. Now, would you like to see the rest of the house?"

It took the girl a second or two to realize he was finished with the subject.

"Oh? You mean upstairs?" The giggle was back.

"If you like." Jeff picked up his glass, and beckoned for her to follow him.

She hesitated at the foot of the staircase. "Are we alone in the house?"

"Except for the couple who cook and clean and run the place."

"I see." She circled the foyer, peering at an antique mahogany hall table by the door. "Your mother had some nice stuff."

Jeff waited patiently at the foot of the stairs. She was either playing for time or sizing up his fortune. It didn't matter because he didn't care about her, either way. If Debbie Grant didn't put out for him then maybe he'd call that little bimbo TV producer who'd bugged him on the plane ride down . . . Steffie. He couldn't remember her last name but he could remember the way she'd made it clear that she was available any time he wanted to talk. "Even if you just want to talk privately . . . first," she'd said. Yeah, maybe he'd see about that . . . Maybe.

The barmaid came toward him with a big smile, and he led the way to the top of the stairs and down to the end of the hallway, passing Marina's master bedroom. He guessed his bags would have been taken to his old room that lay at the end of the hallway.

The door stood open but the room was dark. He flicked on the light switch and glanced around. He saw that one of his bags had already been unpacked. His pajamas lay on the bed and the extra pair of pants he had brought with him were hanging on the valet along with a navy blazer. He wished that he'd told the chauffeur to leave his bags alone. Ignoring the girl he crossed the room and picked up the garment bag, anxiously unzipping one of the side pockets. He slid his fingers inside and felt the hard frames of the three photographs that had traveled with him from Wallkill. He was relieved that, at least, they had not found the photos or thought to display them prominently on his dresser.

"If you're looking for, you know, condoms . . ." Debbie's voice made him jump as she came up behind him, encircling his waist with her thin arms. "I have some. Never travel without them these days."

"No, not condoms." His hand snaked into the other pocket and he brought out a bottle of Shalimar. He held it out to her.

"For me? Wow!"

"Go on, put it on."

She looked at him quizzically but unscrewed the top of

the bottle, and dabbed hesitantly behind her ears. The scent wafted deliciously in the air.

"Do you want me to dab it all over?" She giggled, and he clenched his teeth.

He turned around and backed away a step but she was right on top of him, tightening her arms around him, grinding her hips into his crotch as she nudged him toward the big bed.

"That's it, Jeffie. Lie back, relax. Forget about all the bad things . . ."

She continued to murmur as she reached to unzip his pants. He wished she would stop talking. She was beginning to slur her words. Or maybe she thought she sounded sexy. Either way, it was grating on him. He closed his eyes and tried to drown out the whisper as he felt her warm breath between his legs.

Finally she had stopped talking. But she wasn't making anything else happen. Perspiration broke out on his forehead.

"Take it easy, Jeffie." Her tongue flicked upward as her hands stroked his belly. She brought her head up, sat back on her heels and deftly removed her skirt and panties. She took his hand and guided it between her own legs. "There, maybe that will help."

He gripped her in the palm of his hand, the scent of the perfume invading his nostrils and suddenly, without warning, he was in a different time and place. It was his last night before Green Haven. He kept his eyes tightly closed. He was with Kitty again. . . .

"See, I knew you'd like that."

The voice. Oh God, that awful voice again. His eyes flew open, and he sat up abruptly. "Why don't you shut up!"

"Well!" The girl looked at him, startled.

"I'm sorry. I mean, do you have to talk? I don't like talk."

She moved away from him but her eyes darted to his groin. "You don't seem to like anything I do with my mouth." She slid off the edge of the bed and waited a moment, as if expecting him to protest. But he didn't say anything.

Instead he leaned back against the headboard, watching her pick up her clothes and struggle into the tight little skirt. She was a slut. A thin, scrawny little slut.

Still, it was better if she went without any bad feelings. "I'm sorry, Debbie," he said finally. "Tonight just wasn't the right time. I've got a funeral to go to tomorrow."

She didn't look back as she headed for the door. A minute or so later he heard the front door slam behind her. He walked over to the window, watched the taillights of the little Honda disappear down the driveway.

When he knew she was finally gone, he walked over to where he'd dropped his garment bag. He reached in to bring out one of the photos. He stared at it. It had been taken on Marina's wedding day. He stared at the little group of four: Marina looking the way she always did; Davenport, the asshole, already drunk to the gills; and him with Kitty, both grinning, pretending they were having a good time, sandwiched in between the happy couple.

He groaned and slammed the photograph face down on the floor, a wave of anger, and frustration, and loss, washing over him as he saw glass splinter on the oak floor.

Nothing ever turned out the way he wanted.

He got down on one knee and picked up the biggest shards. Then he carried them, together with the picture, and dumped everything in the bathroom trash can before flipping on the shower and stepping under the cold blast of water.

❧ *Chapter* 20 ❧

Saturday, September 2

*K*itty approached cautiously. The graveside service was already under way. From where she stood, between two black stretch limos, she could see a small group gathered around the raised casket.

Jeff stood in the foreground, his head erect, staring at the pastor. He did not look as gaunt as he'd looked the first time she'd visited him in Green Haven. If anything he looked as if he'd put on a little weight, and his hair was cut shorter than she'd ever seen it.

She did not recognize anyone else in the group standing around him. There were two women—one older, with sleek silver-gray hair drawn back off her face, the other a little younger. Behind them stood two men in dark suits. She imagined there'd been many more mourners at the church.

Across from the family group, herded together along a narrow sidewalk between two giant banyan trees, stood a much larger group of reporters and cameramen. They stood, jostling and shifting, cameras whirring, held back

by a bright pink ribbon strung up between the two banyans. Two uniformed police officers sandwiched the media
group. Right on the edge of the crowd Kitty spotted Frank
with his partner. Then Kitty's eyes skimmed over the
crowd as she tried to place Bernie.

The funeral would make the early evening news shows.
But *Inside Copy* would need its own footage for follow-up
stories during the week.

She had decided not to take the chance of joining the reporters and camera crews. The last thing she needed was
a scene between her and Jeff in front of all those cameras.
She had thought out a different strategy in the early hours
of the morning, and a dawn phone call to Frank had produced the name of the chauffeur.

Now, she stepped toward the first limo in line and
tapped on the driver's window, waiting for it to slide open.
"Mr. Moretti?"

"That's me." The stocky, dark-haired chauffeur stared at
her through a pair of RayBans.

Kitty cleared her throat and extended her hand to shake
his. "Mr. Moretti, I'm Kitty Fitzgerald. I'm supposed to
wait for Mr. Haley in the car."

"Is that right?"

"Yes, I'm a very old friend of Mr. Haley's."

He didn't move. "You're a TV reporter, aren't you?"

"Yes. And an old friend." She reached into her tote for
the copy of the newspaper story she had taken from Frank
the previous evening. "That's me," she said, pointing
to the "Gal Pal" part of the headline and swallowing nervously. "As you can see we're very old friends. Now, Mr.
Moretti, open the door for me."

Her authoritative tone finally budged him and she slid
into the back seat, her heart thumping. If Jeff turned on
her at least the scene would be safe from prying cameras.

In the rearview mirror she checked her hair. She had
brushed it back off her face so that it resembled her old
style more closely. She had also spent an agonizing twenty
minutes picking through her closet discarding one outfit

after another before settling on a black embroidered halter-top vest and black cotton pants. The color was appropriate—if not the style. But the halter top showed some cleavage.

She leaned forward and punched the button to close off the partition between herself and the chauffeur as she saw the small group across the cemetery beginning to disperse. Her heart thumped uncomfortably, watching Jeff walk toward the limo. Moretti was already out of the car and holding the door open for him.

She held her breath as Jeff ducked his head into the limo and then seemed to freeze.

"Jeff . . . I'm sorry . . . I didn't mean to startle you."

He stared at her for a moment and she noted his expensive Porsche-Carrera sunglasses. But she could not see his eyes behind the shades. All she could see was his clenched jaw.

For one moment she thought he was going to tell her to get out of the car, but then he slid into the seat and leaned back, motioning for the chauffeur to close the door.

"So, Kitty, you couldn't stay away, huh?" He smiled thinly. "I suppose I shouldn't be surprised, even though I didn't really expect you to show up. But then again, it is your job. You are here for the story, aren't you?"

Kitty said nothing as her stomach flip-flopped. She had prepared herself for this question and she had rehearsed her lines, carefully. She had figured that if she got a shot at Jeff there was only one play to make, and that was to tell it straight. Jeff was too smart to believe that she was there for any other personal reason.

She turned in her seat and removed her own shades, so that he could see her eyes. "Yes, Jeff, I think you're a good story and, of course, so does Todd. Naturally, he doesn't see why you wouldn't sit down for an exclusive interview with *Inside Copy*. I, of course, know better. I didn't even expect to get this far with you. But you know me, I had to try." She broke off and stared pointedly at him, but his face remained expressionless behind the gold-rimmed Porsche-Carreras.

"Anyway, I've made the pitch. You know you have old friends at *Inside Copy* and we would treat you fairly. That's all I can say except I'm sorry about Marina and I'm sorry that things between us worked out so badly. If I hurt you I didn't do it deliberately."

She hesitated, waiting for some response, but Jeff sat with his head back against the seat, and she thought he had closed his eyes. He seemed deep in thought. Or maybe, she thought, he was just waiting for her to leave. She reached for the door handle.

"You still wear Shalimar," he said suddenly, placing his hand on her bare arm. "Don't be in such a hurry to leave."

She let go of the handle but remained perched on the edge of the car seat.

"Sit back, relax. We haven't finished here."

He turned to face her, unsmiling. "You've had your say so maybe you can let me have mine. There was a time when I felt better about things. And I didn't hate you anymore. I wanted to write to you, tell you I could even think about forgiving you. Then about two months ago the Parole Board decided I'd been a good boy and that they could release me back into society and for a couple of weeks that sounded good, but then . . ." He broke off and she realized he was having difficulty getting the words out.

She gently laid her hand on his arm. "Then what, Jeff?"

He looked away, staring through his window. "Then it hit me, Kitty. I suddenly realized I had nothing to look forward to. I suddenly realized there was no point in getting excited because I had no life to go back to. Not one friend. So . . . I tried to kill myself."

"Oh, God, Jeff." She sat upright again, staring at him wide-eyed. "I didn't know. How did you . . . ?"

His lips set in a thin line. "It was a pretty stupid, pathetic attempt. But then, I didn't have many options. I drank cleaning fluid. Even that was watered down so all I ended up with were severe stomach cramps and a sore throat."

Kitty sat mute. She did not know what to say or what she was expected to say.

She sighed. "I shouldn't have come. You must really hate me."

Jeff smiled sadly. "Hate is a pretty useless emotion, Kitty. But it's a very powerful one. The trick is to turn the force of the negative feeling into something constructive. Focus on what you want and apply that force to achieving your objective."

It sounded like the sort of thing the prison psychiatrist might have said. A piece of useless psychobabble. She didn't say so in those exact words, though. Instead she said, "Did it work for you?"

He laughed. "Well, let's say I tried. But it's not that easy in a cell." His words seemed to drift away along with his thoughts. Then he reached across the seat and patted her hand. "The truth is Marina's death shook me up because it was sudden, and awful. It made me see a lot of things differently. And it put a lot of things in perspective. I don't want to waste my time on nurturing old hurts and grievances, Kitty. I want to get on with my life and start afresh."

Kitty nodded and was about to tell him he was right but Jeff didn't seem interested.

"So, go ahead, make me an offer," he continued. "I'll consider it along with all the others. What is *Inside Copy* prepared to pay me for the interview? *A Current Affair* has already offered fifty thousand."

The mood and the conversation had changed so abruptly that Kitty found herself gasping. But Jeff, evidently, misunderstood her reaction because he added, "I know, it's insane, isn't it? Competition must be brutal these days. But I'm curious to see how high it's going to go. Who's going to make the highest bid."

"And you're going to sell yourself to the highest bidder?"

"I didn't say that." He grinned. "There are other factors to consider. Money isn't everything."

"Especially when you have plenty of it already," Kitty blurted out, trying to picture the disgust on Todd's face when she told him that Jeff Haley was looking to be paid. She shook her head and leaned back, resting her head on the back of the seat. "You took me by surprise, Jeff. I can't make that decision on my own. I'll have to talk to Todd."

"Okay, let me know what he says. In the meantime, do you have any idea what the interview would entail? What sort of questions you want answered?"

"You know we would be fair to you, Jeff."

"I don't want anyone springing anything on me, out of the blue. I'd like prior approval of the questions. That's almost more important than the money."

Kitty was at a loss. Todd didn't like submitting questions in advance any more than he liked paying for interviews. Jeff knew that. She wondered if he was just toying with her. Winding her up and raising her hopes just before kicking her out of the car.

As if reading her thoughts, Jeff said, "I'm not being deliberately difficult, you know, Kitty. I'm just not going to agree to any interview that makes me look like an asshole, okay?"

Kitty nodded, reflecting that Jeff had changed a lot in five years. He seemed harder and more determined now.

"What I'm saying is I don't want anyone springing any silly questions on me. I'd have to have a contract that specifies the areas you want to talk about. If Todd agrees to that we can discuss the rest of the deal."

"When?"

"It's up to you. You're the one with the deadlines, not me."

Kitty glanced at her watch. She was supposed to pick up Jamie in less than an hour. And she hadn't really thought this far ahead. But she was loath to leave things up in the air. "I'd like a little time to speak to Todd, and then I'd like to get right back to you on it."

"So, fine," he nodded, his tone curt. "I'm free for the rest of the day, and evening. We could discuss it anytime, even over dinner, if you like. I'd planned on eating at Bice's. I've been fantasizing about it for months. It would taste even better if *Inside Copy* was picking up the tab." He laughed softly and glanced sideways at her as she grimaced. "It's okay, though, I know you must have other plans. Don't worry, call me."

"No. No other plans," Kitty jumped in quickly. "Just a baby-sitter problem."

"You don't have a live-in?" Jeff looked surprised.

"I have a student, Sharon, from the local university who baby-sits and does a bit of housekeeping in return for a free room—but she went home to Iowa for the summer and isn't back yet."

"Well . . ." Jeff seemed to be pondering. "I suppose you could bring Jamie with you."

Kitty laughed now. "To Bice's? I don't think so."

Jeff shrugged. "So, Bice's can wait. Bring him to the house. I'll have the Morettis cook."

Kitty hesitated. The conversation had taken so many swift turns she found herself wondering how she'd arrived at the point where she was making plans to bring Jamie to dinner at Jeff's house. On the other hand, this was a million times better than getting kicked out of the car.

"Yeah, that's a better idea, anyway," Jeff was saying. "We could talk without people staring at me. Seven? Seven-thirty suit you?"

Kitty found herself nodding. "Seven's fine. See you then."

She knew he was watching as she walked away and she tried to keep her walk steady. But in spite of her effort she could feel her legs trembling as the nervous tension that had been building up since the early hours of the morning dissipated into relief.

She'd cracked it. Her foot was in the door. She had no

way of knowing for sure that he wasn't toying with her. Maybe this was his way of kicking her in the teeth. But at least she could call Todd this afternoon to tell him they were meeting to discuss the interview. Right now she was ahead.

She followed the sidewalk outside the cemetery gates and rounded the corner of the street where she'd parked the Blazer. Then she saw Frank leaning on the hood of her car.

❧ *Chapter 21* ❧

*F*rank glanced at his watch as Kitty walked toward him. He was surprised that only ten minutes had elapsed since he'd seen Kitty getting into Jeff Haley's limo. It had seemed like much longer.

He kissed her lightly on the cheek. "I saw you get into the limo. I thought I should wait in case things got ugly."

Kitty exhaled loudly and shook her head. "Thanks hon, I was expecting him to blast me right out of the limo—but he couldn't have been nicer."

Frank eyed her, staring directly at the exposed V of her cleavage. "I'm sure you used all your charms to make him see things your way."

He was mildly gratified to see Kitty flush, knowing she had not mistaken the look or the meaning of his words.

"I had to give it my best shot, Frank," she muttered, turning away to unlock the door of the Blazer. "At least I've got my foot in the door."

"So long as that's all you've got in the door." Frank grinned to lighten the moment. "Tell me about it."

Kitty leaned into her car and switched on the engine. "He doesn't know if he's going to do any interviews. He hasn't decided yet. But, at least, he's willing to discuss it."

"Great!" Frank made an effort to sound genuinely pleased for her. "So, you're back in the game? When's he going to let you know?"

"We're going to discuss it tonight. Over dinner." She stared at him. "At the house."

Frank made an effort to sound calm. "Why at the house?"

"So that I can bring Jamie. I don't want to leave him at the Baines's for another night. Not over the weekend, anyway."

"I see. That's very accommodating of Mr. Haley." Frank hesitated for a moment, struggling to find the right words. He certainly didn't want to tell Kitty how to do her job, but he was disturbed by the way things were working out.

"Listen, Kitty," he reached for her hand. "I'm not going to tell you how to handle your story but this isn't making sense to me. Last night you were in a panic because you thought you wouldn't be able to get near Haley. You were afraid he was going to blast you out of the cemetery. But the minute you appear on the scene he's all over you, everything's forgiven in an instant, and he's inviting you for dinner at the mansion. Am I missing something here?"

Kitty smiled. "Maybe I am. I don't understand either— except he says Marina's death has changed him. He doesn't want to waste time being petty and bitter. He wants to get back his life." Kitty paused and shrugged.

Frank's jaw tensed. "Does that include you?"

Kitty shook her head firmly. "I doubt it. He never had me. Not in that way."

"Is that right?" He cleared his throat. "Yeah, you were just friends. Never anything more?"

"No! C'mon, Frank, we went through all this last night."

He shook his head. "Yes, we did. But I guess I just

don't get it. You're telling me that he never once came on to you? He laid on limos for you and cooked for you and redecorated your apartment and bought you expensive clothes, and never once tried to get into your bed. He cared for you but didn't find you attractive?"

"I was pregnant for most of the time, don't forget."

Frank brushed off the flimsy explanation. "C'mon, Kitty. You're not asking me to believe he was turned off by that?"

He saw her looking over his shoulder, somewhere into the distance.

"Okay," she said, finally. "Once. He tried once. There. Does that make you happy?"

It didn't make him happy. "Once" didn't sound credible, either. But this seemed closer to the truth. "What happened?"

"Oh, you want all the icky details now?" Her mouth twitched in a smile.

"Are they icky?" He raised an eyebrow.

She twisted a strand of her hair in her fingers. "He tried, okay? But nothing happened. We spent one night together—the night before he went up to Green Haven. He asked if he could stay with me. He was terrified and he didn't want to be alone. And, yes, he came on to me. But, in the end, nothing happened."

"You turned him down?"

"Oh my God, Frank, this sounds like an interrogation. No. Nothing happened because he couldn't do it. He was too nervous. Too upset. Hell, I don't know. Maybe because Jamie was in his crib in the next room and kept waking up. It's not exactly a memory I dwelt on afterwards. It didn't matter to me. It was nothing."

"For you." Frank leaned against her car door. "But I can imagine how Haley felt."

"Oh yeah?" Kitty tossed her head.

"Yeah, and I'm surprised you can't see it. I think he wants you. I think he can't help himself. Trust me, hon. He's a man. He's been inside for five years tormenting himself with a memory of what might have been. Do you honestly believe he ever stopped thinking about that?"

Frank saw the wavering in her eyes and for a moment he felt he was getting through to her. "Kitty, don't go to his house. Call him, tell him you'll meet him for lunch instead, sometime during the week. Don't give him mixed signals."

There was an awkward silence between them for a few moments. Then Kitty shook her head. "And while I'm waiting for lunch, *A Current Affair* and *Inside Edition* will be right in there waving their checkbooks in his face. Nothing's going to happen, Frank. You have to trust me. I promise you if he shows any sign of finishing what he started, I'm outta there. I certainly don't want or need the interview *that* badly." Kitty stepped up to kiss him on the mouth and then climbed into the Blazer and slammed the car door shut. "And I'll come and check in with you after dinner." She winked at him. "You'll see everything's going to work out fine." Then she laughed over the noise of the engine. "Now, go do your work. We're going to need a suspect soon otherwise this story's going to die."

He watched the Blazer cruise to the top of the street, then walked down to where Don was parked and waiting for him. He slid into the passenger seat of his partner's white Buick, slamming his palm down on his thigh. "Damnit! Tell me what's going on here, Don. Haley just invited Kitty for dinner at the house tonight."

"And she's going?"

Frank nodded curtly. "I'd like to drive round right now and meet this guy."

"Play it cool," Don advised. "We're not going to get anywhere if we steamroll him before he's out of his mourning suit. Let's wait for *his* call."

Frank took a deep breath. Don was right. They had discussed all this before the funeral, deciding they would gain nothing by beating down his door and badgering him with questions about his mother before he'd taken care of burying her. So Frank had passed a message to him through his chauffeur, asking Haley to call police headquarters at his convenience.

"What is it that bugs you about this dinner, anyway? It's business, isn't it? I mean, you're not afraid that Kitty will—"

"No." Frank cut him off. "I don't think Kitty's going to fall for his charms. But he'd like her to, I know that much." Frank paused, staring silently out of the window as they pulled away from the curb. Kitty had added another piece to the puzzle—and this had brought the picture into clearer focus.

"Listen to this," he turned to glance at his partner. "That bastard's been stewing inside for five years fantasizing about their last night together. There he was, right in her bed, lying next to that sweet little body. Only he couldn't get it up. That's the memory that is eating away at him. Hey, put yourself in his place."

"It's bad enough when the memory just lasts overnight," Don interrupted, grinning at the windshield.

"My point." Frank nodded. "So what do you think he's going to do as soon as he's out? He's going to try and fix it, that's what." Frank shook his head. "I think he's always had a thing about her. I think he wants her and I'm just wondering how far he'd go to get her back."

"Meaning?"

"Meaning what's one surefire way to get Kitty's attention? Meaning . . . Marina's murder has put him right in the spotlight. He's the big story right now, the way he was five years back when he shot Marina's husband."

"Whoa!" Don interrupted. "Back it up there, pal. Are you telling me you think he might have arranged his mother's murder just to get back with Kitty? That's one bizarre theory." Don let out a low whistle.

"Bizarre things happen," Frank shot back at him, then allowed himself to grin. "Don't you ever watch *Inside Copy*?" He paused. "Think about it. The night he shot Marina's husband was right after they'd had a bust-up. Kitty threw him out."

"Wait! Now you're saying Kitty was his motive for shooting Davenport?"

Frank shook his head. "Not necessarily. But that was the way things turned out. She came running to his side. She got the big interview. They were pals again. She visited him in jail . . . she wrote . . . they talked on the phone. . . .

"Then she meets me, and it's all over. She cuts him off. He writes to tell her he's bitter and angry and he'll never forgive her. She doesn't respond. So maybe he figures what worked before will work again."

"You really don't like this guy, do you, Frank?" Don commented dryly as they pulled into the parking lot behind the station house.

"No, I don't," Frank admitted. "But it's not all personal, Don. There's a lot of things I don't like about Haley. I don't like his timing—the fact that his mother was murdered just a matter of days before he's due out on parole. I don't like the fact that he has such a perfect alibi. I don't like the fact that he's spent the last five years in a place crawling with low-lifes who'd kill their own mothers, never mind someone else's mother, especially if there's big bucks in it. And I don't like the fact that he's now seven or eight million bucks ahead."

"Half of that was his, anyway," Don interrupted.

"Yeah, yeah." Frank nodded. According to Marina's attorney, the TV talk-show host and her son had been joint and equal partners holding joint ownership and equal powers of attorney in all her assets. "But eight million is better than four, especially if you haven't got Mom looking over your shoulder while you're spending the money."

Frank paused and motioned for Don to kill the engine. "All I'm saying is it's worth keeping at the back of our minds. All these questions need to be answered. But you can see how he's already reeling Kitty back in."

Don shook his head. "And how's he going to make her stay with him after she gets the big story? How's he going to get around you?"

"He doesn't know about me." Frank paused. "And the

way I figure it, he's not going to agree to the interview for a while. He'll string her along, holding out the carrot. He'll try to reestablish the relationship. He'll try to woo her back."

Don made no move to get out of the car. "You'd have to be pretty cold-blooded to hire someone to batter your mother to death just for a piece of ass—as gorgeous as she may be," he added quickly.

Frank laughed as he got out of the car. Don was always the voice of reason. The logical one. Frank was the one who worked on gut instinct. It was the Irish way. As Frank had once said, together, they made one helluva detective.

Swiftly, his expression grew serious again as Don fell into step with him. "The man pulled a trigger on a drunk. That's *pretty* hard to swallow, too."

They walked into the station house and took the stairs up to the squad room, where Frank found a note on his desk informing him that Haley had called in response to his message.

He dialed the number immediately and waited. When Haley answered the phone, Frank introduced himself, offered the briefest of condolences, then told Haley they needed to talk as soon as possible.

"Absolutely we must meet, Detective." Haley's tone was polite and agreeable. "But this afternoon is really not convenient, unless you have some positive news on the investigation, of course. I'm getting ready for a dinner date."

Frank clenched his jaw. "I'm afraid I don't have any good news. What I have is a lot of questions and I think you could be of help. It wouldn't take very long."

"I understand, Detective." Haley still sounded amiable. "But when I said I'm getting ready for dinner I wasn't talking about slipping into a tux. I'm cooking tonight, and I'm afraid I'm going a little overboard. Cooking used to be a favorite hobby before—" Haley interrupted himself, then picked up almost immediately. "Well anyway, I used to make a perfect trout amandine, with avocado coleslaw. It's been a long time since I've had a meal like that."

Frank stared nonplussed into the receiver for a moment. There was a strange, crowing note in Haley's voice, as if cooking perfect trout amandine was some sort of incredible accomplishment that he did not expect a mere detective to appreciate.

Frank cleared his throat. "Then what would be a good time, Mr. Haley?"

"Do you work Sundays, Detective Maguire?"

"I can."

"Then how about first thing tomorrow morning? Come as early as you like, Detective. I have nothing else planned."

Yeah. Make sure you keep it that way, Haley.

"I'll be there," Frank said into the mouthpiece, and hung up.

He turned to Don, shaking his head. "He's going to woo Kitty with homemade avocado coleslaw. Asshole!"

Chapter 22

$\mathcal{K}$itty was tempted to call Angela Baines to ask her if she would keep Jamie for another couple of hours. She felt drained and exhausted from nervous tension and lack of sleep. She longed for a nap before the evening loomed up on her. But she was reluctant to impose any further on Angela.

Kitty was always apprehensive when Jamie was at the Baines's home—a spectacular apartment in a gleaming white high-rise on the beach, a block down from the Boca Hotel and Resort Beach Club. Situated as it was on the fifteenth floor, it came with equally spectacular views of the ocean and the Intracoastal. But the thing that made Kitty really anxious was the apartment's decor: Chrome and glass dominated the white living and dining rooms. Unlike her house, where Jamie's toys regularly spilled and wandered into the living room, Kitty had never seen any of Alex's things on the white rugs and couches of the formal apartment.

It was perfect and sleek. Like Angela herself, who had once been an Elite model. Kitty had never seen Angela in the same outfit twice. She did all her shopping in the pricey boutiques of Mizner Park. But Kitty did not hold that against her. Angela was a former New Yorker too, and Kitty got on well with her.

She opened the door to Kitty, wearing a perfectly pressed, bright white embroidered top, tucked into alligator belted aquamarine shorts. The high heels of her white strap sandals clicked over the marble floor as she beckoned Kitty to follow her onto the terrace.

"The boys are playing in Alex's room," she smiled. "Can I get you an iced tea?"

Kitty shook her head. "I don't think so, Ange, I'm sure Jamie's close to overstaying his welcome and I have a million things to do. Let me just go and tell him to get ready. Did you have any problems with the two of them?"

Angela shook her head. "Aside from the fact that they didn't get to sleep till around ten, they were perfect."

Kitty walked across the living room and down to Alex's bedroom, the only room in the apartment, Kitty surmised, that would not have made the pages of *Architectural Digest*. The beds were still unmade and the floor was strewn with assorted toy weapons, action figures, and stuffed animals.

She stood in the door for a moment being roundly ignored by both boys. Their eyes remained glued to the Nintendo game on Alex's TV screen. When she spoke and asked Jamie to put on his sneakers he didn't even turn around.

"Mom! Can't you see we're still playing? We're all the way to Desert Land. We can't stop now!"

She smiled to herself. "Five minutes, Jamie, then we have to leave. Please find your sneakers."

She walked back onto the terrace where Angela had plumped down on one of the patio chairs, her long fingers curled round a crystal water glass. A slice of lemon floated in the water. A breeze wafted in from the ocean.

She patted the lounge chair beside her. "Come on, sit down. You know you're looking at a fifteen-minute wait, at the very least, so sit. You can give me the scoop on Marina Dee Haley. Oh, and I've got something to tell you."

Kitty sat down, stretching her legs out. "You first then because my scoop on Marina amounts to zip at the moment."

Angela leaned closer to Kitty. "I found out what happened to Timmy Myers."

"Oh, that's right." Kitty's hand went to her mouth. "I forgot all about that. Jamie wanted to call Timmy Thursday night. Is he all right?"

Angela tapped Kitty's hand. "Listen, that's what I'm trying to tell you. Jamie and Alex called Timmy and when they'd finished, I talked to Julia. She and Bill were steaming."

Kitty sat forward in her chair. "Over the accident? Jeez, how bad was it? Jamie told me the paramedics came to take him to the hospital."

Angela's lips pursed. "If you'd just stifle yourself for a moment I'll tell you the whole story."

"Okay, okay." Kitty grinned and leaned back in the chaise. "So tell."

"Well, that was the problem. It wasn't paramedics who took Timmy to the hospital. Apparently, when Timmy fell off the jungle gym, a doctor happened to be driving by, saw what happened, screeched to a halt, and went running into the yard to help. Took one look at Timmy, said he should get checked out, and that he himself would run him straight over to the ER."

Angela took a sip of her water. "Okay. So the doctor says ER and you figure Boca Community Hospital."

"Or West Boca Medical Center," Kitty interrupted again.

Angela's eyes narrowed. "Try North Broward Medical Center."

"He drove Timmy to Pompano! Why?"

Angela shook her head. "Probably because that's where the asshole works but apparently either he didn't make that clear to Janis or she wasn't listening because Netta Freeman couldn't locate him and had to call the police."

"The cops had to search for him?"

"No, apparently the doctor eventually did call to ask if

anyone was coming from the school but by that time Julia was going into shock. When I spoke to her later that evening she was still shaken. She spent a whole hour imagining the worst. Of course, Bill threw a fit when he got home and heard what happened. Started yelling about suing the school."

Kitty shook her head. "I can't believe Janis would do that. Letting a stranger walk off with one of the kids?" She paused. "If I were the Myerses I'd go after the doctor, too. That's a pretty irresponsible thing to do—just to whisk a kid off like that, without a parent or teacher."

"According to Julia, Bill was thinking about it, believe me. But the hospital wouldn't give him a name. Said they couldn't find the doctor. Said that Timmy checked himself in."

"Oh, bullshit! They're just protecting him."

Angela shook her head. "No, wait, it's what Timmy said, too. Said that the doctor dropped him off outside the emergency room doors, saying he was late for work."

Kitty jumped to her feet. "Oh, Angela, c'mon! That's total baloney! It's bizarre. Since when do doctors care if they're late for their appointments, anyway?"

Her friend laughed. "You're right. Doesn't sound like a doctor at all."

Kitty felt a chill run up the back of her neck as Angela's words abruptly set off a series of images flashing in her head. One after another they flashed and dissolved in a sudden, vivid replay of the porn video that had landed on her desk. The naked pervert on the video certainly hadn't been a real doctor.

"Anyway, all's well that ends well, I suppose," Angela concluded, shrugging as she rose from her chaise. "Are you sure I can't get you an iced tea?"

"No! No thanks. I have to get Jamie. Have to get going." Kitty turned to walk back into the living room and was relieved to see that Jamie was already walking down the hallway with his sneakers on his feet.

In the car Kitty's thoughts stayed with Timmy Myers.

She was puzzled by the story and outraged by the way the school and the doctor had acted. She wondered, for a moment, if she was overreacting, because the ugly images of the bogus videotape doctor were still strong in her mind. The bottom line, surely, was that no harm had come to Timmy.

Still, she knew that if she had found herself in the same situation, videotape or not, she would have wanted to confront the jerk who'd driven off with her son and then dumped him outside the hospital doors. On an impulse she picked up her cellular and dialed the Myers home. She heard the phone ring out a couple of times and then the answering machine switched on. She left a message for Julia as well as the number of her cellular phone.

"Mom!" Jamie's shriek made her jump. "You drove right past our street. You missed our turning."

"No, I didn't," she glanced at him, grinning. "I've got to stop at Carmody's to pick up a bottle of champagne."

"Oh. Why?"

"Because."

"Because is not an answer."

"Because is not an okay answer for a kid. It's perfectly okay for moms."

She kept up the easy banter while she considered what kind of champagne she should take to Jeff's house. Dom Perignon immediately suggested itself because it would fit the setting and add a little style to her negotiations. But suppose it also sent one of those mixed signals that Frank was obviously worried about? Moet was definitely out. Kitty remembered that Jeff had bought Moet by the case in New York to use for Mimosas. So that left about a half-dozen choices in between.

Pat Carmody, the store's owner, came up with a solution. Louis Roederer Cristal. As good as Dom but not with the same hype. "And the price is right," he grinned genially at her. "I have it on sale this week."

She took two. What the hell? *Inside Copy* would pay for Jeff's. The second she would share with Frank—later.

❧ *Chapter* 23 ❧

*I*t was only a few minutes after seven when Kitty and Jamie arrived at the mansion, sweeping through the gates past a few camera crews still on stake-out in the street. She was surprised when Jeff opened the door himself.

"You're supposed to let the butler get the door, aren't you?" she smiled, pushing Jamie into the foyer ahead of her as she handed over the bottle of Cristal.

"I'm afraid the staff are gone." Jeff shrugged as his eyes settled on Jamie. "Come here, Jamie, let me see how tall you are. Last time I saw you, you were only this big." He extended his hands about a foot apart, and Jamie looked over his shoulder at her, uncertainly.

"Is that true, Mom? I wasn't never that small, was I?"

"Not quite that small." Kitty dismissed his question. She didn't want to start reminiscing about those days. She wanted to get through the evening with as little reference to the past as possible.

Fortunately, Jamie's attention was diverted by the sight

of the ocean through the huge living room windows. "Hey Mom, look! The beach . . . it's right in the backyard. Can we go down there?"

"Sure you can." Jeff jumped in as she hesitated. "Why don't you and your Mom take a walk down there while I finish in the kitchen." He ushered them across the foyer and living room onto the veranda.

"Finish in the kitchen?" Kitty echoed. "You weren't kidding about the staff. Where did they go?"

"Beats me. Mrs. M. came to me this afternoon and said they were going to evening Mass but I noticed their suitcases in the back of their car. Somehow I don't think they're coming back."

"But Jeff, can they leave just like that? I mean the police are still questioning and interviewing people about—"

"I'm sure they haven't skipped town," Jeff interrupted abruptly. "I think it's just me they want to get away from. Mrs. M. asked me this morning if I thought God had forgiven me for shooting another human being or rather for *'speeling blood'* as she so quaintly put it. Hey, it doesn't matter to me. Apparently they were just filling in for the regular staff anyway. I can manage on my own for a week."

Kitty noticed a table had been set up on the veranda under the wooden paddle fans that were already rotating slowly. A centerpiece of fresh roses stood in the middle. A bottle of white chardonnay was chilling in an ice bucket next to the table. Jeff walked over to it, poured some into a heavy crystal wineglass, and handed it to her. "Go on, take a walk down to the beach with Jamie and relax. I'll ring the bell when it's ready." He grinned.

She slipped off her heeled sandals and started after Jamie who was already tearing across the lawn toward the dunes.

"You should have brought a pair of shorts for the beach," Jeff called after her, but she pretended she hadn't heard. She had deliberately dressed formally for the dinner, choosing a butter-colored, shawl-collared shirtdress with a midcalf circle skirt. She had figured that between her formal appearance and the presence of the Morettis, she would be able to keep the mood of the evening on a business-like level. Now, it seemed, with Jeff cooking, the evening could only serve as an evocative reminder of their evenings in New York.

She was pleasantly surprised though. When they were eventually seated at the table Jeff himself steered the conversation immediately to the subject of the interview, wanting to know Todd's reaction.

Before she could answer the question the phone rang and Jeff left the table to answer it.

"It would be useful to have someone around just to answer the phone," he said, returning a couple of minutes later. "The damn thing hasn't stopped ringing. That was a producer for *Dateline*. Second time she's called."

"Well," Kitty allowed herself a smile. "You should just sit down and do one long exclusive interview. Then everyone else will stop bothering you."

"Maybe." Jeff nodded. "So what did Todd say?"

Kitty sipped her wine slowly, recalling her earlier brief and rather one-sided conversation with her executive producer whose reaction had been predictable. "Fuck him! I'm not paying a dime to talk to the little putz. Tell him if he doesn't give us the interview we know enough about him to do a story and make him look like a real turd."

Kitty put down her glass. "I couldn't pin him down on a figure. You know Todd doesn't like opening the old checkbook."

Jeff grinned broadly and, Kitty thought, smugly. "I remember," he said. "I didn't really expect him to make a sensible offer. What did he say about prior approval on the questions?"

Kitty hadn't even raised that one with Todd. "You know we're not going to make you look bad, Jeff. I'm quite happy to tell you what we want."

"Shoot!"

"Mom, can I be excused now?" Jamie interrupted. He

had pushed the trout around his plate but had not touched it, as Kitty had anticipated.

"Sure, hon," she agreed, then turned to Jeff. "Where's the TV? I brought a couple of videos he can watch."

Jeff led Jamie and Kitty into the den. Kitty retrieved the videos from her purse and inserted them into the VCR. Jamie, ecstatic over the large screen, bounced onto the couch and stretched out across the cushions.

"So, where were we?" Jeff cupped her elbow lightly, prodding her back to the table on the veranda. He held the chair for her as she sat down and then he poured more wine into both of their glasses.

"Yes, the interview." Kitty leapt right back to the subject. "Okay. We'd like you to talk about the last five years: your regrets, if any, for taking the deal rather than going for a trial; how you got the news about Marina's death; your future plans; are you going to keep this house? Stay in Palm Beach?"

Jeff laughed. "Well, the last one's easy. I have to stay in Palm Beach for a while. They agreed to let me serve my parole down here. As for the house, I don't know. It depends."

"On what?"

"On whether I'll be needing all this room in the near future. It would be stupid for me to keep it if there's no one to share it with."

Kitty cleared her throat, sensing dangerous ground ahead. "Okay, well, that's the sort of information we're interested in. We'd also be interested in a tour of the house. Hey, if you decide to sell it that would be like free commercial time."

Jeff pushed back his chair. "Come on, I'll give you a tour now, if you've finished."

"Sure." She followed Jeff off the veranda into the living room with its heavy mahogany furniture and Victorian-style drapes, and then they worked their way around the rest of the house through the kitchen, with its genuine wood-burning oven and yards of counter space, and the dining room (more heavy mahogany), and the den—where Jamie, oblivious to everything but the TV screen, didn't even stir when they walked in.

There were more rooms on the ground floor, along a wing that ran out to the pool. They could have been guest suites or sitting rooms but apparently had not been designated for any particular purpose by Marina who had let them stand empty.

"See what I mean about the size," Jeff commented as they returned to the porch, where he poured Kitty another glass of champagne. "I remember coming here as a teenager when Marina first bought the house . . . rattling around in it. I always thought it would be great for hide-and-seek for the kids . . . one day."

Kitty sank onto one of the overstuffed rattan chaises. "It's a terrific place, Jeff," she said, steering the conversation back to a less personal level. "But it does need a coat of paint, some bright breezy wallpaper and new furniture." She hesitated. "Mahogany seems out of place on the beach."

"I know what you're saying," Jeff nodded. "It needs big modern sectional couches and pastels and bright colors to make it lighter and to open it up."

A phone rang out again as Jeff was on his way into the kitchen for cappucinos. This time it was Kitty's cellular, and she immediately recognized Julia Myers's voice on the other end.

Kitty paced across the veranda as she told Julia why she'd called. "I heard what happened to Timmy, and Angela told me you were going to sue the school."

"Kitty, I don't want this story on TV," Julia interrupted quickly. "Bill and I decided not to make a big issue of it, anyway."

"Julia! I'm not calling because I want to do a story. I'm anxious myself, that's all. I mean it just sounds so bizarre. Janis is a dingbat, and we all know that, but for a doctor to behave that way, that's something else. Did you ever track him down at the hospital?"

There was a moment's silence at the other end. Then Julia lowered her voice. "Look, I'll tell you this much: Bill wanted to turn the hospital upside down when they wouldn't produce the doctor. He was very worried, naturally. So was I. But we had a long talk with Timmy and questioned him every which way in case something ... well, you know ... something had happened in this car. But he was adamant. Nothing happened and he's absolutely fine. And Netta, by the way, has suspended Janis."

"So, that's it?"

Julia sighed. "Yes, I guess. It wasn't Netta's fault. She said she would make a report to the police, and she was good enough to give us a semester tuition-free."

"I see. And you're not going to do anything more about the doctor?"

"What am I supposed to do, Kitty? Spend the next few weeks searching for some overzealous jerk intern? I gave the hospital administration people the name and they said they had no doctor or surgeon by that name but they'd check on their interns and other staff. I'm not holding my breath."

"The name? You had a name?"

"Sure. He gave Janis his name. At least she remembered that much."

"Which was?"

There was silence at the other end.

"C'mon, Julia. I'm not going to stir up trouble, but maybe if I call as a member of the media you'll get some response."

She heard the other woman sigh. "Okay, I'll let you have it Monday. Bill's got it written down somewhere but I can't look for it now. Okay?"

Kitty agreed reluctantly and hung up, knowing that Julia didn't want any more fuss. Not now that she had a tuition-free semester coming.

"What's the problem?" Kitty looked up and realized Jeff had returned with their coffees.

"It's nothing. No need for concern."

"You look concerned."

She sighed. "Really, it's not a big deal." She got to her feet, suddenly wanting to be with Frank. "But it is getting late and it's way past Jamie's bedtime. We should be going."

"Kitty!" He laid a hand on her arm. "There's something wrong. That phone call upset you. For heavens' sake." He paused. "I understand things have changed between us. I know you have your own life, and I'll have mine but godamnit, Kitty, I'm not an absolute total stranger. You don't have to be so edgy around me."

Kitty sank back onto the rattan couch. "Okay, okay, Jeff. I didn't mean to be edgy. It's just that it's nothing I can really explain at the moment. Something happened at Jamie's school and it seems I'm the only one who thinks it's a problem."

Jeff stared at her quizzically, and she sighed before sketchily outlining what had happened to Timmy Myers. "It just doesn't sound right to me. Or maybe I've worked for *Inside Copy* too long. I don't know, maybe I'm too suspicious."

Jeff shrugged. "Could be. On the other hand it's better to be suspicious—and safe. Do you think Jamie's in danger?"

"Hell, Jeff! Kids are always in danger. That's the kind of world we live in. Wackos all over the place. I guess that's why I'm upset. That doctor could have been a wacko." She swept her hand over her hair. "That's it, I don't want to talk about it anymore."

She stood up. "I've got to go, Jeff. When can you let me know about the interview?"

Jeff laughed but not unkindly. "Wow, that's a shift in gears. No more sweet-talk. Either yes or no, Jeff. It's make-your-mind-up time. Right?"

She shrugged. "There's nothing more I can add, Jeff. You know my work. You know I'd be fair. But I'd like you to be fair, too. Don't toy with me. Just give me a straight answer."

"Sure, I can do that." His eyes narrowed. "But let's get one thing straight: Since you guys don't want to pay anything, that means I'm not bound exclusively to you, right?"

Kitty sat down again. Yo-yo time. Jeff was going to play hardball. "Go on."

He sat down beside her. "I'll level with you, Kitty. I don't need the money. I'm not going to do an interview for the money. I admire you. I always have and you were pretty ballsy this morning. Just for that I'd do it but I've had other offers."

"You told me that. Fifty grand from *A Current Affair*."

"Yes and *Hard Copy* made an offer of sorts. One of their producers flew down on the same flight with me yesterday. Steffie . . ."

"Newman," Kitty supplied the last name as he hesitated. "I know Steffie. What sort of offer did they—" she suddenly broke off, laughing. "Oh Jeez! I see. An offer from Steffie!" Kitty stared at Jeff, shaking her head, bemused. "Well, I can't compete with that."

Jeff jumped to his feet. "I wasn't suggesting you do." His face suddenly flushed. "Jesus. This whole thing is ridiculous. Marina's only just buried and I'm sitting here discussing offers for interviews. No," he shook his head, "this isn't ridiculous. This is sick."

He paced across the veranda and back again to her. "Look, I'll do an interview with you. I can't refuse you, Kitty, you know that. I was pissed at you but you were my only friend when I needed a friend and I'm not going to forget that. I'll do it tomorrow, then I can tell everyone else to go to hell."

Kitty's pulse raced just as the phone rang again. While Jeff turned away to answer it she picked up her purse and stood up. Smiling, she crossed the foyer into the den where she saw Jamie had fallen asleep in front of the flickering TV.

She scooped him up in her arms and walked toward the

front door. Jeff was already standing in the entranceway. "Thanks," she smiled at him. "What time tomorrow?"

"Call me in the morning. I've got to talk to one of those detectives first. By the way, speak of the devil, that was Steffie Newman on the phone. Persistent little woman, isn't she?" He winced. "I hung up on her."

Kitty shifted Jamie so that he was draped over one shoulder, her purse over the other. "I appreciate that, Jeff," she said as he opened the door.

"Damn!" Kitty saw the rain coming down in sheets. She took a step back. "Let me put Jamie down. I'll drive round into the garage and take him out that way."

Jeff shook his head. "No, give me your keys. I'll pull around. You stay here."

She didn't argue. As he ran out the door she turned and crossed the foyer toward the garage door. Locating the switch, she pressed it to let Jeff pull in with the Blazer.

He jumped out of the car. "It's bad out there, Kitty. Why don't you wait till it eases off? If it's like this all the way to Boca it'll take you hours to get back."

"Oh no, I'm . . ." She stopped, not wanting to tell him she only had a couple of miles to drive to Frank's house. "I'm . . . used to rain."

He stared at her. "Up to you. But this is blinding. It's got to be pretty bad, it's driven all your colleagues off the street out there. I don't want you to misread this, Kitty, but you could stay here overnight. There're plenty of spare bedrooms—and it'll save you the trip back tomorrow."

Kitty shook her head. "No, I can't, Jeff."

He shrugged. "Okay, suit yourself." He turned to open the door of the Blazer for her just as the phone rang out again inside the house.

"Go, the phone's ringing."

"It's okay, they'll call back. Let me get you out of here first."

They'll call back? Who? Steffie Newman?

"Well? What are you doing, Kitty? In or out?" She heard the impatience in his voice.

Maybe he hadn't hung up on her. Maybe he'd told
Steffie to call back.

Stay with the story, Fitzgerald . . .

The rain was still belting down. She could hear it
hailing down on the gravel outside the garage.

Frank would kill her if she stayed . . .

"Come on, Kitty! Let me help you with Jamie."

Anxious now for her to go.

Todd would kill her if Hard Copy *got the story . . .*

"That rain does sound bad," she mumbled the words.

Frank would understand . . .

"I thought I said that about five minutes ago."

Kitty's arm was going numb from Jamie's weight. She
reached inside the Blazer for her tote. She had a toothbrush in there somewhere, and her phone was in her purse.
She'd call Frank to let him know what was happening.

She turned to Jeff. "Okay. You're right. I'll take a room.
Make it a double," she smiled. "I don't want Jamie waking
up alone in a strange house."

Chapter 24

Sunday, September 3

"Come on, Haley. Open the Goddamn door!" Frank mouthed the words under his breath as Don pressed the doorbell again.

The house seemed empty and silent inside and Frank's anxiety rose another notch. He had slept badly, dozing and waking through the night after Kitty's phone call. She'd been brief, telling him that she had a deal with Haley and that she was staying overnight and that she was safe with Jamie.

"See what I mean," he'd commented to Don. "He gives her a maybe and already she's staying the night. You watch, pal."

"Take it easy, Frank. I'm sure Kitty knows exactly what she's doing, and if you didn't believe that you'd have been banging down this door last night."

Frank didn't add that he'd considered doing just that. Instead he walked down the steps. "Come on, let's walk around the back."

The two men followed the gravel driveway around the

garage and along the side of the house to the backyard.
Frank saw Kitty before she saw him. She was sitting on
the veranda, dressed in shorts and T-shirt, slumped back in
a deep rattan chair. A silver pot of coffee on a silver tray
stood on the glass-topped table in front of her.

"Nobody answered the doorbell. Where's Haley? Where
are the Morettis?"

She jumped to her feet, whipping off her sunglasses and
grinning at him. "Well hi there, babes!"

"Hi yourself," he answered a little stiffly. "You look
nice and relaxed sitting there. Kind of at home, too."

"Just thinking about my interview. He's going to do it,
Frank. This morning. Bernie's on his way over."

Frank stared at her, unable to hide his surprise. "He is?
No shit! What happened? He rolled over just like that?
What did you promise him?"

Kitty laughed. "I didn't have to promise anything."

"He didn't come on to you?"

She shook her head. "No. And he's not going to, Frank.
He knows I'm a lost cause. He's got his eye on a *Hard
Copy* producer. That's why I stayed over. She was on the
phone bugging him all evening."

"Really? So how come he's not doing the interview
with her?"

"Maybe he still will." Kitty shrugged. "I don't care. So
long as we have it first. That's all that counts."

"So." Frank mulled this new turn of events for a second
or two. "You do the interview today and that's it, right?
You're finished with Haley?"

"You've got it. Onward and upward, babes." She paused
and they both looked across the lawn to where Jeff Haley
had appeared on the dunes. "He went running on the
beach," Kitty explained. "And I'm waiting for Jamie to
wake up." She paused again. "He's not a bad person,
Frank."

"Sure, easy for you to say," he responded and then
grinned at her. She looked so thrilled with herself and he
was relieved, too. Maybe he'd overreacted just slightly to

the situation. Maybe Haley was just going to get on with his life and leave Kitty alone. Maybe.

"Oh, by the way," Kitty lowered her voice although Haley was still some distance from them. "I didn't say anything about us. I didn't see any need . . ."

He nodded again. "Suits me. He doesn't need to know anything about me." Then he and Don stepped off the veranda and set off across the lawn.

"And before you say anything," Frank began, throwing his partner a warning glance, "I'll believe it when I see it, when she's got the damn interview on tape, okay?"

He waited for Haley to close the gap between them before introducing himself and Don. "You didn't say you would be having company this morning."

From behind his shades, Frank studied the man. He looked in good shape—muscular arms and legs; maybe a little soft around the waistline, though.

"That's not company," Haley retorted without a smile. "She's a TV reporter. I agreed to do an interview for her show. I'm a real popular guy right now, Detective. They're lining up. You'd be amazed at the offers I've had."

Frank couldn't help himself. "That TV reporter back there? What was her offer?"

Haley shrugged. "Nothing. I know Kitty Fitzgerald from way back. We used to work together. I'm talking about some of the others. It's a funny business for sure, Detective, but then who am I to look a gift horse in the mouth, eh?" Haley's lips twitched in a half-smile.

Frank couldn't resist the comment that sprang to him so readily. "It's just a shame that the circumstances of your good fortune had to be so tragic."

And he felt a glimmer of satisfaction seeing Haley's double take before the other man beckoned him and Don toward the house. "Let's walk inside and talk. You have some questions for me?"

Frank assessed Haley as they followed him into the house through a side door. He seemed calm and relaxed. Maybe a little too relaxed for an ex-con meeting two detectives, he thought. But that could be a facade. He would see soon enough.

He and Don perched on stools by the kitchen counter and declined the offer of a cold drink. Frank, watching as Haley poured himself a tall glass of orange juice, decided to shelve his personal distaste temporarily and to ease into the interview gently.

Following Kitty's call the previous night he'd picked up Marina's manuscript and had found the chapter that Kitty had teased him about. In truth, he'd been shocked by it, reflecting that any woman who was ruthless enough to use her own son in that way to boost ratings must have made many enemies along the way.

"The thing is we've got very little to go on, right now, Mr. Haley. Your mother seemingly lived a very reclusive life down here and we have to wonder if there's someone in her past who decided to settle an old score."

"You mean someone with a grudge?" Haley laughed abruptly. "If you've learned anything at all about my mother, Detective, then you must know she wasn't Mother Teresa. And TV is a very competitive business. Very backstabbing." Haley cleared his throat shrilly. "What I mean is, there were probably hundreds of people who hated her. But that was then."

"So? People carry grudges."

Haley shrugged. "I didn't find that in the TV business. It's such a revolving door. People were always being hired, fired, rehired. There's always someone new to hate."

"So you can't think of anyone from all her years in the business who hated her enough."

Haley shook his head. "Who hated her enough to wait until she's been retired for five years? I don't think so, Detective."

"What about your father, Mr. Haley?"

Jeff Haley's eyes widened. "I'd say definitely no on that one. So far as I know my mother never told him about me."

"Did she ever tell you?"

"No. She never told me." The words came out very emphatically. "It was my mother's secret, Detective."

"Did that bother you?"

Haley shrugged. "In the beginning. But I think, maybe, she had a right to keep one secret in her life."

So understanding, Frank thought wryly. But not very helpful. He had considered Haley's father the previous evening. Had wondered if perhaps the man had found out or if perhaps Marina had finally told him. Maybe she had wanted to include him in her book. Maybe Jeff's father had thought it was a bad idea. There were a half-dozen different scenarios in which the father could have figured recently, all of which could have provoked him to murder Marina. But Frank obviously wasn't going to get any clue to the man's identity from Haley.

He found it interesting, too, that Haley was diverting him away from the wide field of possible suspects he'd mentioned so far.

Okay. Let's get back to you, son.

"Did your mother write to you while you were in jail?"

"Yes. But not that often." Haley circled the counter.

"Did she mention any new friends? Men friends?" *Any new stepfathers on the horizon?*

"No and no. I don't think she was interested in making friends here, Detective. She just wanted to do the Garbo bit. 'I vant to be alone,' you know."

"Did she want *you* down here?"

Haley stopped circling. "It was her idea. She suggested it to me and she wrote to the parole board asking them to allow it."

Frank thought he detected the first glimmer of nervousness in Haley's eyes. "Did you like that idea?"

"Come on, Detective," Haley spoke softly, "given a choice, where would you rather be paroled? Royal Palm Beach or New York City? Anyway, this is my home now. Marina sold the townhouse in New York."

"You lived with your mother in New York." It was

more of a statement than a question. But Jeff Haley jumped right in to explain.

"I got on well with my mother. And we owned the properties jointly. We were a business partnership, Detective. Owned everything jointly with equal powers of attorney."

"That's right." Frank paced over to the kitchen window and noticed that Bernie had arrived and was in conversation with Kitty. He let the words hang in the air for a moment or two, aware that the talk of assets had rattled Haley a little more.

"Ever think about striking out on your own?" He turned back to face Haley. "Ever consider taking charge of your own life and doing something without your mother looking over your shoulder?"

Haley's face flushed and Frank thought he saw a glint of anger in the eyes, but then Haley shook his head. "It may sound strange to you but I didn't resent my mother for holding the purse strings, if that's what you're getting at. I had one of the best jobs in TV. I had a nice life. There was nothing I wanted to change."

"Until your mother married Larry Davenport."

Haley's eyes registered a momentary hesitation. Then, avoiding Frank's cold stare, he said, "Davenport ruined my mother's life. She should never have married him."

"Well, you took care of that, didn't you?"

The jaw tensed and Haley's lips pursed. "It wasn't what I wanted to do. . . ." A brief pause, then, "You know, Detective, you're not being very fair. I paid for that. I served my time." He brushed an imaginary speck off the counter and then cleared his throat. "Look, if you've got any other questions for me, please go ahead, Detective, otherwise I'd like to go and shower."

Frank pretended to consider his request, reflecting that Haley was certainly less calm and relaxed now than when they'd started. Then he nodded. "Go ahead. We'll probably get back to you later, Mr. Haley. In the meantime I'd like to have another word with your housekeepers, the

Morettis. I've got a couple of questions I need to clear up with them."

Jeff Haley shook his head. "They left."

"And they'll be back when?"

"No, I mean they've gone. They no longer work here."

"You fired them?"

"Uh-uh. They quit. Something Mrs. Moretti said made me think they weren't very anxious to be around someone like me."

Don jumped in. "I trust they left a forwarding address or phone number. We made it clear they shouldn't leave the area without notifying us."

"Not with me." Jeff Haley shook his head again. "To tell you the truth, Detective West, they left without any niceties whatsoever. They said they were going to evening Mass—and just didn't return. I'm not even sure they've been paid for this week."

Frank was aware of Don's bemused, suspicious glance. He shrugged in response. Who could blame the Morettis for skipping out on Haley? The agency that had sent them would no doubt be able to locate them.

He and Don let themselves out of the front door and crunched down the driveway to Frank's Thunderbird, ignoring the questions thrown at them by the small crowd of reporters and camerapeople.

As Frank revved the engine, Don picked up the car phone and dialed Marina's attorney. Frank heard him ask about the Morettis. Then there was a pause on Don's end. A long pause that Frank found ominous.

"Well?" he asked as Don hung up.

"They didn't come from an agency. According to Jonathan Gates they were friends of the regular staff. The Vascos brought them into the house to cover for them. Apparently, they were nervous about creating a problem for Marina."

"He doesn't have anything on them? No references? No address? No phone numbers?"

Don shook his head. "The Vascos introduced them to

Marina and she seemed happy just to have the problem taken care of."

"Okay. Okay. I get the picture," Frank interrupted. "What about the Vascos? Where can we reach them?"

"Gates is going to check their file in his office. He seems to think they have family in Chile . . . and Miami."

He thought about the Morettis back at his desk. It was one thing to skip out on a jailbird on parole. He could sympathize with that. What he didn't like was the Morettis' leaving without notification. He'd made it clear that he would need to speak to them again. They had not misunderstood, he was sure.

Then again, maybe Haley had lied. Maybe he had fired them. Maybe he didn't want prying ears and eyes around. Either way, the Morettis had to be found.

❧ *Chapter* 25 ❧

Kitty banged on Frank's front door when he didn't respond to the doorbell. But there was no answer to either the bell or the pounding. Not really that surprising, she told herself. He was in the middle of an investigation, after all.

She was disappointed nonetheless. She checked her watch. Just after five in the afternoon. She wondered if it was worth waiting around a little longer. She wanted to share her excitement with him. She wanted to show him the dozen or so tapes Bernie had shot. She wanted to tell him that Todd had promised her a raise and was going to "promo the shit" out of the interview. She wanted to open the second bottle of Cristal and celebrate. Most of all she wanted to tell Frank: *Relax, it's done. It's in the bag. I don't have to see Jeff Haley again.*

She considered poking her head around the door of Bradley's Saloon, but she knew she couldn't leave Jamie in the car. He'd fallen asleep before she was out of Jeff's driveway, seconds after complaining that he couldn't get comfortable with the seatbelt strangling his chest.

She pulled away from the curb outside Frank's house and headed home. Jamie slept all the way, and Kitty did not wake him when she pulled up outside the house. She would open up the house first, and then she could carry him straight in and let him nap a little longer, giving her a chance to start her script.

She slipped the bulging tote onto her shoulder and walked up the path to the courtyard gates. One of the gates had been left ajar but she thought nothing of it, figuring one of the neighborhood kids had come calling for Jamie and had, naturally, forgotten to close it.

Nor was she puzzled to see Flipper lying in a crumpled gray rubbery mass by the side of the pool. Flipper was the third inflatable dolphin she'd bought for Jamie. Each had survived about a year. She smiled to herself. The sun, and Jamie's pummeling, weakened the plastic and eventually they all expired, their air seeping out through the tiny punctures caused by wear and tear.

In the next moment, however, the smile froze on her face as something crackled underfoot and she looked down to see shards of broken glass strewn across the pathway. Almost in the same second she realized what they were.

The kitchen window was broken. Jagged edges of glass stuck out at odd angles from the frame. The window was raised and the screen had been pushed inside. She could see it, through the half-drawn drapes, balancing precariously against one of the kitchen chairs.

"Shit!" Kitty's first instantaneous thought was about bugs. How many of them had flown or slithered in through the open window? Her second thought, coming hard on the heels of the first, was: *I've been burglarized.*

She felt her heart pounding in her chest and her hands suddenly turning clammy. She had not set the alarm because she had not planned on staying out overnight.

She reached inside to touch the drapes that hung limply. They were damp. The window, had, evidently, been broken before or during the storm last night. She pushed the drape aside, peering into the kitchen as her heart pounded harder at the thought of what she might see. But the kitchen area looked undisturbed. The cabinets and drawers were closed. She could even see her Walkman on the counter where she'd left it.

She glanced back through the courtyard gates and saw the top of Jamie's little blonde head still resting in the same position against the passenger-side window. Good. She didn't want him walking into the house with her. She let herself in through the front door slowly, turning the key and letting the door swing open.

Then, she hesitated. She was being stupid. She should not walk into the house. The police always warned against it, in case the intruder was still on the premises. But the house felt empty.

What a stupid thing to think. She took a step inside, glanced at the blinking green light on the alarm pad that signaled that a door or window was ajar. She stood in the doorway, her head turned upward. Then she reached across and without further hesitation pushed the panic button. She would do the right thing, especially with Jamie in the car. She would wait for the police. Then she turned and ran back down the pathway toward the Blazer, slamming the courtyard gate behind her.

The patrol car pulled into the cul-de-sac less than ten minutes later and she ran over to the officer at the wheel.

"Thanks for coming so quickly, Officer." She beckoned him in the direction of the house. "I just returned home and it looks like someone broke into my house."

The young officer followed her through the gates, his eyes glancing over the yard and the house. "Have you had a chance to check on what was taken?"

She shook her head. "I didn't go inside. I didn't want to go in alone."

She glanced back again to check on Jamie. She double checked that the passenger window was open for air. It was better to leave him where he was until the house was checked out.

She saw the cop's hand resting lightly on his holster as he approached the doorway. She followed him in, wondering if he was going to take his gun out. But he didn't.

They stood for a moment in the small foyer, Kitty staring into the living room. Nothing in there seemed to have been disturbed. She noticed that her laptop computer lay on the couch where she'd left it.

Kitty relaxed a little and motioned to her bedroom. "That's the master bedroom."

They walked toward it together, Kitty embarrassed for a second when he stared at her unmade bed and open closet door with her clothes where she had thrown them on the floor. "That's how I left it," she smiled weakly.

While the cop walked across to her bathroom, checking it out, Kitty opened her top dresser drawer. She kept a few pieces of expensive jewelry in a small box in the top drawer. She lifted the lid and checked her mother's sapphire ring and the gold necklace she had inherited from her grandmother.

She let out an audible sigh of relief. "He didn't take anything."

It was the same story in the kitchen. The Walkman and the twenty dollars in single bills she kept in a kitchen drawer were also there. She glanced around the family room. Everything looked normal.

"I don't understand." She looked at the young officer.

He was staring down the hallway.

"There's nothing there. That's just a guest bedroom and my son's room. Believe me if he couldn't find anything to take from here that goes double for down there."

The cop walked over to the kitchen window, staring at it for a while. "Did you close this window before you left the house?"

"Of course." Kitty nodded. "I never open any of the windows during the summer." She laughed. "The humidity would peel the paper straight off the wall."

"It could be vandalism by some of the older kids living around here, ma'am. We've had a couple of reports from this development about smashed car windows, stolen car radios, and patio furniture tossed into pools. Quite honestly, I think that's got to be the answer."

The ringing of the phone made Kitty jump, and she ran to pick it up, hoping it was Frank.

It was Jeff.

"Hey, Kitty," he started. "Your cameraman left a couple of tapes here . . . I—"

"Jeff," she cut him off in mid-sentence, "I'm going to have to call you back. The police are here."

"The police?" She heard the concern in Jeff's voice.

"It's okay. I had a break-in. I have to go, Jeff."

"You want someone with you? I could be right there."

"No," she protested. "It's okay, Jeff. Nothing was taken." Then she realized he'd already hung up. She shrugged and replaced the receiver in its cradle and walked out into the yard where the young police officer was crouched beside Flipper.

He looked up at her and held up the gray mess. "Look at this. Whatever it was, it's been slashed, see here . . ." He showed her the jagged cuts in the plastic. He threw down Flipper's remains with a look of disgust on his face. "It's vandalism as I thought, Miss Fitzgerald. We've put on a few extra patrols in this development." He stood up. "Let me write up some details on this, anyway."

Kitty nodded. "I'll go get my son, he's still asleep in the car."

Jamie was snoring softly and his hair was damp with light perspiration. She hoped she could carry him through to his bed before he woke. She didn't want him seeing the broken window or the cop.

Gingerly, she freed him from his seatbelt and wiggled him into her arms, then carried him into the house. The door to his room was closed and she had to prop him up on one raised knee while she turned the doorknob and nudged the door open with her foot.

She took a step into the room and then froze at the sight before her. She wanted to scream but instantly realized it would wake Jamie. Instead, she clamped her lips together firmly. Then she backed away from the room as fast as she could go with Jamie still in her arms.

She placed him on the family room couch and then, gasping for breath, turned to the cop who'd seated himself at the kitchen counter to scribble out his report.

"Officer," her breath came in short gasps. "Officer, you'd better take a look . . . in Jamie's room."

❧ *Chapter 26* ❧

*D*o you still think it's vandals?" She hurled the question at the bewildered cop as they both stared into Jamie's room.

Kitty clutched her stomach trying to stop herself from shaking at the sight: The room was bare.

Empty and stripped of every single possession of Jamie's.

Only the furniture had been left standing. The little bed, a nightstand, and the desk and chair under the window. But everything else was gone—even the sheets and the pillows had been taken off the bed.

"Look." She waved her hand over the room. "This is my son's room. There was a lamp here. There was a pattern of toy trains on the shade, and his books were here, on the desk. And his videos and video games were stacked up here." She banged her fist down on the window ledge.

Like some madwoman she flung herself toward the walk-in closet, flinging the doors open. "Nothing! There's nothing left! All his clothes are gone!" She felt tears sting-

ing her eyes when she noticed that the toy chest Jamie
kept in a corner of the closet was gone, too. She thought
of all the little action figures, and the Power Rangers, and
all the Zords that had been so hard to find in the stores.
The tears rolled silently down her cheeks. What on earth
was she going to say to Jamie?

"Ma'am?" The officer took a step back into the hallway,
trying to maneuver her out of the room. "Ma'am? I know
this is very upsetting. Believe me, everyone feels the same
way about being burglarized. But please try to calm yourself. Can you give me an idea of what's missing? Was
there anything of real value in your son's room?"

Kitty felt like yelling at him. Real value? Yes! Everything was of value to Jamie. But she realized it would get
her nowhere. It was not the cop's fault. He was trying his
best.

"Yes . . . no . . ." she started. "I mean, none of the
things were priceless. Just regular little boy stuff." She
hesitated, almost choking on the words. "I mean it's all re-
placeable, I guess, but . . . I don't even remember half the
toys that were in here." Her voice rose sharply again, her
shock suddenly turning to anger. "Why? Who the hell
would do something like this?"

The police officer steered her down the hallway toward
the kitchen. "Was your son in any fights, any arguments
with the neighborhood kids recently?"

She stared at him, perplexed. "Fights? My son is five
years' old, Officer. He doesn't hang out with kids on a
street corner. If he goes outside to ride his bike or play,
I'm right there with him."

The officer sighed. "Do you want to give me a list of
some of the bigger items that were stolen? Or would you
like to wait until one of our investigations officers arrives."

Kitty nodded. "Yes, sure," she replied, but she was not
sure, at all, which question she was answering, her
thoughts were jumping so crazily around in her head.

This was not the work of neighborhood teenagers or

vandals. The room had been stripped thoroughly—and meticulously.

But there was no point in discussing this with the young cop. She wanted Frank here. "Sure," she nodded again. "Why don't you have someone come out and I'll put together a list of what's missing."

A few minutes later she watched the officer walk up the path, then she picked Jamie up off the couch and carried him to her bed before grabbing the phone to call Frank again. She speed-dialed Frank's number and, as the machine kicked in, she heard her own phone signaling another call coming through.

It was the security guard at the main gate. Jeff had arrived. A couple of minutes later he was walking to the front door.

"Jeez, what happened, Kitty?" He put two tapes on the kitchen counter.

"Jeff, you didn't have to drive down. I'm sure you've got better things to do."

He dismissed her words with a wave of the hand. "Don't worry about me. Tell me what happened."

Kitty sighed. "Okay, come and have a look for yourself." She beckoned him to follow her down the hall. "This is Jamie's room." She stood back silently. "And that's not the way I left it yesterday."

Jeff took a step inside, glancing over the open drawers and open closet. "They just took Jamie's stuff?"

"You got it."

He shook his head. "That's weird. What did the cops say?"

Kitty told him about the neighborhood vandals theory.

Jeff shrugged. "Did Jamie have a lot of expensive video games? Nintendo or Sega or whatever they call it?"

Kitty shook her head. "Oh for heavens' sake, Jeff, don't you start." She shook her head again, trying to control the quivering in her voice. "If that's what they were after, why take the sheets off his bed, and the pillows and his clothes?"

"Okay, I get it." Jeff eyed her quizzically. "Where is Jamie?"

"In my bed."

"Okay, next thing—do you keep cognac in the house?"

She tried to protest. But he started looking through the kitchen cabinets. She directed him to the right one and watched while he poured her a belt into a juice glass.

"Now ..." He walked over to the window. "Do you have any plywood or even a cardboard box so that we can cover the window?"

"Jeff, I'm not concerned about the stupid window. It's Jamie ..."

He perched on the kitchen stool next to her and put his hand over hers. "Kitty, nothing is going to be accomplished with anger or tears. Now, was there a lot of stuff? Can you make a list? Is there one store around here where we could get it all replaced?"

"No!" Kitty shook her head violently. "It can't be done, Jeff. I can't remember exactly what Jamie had. That's stupid, we can't replace everything and pretend—"

"Mom!"

The sound of Jamie's voice made her freeze. "Oh Jesus!" She glanced at Jeff. "What am I going to tell him?"

Jeff touched her arm gently. "Stay calm. Just stay calm."

"Hey Mom! What happened to the window?"

Kitty jumped to her feet, almost spilling her drink as she reached for her son and took him into her arms. "Listen Jamie, I'm going to tell you what happened but you mustn't get upset. Some bad kids broke into our house last night."

"Bad kids? Bad guys you mean, Mom."

Kitty shook her head. "No. The police said it was some kids. They ... they broke in because they wanted to steal some toys."

She saw Jamie's eyes widen as he wrenched himself free and went careening down the hallway before she could stop him.

"Jamie! Wait!" She ran after him but not fast enough. His distressed shriek cut right through her.

"Mom! They stoled everything! Mom!" He flung himself at her, pummeling her with both fists. "I hate this house! I hate this house!" he shrieked at her. "Why do we have such a stupid house that bad guys can get into?"

"Jamie!" Jeff's voice cut in firmly from behind them. "Jamie listen, come back here." Jeff motioned for Kitty to bring the sobbing boy back into the family room. Then he got down on one knee in front of him.

"Listen Jamie . . . no, I mean listen without crying. I can't talk while you're making all that noise. That's it, you can use your sleeve, if you want."

"Now," Jeff took Jamie's hand and led him over to the couch. "I never saw your toys but I bet some of your stuff was really old. Now you can get everything new. Listen, the bad guys are going to have all the old stuff and your mom will take you and get everything you want—new."

"Oh yeah?" Jamie's lower lip quivered, his eyes brimming with tears.

"Yeah," Kitty agreed firmly. "Jamie, I'm going to get you new toys and videos and video games. I promise, sweets. I'll replace everything those bad kids took."

Jamie turned to Kitty, brushing his wet face with the back of his sleeve. "And can we get some other toys as well, Mom? Like stuff I didn't have? Can we go to Toys "R" Us, right now?"

Kitty pulled him toward her, laughing inside. "Well, not tonight. It's closed right now and, anyway, we first have to make a long, long list of everything we have to buy."

"A long, long list," Jeff echoed.

Jamie giggled. "A very, very, very, very long, long, long, long list. Right, Mom?"

Kitty hugged him. "It'll be such a long list we'll have to spend the whole night at Toys "R" Us."

Jamie stepped back away from her. "Mom, that's silly. You just said they close at night."

Kitty looked over the top of his head at Jeff mouthing "Thanks."

Jeff moved toward the door. "Now, let me go find some plywood to board up that window. You don't want it gaping open all night. I'll be right back."

While he was gone Kitty fussed around Jamie, crossing her fingers as she assured him that the police would find the bad kids and get all his things back, and then he would have two of everything.

She retrieved some pajamas from the dryer, relieved that at least half his clothes were in there, and pushed him toward her own bedroom, supervising his bath while she tried to reach Frank. Only the answering machine was picking up and she left a brief message asking him to call. She thought about trying his cellular phone, even having him paged through the precinct, but she did not want to reach him in the middle of some important interview or meeting.

"You'll have to make up a bedtime story, Mom." Jamie clambered onto her knee as she dried him off. "They took all my books, too, didn't they?"

It was after ten when Jamie finally fell asleep, and when she came into the kitchen she saw that Jeff had finished boarding up the window and was sitting at the counter with his own drink.

"Doesn't look very pretty," he pointed to the plywood, "but at least it's a little more secure." Then he paused for a second. "What do you think's going on here?"

Kitty shrugged but didn't say anything.

"I'm sorry. You don't want to talk about it?"

Yes, but not with you. With Frank. "I'm trying not to think about it. There's not much I can do right this minute."

"Okay." Jeff nodded and got to his feet. "You think you'll be okay?" He looked over her shoulder as if checking his handiwork on the boarded-up window. "Is there anyone you could call to come and stay with you?"

Kitty glanced at the phone, wishing that Frank would

hurry and call. Then she laughed nervously. "Why? Do you think they . . . whoever . . . might come back?"

"Probably not." Jeff shook his head but looked as if he wasn't sure. Kitty wasn't sure, either. The break-in hadn't been just another burglary. She was sure of that. It was some kind of message directed at Jamie. Just like the porn video and note. Someone was obsessing about Jamie. . . . And that someone had been in their house.

She felt chills running up and down her back and shivered visibly.

Jeff sat down beside her. "Would you like me to stick around for a while?"

She didn't reply. What could she say? Yes, stick around till Frank gets here? Suppose Frank was tied up for hours yet?

Jeff, evidently misreading her hesitation, added, "You're not messing up any of my plans if that's what you're worried about. My only concern is getting something to eat, sometime this evening." He grinned at her. "I don't suppose you've got anything in the freezer?"

She laughed, suddenly deciding that Jeff's presence was better than nothing. She wasn't going to take any chances with Jamie's safety. "You've got that right. But I could order pizza."

❦ *Chapter 27* ❦

Monday, September 4

*F*rank woke to the smell of coffee wafting from the galley. He lay with his eyes closed, enjoying the rhythmic lapping of water against the side of the sailboat. The boat rocked gently.

Suddenly, his eyes opened—wide. *Coffee! Who the hell was making coffee?*

In the next second the events of the previous evening came flashing back to him, and he closed his eyes again as he listened for sounds of movement.

Was she in the galley? Was Roberta Mallory still on the boat?

She had finally returned his call around eight the previous evening—several hours after he had attempted to contact her about the Vascos. He and Don had spent the afternoon on the phones trying to track down the couple. Marina's attorney had produced a couple of numbers for them in Miami as well as names of former employers. The calls had produced other numbers and contacts, but all had eventually led nowhere.

Thinking about the Vascos had reminded Frank of Roberta. He had recalled her look of concern over their family emergency. He had figured that she had known them better than the Morettis.

By the time she'd called at eight, reaching him on his cellular phone, Frank was finishing up an interview with the couple who worked for Marina's neighbors. They, too, had known nothing about the Vascos or their plans.

He arranged to meet Roberta, who had just finished a shift at the reception desk of the Breakers Hotel, in the bar of the Brazilian Court. She'd been waiting for him when he arrived.

He came straight to the point as soon as she had her gin and tonic in front of her. "I need to find the Vascos," he told her. "Do you have any idea where their family emergency took them?"

She toyed with her swizzle stick. "Are they in trouble?"

"Why would you think that?" He sipped his beer.

She shook her head. "They're a nice couple. Mrs. V. always had cappucino and brownies for me when I came to pick up Marina's manuscript. I never touched the brownies, of course," she smiled, her hand patting her thigh. "Would have gone straight here."

"Did you know about their family problem? Come on, Roberta, this is important."

She played with the swizzle stick, a frown creasing her forehead.

"Listen Roberta, unless the Vascos crept back in the middle of the night and murdered Marina Dee Haley they're not in trouble with me. Now would you please tell me what you know?"

She sighed. "Okay. There wasn't a family emergency. They went away for a vacation. They didn't think Mrs. Haley would give them time off." She added, as if to justify their deception, "In the three years they worked for her they'd only had two weeks off."

"Any idea where they went?" Frank signaled the bartender to bring her another drink and ordered an Irish coffee for himself.

"Somewhere in the Keys."

"Roberta," he put his hand on her arm, "do you know where in the Keys?"

She nodded. "Mrs. V. showed me the brochure. She was very excited. They must have saved for a long time because it looked like an uptown place. She asked me what kind of clothes she should take."

"Roberta . . . ?"

"Okay. Okay. It was Hawk's Cay Resort."

Frank used the phone at the bar to reach the hotel. Sure enough, the Vascos were registered but were not in their room.

As he hung up the thought had suddenly struck him that surely they had heard about Marina's murder. And if that were the case, why had they not returned or called? The idea of household staff taking off on a vacation in an expensive resort didn't sit too well with him, either.

He had intended making it an early night, planning to drive south to the Keys with Don in the morning. But walking Roberta down Brazilian Avenue to her car, making small talk with her, he'd mentioned his sailboat was berthed a couple of blocks down in the Municipal Docks.

Of course, she'd wanted to take a look. Of course. *Just one little peek. I just love boats. . . .* Then she'd wanted to sit on the deck to listen to the water, and hinted that *a little cocktail would just make things perfect*.

He'd rummaged around and found a bottle of Schnapps in the galley. Roberta had never drunk Schnapps before, but she'd had three or four before she discovered it gave her *a teeny, weeny bit of a headache*. So she'd slid her head down onto his lap, her blonde mane fanning out over his thighs, her hands tightening around his waist. . . .

Frank's head pounded now, as he stared through the porthole above the bunk. Gritting his teeth, he flung back the sheet and slid out of the bunk, hesitating only a second before pushing through the doors into the main cabin.

The galley was empty. But coffee was perking on the little stove.

His cellular phone rang as he took his first sip out on the deck. It was Don calling from his car. "I'm sitting outside your front door. Where are you, pal?"

"On the boat. Pick me up here." Frank hung up and thundered down the steps, stopping to check the closet for a clean shirt and a pair of jeans before heading into the shower.

By the time he was ready Don had arrived and was waiting in the cabin, staring pointedly at a little note lying beside Frank's car keys and an empty bottle of Schnapps.

Frank stared at the penciled scribble, too. "Three strikes—and you're out," it said. Underneath the words Roberta had drawn a sad face, with a downturned mouth.

Frank grinned at his partner. "She's got it wrong, you know. I'm not even at bat."

❦ *Chapter 28* ❦

*K*itty sat at her desk staring into space. She had about five hours before she was due to feed her segment on Jeff Haley to New York. Satellite time had been booked for two o'clock and Todd had told her he wanted seven minutes for today's interview. Since it took approximately one hour of editing to produce one minute's worth of viewing, time was already tight.

But she couldn't focus on the work. She had tossed around all night, getting up and showering by 5:30 A.M., wanting to speak to Frank before she could even begin to think about the work that lay ahead.

She had gotten through on his cellular phone, only to hear a woman's voice at the other end. She had hung up and dialed the number again a couple of minutes later, thinking she had misdialed, and this time it had just rung out.

Where the hell had he disappeared to when she needed him so urgently? He'd obviously not picked up any of his messages, because she'd waited till midnight for him to call. In the end, when Jeff had offered to stay overnight, she'd thanked him and shown him to the guest room.

If Jeff had not been around she would still be at home, dithering around, not knowing whether to go to work or to wait for the window repairman. Not knowing whether to send Jamie to school or to bring him to work with her.

"What good will keeping him out of school do?" Jeff had asked. "Right now, it's probably the best place for him."

"What about the detectives who are supposed to come? And I've got to get the window fixed and . . . then I've got to take Jamie to Toys "R" Us."

"And you'll get nothing done by getting all wound up," Jeff had replied calmly. "Why don't you concentrate on getting the story done. I'll take care of everything else here. I can supervise the window repair and I'll take Jamie to school, and I'll tell you what else I'll do—I'll stop by the school at lunchtime and check on him.

"Go on," he'd urged her as she hesitated. "I've got nothing else to do. This will make me feel useful. Besides, I don't want you to waste all that good stuff I gave you for the interview. Go."

Kitty took a deep breath and forced herself to concentrate on the story, staring at her computer screen, where she'd started inputting:

sfx   *sound up music*

jeff/b-roll/   SOT JEFF/T

The rest was blank space because she could not decide which sound bite to use for the opening. There were two possibilities: One, where Jeff was walking toward the pool. The other . . .

Screw it, she thought. She was not going to agonize over it. The pool shot was dramatic and powerful. She consulted her notepad for the timing, then next to the "T" she typed in 7:12:23. Underneath that she typed the most dramatic part of Jeff's sound bite:

> *How can I stay in this house? Every window looks out onto this pool.* ON CAM: *I'm never going to be able to look at it or swim in it without seeing my mother's battered, lifeless body lying there.*

Okay. She was off and running. If she put everything else out of her mind, she'd make the feed. She paused. Then started typing again, her fingers flying over the keyboard. There was so much good material that the script almost wrote itself.

When she had it ready she faxed a copy to Todd in New York for his approval but knew he'd have no problem with it. Then she got down to the hard part, laying down her audio track, and directing Ben, her editor, to the relevant portions of footage that would cover the voice overs on the audio track.

Editing was a slow, painstaking task and they worked feverishly for the rest of the morning and through lunch, finishing with just enough time for Kitty to race down to the control room with her tape.

By 2:30, she was on her way back to Boca Raton in plenty of time to pick up Jamie. Frank had finally called, leaving a message with Ginny that he was out of town and likely to be gone for the day. Jeff had called, too, to keep her informed that Jamie was fine, that the window was fixed, that the mess left by the repairmen was cleaned up, and that detectives from Boca Raton police department would be by in the early evening.

"I'll probably be gone by then," he told her. "But don't worry about dinner. I made some chicken cacciatore for my lunch and there's plenty left for you and Jamie."

Kitty didn't have the heart to tell him that Jamie would not touch cacciatore in a million years. Jeff had saved the day for her. Now, she looked forward to spending a couple of hours with her son in the toy store.

Jamie was waiting for her in the schoolyard when she pulled up. He was sitting at one of the big redwood tables counting Pogs with Alex Baines and Timmy Myers, whose right arm was wrapped in a gauze bandage. A thicker bandage encircled his knee. She walked across to the gate and waved to Jamie who came running toward her, with Timmy and Alex behind him.

"Mom! Can Timmy and Alex come to Toys "R" Us?"

Kitty ignored her son's question and rumpled his hair. Then she crouched down beside the small group.

"How's the arm, Timmy?" she asked. "And the knee? I heard you had quite a fall last week."

"Look!" he gestured to the bandage. "They put that on in the hospital. I had to go to the hospital."

Kitty smiled. "I heard. But you didn't go in an ambulance did you?"

"Uh-uh." Timmy shook his head. "It was the doctor's car."

"The doctor who took you must have been a nice man."

Timmy looked at her suspiciously. No doubt, thought Kitty, because his parents had asked him the same questions, over and over. Kitty looked around, guiltily, for Julia Myers.

Stop with the questions. Leave the boy alone.

But she couldn't help herself. She wanted to hear about the doctor for herself.

"Did he talk to you?"

"Not much. I told him my arm hurt me and it was bleeding and blood was gushing out all over the place. All over the car, and everywhere."

Kitty smiled at the obvious exaggeration. "It was?" She tried to look shocked and frightened.

"Yeah, it was! You should have seen it." Timmy was warming to his story. "And the doctor was frightened, too. Yeah. He was. He thought I was going to die. He made me count his fingers . . . you know like in the movies . . . after a guy gets hit on the head."

Kitty laughed. "Well, I'm sure he was worried about

you. He sounds like a nice doctor. Did he tell you his name, Timmy?"

She was uneasy about badgering the boy, but she had the feeling that Julia was going to be reluctant to pursue the subject.

"Uh-uh." The boy shook his head and Kitty straightened up, her leg cramping from having crouched beside him. She reached for Jamie's hand and started to walk to the gate.

"But I told him mine," Timmy continued, trotting alongside them.

"You did, huh?" Kitty echoed.

"Sure, I had to."

Something about the way Timmy emphasized the last three words caught Kitty's interest again.

"Had to! Why is that Timmy?"

" 'Cause he kept calling me the wrong name."

"He did?" Kitty stopped walking and stared at him.

"Yeah," Timmy Myers grinned at her. "He kept calling me Jamie."

❧ Chapter 29 ❧

The traffic slowed to a crawl on the two-lane just north of Islamorada and Frank swore under his breath. They were looking at a four-hour ride back to Palm Beach. Five at this rate. But this was Route 1 in the Keys. One lane each way for miles and miles.

"Five-thirty. It's rush hour, pal," Don pointed to the clock on the dashboard.

"Rush hour!" Frank laughed. "No such thing in the Keys. Unless they're all rushing to the bar to watch the sun set." He glanced in the rearview mirror to check on the Vascos. Neither had said a word since getting into Frank's car in Marathon, where they'd dropped off the Vascos' rental at the Hertz office. Now, they sat in the back seat, each in one corner, not touching, not talking, both faces set in glum, resigned masks.

Let them stew over their stupidity—and greed, thought Frank. Because that's what their story boiled down to.

Two words. But it had taken more than a couple of hours to piece together their story as the four of them sat in the corner of the hotel lobby, where Don had approached them as they returned to the resort after a boat trip round the Keys.

The Vascos had known instantly why Frank and Don were there. They'd seen the TV news reports on the murder, they'd said, but the Morettis had called them to say they were dealing with the situation. "They told us the police had not asked for us to return home," Tony Vasco had added, picking nervously at his pencil-thin mustache.

"It's your friends the Morettis we want to talk about," Frank weighed in. "They've disappeared and we need to find them."

He saw the puzzled look that passed between Lisa Vasco and her husband before the woman answered. "Disappeared? They left the house?" She shook her head. "They should have called us."

"Where can we find them, Mrs. Vasco?" Frank prompted.

"Oh, through Eduardo Alvarez. He does the landscaping for Mrs.—" she flushed bright red. "I mean, he used to do it for Mrs. Haley. Vincent Moretti is a cousin or nephew of Eduardo's, I think."

It had taken Don about three minutes on the phone with Alvarez Tree and Lawn Service in West Palm Beach to ascertain that Vincent Moretti was neither a nephew nor a cousin of Eduardo's nor, in fact, a former or current employee of the service.

That was only a story the Morettis had spun for the Vascos on the day they'd turned up in the driveway with a delivery of potted hibiscus for Mrs. Haley. Over a couple of diet sodas in the Vasco kitchen, Vincent Moretti had drawn them into a conversation about finding work as household staff in Palm Beach.

"He said his wife wanted to quit outdoor work. But it was difficult to find decent live-in positions in Palm Beach without references ... and you couldn't get references without doing the job first."

"So?" Frank had prodded but had guessed the rest of the

story before Tony Vasco started stumbling through it: The Morettis had finally offered to pay the Vascos for the chance to establish a solid reference by working for Marina Dee Haley.

"How much?" Frank asked.

"Seven thousand."

Frank heard Don's low whistle as he continued. "That's a lot of money, Vasco. Didn't you wonder about it?"

Vasco shook his head and shrugged. "It's a lot, yes. But it's the way for people like us. You can pay all your savings for green cards, references, recommendations, anything that will help get a good job."

"So you lied about the family emergency to Mrs. Haley, took the money, and ran?" Don had jumped in, shaking his head in amazement. "They paid you in cash, of course?"

Vasco nodded and hung his head. "Lisa always wanted to see the Keys. To have a vacation like rich Americans. We've been in America for five years, three years with Mrs. Haley, and never more than a day off here, four or five there."

Yes, indeed, stupidity and greed were an unbeatable combination, thought Frank, pulling off the road into the parking lot of a diner. He had told the Vascos that he was not arresting them but had strongly advised them to return to Palm Beach where they could be of some help to the investigation.

In the diner he let them huddle together in a booth while he and Don chose stools at the counter to order sandwiches. Stirring his coffee, Frank finally verbalized his anger at himself. "I screwed up, that's for sure. As soon as the Morettis told me they were temps that should have been a flag, right there . . . Jesus!" He raised his palm to his forehead.

"Sure, sure," Don nodded. "Hindsight is always twenty-twenty. You're being too hard on yourself, Detective. Anyway, their story checked out, remember? I spoke to the bartender myself."

"Yeah, right. Bartender in a busy bar. He's watching

Vincent Moretti all evening? How long would it take to drive from that bar to the house, pick off Marina, and drive back again?"

Frank bit into his tuna fish sandwich and chewed without tasting anything. "You're wrong, Don. I should have known. For one thing Moretti was too articulate. That should have tipped me off, too."

"You've got no doubts they did it?"

Frank laughed derisively. "Yes, I have doubts. There are some pieces here that don't fit—"

"For one," Don cut in, "why did they hang out and call the cops the next morning?"

"Yeah, yeah." Frank nodded, draining his cup of coffee. "There's that. There's a couple of other oddities, too."

He paused, staring morosely at the Vascos in their booth. "Maybe the Morettis didn't do it, Don, but I'd put it this way: Right at this moment they've got every other suspect in the world beat for second. The question is, why did they do it?"

❧ *Chapter 30* ❧

$\mathcal{K}$itty looked in on Jamie just after eight, a few minutes after Detective Jim Beaufort from the Boca police department had left. Her son was sprawled on her bed surrounded by packages and discarded boxes. Action figures of all shapes and sizes were strewn all over the bedspread except for the Power Rangers, which Jamie was lining up on the nightstand.

"Jamie," she approached the bed. "Time for lights out, honey."

"Mom! Just five more minutes."

She laughed. "You said that last time I came in. Come on. Get under the covers. You're going to have plenty of time to play tomorrow."

She perched on the edge of the bed and absently picked up the red-colored Ranger. Jamie had been thrilled with the new karate-kicking, swivel-action models.

"Look Mom!" He fiddled with something and the black Ranger's leg kicked out. "See, my other Power Rangers didn't do that. These are great, Mom!"

She grinned and held the covers open. "Come on, into bed." She dimmed the bedside light and for a moment she sat with Jamie as he burrowed down, making himself comfortable. Then she kissed him good night and walked out of the room, back to the kitchen where Jeff was pouring himself a glass of club soda.

He had been walking out of the front gates to his car when she'd pulled up with Jamie after their shopping trip. "The security guys only just left," he told her. "They reconnected the sensors on the new window. Everything's back in working order."

Then he'd helped her and Jamie with the packages and when everything was in the house he'd poured her a large glass of iced tea, which he'd obviously prepared earlier in the day.

The little gesture had touched her and she had slumped back on her couch, finally abandoning the brave face she'd put on for Jamie's benefit throughout their shopping.

"Jeff," she put her glass down on the table, horrified to see her hand visibly shaking, "the pervert who took Timmy Myers from the schoolyard thought he had Jamie. It's Jamie he wanted. I spoke to Timmy this afternoon."

Jeff's eyes had narrowed. "The boy told you that?"

"Wait!" Kitty silenced him. "That's not the only thing." She proceeded to tell Jeff about the porn video and note she had received the day after Timmy's accident in the schoolyard. "He sent it Fedex, Jeff. He must have dropped it off when he had Timmy in the car. Only at the time he thought it was Jamie. It all fits. And listen to this." She paused as a chill ran up her back. "I cornered Timmy's mother outside school and made her give me the name of the doctor. Or at least the name he gave to Janis."

"And?" Jeff prodded gently.

She closed her eyes. "It was the same name that was on my Fedex envelope . . . Stroud."

Jeff's reaction had been swift. "That's heavy, Kitty! It puts the break-in into a whole new perspective. You've got to tell the cops. You've got to get them here right now."

"No kidding, Jeff!" She had smiled weakly. "I already called them," she said. "Detective Beaufort is coming."

Detective Beaufort had come—and stayed for two hours. Five minutes after his arrival the phone had rung and she'd been relieved to hear Frank's voice. Only to learn that he was still several hours from home and that he anticipated a busy night. She had wanted to tell him what was going on, but he'd warned her off the idea by saying he was on the car phone and not able to talk freely. She hung up disappointed. She had hoped he would arrive in time to talk with the Boca detective. She would have liked Frank's input.

Beaufort had taken methodical and careful notes of everything she'd told him. Had asked for the video and the note and the Fedex envelope. She had told him everything was in her office and she would have it delivered to him the next day.

He had asked her if she'd received any other kind of threats or phone calls. Or if she could name anyone who had a grudge against her.

"Why against me?" Kitty had asked. "It's Jamie he's fixating on. He's a pervert. I would think the video makes that obvious."

"Not necessarily, Miss Fitzgerald," the young detective spoke slowly. "Pedophiles . . . perverts, are usually looking for kids who aren't that strictly supervised. It's too much hassle for them to abduct a child from a schoolyard. The second point that bothers me is the note he sent you. Another thing they don't do usually is tip off the mother. My feeling is that your son may have been targeted by a kidnapper—possibly for ransom."

Beaufort paused and Kitty found herself thinking his slow manner of speaking was misleading. He seemed, anyway, to have some grasp on the situation.

She had waited for him to continue. "What I'm saying, Miss Fitzgerald, is there's nothing to be gained by jumping to conclusions. I'd like to speak to the teacher at the academy, and the boy, too. You send me the video and we'll take it from there."

"What about the break-in?" Kitty had asked. "Why would he take Jamie's things? Just Jamie's? Do you think we're in danger here?"

Beaufort had shrugged. "The only reason I can think of right now is that maybe he was dealing with his frustration. He obviously went to a lot of effort to plan the abduction attempt and he came away empty-handed. That's only a guess, though."

As for the danger, Beaufort had promised to lay on extra car patrols but had suggested she might want to stay with a friend for a few days.

Now, returning to the kitchen, Jeff handed her another glass of iced tea and said: "So, where do you go from here?"

"Oh Jeff, how the hell am I supposed to answer that?" She flung the words out irritably, slumping down on the couch.

Jeff turned away from her and rinsed his glass out under the faucet, then wiped it and put it away in the cabinet. He closed the door with a gesture that suggested to Kitty he was all done and finished . . . and ready to leave.

A momentary unease seized her. She didn't want to be alone, not just yet. She didn't want to sit in the house listening for every little sound and creak.

"I'm sorry," she blurted out. "I didn't mean to snap. There's no excuse for taking it out on you. I want you to know I really appreciate what you did today."

Jeff stood in the middle of the kitchen, looking uncertain of what to do next.

"Come on, sit down for a minute," she urged him. "You're right. I need to think about this. What am I going to do with Jamie? How am I going to let him out of my sight ever again?"

"It won't be forever, Kitty. Just till they catch this weirdo." He perched on the edge of the kitchen stool, jangling his car keys in his hand. "I don't know what else to tell you except that maybe you should consider hiring a bodyguard for Jamie. For a couple of days, at least. I'm sure there are security companies around here who provide that sort of service."

Kitty considered the idea. "You mean like they do in Hollywood?" Her lips twitched in a smile. "I don't know that it's a big business around here."

"Well you should check it out," Jeff said, standing up. "I wouldn't take any chances with that little boy's safety."

Kitty's throat tightened. "Do you think he . . . we are in any danger staying here?"

Jeff shrugged. "I don't know. I would say probably not. All your doors and windows are wired to the alarm system and there'll be a police car cruising outside."

Kitty shivered.

"Listen," Jeff walked over to the couch and crouched down beside her. "I'll tell you what I think. I think I should stay here tonight. Tomorrow, *I'll* play bodyguard. Take Jamie to school and hang out on the premises, bring him home and generally make myself visible so that if there's anyone out there with bad intentions they'll know there's a man around they have to deal with."

"Jeff," she interrupted to tell him that she already had a man who could play that role but Jeff ignored her.

"Try it for a couple of days, and let's see what the cops come up with. I gotta couple of days to spare." He grinned suddenly. "And you know I would protect Jamie with my life."

She heard the decisive ring in his voice and was reminded for a fleeting second of the take-charge Jeff she'd known in the old days. Yes, she knew he would protect Jamie. Just as she knew that she could not rely on Frank right now. He was obviously bogged down in the investigation and she couldn't expect him to come running at a moment's notice. But Jamie's safety came first.

"Okay, but . . ."

"But?"

She grimaced. "Don't get bossy with me, Jeff. No cooking fancy meals or hanging lists of basic food groups on the refrigerator, okay?"

"I hear you, Kitty. I'll stick with Jamie, that's it. You can rest easy I won't take my eyes off him, except for about an hour tomorrow when he's in class. I'll run up to the house and get some clean socks and underwear . . . maybe check in with the cops up there, see what's happening."

He walked over to the refrigerator and opened the door, taking out his leftover cacciatore. "Now, I'm starving. Mind if I heat this up?"

She shook her head, eyeing the bowl and suddenly realizing how hungry she was. "Know what?" She shrugged. "If there's enough, I'll join you."

Chapter 31

Tuesday, September 5

*F*rank didn't have to wait more than a few seconds for Lisa Vasco to open the door, even though he was a half-hour early. He had told the Vascos to expect him around eight and to let Jeff Haley know that he would be bringing a team of crime scene technicians back to the house.

He and Don had dropped off the Vascos at the front door around eleven o'clock the previous night, cautioning them not to use the staff apartment. To serve as a reminder, Don had strung a length of yellow crime tape across the door.

"Is Mr. Haley up?" Frank asked, but without waiting for an answer he strode into the foyer, beckoning the team of technicians to follow. "Maybe you could lead the way to the apartment, Mrs. Vasco."

He had discussed the job with Will Maynard, the chief technician, back at the station house, making it clear that he wanted the apartment turned over for anything that could help link the most recent occupants, the Morettis, to the murder of Marina Dee Haley. The search for hairs, fibers, skin tissue, and in particular bloodstains or drops would start with the sink and shower drains in the apartment but would possibly have to extend throughout the house: The Morettis, after all, had had the run of the entire place for several hours after Marina's death.

At the apartment door he asked Lisa Vasco about Jeff Haley again. He had not been home the previous night when Frank and Don had arrived with the Vascos.

"I have not yet seen him this morning," the woman replied. "He must have come in very late."

"Maybe you could wake him and tell him we're here," Frank suggested. "I'd like him to know what's going on."

Frank followed the technicians into the sitting area of the small apartment, noting how neat and tidy it looked. Spotless almost, he reflected, as Mrs. Vasco returned to inform him that Jeff Haley was not in his room and his bed had not been slept in.

He took in the information with a curt nod and resumed his study of the room. A faded Berber rug lay in the center of the wood floor. An oak veneer coffee table stood on the rug. Frank noted that the tabletop looked clean and polished. He leaned over and caught the faint whiff of lemon-scented Pledge.

A door off the sitting area led into the bedroom, where he caught the same scent off the nightstands. He wondered how methodical the Morettis had been about wiping down counters and tabletops in the rest of the house.

"Frank, he's here." Don walked into the room, gesturing for him to look out of the window. Frank saw a red Mustang convertible pull up the driveway. He wondered if the car was newly acquired. He did not remember seeing it in the garage on his previous visits.

He turned and walked down the long passageway, reaching the top of the staircase just as Haley walked into the house.

"What's going on, Detective?"

Frank walked downstairs, noting the other man's outfit

of plaid shorts and canary yellow Ralph Lauren jacket, then gestured for Haley to lead the way into the den.

"So?" Haley faced him across the room. "What's going on here? What are you doing?"

Frank waited for Don to join them before answering. "Right now we're treating this house as a crime scene." Frank let the words hang in the air for a second or two, but seeing only a puzzled look in the other man's eyes continued. "We may be here for a while. At the moment we've confined it to the staff apartment but it's possible we may have to spread out."

"The staff apartment!" It was an exclamation rather than a question.

"Yes. We now have information that leads us to believe that the Morettis—the couple who were here when you arrived—conned their way into your mother's house."

"Conned? Meaning what?"

"Meaning they paid the Vascos to go on vacation while they moved in." Frank paused for a fraction of a second. "When did you meet the Morettis, Mr. Haley?"

Jeff Haley blinked. "Saturday—no—I mean Friday evening. Moretti came to pick me up at the airport. I met Mrs. M. the next morning."

"You'd never seen or met them before? You didn't recognize them?"

"No." Jeff Haley shook his head and then sat down heavily on the couch. "You're saying they conned their way in here to kill her?"

"Maybe, although there's a couple of other possibilities."

"Like what, Detective?"

Frank didn't answer the question immediately. In the early morning hours he and Don had considered the other scenarios, including the likelihood that the Morettis had been involved in some sort of scam. Conning rich, old employers was the most popular game in town. In which case, Marina might have stumbled onto the scam.

"What do you think, Mr. Haley? If your mother had discovered that her temporary household staff were stealing from her, would she have confronted them herself?"

Haley seemed to give this some thought but after a few moments he shook his head. "I'm not sure. In the old days I would have said yes. But today? I just don't know." He lapsed into a pensive silence and Frank watched him get to his feet and pace across the room. Then he paced back and looked at Don. "What do you think, Detective?"

"I think not," Don shook his head. "They paid seven thousand dollars to con their way into this house. If they were involved in any kind of scam it wasn't to steal those Lladros off that shelf over there. It would be a little more sophisticated than that, and I doubt that your mother would have stumbled on it without the help of her accountants or attorneys."

Haley nodded. "So you're saying they came in with the intention of killing her?"

Frank jumped in. "That's the way it looks to us."

Haley considered this for a moment. "Why go to the trouble and expense of getting into the house and then killing her out in the backyard?"

Frank smiled. "Good question." Then he inclined his head toward the door. "Come with me, Mr. Haley. I'd like you to see something."

Frank strode across the foyer toward the door that led to the backyard. He stopped along the path Marina had walked to the pool and waited for Don and Jeff Haley to join him.

"Here, take a look at this. Your mother, Mr. Haley, was accosted here by someone who slammed her head into this wall. That first assault probably stunned her slightly but she came back at him. We know that because her broken fingernails suggest she tried to fight him off. But he slammed her into that wall again and probably again until he fractured her skull . . . right here." Frank paused and stared at Jeff Haley, who was rubbing his eyes as if he didn't want to look. Frank wanted him to look—and hear the details.

"Then the killer or killers dragged her down this path to the pool and left her there by the steps, her face down on the concrete. As if she had slipped and fallen and accidentally banged her head. Does all that suggest anything to you, Mr. Haley?"

Jeff Haley rubbed his eyes with one hand again, and Frank noticed stains of perspiration around his armpits.

"It suggests the work of a psycho to me, Detective. A total nut."

"Not a professional hit, right?"

"No! Not at all." Haley's complexion had returned to its normal pink color.

Frank nodded. "Unless the killer or killers were told to make it look that way. To confuse the investigation."

"Told by whom?"

Frank stared at Haley pointedly. "Whoever paid them to murder your mother."

"Them? You mean the Morettis?"

"Looks like."

"So you're saying they carried out a hit, and then they waited around for the police to show up knowing they'd be questioned? That's a ballsy thing to do."

"Yep." Frank nodded. "Ballsy. Cool. Smart. It diverted suspicion from them for a while. Allowed for their fingerprints to be found all over the crime scene." Frank paused. "And maybe they were waiting to be paid for the job."

He noticed the muscles in Haley's neck visibly tautening.

"You're looking at me, Detective, aren't you?"

"Give me a good reason why I shouldn't."

Jeff Haley shook his head. "Because I didn't hire anyone to kill my mother. I swear, Detective." He wiped his forehead with the palm of his hand. "I thought I explained everything. There was no reason on earth why I would want her dead. Marina and I had a very good relationship. I told you that the other day."

"I remember." Frank nodded curtly and then turned to

walk back into the house where Mrs. Vasco was waiting for him in the foyer.

"Detective," she gripped his arm. "You asked me last night to check through the house for anything missing. I found something. Please follow me."

She hurried him into the den and pointed to a shelf of videotapes. "Over there she kept her hurricane money, and now it's gone."

"Hurricane money?" he echoed.

"Yes. Her emergency stash," Haley explained, walking into the room behind them. "You know, in case she couldn't get to the bank."

"How much?" Frank asked.

"Five thousand." Mrs. Vasco nodded.

Frank sighed, his interest in the money deflating suddenly. The Morettis had not invested seven thousand dollars to steal five.

He turned his attention to Jeff Haley, who was now staring out the window, a curious expression on his face that Frank couldn't decipher but seemed to suggest either anxiety or pain. "Mr. Haley, you wouldn't by any chance have used this cash, would you? This weekend, perhaps?"

"No." Haley sighed. "Mr. Gates, our attorney, made funds available to me on my arrival." He glanced at his watch and his mood suddenly seemed to lighten.

"I have a number of things to take care of, Detective. Would it be okay if I left now?" He paused and looked at his housekeeper. "Mrs. Vasco, please let Detective Maguire have anything he needs."

Frank got the impression he was leaving for a while. "You're not leaving town, Mr. Haley?"

"Not entirely." He reached into his jacket pocket and brought out a slip of note paper. "I'm just staying with a friend for a couple of days. She needs some help." He handed the slip to Frank. "But here's the number where you can reach me."

He handed the note to Frank, who glanced at the

number . . . and then glanced at it again, recognizing it instantly.

Kitty's home phone number? Haley was staying at Kitty's house! What the hell was going on?

Haley stood uncertainly in the doorway as if expecting another question. "It's in Boca Raton," he added.

Frank nodded. "Okay. You're heading there now?"

"Is that all right, Detective?"

Frank turned away without answering the question. "So long as we know where to reach you."

He watched Jeff Haley walk down the driveway to his red Mustang, then he sank down onto a high-backed antique chair behind the desk. Fingering the note Haley had handed him he tried to make sense of what he'd just heard.

But Don's voice cut through his murky thoughts. "I thought we agreed not to push Haley that far today. You were very, very hard on him out there."

Frank shook his head. "Not as hard as I might have been if he'd given me this note before we started." He passed the note to his partner. "That's Kitty's home phone number."

"Oh shit!" Don's face registered total bemusement. "Do you know what's going on?"

Frank shook his head.

Don crossed the room and perched himself on the corner of the desk. "I'm sure there's a good explanation. You know there has to be." He paused and blinked. "Listen Frank, you've got to get a grip. You can't let personal business screw up this investigation."

Frank balled his fist and got to his feet. "No! You listen, Don. There's the personal and there's the professional and I know how to keep them separate. We discussed this already: If the Morettis killed Marina they were probably hired to do it. And if they were hired then we agreed that Haley is right up there as a contender for doing the hiring. So I did what had to be done, okay?"

"It's early. We could be wrong, you know. And you put Haley through the wringer."

"I don't think we have to lose any sleep over his feelings. Both times we've talked to him he's told us he was close to his mother. 'We had a close relationship,' he says. But I've yet to hear him say he loved her. Think about it, Don." He paused for a breath.

"Even when I stood there, pointing the finger at him, the best he could come up with was: '*We had a good relationship.*' Hell, I could use warmer words about the bartender at Bradley's."

❧ Chapter 32 ❧

$\mathcal{B}$ernie had finally arrived at work and was napping on her couch when Kitty emerged briefly from the edit bay around lunchtime. She had spent the morning working with Ben on the second part of the Jeff Haley interview and they were moving along speedily.

"Nice of you to stop by—if only for a nap," she commented in Bernie's direction. "Did you take a look at our overnights for last night's interview?" She picked up the page that had been faxed from New York. The overnights, ratings for some dozen key cities around the country, showed that they had gone into double digits in almost all the markets. "And we got a twenty-five share in New York. Now that's incredible. That's better than *Roseanne*."

"What are you using for part two?" Bernie sat up on the couch.

"Jeff talking about prison, and the last five years, and the interior footage from our tour of the house. Todd sent the shots from Wallkill so Ben's working on the dissolves from jail to house now. I figure another hour or so and we'll be done."

The phone rang on her desk. "Oh yeah," Bernie started, his memory evidently jolted by the sound. "I forgot, but Frank called while you were editing. Said he'd call back."

But it wasn't Frank calling back. Kitty had to hold the receiver an inch or two from her ear as Rick Tyler's voice boomed down the line.

"Nice going, Fitzgerald." The reporter for *Inside Edition* congratulated her. "Nice interview. Great ratings. You're cleaning up on this one."

"Thanks, Rick." She smiled into the mouthpiece. "Be sure to look out for part two tonight."

"I'm working on a cracker of a Haley piece myself," he announced. "As a matter of fact it's why I'm calling. Maybe you can help me—off the record."

"Sure, Rick." She laughed. "If I can."

"See I have to throw something together on Haley, and since you've got him tied up. . . . Oh, by the way, I hear you've got him stashed at your place. Must be nice and cozy. Anyways, going back over Haley's clippings I came across a curious snippet."

Kitty heard a warning bell start to clang in her head. She took a deep breath and leaned back in her chair. "Spit it out, Rick."

"You know what I'm getting at, right? You remember that *Post* story, the 'Gal Pal Helps Police in Investigation' story? The one that implied that Haley and you were kind of cozy for a while that year . . . the year your son was born . . . ?"

"Get to the point, Rick." Her tone was cold but the receiver felt hot and sweaty in her hand.

"Okay. I need some sort of comment from you, Kitty. Are you, in fact, reconciling with Jeff Haley? And are you prepared to confirm now that he is your son's father?"

"Are you trying to make me part of the story?"

"You are part of the story, Kitty. Come on, it's there in black and white."

Kitty's thoughts raced. She knew the damage Rick could do by simply repeating the old story.

"You've done your homework pretty thoroughly, Rick."

"Is that a confirmation, Fitzgerald?" She heard the satisfied note in his voice and felt a tightness in her chest.

"Am I supposed to interpret your silence as confirmation?" A pause. "Okay, Fitzgerald, I'm going to hang up."

She took a deep breath. "Listen, Rick, I'm going to give you a statement, okay? But ... I'm going to tape it, and I think you should too just so there's no misunderstanding."

"Hey, you've got it, Fitzgerald. I'm on, shoot."

Another deep breath. "Okay, Rick, now listen up. Any inferences you drew from that story are incorrect. Jeff Haley is not Jamie's father and blood tests can ascertain that. I'm willing to provide you with the results of those tests." She paused.

"What's more if you disregard my offer to help you establish the facts and if you use that old *Post* story to fuel fresh speculation about my son, I will sue you and your show for publishing information with a careless, reckless, and malicious disregard for the truth. Not only that but I will also sue you for invading the privacy of a child who is not a public figure and for causing grave emotional distress to his mother."

There was silence at the other end of the line. Then she heard Tyler clear his throat. "Okay. Okay. I think you've made your point, Fitzgerald. But you can't blame me for trying."

"Tell it to some sucker who's not in the same business, Rick." She banged down the receiver. "Putz! What a putz!" She slumped back in her chair.

Bernie crossed the office and sat down on the chair in front of her desk, his face beaming.

"That was quite a performance, chief. What's going on?"

"Oh, sour grapes on their part. And they've gotten wind that Jeff's staying at my place."

"He is? What are you doing? Protecting him from the rest of the pack?"

"He's protecting Jamie." Kitty sighed. "Remember that video and note I got last Friday? Well the pervert who sent it tried to abduct Jamie. That's what the note meant."

Bernie's eyebrows shot up. "The perv in the video?"

"I don't know if the one who appeared in the video is the one who *sent* the video."

"When the hell did all this happen?"

She grimaced but decided to recap the story for Bernie, giving him a brief summary up to the visit from the Boca detective. "Beaufort's the one who suggested it was a kidnap attempt rather than some pervert obsessing about Jamie."

"Did you tell him about last Thursday night?"

Kitty stared at her cameraman blankly. "What about it?"

"You don't remember the Bufo? You said you thought someone was out there."

"Oh my God! I didn't even think of that, Bern. I just put all that down to being spooked by Marina's murder."

He looked at her pointedly. "Go back to that *Boca Raton Magazine* article. Aside from having your picture and Jamie's prominently displayed it also had that caption where you said you liked panhandlers more than Bufo toads. Think about it, Kitty."

She felt goosebumps popping out on her forearms. "Bernie you've got a really twisted mind, you know that?" She paused. "But it makes sense. He got the wrong boy in school so he dumps him and then comes after Jamie again at home."

She rubbed her eyes with one hand. "Know something else, Bernie? When I was driving back from Frank's some creep followed me. That was Friday night. I thought he was a drunk. But he came after me, down that road to Everglades Island—" she broke off and shivered, feeling clammy and cold.

Putting it together with Bernie, she could see a distinct pattern of too many inexplicable incidents.

Then she thought about the big car again, and her pulse quickened as she remembered repeating the license plate number to herself. Repeating it under her breath till she'd reached the gas station in West Palm where she had finally assured herself that she was no longer being followed. She had scribbled down the number on a scrap of paper.

She was aware that Bernie was staring at her with total bemusement as she grabbed her tote from under her desk, and in one swift movement emptied the contents onto the floor between her feet.

She tossed aside gum wrappers and used pens, her makeup, and Jamie's blue yo-yo before ferreting out the yellow dry cleaner's invoice on which she had scribbled the number.

"I'm going to check it out, Bern. It's worth a shot." She grabbed for the phone and dialed the number of the Palm Beach police department. Frank would get her a trace on this, in no time.

She got his voice mail and promptly hung up. Then she dialed the number of a precinct in Fort Lauderdale. Detective Bobby Springer—the one who'd tipped her off to the Singer story—would do the job just as well for her.

Bobby picked up on the first ring, and she went back and forth with him for a few seconds, exchanging pleasantries. Then she got to the point, giving him the license number. "I also want to know if the driver has a record."

"Mmmmm." Bobby Springer sounded as if he was considering the request. She knew he was not supposed to give out that information.

"Tell you what, Bobby. Get me a name and address, as soon as you can, and don't worry about the rest of it for the time being."

"Done. That's no problem. For you, anytime."

Kitty replaced the phone in its cradle before bending down to stuff the contents of her tote back in the bag. Then she stood up.

"Listen Bern, I'm going to finish up with Jeff's interview. If Springer calls back, come and get me, okay?"

She was almost finished with editing when the phone call came through.

"Piece of cake," Bobby Springer laughed. "The car is registered to a Gordon Slades."

"Slades?" Kitty repeated aloud, raising an eyebrow in Bernie's direction, as if to ask if the name sounded familiar.

He shrugged.

Bobby's voice boomed on the line. "Yeah, Slades. It's a 1993 white Cadillac. The address is fourteen Arlington Drive, Serenity Lakes Village, Pompano. Okay?"

"Spell the name for me, would you?"

"S-L-A-D-E-S. Doctor Gordon Slades."

Kitty's grip on the phone tightened and her heart thudded so hard against her chest she had trouble catching her breath. "Did you say 'Doctor'?"

"Affirmative. And you owe me a lunch or at least a beer, Miz Fitzgerald."

Kitty muttered her thanks and assent into the phone and then hung up.

"Did you get that, Bern? *Doctor* Gordon Slades. Jesus! It's him."

"With an address at Serenity Lakes?" Bernie sounded skeptical. "That doesn't sound right."

Kitty ignored the comment. Serenity Lakes was one of the biggest retirement communities in Broward County. As in most retirement communities, there was a minimum age requirement for owners. It was usually fifty-five. And, as in most retirement communities, where so many elderly and frail were gathered, security was among the tightest of any gated development. She knew she would not be able to just sail through the gatehouse.

She snatched at the phone again and dialed information, and then immediately dialed the number for Serenity Lakes.

"Administration office, please," she said, as soon as she was through.

"You have it." The woman on the other end sounded harried, irritable.

Kitty identified herself quickly. "I'm putting together a piece for *Inside Copy* and we'd like to shoot some footage on the grounds of Serenity Lakes."

"*Inside Copy?*" The woman sounded immediately suspicious. "Is that the show . . . ? What kind of piece exactly?"

Kitty cleared her throat. "Oh, just a general crime piece. We want to show the safest communities in Florida." She crossed her fingers behind her back. "I suppose we could get our footage by renting a helicopter and taking aerial shots," she continued as the woman hesitated, "but I really wanted to get a full frontal view of that magnificent clubhouse."

There was a short silence at the other end then the woman sighed. "Well, I suppose that'll be okay. When are you coming? Today? The weather is perfect today."

Kitty nodded. "Uh-huh."

"I'll call the gatehouse to let you in, then, but you'll have to stop by at the Administration office for visitor passes. Do you understand?"

"Oh, of course," Kitty gushed. "We'll be by for them within the hour."

"They're three dollars per person," the woman added but Kitty was already hanging up.

Bernie adjusted his cap nervously. "Why don't you let the police handle it?"

Kitty shook her head. "No. I want to check it out myself. And you're coming with me, Bern. As soon as I've fed part two to New York. I want to take a look at this sicko.

"Come on, Bernie," she prodded. "The police aren't going to storm in there because this guy happened to be driving behind me on South County Road. But if I meet him, I'll know."

❧ *Chapter 33* ❧

Serenity Lakes Village was a six-mile drive west of I-95 in Pompano. The community took up a forty-acre site, had a golf course and a clubhouse, and three community swimming pools. Trolley buses ran between the clubhouse and the rest of the development. Residents lived in condos that were housed in low-rise gleaming white blocks. Streets and blocks were alphabetically arranged with Arlington Drive being the nearest to the gatehouse. The streets were tree-lined and wide. The speed limit was set at 15 mph.

"Wait, Kitty." Bernie regarded her anxiously. "Do you know what you're going to say? Or do?"

She shook her head. "You ring the doorbell, Bern. We'll take it from there. Oh, bring your camera."

They parked in a spot marked "Guest" outside the building and walked to the door. Kitty stood to the side while Bernie pushed the buzzer and waited. There was no sound from inside. He pressed the doorbell again, holding his finger on it for a few seconds longer.

Kitty stared along the walkway that ran the entire length of the block. An older woman was walking toward them, progressing slowly with the help of a tripod-type steel frame that she used to inch herself forward. Kitty motioned for Bernie to ring again. "Maybe he's napping and has taken his hearing aid out."

"Maybe he's out looking for little boys."

The woman stopped as she came up behind Bernie. "He's not in, you know."

Kitty whirled around.

"Gordon's not here," the woman repeated. She was neatly dressed in a floral skirt and white blouse. Her graying hair was pulled back into a bun. Kitty stared at the woman's slippered feet. The left foot was misshapen, bandaged and stuffed into a brocade slipper that was bursting at one side-seam.

"Do you have any idea when he'll be back?"

The woman squinted at Kitty, her eyes narrowing, seemingly more from suspicion than the sun. "Who wants to know?"

Kitty introduced herself and Bernie, not mentioning *Inside Copy.* "We need to speak to Dr. Slades," she added firmly.

"Well you can't, dearie. He's not here. Gordon won't be down for . . ." she paused, "oh, not for another month, at least."

"He doesn't live here?" Kitty's disappointment showed in her voice.

"He does during the season. He's usually here by mid-November. But he stays up north for most of the fall."

"You're sure?"

Kitty saw the woman's jaw tighten. "I may look old, dearie, but I'm in possession of my faculties. Of course I'm sure. I take in Gordon's mail and keep an eye on his apartment. I wish he was here as a matter of fact. When Gordon's here I never have to worry about getting to the supermarket. He's a good neighbor. Not like some around here who'll charge you five dollars just to drive to Publix."

"He sounds like a kind man."

"Who, Gordon? Of course he is. He's a gentleman. Always was. Even when his wife was around. If there was a dance or some such function at the clubhouse he'd always say, 'Vera, you're coming with us. You can't just curl up in that apartment of yours and die. We'll be one of those ménages à trois.' "

Kitty took a deep breath, wanting to get the conversation back on track. "So, Vera. Mrs. . . . ?" She stared quizzically at the woman.

"It's Mrs. Dolan. Vera Dolan."

"Mrs. Dolan, does he usually drive down here in November?"

The woman looked confused for a moment, then she shook her head. "Drive all the way from up north? Oh no, no. That's a long drive, dearie. Of course he did that a couple of times when Doris was alive."

Kitty felt like screaming. She decided she would just have to be direct. "So he leaves his car here, Vera?"

"Of course he does. Not here exactly. Not in his regular spot by the apartment. He drives it to the main lot by the Clubhouse and parks it there because it's next to the bus stop, and then he can take the bus to Pomapano Village Square and another one from there to the airport—"

"Mrs. Dolan," Kitty interrupted. "Would you happen to know? Does he have a designated parking spot near the Clubhouse?"

The woman shifted her weight to her bandaged foot, winced, and shifted back again. "Why are you asking?"

Kitty was ready for the question and launched into a convoluted story about hitting a white Cadillac while pulling out of a supermarket parking space. "I took down the license plate number, and I left a note behind one of the windshield wipers. But I never heard back so I had the license traced."

Vera Dolan nodded to herself. "That's very honest of

you, dearie, but like I say Gordon's been gone all summer."

"Maybe someone borrowed the car, Vera," Kitty interrupted pointedly but kindly. "Look, could you do me an enormous favor and give us an idea where he parks so that we can check out the car. I left a horrendous dent in the front bumper."

The woman lookd down at her walker and up again then sighed. "I dare say if you'll help me into your car I could do that. But I know it was in one of the spots closest to the busstop. I saw it there a week ago when I was waiting for the bus to go to my podiatrist. I remember thinking that Gordon was lucky he'd found a spot right near the busstop so that he didn't have far to walk with his suitcase."

In the Blazer, Vera directed them to the clubhouse and the parking area in front of it.

There was no white Cadillac in the spot she directed them to first. "Well, that's where it was on August fifteenth."

"The day you went to your podiatrist?"

"That's right." .

"That was more than three weeks ago, not one week ago." Kitty looked across at Bernie and rolled her eyes. "Let's cruise around," she said. "Maybe you were mistaken about the spot, too."

Ten minutes later, however, there was still no sign of the white Cadillac they were looking for. They drove back with Vera to Arlington Drive.

"That's really strange," she muttered in the back seat. "I'll ask Gordon about it when he calls. Maybe Teddy borrowed it."

"Teddy? Who's Teddy?" Kitty's question came abruptly and sharply.

But Vera didn't seem to notice the urgency in her voice. "Teddy's another neighbor. He lost his license last year. Along with his left leg. But he just refuses to take the lolly buses." She shrugged. "Teddy claims he hasn't ridden a bus since he was sixteen and he's not going to start again at eighty-two. Sometimes Gordon lets him borrow the Caddy just to run up to the Clubhouse and back. . . ." Vera droned in the back seat but Kitty had lost interest in what she was saying. An eighty-two-year-old with one leg was not the man she was looking for.

Neither Kitty nor Bernie said anything until they had escorted Vera back to the walkway. Then as the old woman moved away Bernie took Kitty by the arm, leading her back to the Chevy. "Let's drive around just in case Teddy's parked it around here somewhere."

Kitty didn't resist but shook her head. "No, I think it's gone," she said. "I bet the pervert isn't even anyone who lives in here. You could sneak in here on foot easily enough. I bet he walked in and stole it. And it's got to be someone with local knowledge who knows there's plenty of seasonal residents who leave their cars here when they go back north."

When she stopped at the end of the street, Bernie reminded her that they were supposed to get their visitors' passes from the Administration office.

"To hell with the admin office," Kitty retorted and turned sharply toward the main gates.

"Why don't you pass this license number on to Frank, or Beaufort in Boca? They'll find the car."

Kitty laughed harshly to mask her disappointment. "Sure they'll find it. But not the driver. I bet he's dumped it by now."

🦋 *Chapter 34* 🦋

F rank finally got through to Kitty in the late afternoon, by which time his bewilderment over Jeff Haley's
little bombshell had turned to a slow-burning indignation.

She needs some help, Haley had said. With what? The
interview was in the bag, as Kitty would put it. He'd heard
it promoed on the radio driving down to the Keys yesterday. So what was left to help with?

He intended to come straight to the point when Kitty
answered her car phone on the second ring, but he heard
the muted strains of Donna Summer's "Hot Stuff" in the
background and he mellowed. Kitty had once told him that
she played the cassette because the song always reminded
her of him.

"I miss you too, Hot Stuff," he began instead. "But I
had a nasty surprise this morning. I talked to Haley and he
told me I could reach him at your number over the next
few days. Is he going crazy or am I?"

"Neither." He only just caught Kitty's response. "I've
been trying to reach you since Sunday evening, Frank, to

let you know. This has been a very bad couple of days. You can't even imagine." The strain in her voice came clearly over the line.

"What is it, Kitty? What's happened? I'm sorry love, I know I've been out of touch but I've been working round the clock."

"I know. I'm not blaming you but I had to make a decision. I had to do something and Jeff was there."

"And now he's staying with you!"

"For a couple of days."

"So would you mind telling me what's going on?"

"How long have you got now?"

He stared into the speaker of his car phone, wondering if the remark had been meant accusingly. "I'm driving over into West Palm with Don so I've got some time."

He sensed her hesitation at the other end. Then she said, "I had a break-in Sunday evening, Frank. Someone got into the house and took every single one of Jamie's things—his toys, videos, books, clothes, even the pillow and sheets off his bed."

"Christ! Did you call in Boca PD?"

"Yes, hon." He noted the weary tone of her voice. "Of course."

"Who did they send?"

"A Detective Jim Beaufort. There's more to it, hon. There were some other incidents, one at Jamie's school . . . anyway the bottom line is that some creep is out to get Jamie."

He felt the blood pound in his temples. "Was Jamie hurt? Kitty, I can't believe you didn't tell me." Frank couldn't keep the hurt and shock out of his voice.

"Jamie's okay. I'm sorry, perhaps I made it sound more dramatic than it was, but you know it's really difficult to explain it over the phone. It was all different little incidents, which didn't make any sense until yesterday."

"Like what?"

"Well," he heard her laugh suddenly, "take last Thursday night. Remember when you called and I told you about the Bufo toad leaping out at me? I think this creep was in the backyard that night."

"Jesus! Kitty! How could you not have mentioned any of this?" He glanced over at Don, who could hear every word on the speaker, and shook his head in bewilderment.

"Listen, Frank." The sharpness of her voice startled him. "I didn't know. And when I did realize what was going on then you were on your way to the Keys or from the Keys and you said it wasn't a good time to talk."

"Let me spell it out for you, Kit," he interrupted, aware that his own voice sounded sharp, too. "Marina Dee Haley is dead and will remain so whether I find her killer or not. Jamie and you are alive and I'd much rather that's the way it stayed. Jesus! I should have known all this. What are the Boca PD doing?"

"They've put on extra patrols at the school and around the house."

"And what's Haley's role in all this?"

"He's looking out for Jamie. He stays with him in school and brings him home, and he's staying overnight . . . in the guest room. He was there, Frank. We were talking about bodyguards and he offered to do the job for a couple of days."

"How did he happen to be there?"

There was a pause on the other end. "Oh, he . . ." She paused, as if trying to remember. "Yeah, I'd just arrived home on Sunday and discovered the break-in and he happened to call about a couple of tapes I'd left behind at the house."

There was an awkward silence between them for a few seconds. Then Kitty said; "Please, Frank, don't make a big deal out of this. I can trust him with Jamie and I don't particularly want to be alone in the house at night. It's only for the next few days until Sharon gets back."

"There's no reason why I couldn't come back to Boca every night."

"No, Frank. Don't even think about it. You're working

all hours. You can't play bodyguard. That's plainly ridiculous. You've got a job. Jeff hasn't."

Frank shook his head resignedly. Kitty had made up her mind and he could tell he wasn't going to get anywhere by arguing with her over Haley. He considered telling her about his suspicions. But then discarded the thought. Hell, he couldn't even convince his own partner without getting an earful about the way his personal feelings were interfering with the job. So what chance did he stand with getting through to Kitty?

His thoughts were interrupted by what sounded like a brusque laugh at Kitty's end. "Besides, if you stay cool about Jeff, I won't ask about the woman who answered your cellular phone on Monday morning."

Frank laughed too. "Very funny, hon. But, okay, I'll stay cool so long as he's gone by the weekend. Deal?"

"Deal," she replied happily.

It was only after he hung up that Frank realized that what he had taken as a joke could easily have been the truth. Monday morning he had awakened on the boat. Monday morning, Roberta Mallory had made coffee in his galley. She had, evidently, also answered his phone.

But he dismissed the thought instantly. It was minor league compared to the news Kitty had dropped on him.

" 'Jeff was there.' " Frank repeated Kitty's words aloud with a touch of sarcasm. "He's always there, godamnit! Leave it to Jeff. You need an interview, he's it. You need a bodyguard, he'll do it."

"No end to the man's talents, is there?" Don interjected glancing sideways at his partner. "Do you think he also hired someone to spook Kitty?"

Frank returned the glance, his eyes narrowing. "Now you're yanking my chain, West, aren't you?" Then abruptly he looked away and stared out the window.

❧ *Chapter 35* ❧

Friday, September 8

*J*amie Fitzgerald loved Fridays. It meant there was no school the next day or the day after that. He could watch TV all afternoon on Fridays if he wanted more than the couple of shows his Mom allowed him to watch during the school week.

Today, though, Jeff had driven him to karate class first. So he was going to have karate *and* TV, and Jeff, who was Mom's friend from New York, knew all about TV, and had taped his favorite show, *The Mighty Morphin Power Rangers,* throughout the week so he could watch them all over again, this afternoon. Mom never allowed him to do that.

Mom never took him to karate two times in one week either, and she didn't let him practice his kicks and knife-hand blocks on her.

Jamie waited till Jeff walked around to get into the driver's seat. Then he decided to ask the question that had been on his mind but he started carefully. "Can I ask you a question?"

"Shoot." Jeff switched on the engine and Jamie put his face up to the cold air vents like he always did after getting into a hot car.

"How long are you going to stay with us?"

Jeff laughed. Then he said, "How long would you like me to stay?"

Jamie hated it when grownups did that. When you asked a question they always asked you one back. And he never knew the answer. He liked Jeff okay. Jeff was like a new friend. Not like Frank who was going to be his dad. Frank sometimes stopped him from eating too much ice cream, but he had a cool boat and, when he was around, he always sneaked in after lights-out to read Jamie an extra bedtime story. But Jeff had a neat car with a roof that could disappear.

"Well," he nodded, "maybe till my birthday." He paused, then, "Jeff, can you put the roof down?"

"Sure can. But you have to put on your seatbelt." As Jamie reached for the belt Jeff pressed the button that made the top of the car slide back. Then he checked his rearview mirror before reversing out of the parking space.

"Till your birthday! You just had one. You want me to stay for that long?"

Jamie had to think about that. What he really wanted was for Jeff to be around for his birthday. The day before when they were at Discovery Zone with Alex, Jeff had agreed that it was a really awesome place to have a birthday party.

"Well, you see," he began and then suddenly yelled, "Look out! Jeff, look!" The white car had appeared as if from nowhere.

The yell turned to a scream as the other car hit, making a horrible crunching sound. "Oh no!"

He squirmed, open-mouthed, in his seat to look at Jeff and saw that Jeff was leaning forward on the wheel, his eyes closed, his arm hanging by his side.

"Are you okay?" Jamie tugged at his arm. He could see

the driver of the other car getting out and coming toward him.

"Jeff! Wake up!"

The man came over to Jamie's side. "It's okay, son. Are you all right? Come on out, let me see."

He opened the door of the Mustang, reaching in to help Jamie out. "Come on, let's see, make sure there are no broken bones."

Jamie was about to do as the man said when he suddenly felt Jeff's hand on his arm. "Don't get out of the car, Jamie."

He looked over at Jeff who was holding his head with his other hand. He turned back to tell the man that Jeff needed help but the man was already hurrying back to his own car.

"Where's he going?" Jamie watched the man jump into his seat and drive away.

Jeff had his eyes closed again but he was sitting up, putting his sunglasses back on his nose. "That's better."

Then he got out of the car to check the damage.

"It's not so bad," he said, getting back into the driver's seat. "A little fender bender, that's all." He turned the key to switch on the engine. But before driving off he turned to Jamie.

"Listen, Jamie, I want you to keep this a secret between us. Don't tell your mom what happened with that other car. Okay?"

Jamie frowned. "Why shouldn't I tell her?" He suddenly perked up. "I want to tell her, Jeff. That was awesome. Did you hear that yukky noise when that car smashed into us?"

"No." Jeff shook his head. "No, you mustn't Jamie because she'll be angry and then she won't let me take you anywhere again."

"But . . . but . . ."

Jeff stopped him. "I mean it, Jamie. She won't let me take you to karate again or Discovery Zone or anywhere. Do you understand?"

Jamie nodded his head. "I understand. But can I tell Alex at school?"

Jeff sighed.

"Oh please, please, please."

Then Jeff laughed and brushed the top of Jamie's head. "Okay, okay."

✤ Chapter 36 ✤

She was in the pool, drifting lazily, when Jeff and Jamie returned from karate. Her son came running through the courtyard gate in his white pants and jacket with the belt flapping. Jeff followed him at a slower pace.

"Mom! Mom! I'm coming into the pool with you," he shouted, racing past her into the house.

"Sounds like a good idea," Jeff chimed in. "Looks refreshing."

"It's not," Kitty replied, heading for the steps. "The water's too warm." She dripped onto the deck and took the towel Jeff handed her. Then wrapping it around herself she perched on the chaise.

Jeff sat down on the chaise next to her. She noticed his legs had lost some of their pallor and were getting tanned. "It's been quite a week," he began. "Great week, Kitty. Great for you and *Inside Copy* and a great eye-opener for me being around Jamie."

Kitty nodded. The interview with Jeff had been a ratings grabber. Then to top it all he'd given her the tidbit about the Morettis conning their way into Marina's house. It didn't matter that the next day the police department had held a press conference to announce they were looking for the couple "for questioning in connection with Marina Dee Haley's murder." She had already scooped everybody.

". . . So I thought," Jeff was saying, "that you and I and Jamie could go out tonight and celebrate. Somewhere fancy, of course, like the Boca Hotel, or maybe we could drive to Palm Beach."

Kitty wondered where Jamie was, and looking over her shoulder spotted him in the family room engrossed with his new Power Rangers evidently having forgotten all about swimming. She turned her attention back to Jeff. "Oh, I don't think I'm up for it. Friday night is pizza night anyway—" she broke off. Frank was coming over later and she wanted Jeff out of the house by then.

"You should go ahead though. Go on, call someone up and make dinner plans. I can't expect you to play body-guard forever."

"I see." His eyes narrowed. "Playing? Is that how you see it?"

"Come on, Jeff. That's not how I meant it. You've been terrific with Jamie but I know you have things to do and take care of. I don't want to be unfair to you."

"Why don't you let me decide what's fair to me? It hasn't been a chore, you know, Kitty. It's made me feel useful. I don't just want to be a Palm Beach playboy. Anyways, I was having a fun time with Jamie. He's a helluva little guy."

"Yes, I know," Kitty nodded. What she also suspected was that Jeff had enjoyed taking care of her and Jamie more than he was even prepared to admit. She had seen it in his face these last few days. He was doing what he did best. Taking charge and making sure everything was just right.

"Come on, Kitty. Truly, I'm in no hurry. I thought it would be pleasant and relaxing to go out, maybe sit somewhere by the water and have a few drinks and dinner."

She fiddled with the towel she'd wrapped around herself. Then she got to her feet. "Listen, I'm sorry if there was a misunderstanding, but we did talk about Sharon returning over the weekend and I thought you'd be anxious to get going. I made other plans . . ."

She hesitated as he slumped back against his chaise and leaned over him. "Jeff, come on, it's time to get on with your business, your life. There're thousands of women out there waiting for someone like you."

"But not you, right, Kitty? Because you want to waste yourself on some flatfoot cop."

"Huh?" She stared at him, her eyes widening.

He shrugged. "Jamie mentioned Frank the Detective several times, and I guess I figured it out, but I didn't know you'd made plans for tonight."

Kitty looked away. "Yeah. Tonight and for the weekend." There was a silence between them and Kitty didn't know how to fill it. She didn't want to seem ungrateful but Jeff was acting the way he'd done in the old days. He'd never really known when to quit. Had never accepted that she needed her own space. Now he was criticizing Frank, too.

Well, the old days were gone. "Jeff," she said firmly. "I don't want you to leave hurt or angry or think that I don't appreciate how much you helped me this week but I've got to go in now to shower."

He shrugged and eventually she turned away from him and walked into her room through the sliding glass doors. Stepping out of her damp towel she walked in her bathing suit into her bathroom and turned on the shower.

"Wait, Kitty!" She looked through the doorway to see Jeff had followed her into her room and was standing by her dresser. "Please, let's talk about this. You're not being fair to me. I'm here because you and Jamie needed me. I've looked out for Jamie all week. I've taken him places and I've cooked dinner for him, and now it's just thanks and good-bye."

"I didn't ask you to cook, Jeff. Nor to do the laundry.

It's difficult to say this without seeming ungrateful but I did ask you *not* to do these things. You can't help yourself though, can you? You have to take charge and do things your way."

"Certainly," he interrupted, taking a step toward her. "What was I supposed to do, wait around to have macaroni cheese every night? I had to cook for myself, anyway, and I didn't hear you complaining during the week." Suddenly he laughed. "Look at us arguing like an old married couple over who does the cooking and who does the laundry."

She didn't want to hear any of it and turned away but in the same moment Jeff moved toward her, his hands suddenly on her arms. His fingers felt hot on her skin and she tried to back away but his grip was firm. His eyes swept over her making her feel naked in her skimpy wet suit.

"Kitty, you're not thinking of what's right for Jamie. You've got a date. That's fine. But what's going to happen next week? Your date won't be around to make sure Jamie's safe. And don't you think Jamie likes to come home from school and have someone who'll take him to karate or out to a playground?"

He broke off drawing her to him so abruptly she was encircled totally by his arms with his body molding into hers. Instantly she wrenched herself free. "What the hell are you doing, Jeff!"

"Oh, excuse me!" He backed away looking as if she'd slapped him. "Jesus, Kitty! Don't look as if I've committed some major crime. I've spent a week in the same house and kept my distance, and considering I just came out of an all-male institution after five years maybe you could cut me a little slack here."

She picked up the towel from the floor and wrapped it around herself again. Her voice was cold when she spoke. "How much slack exactly were you thinking of?" Then without waiting for an answer she shook her head. "Don't you see, Jeff," she added more kindly, "it's not very healthy for you to stay around any longer. I'm the only woman you see and you're not giving yourself a chance to meet anyone new."

Jeff looked as if he hadn't heard a word she'd said. "You want me to leave Jamie in danger? You're not acting in his best interests you know." He shook his head. "That pervert tried to get at him again today."

"What!"

"The stalker ... the would-be kidnapper. I'm sure it was him. He sideswiped me in the parking lot after karate. I winded myself on the steering wheel and in that couple of seconds he was right there, telling Jamie to get out of the car."

Kitty felt a chill run up her spine. "You're making this up, Jeff. Jamie would have told me about something like that as soon as he came home."

"No. I asked him not to worry you. Not to upset you. But you can ask him now."

She felt anger surging inside her. "You told my son to keep that from me? How could you?"

He looked embarrassed. "I didn't want to worry you."

Her anger exploded. "I'm not a goddamn child! You can't keep something like that from me! Were you going to tell *anyone* about it?" She paused. "Oh, never mind. Did you get a look at this creep? Did you see the car? The license plate?"

Jeff laughed harshly. "I was winded, Kitty. For a couple of minutes I couldn't get my breath. I couldn't even see straight. No, I didn't get a license plate. It was a white car, that's all I saw. Maybe a Cadillac."

She sank down on her bed, breathing rapidly, knowing that Jeff could not be concocting the story. She had not mentioned the white Cadillac to him. She hadn't even mentioned it to Frank. She had put it out of her mind after running into the dead end in the Serenity Lakes Village.

"I'm sorry I didn't tell you. I thought I'd be around to keep an eye on things. I didn't think I'd have to abandon him, like this." He made an attempt to reach for her hand but she shrank back from him.

Finally, he turned away from her and walked out of the room.

Kitty ran for the bathroom and slammed the door closed. As she stared into the mirror she mouthed Jeff's words silently at her reflection.

It was a white car. Maybe a Cadillac.

Was it really possible the sicko was still driving around in the same car?

❦ Chapter 37 ❦

She had to tell Frank the whole story from beginning to end as soon as he walked through her front door. He had arrived within an hour of Jeff's disgruntled departure. Frank wanted her to recount every single detail even though he said that he'd already talked with Jim Beaufort at the Boca police department.

"You didn't think I'd just leave it at what you told me on the phone, did you?" he grinned at her, placing his glass of Dewar's on the coffee table and taking her in his arms.

"Is that why they put on a patrol car outside for the entire night?"

Frank's grin broadened. "Professional courtesy. I guess I didn't trust in Haley's talents as a bodyguard as much as you did."

Kitty made a face. "Well, the less said about that the better."

Frank didn't pursue the point. Instead he said, "Let's get

back to the Cadillac. You didn't mention it to Beaufort, did you?"

"I didn't remember it till the day after he came here. Then after Bernie and I checked it out and figured the creep had dumped it somewhere I didn't think it was worth mentioning."

"But you're sure you never said anything about it to Haley?"

Kitty nodded.

"And you're certain he wasn't making up the story about today's incident. Jamie didn't say a word about it to me when I looked in on him just now."

"No, because Jeff told him to keep quiet about it. He only told me when I pressed him. I remembered something else too. The day Marina was found dead was the same day Stroud picked up Timmy Myers. I remember I was rushing to get to the crime scene and I almost collided with a white Cadillac pulling out of the school gates."

"Fra-a-ank!" Jamie's little voice sailed down the hallway, interrupting their conversation.

"Go on, go," Kitty nudged him as Frank jumped to his feet. "I can wait to tell the rest of it and Jamie's missed you. He's waiting for you to finish that *Berenstain Bears* book you bought him." She grimaced. "He's been carrying it around with him so luckily it didn't get taken with the rest of the stuff."

It was a while before Frank returned. Sinking into the couch he grinned. "I had to see all the new toys. Every single one. Now, how about getting me a fresh drink, woman, and getting on with the story?" He winked and patted her behind as she got up and then asked, "Do you think Vera Dolan knew for sure that the doctor was away or that he hadn't returned some time during the last month?"

Kitty nodded from across the room. "She gave the impression that they were very good neighbors and that she kept an eye on his apartment while he was away. But," she returned to her seat beside Frank, "you think he could have returned without her knowing?" Then she shook her head. "Frank, his car was gone and the way she described him he didn't sound at all like—"

"The criminal type?" Frank's mouth turned up at the corners in a half-smile. "Sure, Kitty. You can always tell a pedophile or an abductor by looking at them, right?"

She laughed out loud. "Point taken, sweets."

"I think we should check him out, anyway. Maybe call him and you can use the same story about the fender bender with his car. Then if he sounds on the level I'll tell him we're going to put out an APB on the Caddy."

As he spoke Kitty had jumped off the couch again to fetch the telephone directory for Broward County. "Did Beaufort tell you if he was making any headway with his inquiries?" she asked, reaching onto the top shelf of the hall closet for the book.

"He only just started, but I believe he spoke to that teacher's aide, Janis, and the Myerses—and he checked with North Broward Medical Center—and came up empty on a Dr. Stroud or any Stroud on the staff."

There were a half-dozen Dolans listed but only one V. Dolan, without an address. She dialed the number.

Vera Dolan answered on the first ring and Kitty introduced herself. "Remember we spoke the other day, about Dr. Slades's car? I was wondering if you had spoken to the doctor about it."

"Yes, of course I remember, dearie. As a matter of fact, I mentioned it to Gordon when he called last night. But everything's okay. He said he loaned it to his brother for a few weeks. So I said, Gordon, I wish you'd tell me these things because I was about to report it stolen."

"His brother?" Kitty interrupted, taking a deep breath. "Is his brother staying at the apartment?"

"No, definitely not. Gordon said he was . . ." She paused. "What *did* Gordon say about him? You know, I can't recall exactly because then we got talking about all sorts of other things."

"Vera," Kitty interrupted again, rolling her eyes.

"Would you be kind enough to give me Dr. Slades's phone number? I'd really like to settle this fender bender matter with him."

"Hold on a minute, dearie, I should know the number by heart but . . ." Her words trailed off and so apparently had Vera. It seemed a long time before she returned to the phone.

"Here it is: Area code five-one-eight, five-five-five, one-seven-two-zero."

Kitty scribbled the number down. "Five-one-eight?" She thought aloud. "Where's that?"

"It's somewhere upstate New York," Vera jumped in with an answer. "Makerley. That's the name of the town. It's about seventy miles north of the city."

Kitty thanked her again and hung up. Vera had pronounced the name of the town as "Mekkerley," but Kitty knew it was Makerley, New York.

She ignored Frank's quizzical expression as she stared at the name she'd scribbled, struggling to remember something she felt was important about the name.

Makerley? She repeated the name to herself. She knew the name. She knew how to spell it. She'd heard of it before. A long time ago.

"Makerley!" She shouted the name at Frank. The memory freed itself suddenly. "Jesus!" She felt the hairs standing up on the back of her neck.

"What? For God's sake, what, Kitty?" Frank looked alarmed by the expression on her face.

"Makerley," Kitty repeated. "I know that name, Frank. Marcy did a story—" she broke off again, her eyes narrowing, as she tried to recall the conversation when she'd first heard the name. Her sister had mentioned it to her during a phone call.

"Yes," she spoke slowly, hesitatingly, dredging up the distant memory. "Marcy did a story. Around the time Jamie and I moved down here. I never saw it on TV. But she got an Emmy for it. That's why the name sounded familiar." She gripped Frank's hand. "That's it, Frank. Marcy called to tell me she'd gotten another Emmy."

Kitty broke off, the blood rushing to her face as Marcy's words came hammering back: "That sunuvabitch Slades got me an Emmy, Kit. Can you believe it? The Monster of Makerley got me an Emmy!"

"The Monster of Makerley?" Frank echoed the name as he put his arm around Kitty's trembling shoulders. "Who was he? What did he do?"

Kitty shrugged and shook her head. "I don't know, Frank. That's the part I'm not sure about. I didn't watch the show. I mean, both Marcy and I were churning out stories by the dozen and they always had these screaming titles, hyped-up titles. I was just happy for her about the Emmy."

She reached for the phone again.

"Who're you calling?"

"Marcy, of course," Kitty smiled wryly. "She's only gotten three Emmys. I'm sure she'll remember this story."

❧ Chapter 38 ❧

There was no way Kitty was going to wait for an answer. She glanced at her watch as Marcy's phone rang and figured if her sister didn't pick up she would call the news department at WPEN in New York and have them check out the Monster of Makerley. Or she would have Frank call the sheriff's department in upstate New York.

"Hello!" Marcy's cheery voice finally echoed down the line.

"Marcy! Hi! Did I get you at a bad time?" Kitty breathed a sigh of relief and put her sister on the speakerphone so that she wouldn't have to repeat the conversation to Frank.

Marcy laughed. "I'm dripping all over the rug. I just got out of the shower. What's up?"

Kitty came straight to the point. "I need information about the Monster of Makerley. Remember you got an Emmy for a story on him? It was about three years ago?"

"Hmmm. . . ." There was a brief silence on the other end of the line, then Marcy said, "Oh, sure, I remember.

I don't know if it was three *years* ago. But it was three *Emmys* ago."

Kitty smiled. Marcy deserved her success. No one could say she had not been single-minded about her career. "So, what was the story?"

"Hold on. Let me just get a bathrobe." Her sister was back in a few seconds. "There, that's better. Now, let me think. The story was about the parole system and I chose the Makerley Monster as an example. What the hell was his name?"

"Slades?" Kitty offered as Marcy paused to think.

"Yeah, that was it. Slades. Bill Slades. I chose Slades as a specific case history. He was serving a life sentence in Attica for murder and I believe he'd already served some twenty-odd years when he came before the parole board. Anyway, to make a long story short—when the good citizens of his hometown saw my story and realized he might be getting out they created such a big stink that the parole board backed off. Yeah, it was a good story."

Marcy broke off and Kitty heard her talking to someone at her end. Daniel, no doubt, she thought.

Then Marcy was back. "That's right, Dan just reminded me that we did an update on our show, a month or so ago, when we found out that he had actually been released. They tried to do it very quietly and they moved him around a bit to confuse the press. We might not even have known about it if someone in Makerley hadn't called us with the news."

"So, he *is* out?" Kitty asked the question of her sister but stared wide-eyed at Frank.

"Oh definitely. It had to happen, of course, our justice system being what it is but I didn't do the update, myself. I think I was in L.A. on some other story. That's why I can't tell you too much about it. But if you want . . ." She paused suddenly. "Why the interest in Slades, anyway?"

Kitty cleared her throat. "There was a rumor that he was sighted in Florida. Tell me, Marcy, do you think Slades blamed you for his parole being denied at the time?"

Marcy's laugh pealed out again in the room. "I don't think. I know so. I've still got a couple of letters he sent me."

Kitty felt her heart beating faster and harder. "You mean threats?"

"Not exactly. I mean he didn't say 'I'm going to rip your heart out' or anything like that but he made it clear that he considered me responsible for ruining his chances. As a matter of fact he phrased it a little better. Quite eloquent, our Mr. Slades, you know—"

"Who did he murder?" Kitty interrupted.

"An eight-year-old boy."

Kitty's heart was thudding so hard she couldn't even phrase the next question, but thankfully Marcy didn't have to be prodded.

"That was just the tip of the iceberg, by the way. The boy had been sexually molested and abused and when they eventually picked up Slades other parents started coming forward to tell the cops that their children had also been molested by him."

Marcy's voice was grim. "He'd been molesting kids from nearby towns for years, without anyone ever finding out. You know how it was back in those days. Who knew from child abuse and molestation? Half the kids didn't even know what he was doing to them. And even when they said something, a parent was just as likely to think they were making it up, especially if the accused was a doctor. But when he was arrested everything came out."

Kitty swallowed with difficulty. "Slades was a doctor?"

"No, but his brother was and he lived with the brother, and he'd lure the kids back to the house, to his brother's office. The cops found hundreds of porno pictures and tapes taken in that office."

Kitty felt her stomach churning. "You mean the brother was in on it?"

"Oh no! No. But the kids thought Bill Slades was the doctor. In fact, if I remember, it was the brother who eventually came forward with some crucial evidence against

Bill Slades. Don't ask me details now, Kit, but if you're really interested I'll send you some dubs of the original show." Marcy paused. "I'll tell you one thing, though, Bill Slades is not a stupid man. He was supposed to have some exceptionally high IQ—which he apparently put to use by coming up with foolproof schemes to lure these kids to his home."

"Which was how?" Kitty interrupted impatiently.

"Not with candy." Marcy laughed. But it was a hollow laugh. "I tell you when I was doing my research on him it just made me sick to my stomach. Apparently, he hung out in the playgrounds and parks and watched for kiddies on bicycles or scooters. Then he'd follow them home in his car and on the way home he'd create a little accident. Nothing serious—just a skinned knee or a grazed, banged-up elbow that needed to be cleaned and bandaged, which, of course, he offered to have done at *his* doctor's office. One time, he even used a slingshot to knock a kid off one of those playground carousels."

Kitty took a deep breath and she stared at Frank, whose face was set in a dark, grim mask. She had more questions for Marcy but she was afraid she'd be unable to speak if she stayed on the line any longer. She thanked her sister hurriedly and hung up.

Frank crossed the room to the wet bar and fixed her a Bailey's Irish Cream. "Go on. I think you need this."

She took it, sipping the liqueur slowly. "Well, any doubts now?" She stared at Frank. "I think it's all there, don't you? The car link to Slades and even the same MO. He used a slingshot to make a kid fall off a carousel." She paused. "I'll bet next week's salary that's how he made Timmy fall off the monkey bars."

"That does make a lot of sense," Frank agreed. "Otherwise he'd have to be hanging out at the schoolyard in his doctor's outfit waiting for an accident to happen and waiting for it to happen to Jamie. I don't think so."

Kitty took a large gulp of Bailey's and swallowed quickly. "God must have been with us," she murmured

more to herself than Frank. "It was just lucky for Jamie
... for everyone, really, that the boys were wearing the
same T-shirts that day."

She shook her head and swirled the drink in her glass.
"And there's a motive, Frank, since he blames my twin
sister for having his parole denied."

Frank nodded, then frowned. "It certainly looks that
way, doesn't it. If he was simply going back to his old
ways, I guess any child would have done. Timmy would
have been as good as Jamie."

He paced across the room again. "But does that mean
he confused you with Marcy? I find that a little hard to believe. He'd have to know the name of the sister responsible for keeping him behind bars."

Kitty brushed off his question. "I'm an easier target than
Marcy. I have a child. Marcy doesn't. Jamie is Marcy's
nephew and if he went for Marcy, it might be easier to
trace back to him. This is more subtle ... I say, close
enough, Batman."

She leaned back against the couch, feeling chilly even
though the air in the room was comfortable. The chills got
stronger when she thought of Timmy Myers in Slades's
car. It *was* a miracle that he had returned Timmy unharmed. She jumped to her feet and paced across to join
Frank. "We've got to get that animal, Frank. We have to
find him and make sure he's put away for the rest of his
life."

Frank didn't respond immediately. Instead he stood, sipping his Scotch. Then he said, "We should get Beaufort in
on this. He can call the good brother and see if Dr. Gordon
has any ideas about his brother's present whereabouts. He
can also get Timmy Myers and Janis to ID Slades from
mug shots. Then the Boca PD can launch a full-scale manhunt."

He put his arm around Kitty as she opened her mouth
to interrupt. "Don't argue, hon. I'll talk to Beaufort, myself. I'll handle it."

"I wasn't going to argue, but ..." She stopped and

shook her head "Just hear me out on this: If you get Beaufort and the Boca PD launching a manhunt the news is going to leak right out. Slades's face will be plastered all over the papers and TV."

Frank nodded. "That's good. He won't be able to hide anywhere in South Florida."

"No! That's not good." She shook her head firmly. "Don't you see? If Slades is alerted, he'll go to ground. You heard Marcy: He's not stupid. And then what? He'll disappear and the Boca PD will lose interest eventually, especially since neither Timmy nor Jamie actually came to any harm. Meanwhile Slades will still be out there."

Frank paced back to the couch and slumped down on it, shrugging his shoulders. "I don't get it. What else do you want us to do?"

Kitty took a deep breath. "Listen to this: Right now, Slades doesn't have a clue that we've got his number. He tried to get Jamie again yesterday so we know he's still driving the same car. That means he's right here and still stalking Jamie—and me."

"Oh come on, Kitty! What are you suggesting? That you and Jamie become decoys? That's ludicrous. I couldn't allow that."

Kitty flung herself down on the couch beside Frank, encircling his waist with her arms. "I don't want that, either. But I can't spend the rest of my life looking over my shoulder wondering when he's going to reappear. What I'm suggesting is that you could talk to Beaufort ... get some more of that professional courtesy and have them tail me for a while, and when they spot the white Caddy ... whammo!"

Frank cleared his throat. "And if he abducts some other little boy in the meantime?"

Kitty groaned. "Please, honey! I'm just suggesting we try it this way for a couple of days. He may be getting antsy ... and careless. You can always do it your way later. But let's try without the risk of scaring him away."

Frank sighed, and Kitty was relieved that, at least, he

seemed to be considering the idea. Finally, he nodded. "I'll tell you what I'll do. I'll talk to Beaufort and his captain. See what they think. See if they're comfortable with that idea. It's their case and their territory. I agree you have a point about scaring him off, but the thought of you out there with Jamie as targets is not very appealing."

"Honey," Kitty wrapped her arms around his neck. "Don't forget we do have an advantage. We know who he is and we know it because I got the license number. And, he'll show again, in the next couple of days. Guaranteed. He can't help himself."

❧ *Chapter* 39 ❧

Friday, September 15

*K*itty was on the phone to Todd when Ginny brought in the morning mail. She glanced at the bundle Ginny placed on the desk in front of her, noting that the top envelope had come from Gates and Welles, *Attorneys-At-Law.* She remembered that Jonathan Gates was the Haley family lawyer and she was instantly curious—and apprehensive.

She knew they could not possibly have any complaints about her reporting on Marina Dee Haley's murder, unless the Vascos had complained about invasion of privacy. Her segment on the Morettis the previous week had included Jeff's information that the Vascos had accepted money in return for letting the Morettis into the house. Jeff had given her permission to enter the property and Bernie had caught the Vascos on video as they worked in the house, without telling them what the footage would be used for.

She stared at the envelope as Todd hollered down the line from New York. "What do you mean you're out of ideas? This is the biggest effing story to come out of Palm

Beach since the Kennedy rape trial. Don't the cops have anything?"

"They're still looking for the Morettis," Kitty said quietly.

"Are you sure? I thought you said you had a good contact in the police department. They can't just be sitting on their butts doing nothing. We've got to keep this story rolling."

Kitty chewed her lower lip. "I've covered all the main angles down here. It seems to me the one thing that's left to reveal about Marina is the identity of her secret lover, Jeff Haley's father, and that's on your patch in New York, Toddy."

She heard a spluttering sound at the other end of the line. "You think I haven't got that covered, Fitzgerald? I put Sanders and Clark on it a week ago."

"And?"

"Zippo so far. They found the family in Connecticut where Marina's mother worked as a live-in housekeeper but she already had baby Jeffie with her when she started working there. She told the family that her husband had left her and the baby. Are you sure Haley doesn't have a clue about his old man?"

"Positive." Kitty paused, thinking. "What about Marina's father? What happened to him when the mother moved to Connecticut?"

"Listen, Fitzgerald, we've turned up everything we can. Marina's father died when she was thirteen. The mother remarried a few years later. By that time Marina had moved to New York—where, I presume, she got knocked up. Then I guess Marina's mother said she'd take the baby, and I also guess her new husband didn't much like the idea. Which is why she ended up on her own in Connecticut."

"But isn't it likely he knows something? They must have, at least, discussed taking in the baby?"

"Forget it," Todd cut in brusquely. "We've tried to find him and can't. It isn't exactly as if he was high profile. His comings and goings weren't documented on the social pages of the local paper."

Kitty sighed. Jeff's father was a dead end. Since Marina had never told Jeff about him it was likely she'd never confided his identity to another living soul, either. Kitty could certainly understand that.

"Anyway, this isn't getting us anywhere Fitzgerald. How about you just get Haley again and get him to blast the cops for falling down on the investigation?"

"I'll try it. I'll see what I can do," Kitty replied, suppressing a hysterical giggle. *Oh sure, Todd! Get Jeff to blast Frank on national TV!* As if she didn't have enough personal problems right now.

For one, Slades had gone underground. Vanished off the face of the earth, it seemed. . . .

"Oh, and by the way, Fitzgerald, where's that story on the bisexual attorney who got slashed to ribbons by his male lover?"

Kitty took a deep breath just as Bernie walked into her office. "I asked Platzer to send it back. I think the police might be on the verge of making an arrest. We should wait for that."

She hung up as Todd grunted into the phone, apparently buying her lie. She wasn't happy about lying to Todd but it was a delay tactic. Eventually, she figured he'd lose interest and forget about it. She wasn't going to worry about it, anyway.

Her thoughts returned to Slades. It was exactly a week since she and Frank had discovered Slades's identity. In the last seven days not one single lead had materialized and the waiting was getting her down. She found herself driving around with her eyes perpetually glued to her rearview mirror, praying that she would glimpse the white Cadillac.

Being able to put a face to Jamie's stalker made it a little easier to cope. She had called Marcy and asked her sister for dubs of her TV show and pictures of Bill Slades. She stared at the pictures and watched the tapes over and over committing the Monster of Makerley's face permanently to her memory. It was a jowly face with mean, small eyes. But the face didn't scare her.

Somewhere along the way Kitty's anxiety and fear had been replaced with anger and determination.

On Monday morning she had rummaged around her desk drawers to unearth a .38 revolver. She had bought it months before while researching a story on gun control. She had asked Frank to check it out for her and had insisted he show her how to use it.

She was not squeamish about the gun. She knew that if she came face to face with Slades, if she found herself in a situation where Jamie needed her protection, she would have no hesitation about using it. She carried it with her in her tote to work but stashed it on the top shelf of her closet when she was home.

Sharon had returned the previous Sunday night and even though Kitty felt the girl would be more of a hindrance than a help in any crisis situation she was comforted by her presence in the house.

She had a suspicion, however, that Slades had been scared off after all. In the end Beaufort and Frank had gone along with her idea, but only up to a point. They had agreed not to make a public appeal on Slades but they had both been adamant about the beefed-up patrols. A police car arrived every night at 10 P.M. in the cul-de-sac and stayed till 6:00 in the morning. Another patrol car appeared in the school driveway at the start of the school day.

Just before dawn this morning, Slades had found another way into her life by appearing in her dream and turning it into a nightmare: She had been running down a long hallway, running away from Slades who was pointing a videocamera at her like a gun. In the dream her heart pounded as she ran toward a figure at the other end of the hallway. She couldn't see the face of the man who stood there but in the dream she knew it was Jeff and in the dream she was running into his arms for safety.

She had felt safe and secure when she reached him. She had collapsed against him as his arms tightened around her. But then her relief had turned into terror as she'd looked at Jeff's arms and seen that they were not flesh but long thorny stems, like rose stems with thick sharp thorns that pierced into her, cutting her, tearing her skin.

She had awakened, sitting up abruptly with her heart racing, her body soaked in perspiration. She'd had no trouble interpreting the image of the thorny stems.

Jeff had sent her a dozen long-stemmed roses, in a lead crystal vase, at the beginning of the week. A note had arrived with the flowers. It had simply read: "Kitty! Don't turn your back on me." She had thrown away the note and given the roses and the vase to Ginny.

Somewhere at the back of her mind the thought had niggled that the note sounded like a threat. She had expected him to follow up by bombarding her with phone calls and messages. But nothing more had happened since Monday and she had considered the silence ominous.

Now, sitting in her office, she ripped open the envelope from Gates and Welles and took out the letter. It was short. No more than five paragraphs, but she had to read it three times before she grasped the full meaning of it. When she did, her anger exploded.

"Ginny!" she yelled through the door. "Get me Tillie Berg on the line. Right now! I don't care what she's doing, please find her. Now!"

Bernie leapt off the couch where he had stretched out as usual, obviously alarmed by the urgency in her voice.

Kitty forestalled his inevitable question. "No, Bernie, don't even ask. Please, just give me five minutes. Go! Go!" She bounced off her chair and paced to the window and then back again, trying to control her fury as she waited for Tillie Berg to get on the line.

Tillie was the attorney whom Kitty used for *Inside Copy* business. She was an expert on matters of libel, slander, and invasion of privacy issues and though Kitty had no idea if Tillie had the expertise to handle the problem that had just landed on her desk, Tillie would, at the very least, know where to go for help.

She paced over to the desk and picked up the letter again. Her eyes focused on the words even though her anger made her hands shake.

> *Dear Ms. Fitzgerald,*
>   *I am writing on behalf of my client, Mr. Jeffrey Haley, who has advised me of the situation regarding Jamie Fitzgerald, a minor of whom you have sole custody. According to my client, who intends to file a paternity claim regarding said minor child, you have denied him access to the child, despite his wholehearted efforts to exercise his rights and obligations toward his son since his arrival in Palm Beach.*
>   *Having considered all the facts, and having advised my client of his legal recourse, I must now advise you that unless you and my client can reach some amicable settlement concerning custody and visitation we will pursue this matter by exploring the alternative of legal redress.*

Bastard! Kitty mouthed the word with venom. He's flipped! Freaked out! She wanted to pick up the phone and call him and vent her anger on him directly. But she held back. That's probably what he expected her to do.

She had no idea of what Gates meant by "facts." What facts? She hadn't a clue as to the story Jeff had spun for the attorney. But there was no legal recourse. There could be no legal recourse.

Jeff was just simply and plainly goading her to react. To respond to him. He was probably waiting by his phone right now. But she wouldn't give him the satisfaction.

"Tillie's on the line," Ginny called out.

Kitty snatched at the phone, letting her words come tumbling out hurriedly and anxiously.

Tillie listened without interruption as Kitty read her the letter.

"For the record, Jeff Haley is not, I repeat *not*, Jamie's father, and he very well knows it," she concluded. "Maybe you can get that point across to his attorney."

"Fax me the letter I'll take a look at it," Tillie said.

"Can you handle it for me, Tillie? I don't want to talk to him or his attorney. I just want him out of my life. I've got enough on my mind at the moment without this sort of bullshit. Maybe you can threaten his attorney with a countersuit for harassment."

"Calm down, Kitty," the attorney spoke soothingly. "Fax me the letter and I'll get back to you as soon as I figure it out."

Kitty spent the next hour pacing the floor, muttering to herself angrily. She wondered it Tillie had forgotten about her and had gone off to take care of other business. What else could be taking so long?

It was noon before Tillie got back to her. "Sorry it took so long," the attorney apologized. "But I've been on the line with Gates."

"An hour? Did you get it cleared up? Is it all taken care of?"

Tillie was silent at the other end for a moment too long, and Kitty stared perplexed into the mouthpiece. "Tillie?"

The attorney finally spoke. "Can you come over to my office this afternoon. I think we should discuss this."

"Tillie! I don't want to discuss it. I want to forget about it."

She heard Tillie sigh on the other end. "Listen, Kitty. You asked for my advice. I've spoken to Gates and he seems like a reasonable man, but I have to tell you that he also believes that Jeff Haley does have some grounds."

Kitty shook her head and wondered if she was still, perhaps, in the midst of her nightmare. "How, Tillie? What grounds? Listen, I appreciate your help but I don't want to waste my time on this nonsense. Any simple blood test will prove he's not Jamie's father. Did you explain that to Gates?"

The attorney was silent for a moment on the other end. Then she resumed talking as if Kitty hadn't interrupted. "I made extensive notes during my conversation with Gates. And, as far as I can see, the issue won't necessarily be resolved by a blood test. I don't have expertise in this field but I do know there was a similar case in California recently. Some guy who discovered through blood tests that he was not the child's father claimed he'd been led to believe he was—and he eventually got custody."

Kitty laughed. "Well, that's not similar at all. I've never led Jeff Haley to believe anything of the sort."

Tillie allowed another pause before continuing. "Gates said, and I quote—'There's extensive documentation to show that Miss Fitzgerald led my client to believe he is the boy's father'—end quote."

"What! What documentation?" Kitty gripped the phone tightly. Then she slumped back in her chair, clapping her hand to her mouth and groaning as if in pain.

"Kitty?"

She took a deep breath. "Okay, Tillie. I'll be right over."

❧ Chapter 40 ❧

Kitty arrived in Tillie Berg's office just after one o'clock. The attorney was on the phone but motioned for her to come in and sit down as she wound up her conversation. Kitty chose to stand, then paced over to one of the big windows.

From Tillie's office she had a clear view of the Intracoastal below. A sleek cigarette boat coasted toward the inlet. A sailboat followed. Even from the fourteenth floor she could see the beautiful teakwood of the sailboat glimmering in the sunlight. The teak deck shone. The paintwork of the hull looked new and sparkling white. She imagined the sailboat bound for some exotic island in the Bahamas, and she felt a sudden envy for the party on board.

"So?" Tillie hung up the phone and came around from behind her desk, walking toward the doorway. "Tess!" she called out to her secretary. "Could you get some tea for us?" She glanced over at Kitty. "Or maybe coffee or soda?"

Kitty shook her head. "Iced tea is fine."

"And Tess, are there any donuts left?"

The attorney smiled at Kitty, flattening down her smock top over the flowing pants that covered her wide hips. "I know I shouldn't, but what the hell? I've got a dinner date at the Cafe Arugula tonight and nouvelle cuisine isn't exactly filling."

"Tillie," Kitty interrupted. "What's this extensive documentation that supposedly shows I led Jeff to believe he's Jamie's father? Is it the letters I wrote to him when he was in jail?"

The other woman beckoned her over to two oversized armchairs in the corner of her office bringing a manila folder with her. She sat down opening the folder. "In a nutshell, yes. Gates was kind enough to tell me that he has about twenty letters from you to Haley. One snippet that particularly impressed him goes as follows . . ." Tillie adjusted her glasses and looked down at the yellow legal pad on her knees.

"Quote: I know you'll get a kick out of this: Yesterday Jamie was crawling around the apartment and grabbed at the picture of you and me at Marina's wedding. He stared at it and then said: 'Dada.' Unquote."

"Oh, please!" Kitty jumped to her feet. "That makes me want to puke." She paced across to the windows again. "I used to write about Jamie because he was the most interesting person in my life and because, I suppose, I was showing off about him. I wrote that to Jeff . . . don't you see? That bit . . . 'you'll get a kick out of this' is precisely because he *wasn't* his father—" she broke off, her words trailing as she looked helplessly at Tillie, realizing how inane the explanation sounded.

Tillie Berg stared back over the top of her glasses. "You see the problem, don't you? You have to hear it the way a total stranger, like a judge, might be hearing it."

Kitty returned to her chair and slumped down, shaking her head. "This is crazy, Tillie. It's a lie from start to finish. I was three months pregnant when I met Jeff. I told him that the first time we had dinner together."

"Well, apparently he's willing to overlook that minor detail," Tillie commented dryly. "But as a matter of interest was Jamie's real father around at the time? Would there be any point in contacting him?"

Kitty shook her head firmly. "No! Forget Jamie's real father. He'd be no help in this at all. I didn't even tell him about Jamie. He never knew. He doesn't know. He wasn't around. End of story," she added emphatically.

"Pity," Tillie Berg grimaced, taking off her glasses to rub her eyes with the back of her hand. "Since Haley's basing everything on the claim that you led him to believe he was the father, it would have helped if you could point to an occasion when you, perhaps, introduced him to the real father."

Kitty shook her head again. "It never happened, Tillie. I never spoke to Jeff about him and Jeff didn't pry. He was just there for me, being a nice guy, lending a helping hand. I never thought he'd use it like this."

"Tell me more about it," Tillie prodded, and Kitty took a couple of minutes to recount the various ways Jeff had helped her out. "I didn't actually ask him to do most of these things. He just seemed to take over."

Tillie nodded. "I can see how he's twisted that around to suit his claim. To quote Gates 'my client accepted his duties and obligations as Jamie's father as soon as he learned of the pregnancy and continued, insofar as he was able, during his incarceration, and thereafter.' "

Tillie flipped through the manila folder and brought out another sheet of paper. "According to Gates, Haley has receipts and canceled checks for . . . ," she paused and then itemizing on her fingers, "one, the construction of a nursery in your New York home. Two, the purchase of nursery furniture and related baby items around the time of the birth."

Kitty buried her face in her hands as Tillie continued. "Most recently, according to Gates, his client claims that the two of you resumed living together and that he assumed parental duties with Jamie." She looked down into the folder again. "Taking him to and from school, and to and from afterschool activities, providing his meals and caring for him."

Kitty jumped to her feet. "Now, that's bullshit! Pure bullshit, Tillie. He stayed over at my place for a few nights. He offered to keep an eye on Jamie."

Tillie raised an eyebrow. "This is after he did the two-part interview for *Inside Copy*?"

"Yes," Kitty sighed. "I had a problem last week." She laughed harshly. "I suppose I still have it. The thing is while I'm running around covering the biggest story of my career some creep is lurking around Jamie's school trying to abduct him."

Tillie's eyebrow rose again.

"Yeah, some child molester who has a grudge against my sister, Marcy, because she did a story about his parole hearing. Anyway, he also broke into the house and removed all of Jamie's things. So all this is going on and Jeff was around because we'd just wrapped the interview—and that's how he came to stay over."

"Go on, don't stop now," Tillie smiled at her.

"Well, in the end, I had to tell him I didn't need him anymore because Sharon was coming back and Frank was going to be around, and he took it badly."

"What do you mean?"

"He didn't think Sharon or Frank could do the job as well as he could."

Tillie nodded and shook the manila folder. "Okay, I see how we got to this point. But . . . ," she paused, shaking her head, "I haven't even got to the kicker." She motioned for Kitty to sit down. "You're going to just love this: Gates tells me that last week Haley came into his office to set up a trust fund, making Jamie sole beneficiary of his estate."

Kitty felt the color drain from her face. "He named Jamie as his sole beneficiary?"

"As Gates remarked: Why would you do that for a child unless you believed he was yours?" Tillie laid the folder aside, tapped on it with her fingers. "He's done quite a number on you here, Kitty."

Kitty bit the inside of her lip, shaking her head. "It's outrageous, Tillie. Totally off the wall. There's a pervert out there somewhere who wants to abduct Jamie because of a story my sister did about him. Now Jeff seems to have an airtight case for taking Jamie away from me—legally. I don't know if I can handle it."

Tillie moved over to Kitty's chair and perched on the armrest, putting her arm around Kitty's shoulders. "Don't freak out just yet." She patted her arm. "I've given you the sum of their case."

"And what's mine, Tillie?" Kitty stared at the attorney. "A blood test? A DNA matchup? That's something I can produce but you just told me that's not relevant here."

Tillie walked over to her desk and picked up a printout that she brought over to Kitty. "I had Tess search Nexis for the California case I mentioned to you and this is it: You can see the plaintiff had an ongoing relationship with the woman and the child. He'd lived with them continuously for three years. Also the boy believed the plaintiff was his father. That's obviously somewhat different from your situation."

Kitty slumped back in her chair, breathing out loudly. "So what do we do now? Let him go ahead? Call his bluff?"

Tillie Berg got to her feet and walked back to her desk. She plumped herself down in her big leather swivel chair, her fingers drumming on the polished dark wood, a smile playing on her lips.

"Not our best option, Kitty. Going to court is time-consuming, nerve-wracking, costly, and messy."

Kitty returned the smile in spite of her grim thoughts. "I thought that's what you lawyers liked—costly and time-consuming."

Tillie grinned. "Well, I wouldn't be the one making the

money on this one. I'd have to hand you over to an expert in family law. And speaking as a friend, I'd hate to see you enmeshed in a court action if there's a way to avoid it."

"Is there?"

"Of course," Tillie smiled. "It's called negotiation. What does the other side want? How far can you go to compromise? What can you offer?"

"That's out of the question," Kitty interrupted. "Jeff wants . . ." She hesitated. "I guess what it boils down to is that he wants to hurt me."

"Exactly." Tillie stared at her pointedly.

Kitty laughed. "Well, that doesn't make it any more negotiable."

Tillie tut-tutted. "You're not thinking logically, Kitty. Why does he want to hurt you?"

"Because he can't get his own way?" It was more of a statement than a question.

Tillie shook her head. "Look at it the way I have to look at it as an attorney. See it from his point of view, for just a moment. I'm not making any judgment here because I've never met Jeff Haley and he sounds like a pain in the ass, if you ask me, but this is how I see it based on what you've told me." Tillie paused to sip her iced tea.

Then she continued, "You were close friends before he went to jail. Then, irrespective of what happened in the meantime, when he came out you were there again. You wanted the interview."

Tillie held up her hand as Kitty started to speak. "Let me finish. I know it was your job. But the fact is you needed something from him and he gave it to you. Then you were freaked out over Jamie and he was there to help out. He felt needed again. He had a purpose. He stepped out of jail after five years and he sees that maybe he can walk right back into his old life. Then he finds out that's not so." Tillie paused. "He's going to feel a little sorry for himself, don't you think? And he's going to want to cling

to something he knows rather than make a new life for
himself."

"So he's threatening to take me and Jamie to court!
That's a wacky way of going about it."

Tillie grinned. "Who said rich people were sane? Listen
hon, I'm not saying he sounds like the world's most ratio-
nal man but he's got money and people with money think
they can buy whatever they want. You know that. And if
you know what the other side wants you can play it so that
you won't have to go to court.

"Look, a man with his money is not going to be alone
for long, guaranteed. All he needs is time to make the
break, then you and Jamie are going to be history, Kitty."

Kitty considered the idea. Jeff's remarks about Steffie
Newman sprang into her thoughts. Jeff would probably
have moved on to Steffie if she hadn't accepted his offer
to stay and help her with Jamie.

"So what do you suggest?" she asked Tillie calmly.

"I suggest you talk to the man. Don't make him feel as
if you're never going to take another one of his calls."

"Make nice after he's put me through this bullshit?"

Tillie grinned. "I know. It goes against the grain for
you, doesn't it? But think of it this way: You don't want
to let this get out of control. You don't want to force him
to play his hand."

Kitty nodded. The memory of Rick Tyler quizzing her
about Jeff and Jamie on the phone a week ago flashed into
her head. God, would Rick ever go to town on this. The
moment Jeff filed anything in court, it would become a
matter of record.

She glanced at her attorney and smiled weakly. "Yes, I
hear you, Tillie. You mean lose the battle, win the war."

Tillie grinned. "I think it's worth a shot, don't you?"

Kitty nodded again. "Since you put it that way, I guess
so."

❧ *Chapter* 41 ❧

$\mathcal{F}$rank paced over to the window of the quiet office and recalled times when the mood and atmosphere in this room had been more relaxed.

The captain in charge of the investigations unit sat behind his desk, his face a study in intense concentration. "Let's go over this one more time, Maguire."

Al Parkins's even tones were misleading. Frank knew under the cool exterior the man was steaming and had been since the early morning when he'd taken a call from the senior correspondent of *A Current Affair.* The reporter had asked Parkins to confirm rumors that the investigation was now leaning toward a theory that Marina's killer was a "psycho who was still on the loose in Palm Beach."

"You get the picture, Maguire," he'd confronted Frank. "The press are running out of facts. Now they're going to start with the bullshit. We don't need this kind of publicity."

Parkins's annoyance did not faze Frank. He was satisfied that over the last two weeks he and Don had done everything possible to find the Morettis: Fingerprints lifted from the apartment and checked through the AFIS data base and the FBI's computers had led to a dead end. The Morettis evidently had no criminal records. Neither of them apparently held Florida drivers' licenses. Nor were they listed on any tax rolls or as clients in any of the major employment agencies in Palm Beach County. Identikit pictures reproduced on TV screens and newspapers in South Florida had not produced any useful response from the general public or informants. And the Vascos had spent hours pouring over mug shots of known scam-merchants in the attempt to track down the couple. Hundreds of man-hours had also gone into tracking down and eliminating other couples with the same last name.

"If there's some place we haven't looked," said Frank, "I'm open to suggestions."

"But where does that leave us?" Al Parkins wanted to know, looking first at Frank then at Don.

"There're two possibilities," Frank jumped in. "One is that the Morettis were who they said they were, that is domestics, but most likely illegal aliens looking for employment and green cards. In which case they've most probably fled back to their native country."

"Which might be where?"

Frank thought about Vincent Moretti's demeanor and way with words. "Maybe Cuba," he offered.

"It might also explain the missing five grand," Don interjected. "If they found it, maybe they saw it as a way of recouping their investment."

"Does it also explain the missing chapter?" Parkins asked incisively.

"Not in any satisfactory way." Frank shook his head. "Though there is always the possibility that it's our proverbial red herring. We have no real way of knowing whether she wrote anything at all that night. Could be she was suffering from writer's block and decided to take her swim before getting down to it again."

The captain pressed his fingers together, forming a little

steeple. "And if they were illegals who were scared off by the police activity, where does that leave us with suspects?"

There was a silence in the room. No one, not Frank nor Don nor Chris Roberts, the detective-sergeant, wanted to return to the subject of a psycho on the loose.

"Let's consider your other theory about the Morettis, Frank," Al Parkins prodded.

"The best hit team money can buy," Frank replied simply and decisively. "Look at the way they moved in. They had money. They made the hit. They were cool enough to wait a day or two to divert suspicion. Then they moved out and are gone without a trace. Vanished off the face of South Florida."

"And no evidence that they were into any other scam?"

"Not that we can find." Frank lapsed into momentary silence. Marina Dee Haley's attorney and accountant had reviewed all her files, her bank accounts, her stock portfolio, and all had seemed in order. There had not been any hint of any irregularity. No inexplicable withdrawal of large sums of money or transfers of any kind. Her insurance company had handed over a detailed list of all her jewelry and valuables. Everything was accounted for except the five thousand dollars in cash.

"It wasn't burglary. It wasn't embezzlement," Frank repeated.

"It was an assault, though. Brutal, upfront, and personal," Parkins paused, collapsing his steeple.

"A cold-blooded killing made to look like a killing of rage," Frank interrupted, "to divert suspicion from the only possible suspect with motive enough to arrange for Marina's murder. Which brings us back to Jeff Haley."

Al Parkins nodded. "Tell us about the motive, Frank. Give me your thoughts on that."

Frank exhaled audibly. "Where do you want me to start? There's the estate, obviously. It's all his now. Eight million dollars worth of it. Then there's Mom herself. She's kept him tied to her apron strings for all his adult

life. Now he's almost forty and she's still dictating to him
. . . telling him where he should serve his parole and so on.
There's also the revenge factor."

He noticed Parkins stiffen in his seat. "What's that?"

"Nothing we can pin down at the moment. It's more of
an impression really, which we've been picking up during
our interviews with Marina's friends: that Haley's big gesture of copping a plea for shooting his stepfather was just
that. It seems Marina may have actually refused to testify
for him. But apparently only she and Haley ever knew the
truth about that."

Frank looked across at his partner and noticed the raised
eyebrow. "Don doesn't buy into this a hundred percent, by
the way."

His partner cleared his throat. "I think there are still
some avenues to check so far as other individuals who had
reason to feel aggrieved toward Marina," Don spoke
stiffly, and Frank knew he was choosing his words carefully. Don would not, in this office, verbalize his suspicion
that Frank was letting his personal feelings get in the way
of the investigation.

Parkins looked from one man to the other, his eyes narrowing as if debating, Frank thought, whether or not to
pursue the opening Don had given him. But the moment
passed. The captain, too, evidently liked the sound of
Haley as prime suspect.

"But unless you find the Morettis and get one of them
to squeal, Haley's going to be a bitch to nail."

Frank nodded. "But if we're agreed that Haley is a
prime suspect, then obviously he arranged the deal while
he was still inside. Which means that's where we're going
to pick up any useful lead."

Parkins closed his eyes and appeared to be engrossed in
thought. "Anything to go on at the moment?"

"A half-dozen names of recently released inmates for-
warded from Wallkill. And there's Haley's former cell
mate. He's awaiting release in a work furlough center at
the moment. He'd be a good start if Haley was asking

around—and he might cooperate in exchange for a speedy discharge."

Parkins hesitated for only a moment longer, then he nodded curtly. "Okay, go do it, Maguire. Let's not have another Brant Davidson on our hands." Frank thought about Brant Davidson as he walked back to his desk. The Palm Beach millionaire had been indicted for arranging the murder of his estranged second wife. Ellen Davidson had been gunned down in her townhouse by someone posing as an electric company repairman, just days before the Davidsons were due in court. Ellen had asked for half of Davidson's assets. Despite evident motive and the testimony of Davidson's former girlfriend, who claimed the millionaire had talked openly to her about getting rid of the second wife, the hitman had never been found and a judge had dismissed the charges against the millionaire.

Frank needed a better break than they'd had on the Davidson case. He reached for the phone to book himself an evening flight to New York but in that same moment his second line rang out. It was the desk sergeant from downstairs, telling him that Kitty Fitzgerald was waiting to see him.

He stared at her legs as he came up behind her, gripping her in a bear hug.

But when she turned around he was startled to see that her eyes held none of their usual brightness or sparkle. "Got a minute, Detective?" Her voice was flat, too.

He put his arm around her. "Several," he grinned at her. "Want to grab a cup of coffee?"

She shook her head. "Let's walk to the beach. There's something we have to discuss."

They turned right, and right again onto Australian Avenue, heading toward the ocean. Frank was aware of his anxiety as he strode beside her. Had Slades surfaced again? Doubtful, he reflected. Kitty would have Jamie in tow if that were the case.

As they crossed A1A he muttered something about a

tropical storm out over the Atlantic. Kitty nodded without interest.

"At least there's a breeze today," he said, turning his back to the ocean, and leaning against the low stone sea-wall.

"Yeah, for a change," Kitty brushed her curls back, low-ered her shades, and reached into her tote. She brought out a long white envelope and handed it to him.

Frank glanced at the return address, instantly recogniz-ing the name of Marina Dee Haley's attorney.

"What is it? What does it say? Did Marina leave you something in her will?"

"They're Jeff's attorneys, too," Kitty answered without a smile. "Read it, Frank. I want you to read it."

Frank took out the letter and focused on the print. The words *Jamie . . . paternity . . . visitation and custody* all seemed to jump off the page at him in the same moment.

He forced himself to read it twice to make certain he'd understood it correctly. Then he looked up at Kitty.

"I don't understand this."

"Neither do I," she replied making an attempt at a smile. "Tillie Berg says he's mad at me."

Frank stared at her in silence, aware of a tightening sen-sation in his chest. "But he's suing for custody? Am I missing something here?"

Kitty sighed and he was alarmed to see her eyes well with tears. He drew her toward him and put his arms around her. He felt her trembling against his chest and his arms tightened.

"I just don't understand, Kitty."

"Tillie thinks he's trying to hurt me because I used him and then threw him out of the house. His attorney has all the letters I wrote to Jeff in jail, and receipts and stuff that he's using as evidence that he supported Jamie, *and* he's made Jamie the sole beneficiary in his will."

Frank listened with a growing sense of horror. Jeff Haley had willed his eight-million-dollar estate to Jamie! None of this was making any sense to him at all.

"Tillie suggests I meet with him and talk to him."

"Baloney!" Frank interrupted. "There's nothing to discuss. If he's not Jamie's father, he doesn't get to see him again or see you again. He can see us ... both of us in court. Listen Kitty, I understand you're worried about the headlines. But it wouldn't last. Once the results of the blood test were published, Haley would look like the fool, like the jerk he is. And, even if he pursued all that other bullshit about being led to believe this and that, well, it would take months to get to court by which time we'll be married and I'll be the father who's established the strongest relationship with Jamie. It will all blow over, you'll see."

Kitty leaned into his chest, shaking her head. "That's how I figured it, at first," she whispered. "But now that I've thought about it, it scares me, Frank." She paused and backed away a step. "I know what I would do on a story like that. The minute those blood test results came out I'd be right back in there asking: 'Well, then who *is* Jamie Fitzgerald's father? It would open such a can of worms. All those reporters would be digging around. Jamie would start asking questions. Don't you see that?"

Frank didn't. "The only one that matters in this is Jamie and you're going to have to tell him one day, anyway. Look, worse things happen to kids than finding out your dad is an Australian who returned to the Outback without knowing that you existed. You had your reasons, and Jamie will understand them one day—"

"Frank! Stop!"

The pain in Kitty's voice startled him. "Kitty, honey." He took her hand in his. "I'm sorry. I didn't mean to put it so bluntly. Look, all I'm saying is, I'll be there with you every step of the way."

"It wasn't an Australian reporter."

She spoke so softly that Frank thought he'd misheard. "You don't have to say it was."

"No, Frank, I'm telling you that Jamie's father was not an Australian reporter." Her eyes teared up. "I'm sorry I lied but I couldn't . . . I just couldn't tell you the truth, not on our second date."

"Third," Frank corrected her, then lapsed into silence. For a long while he stared into the distance, focusing on a tiny sailboat bobbing on the waves.

"So, okay," he said finally. "Not on our third date, even. But will you tell me now?"

She breathed in, long and deeply. She sighed. She fidgeted with the tissue in her fingers. She stared out at the same sailboat. "I don't really want to," she replied, her voice small and hesitant. "I always promised myself that I would tell only Jamie when he was old enough to understand, and then he could decide what to do about it."

Frank shook his head. "That's not good enough, Kitty. I'm part of your life now, too, and I need to know. Look at the mess we're in. There's a child molester threatening and stalking your son and a former would-be friend threatening a court battle over him. I want to get rid of all these shadows around us. And I want to know that you trust me. I want to know the truth."

She pulled away again and he thought she was going to resist even this impassioned plea, but then the fight seemed to go out of her. Her eyes strayed momentarily into the distance, then back to his face.

"How much time have you got? Because if I'm going to tell the story I want to tell it all."

Frank didn't even glance at his watch. He could take the first flight to New York in the morning if necessary. Kitty was at the top of his list right now. "Want to tell it over a drink at Charley's?"

She nodded. "I don't think I can begin without a little help."

"That bad, huh?" Frank said, bantering, as he took her arm and steered her across A1A, toward Charley's Crab.

She didn't return his smile. "It's not that bad, but it's not that pretty either."

❦ *Chapter 42* ❦

She didn't know how or where to begin and was glad they had to wait a few moments before Frank caught the bartender's eye. She ordered a Bailey's, Frank a Dewar's.

He sat and waited, making her even more nervous. Then he reached over and stroked the nape of her neck. "You know you can trust me, Kitty. How bad could it be?"

When she still didn't reply, Frank continued, "So, okay. He's well known, a famous household name, and his career would be ruined if this got out?"

Kitty sipped her drink. "Yes to the first part. Not necessarily, to the second part."

Frank grinned. "Good, then he's not a bishop or cardinal. He's in TV?"

She laughed out loud. "Yes. The TV part, I mean."

"And he's married ... was married at the time?"

"Correct."

Frank smiled. "C'mon, it's not sounding that bad so far.

In fact, compared to some of the stories you've covered on your show it sounds pretty tame."

Kitty laughed nervously. "That's because I haven't gotten to the relevant part yet."

"Okay, why don't you give it to me as if it was a promo for your show? Did I get that right? Promo?"

She reached for his hand and squeezed it. "Yeah. You got that right." Then she took a deep breath, lowered her voice. "Okay, here goes. How about this: *Incredible and shocking: A five-year secret will tear this family apart. Stay tuned and we'll tell you what happened the night the TV anchorman ... got ...,*" she faltered, took another deep breath, *"the wrong twin sister pregnant."*

She sat back on her stool and stared at Frank. She felt nauseous. His eyes had narrowed, as if he was trying to figure it out. But of course he had understood her immediately.

"Your sister's husband? Daniel Stone?"

His voice seemed to boom out all across the restaurant, and Kitty looked around to see if anyone was paying attention to their conversation. The bartender stood at the other end but it didn't make her feel any better. Everyone knew bartenders had keen ears.

"Frank! Not so loud."

Frank waved away her concern, but his voice was a whisper when he spoke again. An incredulous whisper. "And he doesn't know? He never suspected?"

Kitty's face flushed as she shook her head. "I know, now it's going to sound much worse than it was. That's what I was afraid of."

Frank signaled the bartender for another Scotch. "Forget what it sounds like, Kitty. I'm not shocked. I've got an idea what you TV people are like, you know." He grinned as if to let her know he was teasing.

"Well, I saw him first. Marcy was on vacation when he started at Channel Eight. They brought him in from Chicago to join the local anchor desk and ..."

She hesitated, deliberating how to phrase the next couple of sentences. Then she shrugged. "I was young and impressionable and just full of myself at having arrived in the Big Apple and Dan was so polished and professional and just . . ."

"A hunk?" Frank offered. "Is that the word you're looking for?"

Kitty grimaced. Frank had seen Daniel Stone on TV. There was no point in trying to downplay his physical attraction. "Yeah, a hunk," she agreed. "But anyway, it didn't matter because as soon as Marcy returned from vacation all glowing and tanned and rested and drop-dead gorgeous, that was it."

"And you were pissed?"

"No!" Kitty laughed. "There were plenty of other hunks to go around in TV. I didn't even think that Marcy would stick with Dan for long. But then they teamed her and Dan for a newsmagazine show and a couple of months later they were married. And a year after that they were both on network TV, doing the same sort of thing except that Dan anchored the show and Marcy was brought on as a correspondent."

Kitty picked up her Bailey's and crunched the ice between her teeth.

"Anyway," she set her glass down. "Fast forward a couple of years to which time my gorgeous, ambitious sister is on her way to having it all—a Park Avenue penthouse, jetting around the country for a TV network, and a devoted husband to boot."

"Devoted, but not entirely, right?" Frank interrupted.

Kitty laughed. "Wrong. Just hold on, I'm getting to it, okay." She took another deep breath. "Okay, so now it's the evening of their second anniversary and Marcy is jetting back from L.A. or Dallas or somewhere so they haven't planned a big night out. But Dan has organized someone to cater a little candlelit dinner in the penthouse, and I stop on my way home from WPEN with a bottle of champagne for them . . . and while I'm sitting there with Dan, waiting for Marcy to waltz in, she calls and tells Dan her plane's been fogged in . . . so then, Dan pours himself another Chivas and says to me: 'Why don't you stay? The caterers did a magnificent job with dinner, and it's all ready to serve.' "

Kitty stopped, and shook her head. "Do I need to go on?"

Frank looked at her in mock horror. "You're going to stop, now?"

Kitty laughed and buried her head in her hands. "What is it with you? Do you always have to be such a detective?"

He leaned back in his chair, his eyes laughing. "I just want to know who made the first move."

"Ah," Kitty sighed. It was a question she couldn't answer even for herself. Had never really been able to answer it. Had she made the first move when she'd jokingly suggested to a morose Dan that she would brush her hair back off her face and he could pretend that she was Marcy?

Or had he when, after dinner, during which they'd polished off the whole bottle of champagne, he'd suggested that if she was going to stand in for Marcy then she should change into the rose-pink teddy that was hanging in Marcy's closet?

"Bottom line," Kitty concluded. "After all the champagne and the Scotch, one thing led to another."

She sat back and sipped the water that the bartender had placed next to her Bailey's. She was finished with the story. She was not going to tell Frank anything more. She was certainly not going to tell him that Dan had pulled her down on the living room floor and that when he'd called her Marcy she had not been sure if he was still playacting or if by that stage of the evening he was genuinely confused.

"Now are you shocked?" she asked quietly.

Frank shrugged. "But you're telling me he never put two and two together?"

Kitty waved away the question. "He never asked me

about it. I think he blanked the whole thing out of his memory. I'm not even sure that he remembered it the next morning."

"And you never told him about Jamie?"

"Why would I? It would ruin my sister's life and marriage. You know what I've always said: You play, you pay."

"But Daniel Stone played, too."

Kitty shrugged. "I didn't want him to know. Believe me Frank, I have no regrets. I know I did the right thing. Marcy and Dan are still happily married, and Jamie and I are happy. What would have been the point?"

She had not been in love with Daniel Stone. She had never fantasized about him divorcing Marcy and marrying her. She had absolutely never considered telling Daniel about Jamie simply because she had never been able to figure out how it could have worked. Would she and Daniel know—and keep Marcy in the dark? Or would they confess to Marcy? It had just seemed too messy and useless to wreak havoc in three separate lives because of one moment's drunken charade. Above all she had always wanted to protect Marcy from the truth.

"Really, the three of us did not see each other very much. We led separate lives, and I'm sure that Dan, like Marcy, assumed eventually," she cleared her throat nervously, "that Jeff Haley was probably responsible. Maybe now you can understand why that was fine with me at the time."

"It brings us back to the current problem, though," Frank said, looking pensive. "It means you can't produce Jamie's real father for a judge. Jeff Haley is the front contender and it would be a case of your word against his as to what you led him to believe."

Kitty had shredded her cocktail napkin. "That's why I think Tillie has a point. I should call him and talk to him."

Frank stirred the melting ice in his Scotch with the swizzle stick and Kitty thought he was quiet for a very long time. It seemed he was considering her idea, but he looked so deep in thought and distant. Finally, he took her hand in his. "I want you to promise me something, Kitty. Don't arrange anything until I can be with you, okay? Then I think we'll be able to take care of this little problem."

"Oh," she hesitated. "I'm not sure that the two of us together meeting Jeff would be a good idea."

Frank shook his head. "Trust me on this one and don't do anything until I get back. I have to fly to New York tonight—"

"On the investigation?" she interrupted.

"What else is keeping me awake at nights?" he laughed.

"New lead?"

"Just closing some gaps—"

"On Marina?" she interrupted again.

"The whole investigation is about Marina. Anyway, I should be back by Sunday noontime at the latest, and Haley can't do anything between now and then."

"Okay, okay," she laughed. "I wouldn't have time for it tomorrow, anyway. There's Angela's annual apartment complex party and I've promised to take the boys while she gets things ready. Then I've got a million errands to run, and then I've got to get myself to the party." She paused and brushed his cheek with her fingers. "I was hoping you'd be there."

He gripped her hand. "Maybe I'll make it if things turn out right . . . though there's one other thing I'd like to do while I'm up there."

"Oh?"

He drew her head closer to his. "Just between us, I'd like to visit Slades's brother. I just feel he must know more than he's told Beaufort on the phone." Frank sat back against the bar stool. "So, maybe if I get lucky, we'll deal with all our problems in one fell swoop and be able to get on with our lives."

Frank signaled for the check. "In fact, let me move and get on a flight tonight. The sooner I go, the sooner I'll be back."

They walked back to the station house in a companionable silence. Then Frank gave her a long hard kiss before walking away.

Kitty stood on the sidewalk for a moment, feeling better than she had all day. *If I get lucky, we'll deal with all our problems in one fell swoop,* Frank had said. She suddenly wondered what Frank had meant by that. How could his trip help her battle with Jeff? But by the time the thought struck her she realized Frank had already disappeared inside the station house.

❧ *Chapter 43* ❧

Saturday, September 16

*M*akerley was a two-hour drive, north of the city, through Westchester and Putnam counties. It had taken Frank a little longer because of his unfamiliarity with the area, and he had arrived late the night before.

The town had no hotel or motel but the restaurant and bar at the top of Main Street offered a bed and breakfast. Frank had settled for the little room on the third floor of the big rambling house even though he was told he'd have to share the bathroom if any other guests checked in.

He had ignored his shabby surroundings but the bed had been an uncomfortable, narrow twin, and he woke before seven o'clock. That was fine with him. He needed an early start. He wanted to meet with Dr. Gordon Slades before continuing on to Wallkill. It looked like it would be a long day.

He had pinned his hopes on Tony Gardino, but Jeff Haley's former cellmate had been uninformative. The sullen youth, who'd been sentenced for his part in a liquor store holdup, had shown no particular interest in helping

Frank. Not even on the promise that his cooperation might shave some time off his stay at the work furlough center.

"Big deal. I ain't in a hurry to leave," Gardino had told him. "I get my three slops and a flop here. Anyways there's nothing to tell. He kept to himself. Thought he was too good. Had some big TV job before he landed in the slammer."

"He didn't speak of any plans for when he came out? Didn't ask any questions? Didn't try to make any connections?"

"What kind of connections?"

"Like looking around for a hitman?"

Gardino's eyes had widened momentarily. Then he'd laughed, showing very even, very white teeth. "Who, Haley? I don't think so. No one would have talked to him anyway. He was too far up the warden's ass. He had connections okay, but it wasn't the kind you're looking for."

"The name Moretti mean anything to you?" Frank had persisted.

"Wasn't on C-block. Not while I was there, anyway."

So now Frank was on his way to Wallkill by way of a detour through Makerley.

It was a small town that had seen better days when the paper mill, now disused and abandoned, had been a thriving concern. He drove slowly along Main Street—a shabby collection of run-down storefronts. Some of them empty, their windows whitened.

The first person he stopped, a woman with a toddler in tow, just shook her head when he asked for Gainsborough Drive.

The second pedestrian, an older man, hesitated until Frank added, "I'm looking for Dr. Gordon Slades."

"Why didn't you say so? It's Ginsburr Drive you'll be looking for," the man added, correcting his pronunciation.

The doctor's house was, in fact, just a few blocks west of Main Street, on a quiet, tree-lined avenue where all the houses, big and rambling, had wide wraparound porches and shutters.

The doctor's house had seen better days, too. The paint-work on the outside was peeling, some of the window shutters were missing, and the middle step up to the porch was splintered. But the plaque that hung on the gate, indicating that this was the residence of Dr. Gordon Slades, Family Practitioner, was polished, gleaming brass.

Frank pushed the doorbell and heard the chimes ring inside. He waited a few seconds and pushed again.

"All right, all right, I'm coming. Hold your horses."

Gordon Slades was tall and thin. In good shape with a full head of gray hair. He stood erect in a buttoned navy wool cardigan.

Frank introduced himself and saw the doctor's jaw tighten.

"You're here about Bill? Someone already called from the parole office. I told him I don't know a thing. And I don't." He started to close the door in Frank's face but Frank took a step toward him. "Dr. Slades, please, I flew all the way from Palm Beach last night."

The doctor hesitated. "That's not such a long way. I do it all the time. You're up—and then down before you know it. Not even time for a decent breakfast." He paused, sighing resignedly before motioning Frank to walk in. "Oh, come on in. You may as well."

Frank followed the man down a narrow, dark hallway to the back of the house into a surprisingly cheery kitchen. Frank noticed a woodburning stove in the corner and a kettle boiling on the range.

The doctor switched off the burner and took two china cups and saucers from a cabinet above the kitchen table, setting one down in front of Frank. "If it's coffee you want, I only have instant."

Frank shook his head. "Tea will be fine. Doctor, We need to find your brother."

Gordon Slades's mouth twisted into a grimace. "So I understand. But I really can't help you, Detective.

"Can't or won't, Dr. Slades? You told your neighbor, Mrs. Dolan, that your brother had the loan of your car."

The doctor busied himself with teabags, not responding to the question. Frank let it go for the moment. "Your brother tried to abduct a child, a five-year-old boy, in Boca Raton. Did you know he was going to Florida? Did you try to stop him from violating his parole?"

The doctor pushed one cup toward Frank, who saw the old man's hand was shaking. "I don't know what to tell you, Detective. He stayed here a couple of days. Then he took off. He borrowed a bit of money from me. Said he wanted to lie on a beach for a while. After he was gone I noticed that my car keys, the Cadillac keys, were missing."

"What about the keys to your condo in Pompano? Were those missing, too?"

The doctor shook his head. "I don't bring those here with me. Mrs. Dolan keeps them."

"So, he didn't mention he was going to Florida, and you had no idea where he was going until you noticed the keys were missing?

Another shake of the head.

"How much is a bit of money?"

"Five hundred dollars. That's all I could give him."

Frank got the impression that Gordon Slades had given it willingly and wasn't sorry that his brother had taken off. No big surprise there.

"What happened to the little boy?" Gordon Slades asked suddenly.

"Luckily nothing. The boy's name, by the way, is Jamie Fitzgerald. Does the name mean anything to you?"

"Fitzgerald?" The doctor thought about it for a second. "As in Marcy Fitzgerald? The reporter who forced the parole board to reconsider its decision. Was it her son?"

"Nephew."

Slades blinked.

"You look surprised."

The older man shrugged. "He was angry about that for a while, but he'd had so many setbacks on parole in the past this didn't seem to bother him much more than any of the others."

Frank sipped his tea. "You turned him in, didn't you, Doctor?"

Gordon Slades nodded. For a moment he looked away through the kitchen window where a tall maple tree dominated the backyard. He seemed to be weighing up something in his mind. Finally, he turned back to Frank.

"Yes," he said. "I turned him in. He's my half-brother, by the way. I was eighteen when he was born, a few months after my mother married a man who turned out to be a useless drunk. He turned my mother into a drunk, too. And Bill, well he was allowed to run wild. But I was on my way to college and glad to be out of there. Ten years later I returned to set up my practice in Makerley. My stepfather was dead by then so I took on the responsibility of looking after my mother and Bill while building a practice. Then, when my mother died four years later, it was just Bill and me."

Frank thought he detected a glistening in the doctor's eyes as he continued to stare out of the kitchen window.

"He was as smart as a whip, Bill was. He could have been a doctor like me or a lawyer or anything he wanted, I suppose. But he didn't do any of that. He just stayed here in Makerley."

"Molesting children," Frank interrupted. "And you found out about it?"

Gordon Slades looked away. "Too late, I suppose. It had been going on for years but I was always working all hours, not only here but also in a clinic in Hudson. Then, when they found little Billy Wright dead, well, there was one hell of an uproar. Pictures in the paper, and so on, and I remembered seeing Billy in our house the day before he died. I had to tell the police, Detective. Of course you'd understand that."

"Are you afraid of your brother now?" Frank prodded gently.

Gordon Slades shook his head. "No. But I don't really

want him to come back here. Neither does anyone else in this town."

"That's why you gave him the money, Doctor?"

Slades nodded and got to his feet. "And, believe me, I would have sent him more, if I'd had it." He stared at Frank with a dismal look on his face. "I suppose that's aiding and abetting a parole violation, or something like that, isn't it, Detective?"

Frank waved his hand dismissively as he, too, rose hurriedly. "What do you mean you would have sent it? How could you have sent it if you don't have an address?"

"No, he wanted it wired, but we didn't get as far as addresses, although—" He broke off, and shook his head. "No . . . that's not going to help, either."

"What's not going to help?"

Gordon Slades shook his head. "No, it wouldn't help. He sounded as if he was calling from some kind of diner or bar. There was a lot of noise in the background, glasses or plates. It wasn't a private phone . . . I—"

Frank interrupted. "What wouldn't help, Doctor? Please let me decide."

Gordon Slades stared at Frank, then shrugged. "He called me collect. Both times."

Frank clenched his teeth, ran his fingers through his hair in exasperation, and cautioned himself to count to ten. . . . Then he took a deep breath. "When did he call?"

The doctor seemed to think for a long time before answering. "I would say about a week ago, maybe ten days ago."

"Did you get your phone bill yet, Doctor?"

Slades shook his head. "But if you'll wait a minute, Detective, I'll get you the business office number. I'm sure you'll have no trouble getting your information from them."

A few moments later the two men stood on the front porch and Slades extended his hand to Frank. "Good luck, Detective, and I mean that."

Frank gripped the other man's hand. "I know you do, Doctor. I know how difficult this is for you."

Now that Frank was leaving, the other man seemed reluctant to let him go. He followed Frank down a step from the porch.

"You know, I really don't think they should have let Bill out without getting him some kind of help."

Frank glanced at his watch, but Slades did not seem to notice as he continued. "Although I'm not convinced there is a treatment for his sickness, they didn't even try. Certainly not in Attica . . . not in Wallkill."

Wallkill? The facility where Jeff Haley had cooled his heels! Frank spun around. "Wallkill? Did you say he was in Wallkill?"

The doctor looked startled by Frank's abruptness, but nodded. "Yes. He was transferred from Attica at the beginning of August, about a month before they paroled him. Supposedly for some psychiatric evaluations, but I think they were just moving him around to divert media attention from his release. I'm not really sure, though."

"That's okay," Frank jumped in, his pulse quickening. "I just want to know: Are you absolutely positive your brother served time in Wallkill?"

"Of course I am, Detective." Gordon Slades looked slightly affronted. "That's where I picked him up when he was released—Wallkill."

Frank waited till he was on the highway, heading south back to LaGuardia, before picking up the car phone to call Don. "I think we're onto something," he told his partner, pausing for a beat to steady his voice. "Forget the Morettis for a moment and consider this: Jeff Haley and Bill Slades. They were in Wallkill at the same time last month. It makes a lot of sense to me, Don. Even the cause of Marina's death fits when you think about it. Murder is not Slades's specialty. He's a pedophile, not a killer . . . that would explain a bare-fisted assault. It all fits. Haley hired Slades to kill his mother."

Don was silent on the other end of the line. Then Frank

jumped in again. "Come on, Don. Haley and Slades *happened* to be in the same jail. Slades *happens* to be in Florida when Marina buys the farm. Slades *happens* to attempt the abduction of a boy whose mother pissed off Haley bigtime . . . ?"

"You think Haley was behind the abduction attempts, too?" Frank could hear the incredulity in his partner's voice as Don continued: "I can't see that. Haley hiring a pedophile to snatch a boy he presumably cares for? I heard Kitty on the phone with you the other day, Frank. She trusted him with Jamie's life. She knows Haley better than you do."

"I don't know how he feels about Jamie," Frank responded coldly, thinking about the custody letter Kitty had shown him. "I do know he's got some delusion about Jamie being his son. Maybe he feels they have a special bond. Maybe he sees Jamie as his little twin or something. Both fatherless kids growing up without knowing or seeing the men who fathered them. Maybe he planned on taking Jamie away . . . to have all to himself. God knows what was going on in Haley's mind. But I do know one thing—unless we pick up Slades we ain't ever going to know."

Frank reached into his jacket pocket for the telephone information on the note from Gordon Slades. "Slades made two collect phone calls to his brother in Makerley at the beginning of this month asking him to send money. We need locations on both those numbers, Don, and then I think we've got an identifiable area where Slades may still be hanging out. We can put out the APB on the Cadillac, too."

"Okay," his partner agreed. "Next?"

"Next," Frank took a deep breath. "I want the ident guys to get Slades's fingerprint cards and check his prints against any unidentified prints or partials we lifted from the Haley crime scene. And then see if you can get some explanation from Wallkill as to why Slades's name didn't appear on their list of recently released inmates. It would have saved us a lot of time and aggravation if it had."

"Ah, listen," Don interrupted. "You say Slades called his bro for money. How come? Wouldn't he have been paid off by Haley if there was a deal between them?"

Frank shook his head. "You've got a point . . . perhaps. But like I say we're not going to know anything until we pick up Slades, right, pal?"

"Do you want me to bring in Haley, too?"

Frank considered the question. He didn't believe they would crack Haley without getting Slades first, but maybe they'd get something out of it and it was better for Don to handle Haley on the initial go-around. Frank knew he might not be able to restrain his temper if he was there.

"Why don't you? Just bring him in for a chat. Let's just throw the name at him. See how he reacts, what he knows about Slades and what sort of contact they had." Frank paused, checking the time on the dashboard clock. "I'm racing back to the airport now. Hopefully, there'll be a flight back to West Palm around noon. I'll see you then."

He hung up and glanced out of the window. Fall was arriving in the North. It was the one thing he missed in Florida. The changing seasons and the fall colors: the reds and yellows and browns and golds. Everything was always green in Florida.

Then he turned his attention back to the road and wondered if he should also call Kitty. He felt he ought to give her some clue about the latest development. Maybe to warn her.

But no, he decided. Kitty wasn't in any danger. Haley would be spending the next hour or two at the station house and Kitty had a busy day planned. She was safe enough right now. It would keep for another couple of hours.

Chapter 44

*K*itty shoved aside the hangers in her closet, surveying her outfits one after the other. Her annoyance with Jeff was growing by the minute. She did not want to meet him for lunch today. She had made different plans. She had promised Jamie and Alex to take them for a tennis lesson at the clubhouse. She had no time but Jeff had called early, catching her off guard.

"My attorney said your attorney told him you were going to call me. I understand we can work things out, Kit. I really want to. I've behaved stupidly but I know how we can resolve this quickly."

"Really?"

"Yes. I mean it, Kit. Let's discuss it over lunch. There's no point letting this fester, and I've got permission from my parole officer to take a trip back to New York next week so today would be the best for me."

Kitty had hesitated, remembering her promise to Frank. On the other hand, Jeff sounded eager to resolve matters and if that was so she should take the opportunity. By the time Frank came home they'd have one less problem to handle.

But now she was stuck in her closet, wasting time dithering over outfits. She flung aside a cool lime-green dress with a halter top. The skirt was too short and the top too revealing. Ditto for the next three outfits. She felt pants would be more appropriate for the occasion, but she would swelter in them on the terrace at the tennis club.

Jeff had suggested they meet at his house, which he had put forward as his first preference. More privacy, he'd said. And we won't have waiters butting in every minute.

No way. She'd refused.

Then he'd suggested the Top of the Tower at the Boca Resort and Hotel. She hadn't liked that idea much either. She didn't want a place that smacked of an expensive, romantic date.

She had told him that if he really wanted to meet for lunch, it would have to be somewhere she could bring Alex and Jamie. She didn't want to alter all her plans.

She reached into the recesses of her closet for a white cotton pants outfit that suddenly struck her as perfect. The jacket buttoned to the top and it had military-style gold and navy piping around the collar and cuffs. Frank had once said it made her look too severe. Which made it perfect for the lunch.

She wanted to look cool and businesslike and she wanted to behave in the same way. What she had to guard against was her anger.

But she could already feel it bubbling just under the surface as she walked toward him.

He was seated at the table on the terrace when she arrived at the clubhouse with Jamie and Alex, fifteen minutes late. She watched as they ran happily across the court to their coach, then she walked up the steps to Jeff.

She noted his lilac jacket and the ice bucket holding a bottle of champagne beside the table, and it was all she could do to greet him civilly.

"Sorry I'm a little late."

"No problem," he waved away her apology. "I only just got here myself. I had an unpleasant little piece of business to take care of with the local police." He sighed. "But thankfully it's all sorted out now." He beamed at her and stood to hold her chair as she sat down. Her interest was piqued by his comment, but she reminded herself she was here to discuss only one issue. Anyway, if there had been a major turn in the investigation she would have heard from Frank.

She waited as he turned to the waiter, who was already hovering. "Please, pour the champagne."

"No. No thank you," she cut in as the waiter approached her. "I'll stick to Perrier." She glanced at Jeff. "I'm sorry I can't start with champagne this early. I've got a million errands to run this afternoon." Then she took a deep breath. "I'm glad you realize you behaved stupidly," she weighed in without any preamble. "Jeff, you must know you couldn't possibly win. For heavens' sake, the whole thing is a farce. You and I both know it's all a lie. I never led you to believe you were Jamie's father. You know that."

He waited till she'd finished, then he shook his head. "It's not all a lie, Kitty."

"Oh damn it! Listen, I'm not wired. I haven't got a tape recorder hidden in my purse." She threw her pocketbook on the table. "Go on, take a look. You don't have to keep up the pretense with me. We both know very well that I told you I was three months pregnant the first time we ever had dinner together."

"Wait." He held up his left hand. "Let's just take care of things one at a time. Let's decide what we're going to eat. I'm starving, aren't you?"

Kitty stared across the terrace at the boys on the court. It was difficult for them to place the balls across the net, and she thought they were still too young for lessons. But they had pleaded so hard.

Jeff took his time reading the menu; Kitty didn't even

bother picking up hers. She knew the staple items. But she wasn't even interested in eating.

"Jeff."

He looked up at her. "Please Kit, indulge me. You have no idea what it means to have the freedom to actually pick what you want to eat."

Jeff stared undistracted at his menu for a moment longer, then laid it aside as their water appeared. "Kitty?"

"The house salad will be fine," she mumbled.

"Anything else, ma'am?"

Kitty shook her head.

Jeff leaned back in his chair. "I'll start with the clam chowder, and I'd like the Caesar salad, and then I'll have the grilled red snapper with a baked potato."

He turned his attention back to Kitty as soon as the waiter walked away. "You were saying, Kit?"

She sighed. "I said you can't win."

He nodded somberly. "I know, I can't. I can't win, Kitty, because you'll despise me if I go ahead with this, and that's not what I want."

Hallelujah, now we're getting somewhere, she thought, but in the next moment her hopes were dashed again.

"Do you think it would give me any satisfaction to get a court to award me visitation rights, knowing that you were hating me, maybe even wishing me dead, every moment that I spent with Jamie?"

She laughed. "Getting visitation rights to Jamie is a fantasy, Jeff." She pushed aside her water glass and leaned across the table, tapping her finger on the tablecloth to emphasize her points. "Fact: You are not Jamie's biological father. Fact: I did not lead you to believe that you were. Ever."

Jeff shook his head. "Biology doesn't make fathers. The truth is, Kitty, I've been more of a father to Jamie than his real father. Think about it."

Kitty stared at him calmly, not answering as the waiter reappeared with Jeff's clam chowder.

Jeff tasted the chowder, and they sat in silence for a few

moments. Then he pushed his bowl aside before continuing. "But I realize that, in all of this, Jamie's the one who will be hurt the most. Do you think it didn't occur to me what the headlines will say: 'TV Reporter in Custody Battle with Talk Show Host's Ex-Con Son'?" He punched the air with his fingers, emphasizing each word.

"Don't you think I had second thoughts after my attorney sent the letter? Even the existence of that letter could be leaked to the press. You know how lawyers' offices are. It was dumb of me to do that. I realize that now."

Kitty sat back in her chair, her eyes narrowing, as she tried to decipher the message Jeff was sending her. Was he being sincere? Or was he, in effect, threatening her? Jeff knew which of her buttons to push.

Her anger surged again. No. She wasn't going to allow him to get to her that way. She refilled her glass from the bottle on the table. "Okay, Jeff," she said finally. "You're going to have to decide what to do for the best but let me make a couple of things clear to you. I can live with the headlines. I'll be the flavor of the month for a while but the media will lose interest eventually and when everything comes out you're the one who will look foolish." She broke off as their waiter arrived with the entrees, and she was gratified that Jeff made no move to touch his red snapper.

"What's more, Jeff, by the time this gets anywhere near a court, Frank and I will be married. You talk about being more of a father to Jamie than his real father. Well, consider this: You were around for about a month after Jamie was born and last week you spent four days with him. That's it. You have no relationship with him. No bond. Frank has spent the last two years around Jamie. Jamie thinks of Frank as his dad. Frank is the only dad he's ever known and Frank is going to adopt him as soon as we are married. There's nothing you can do to stop any of that. But if you want to take us on, give it your best shot."

Jeff's face had hardened. She saw the clenched jaw and the way he was staring at her through narrowed slits. She thought that maybe she'd gone too far . . . when suddenly he reached across the table and covered her hand with his.

"Let's stop this right now, Kitty. This is not what I intended."

"Really? What did you intend? That I would roll over? That I wouldn't put up a fight?" She drew back her hand.

"No! Like I told you, I regret going to my attorney and asking him to send the letter. But when I thought of all the things I've done for you and all the times I've been there for you . . . okay, maybe you didn't ask for them. But when it's suited you, you've taken my help and support. All I've ever done is been good to you, but you're unfair. You have this knack of turning around and kicking me in the teeth. Think back, Kitty. I've always been there when you most needed someone, but I'm not good enough to have around all the time, and that hurts. This was the only way I could think to make you sit up and realize what part I've played in your life and Jamie's. I cared for both of you so much and for once I decided to fight back for something I thought was worth it. Why does it make you so angry that I want to be your friend?"

Jeff lapsed into a silence, and to her horror Kitty thought she saw his eyes welling up.

"Jeff . . . your lunch is getting cold."

He pushed his plate farther away across the table. "I've lost my appetite, Kitty. You're right I am foolish—and I'm pathetic."

Kitty's throat tightened. She thought how right Tillie had been with her take on the situation. She also realized that what Jeff had said was partly true.

"No, you're not pathetic Jeff. And you have been a good friend. It's just that . . ."

"What?"

She sighed. "I guess what scares me a little is that you always try to take over. You like to take charge. You push too hard. You won't listen to what I have to say. I tried to tell you at the house as gently as possible that I had other plans and you accuse me of putting Jamie in danger."

She thought his face flushed. "I know, and I'm sorry about that. That was crass and dumb of me." She saw his mouth twitch into a smile. "As for taking charge, it's a fault, I admit. I know I'm pushy but that comes from years of working with Marina. It was the only way to get through to her and get things done." He shrugged. "I don't want to lose a friend, Kitty, especially not at this time."

Kitty nodded and looked out across the terrace to the courts, realizing that the boys' lesson was coming to an end. She took a sip of Perrier and got to her feet. "Let me go and get the boys, Jeff."

She crossed the terrace and stepped down to the path leading around the courts, hoping that her steps looked steadier than they felt.

She walked down the path to the court and pressed her face against the wire fence. "That was great, boys," she called out. "You're really getting good."

"Mom, can we practice a while longer?"

She looked at her watch and back toward the terrace. Had she and Jeff resolved the issue? Was he going to back off now? She wanted some sort of assurance from him that he would drop the whole matter. But what did he want from her?

"Mom! Can we stay longer?"

She nodded, noticing that Jeff was walking down the terrace steps to the path.

He came up behind her. "Can't get them off the court, eh? They have no sense of urgency, do they?"

"No," Kitty agreed checking her watch again. "And I'm running out of time."

There was a moment's silence between them, and then she felt Jeff's hand on her arm. "Kitty, I apologize. I would never hurt you, you know that. It's just that things aren't easy for me right now. I'm trying to work out my future and it's difficult without having another soul to share things with . . . that's all." He broke off, pacing a little way down the path and then back again.

"I'm really trying, you know." Jeff picked up the conversation again as if there'd been no pause. "I had an interior decorator in to look at the house. She made a lot of good suggestions and I had some contractors come in to do some work in the master bedroom. And I went shopping on Worth Avenue, and it's a lot of fun being able to say: 'Oh yes I'll have that and I'll have this and charge it.' I know I'm going to get it together one of these days, Kitty."

She nodded. "Yes you are, Jeff. You just need to give yourself time to adjust."

"I know, and I realize it's stupid of me to be burning bridges with the few friends I have left. I'd like to think there'll come a day when I can pick up the phone and call you and suggest we have lunch or even dinner and—"

"Jeff," she interrupted. "I'd have no problem with that."

He beamed at her words and she turned to wave Jamie and Alex off the court. "Come on, guys, we've got to move now."

"I'm glad we've straightened it out," Jeff was saying. "I was afraid I'd screwed everything up."

"Hi, Jeff!" Two little voices chanted in unison behind her as Jamie and Alex flopped down on the grass verge by the pathway. "Mom! We're really, really thirsty."

"Okay," she smiled. "We'll be home in a couple of minutes." She turned to Jeff. "I'm going to have to get going."

He nodded. "I'll tell you what I'll do, Kitty. I'm going to get all your letters back from my attorney and I'll return them all to you and I'll have him draw up some sort of affadavit saying I'm withdrawing all my claims. I know that'll make you feel better."

"Mom!"

Kitty waved her hand at Jamie, motioning for him to pipe down. "I'd appreciate that, Jeff." She smiled at him, wanting to push a little more to pin him down on a time and date—and the sooner the better—but she didn't want to appear overly anxious.

As if reading her thoughts, however, Jeff added, "I'll have that ready for you tomorrow, if you want to take a drive to Palm Beach. Then we'll have everything squared away. You could even take a peek at some of the renovations."

"That would be great," Kitty replied. If Frank was back they'd probably grab some brunch in Palm Beach, anyway. She glanced at her watch again and realized by now she was running really late.

"Why don't I call you first thing in the morning, Jeff. I'll probably be in town for brunch or something anyway." She looked around and realized that Jamie and Alex were wandering away, down the path toward the clubhouse. She called them back.

"Jeff, I'm going to have to run. I've got to get to the dry cleaners and pick up some things at the supermarket . . . and I've got to stop to get these fellas a soda at the house. They're going to drive me crazy!"

Jeff laughed. "Calm down, Kit. It's their weekend, too, you know. Look, do you want me to drive them back to the house for the sodas? Then you can run your errands without them dragging around with you."

"Oh . . ." She hesitated.

Jeff grinned at her. "Don't worry, I won't accuse you of using me."

Oh God! Let's not go back to all that again, she thought. "Okay," she nodded quickly. "I won't be very long anyway. Sharon's away for the weekend but Jamie has a key in the pocket of his racquet cover."

She hurried to tell the boys as they ambled back.

"Hey great!" Jamie let out a squeal. "Now we can drive with the roof down. Hey Jeff! Can we? Can you take the roof down?"

For a couple of moments she watched them jumping around, throwing their racquets in the air with Jeff in the middle, ducking his head and laughing. Then she hurried across the grass to her car.

❧ *Chapter 45* ❧

*D*on was waiting for Frank at the end of the jetway.

"Hey, thanks pal." He grinned at his partner. "I wasn't expecting a welcome committee."

Don shrugged, grinning back. "We got a place to go."

"Yeah?" Frank hitched his garment bag over his shoulder and followed Don through the airport. "Good news?"

"Good—and better."

"Give me the good first."

"We've got a lead on Slades. I traced the two phone numbers to two different bars in Delray. They're about a block apart, and I put out the APB on the Caddy for the South County area as soon as I hung up with you. About an hour ago Delray Beach police called it in. They found it in the parking lot of an apartment complex."

"And Slades was in it?"

"He wasn't. But we're working the area. It's likely Slades is holed up around there somewhere."

"I trust that's where we're heading now?"

Don nodded.

"So, what's the better news?"

"Haley and Slades."

Frank glanced across at Don at the wheel but his partner
kept his eyes on the road ahead, pulling out of the airport
exit onto the feeder road.

"You brought Haley in?"

"Yep, and he arrived with his attorney. Old Gates. I
threw the name at him. Said—" Don broke off. "Oh, let
me back it up a little. First I called. Wallkill to find out
what the deal was with Slades. Why his name wasn't on
the printout they sent us. They said he wasn't an official
inmate or some such bullshit. Apparently they had him
there only for about a month, supposedly for some evalu-
ation."

"Yeah, yeah," Frank interrupted. "I got all that from the
brother."

"Anyway, they claim he wasn't in contact with any of
the inmates. They kept him in an isolation unit in the infirmary."

Frank leaned back in his seat, disappointed. "So Haley
had no recall of Slades?"

But Don laughed out suddenly. "As a matter of fact
that's where it gets interesting. I threw the name at Haley
and his attorney, and at first Haley said he had no recall of
any such name.

"Then I mentioned that we were checking through a list
of recently released inmates just in case one of them had
taken a dislike to Haley, so on and so on, and I pointed out
that Slades's name had popped out in the process and that
we had information leading us to believe that Slades was
in this area." Don paused again. "I've got this on videotape, by the way. You might be interested in seeing the reaction."

Frank sat up in his seat. "What was it?"

"Well, at this point Haley shakes his head, scratches his
head, and then says something like maybe Slades was the
nutcase who was in the infirmary with him. Said there was

a wacko in with him and that he'd had to punch him out. But he couldn't recall why. Said he was in there with severe stomach cramps several weeks before his release. He was in severe pain and this guy was bugging him."

"And you hadn't said anything about Slades being confined to the infirmary?"

Don shook his head. "Not a word. But listen, it gets even better because then he turns to Gates and asks him for 'the note.' "

"The note?"

Don took one hand off the wheel and reached inside his jacket pocket. "This note." He handed it to his partner.

Frank opened the sheet of plain paper that was folded in half and stared at the crudely printed letters: I'M GOING TO GET YOU AND YOURS, COCKSUCKER.

" 'I'm going to get you and yours, cocksucker'?" Frank repeated the sentence. "What's this supposed to mean?"

Don's grin widened. "His attorney then tells me that Mr. Haley brought the note in to him about a week ago when he came into the offices to draw up his will."

"The one where he made Jamie Fitzgerald his sole beneficiary," Frank interrupted. "And?"

"Gates then says that Mr. Haley is worried because the police investigation isn't going anywhere and he's worried now for his own safety because of this note he got while he was inside."

"A note he never bothered telling us about?" Frank interrupted again, not attempting to disguise the scorn in his voice.

"That's what I said. So then Haley explains that he 'forgot about it' when we fingered the Morettis. But it was 'rattling around' in the back of his mind."

Frank shook his head, grinning. "When did he get this note?"

"He says he found it in the folds of his towel when he came out of the shower in the infirmary."

"That prick's got it all figured out, hasn't he?" Frank leaned back in his car seat. "We start asking pointed questions so he figures Slades might be picked up any moment. And, he thinks ahead, right? Figures if we pick up Slades and the molester sings, how's he going to distance himself? You think we've got it right?"

"I think so," Don said quietly. "I think you've been right on the money all along, pal. The only problem is we do need Slades. Otherwise we're going to watch Haley walk, free, the way I did this morning after he handed me the bullshit."

"We'll get him," Frank said quietly, as his partner exited the interstate at one of the Delray exits.

The Cadillac had been spotted in the parking lot of a seedy apartment complex off Federal and Don pointed out the car to Frank as they turned off the main highway. "We got lucky, Frank. It was a quiet afternoon in Delray. And I got Boca to send mugshots of Slades. Delray PD is helping us canvass the area."

Frank glanced across at the apartment complex noting the peeling beige paint and the cheap doors. The two-story building was arranged courtyard style around the obligatory swimming pool. A lone palm with brownish-gray fronds drooped in the corner of the yard. No doubt management conserved water by turning off the sprinkler system in a dump like this, thought Frank.

"He's not a tenant. We checked with the manager but it's a transient sort of place. Tenants come and go, and sublet their apartments to whomever."

Frank nodded. It would be too easy if Slades were here, he thought wryly. "It might be a good idea though to get some of these patrol cars out of sight. And I'd like to check out the two bars where Slades made the calls. Maybe someone will remember him, maybe they talked to him. He's obviously hung out in this area for a while."

Frank picked up the phone to call Kitty. He could see a long night ahead in Delray and no way would he make the party at Angela's. He was in the middle of leaving a message on her answering machine when a tap on the window

from a patrol officer in uniform interrupted him. Frank
hung up and rolled down the window.

"Sir, we may have something. There's a motel a couple
of blocks down. The manager there says he recognizes our
man. Says he checked in a night or two back—with his
son."

Frank's pulse quickened as he motioned for the officer
to jump in.

The motel stood off the street and down a side alley.
Just one row of about a dozen separate rooms. The last
room at the far end was the office. The manager, a small
fat man wearing a gray-looking undershirt and puffing on
a Camel, nodded when Frank asked him to identify Slades
from his mugshot.

"It looks like him. Is there going to be trouble?"

"Not if you help us. You said he checked in with his
son?"

"Yeah, young boy. Maybe twelve, thirteen."

"When did you last see them?"

"This morning. The boy came in here to ask for some
ice. Said his dad had a hangover."

"The boy came in alone?"

"Yeah. I just said, didn't I? Then he wanted to know if
there was a 7-Eleven or anything like it around here. Said
he had to get cigarettes, too."

"When did you last see the father?" Frank emphasized
father with sarcasm in his voice but it was lost on the
manager.

"When they left a while later. About an hour or two
ago. I saw them cut through that parking lot next door . . .
walking, that way, towards the marina."

"Okay, now listen." Frank leaned over the counter so
that he was face-to-face with the manager. "I want you to
take us to his room. You're going to let us in and if you
see him before we do you're not going to let him in on the
secret. Understood? That way things can stay nice and
quiet around here. Just in case, I'm going to have an un-

marked car with two officers parked right across from
your window here."

The man nodded. "Okay, okay. I don't want any trouble.
I've never had any trouble here. This is a quiet little
place." He turned to reach for a set of keys off the back-
board and then shuffled his way down the concrete
walkway to the room at the other end.

"This is it." He opened the door.

Frank took a step inside. The darkened room stank of
stale smoke.

He glanced at the double bed, dresser, and chair that
filled most of the room. Through a doorway he saw a
shower stall and a pair of shorts lying on the linoleum
floor. More dirty clothing lay in a heap by the dresser, on
which he saw a stack of about a half-dozen photographs.

They were Polaroids. He picked them up, flipped
through them, his lips tightening as he studied each of the
photos in turn. A dark-haired boy appeared in all of them
in progressively more pornographic poses. "Scumbag!" He
spat the word out. "When we get him stop me from beating him to a pulp, okay, pal?"

He passed the Polaroids to Don except for one of the
boy, sitting up on the bed, grinning, blowing out a smoke
ring. This one he showed to the motel manager. "This is
the son?"

"Yep. That's him. Sam. That's his name."

"Okay," Frank nudged him toward the door. "You can
go now."

He closed the door behind the man and retrieved the rest
of the photos from Don. "Filthy scumbag pervert! Look at
this."

"I saw." Don shook his head. "But the boy looks like
he's a willing victim. Maybe Slades paid him."

"We'll see," Frank replied grimly. "It looks like they'll
be back. So we'll be able to ask Sam ourselves." He paced
across the room, picked up the chair, and positioned it by
the window where the drapes fell away, leaving a narrow

gap. He sat down. "Okay, partner, make yourself comfortable."

"Yeah right." Don laughed, glancing across at the unmade bed. Then he moved to the dresser where he perched on the edge. "Next hour I take the chair."

"Sure thing." Frank nodded. "I owe you, pal."

❧ *Chapter 46* ❧

*J*eff had left a note for her—taped to the door leading from the garage into the house. Kitty saw it as soon as she pulled in, just before five o'clock. Jumping out of the Chevy she ran to read the brief message, just as the phone rang out inside the house. She hurried down the hallway, grabbing it before her answering machine kicked on.

"Kitty! I called about fifteen minutes ago and spoke to Jeff." Angela's voice echoed on the line.

"Yes. I just got home and found his note. It says you suggested he drive the boys over?" Kitty took a deep breath to steady the racing of her heart. Then she laughed. "Jeez, when I didn't see Jeff's car outside and then I pulled in and saw the note taped to the door, I thought one of the boys had had an accident or something."

"Sorry, Kitty. But I was all done with the preparations here, and it sounded like the boys were getting a bit antsy. I was just wondering if they'd already left because I wanted to make sure Alex brought his tennis racquet home."

"Oh, okay." Kitty glanced around the kitchen and family room. "I don't see it lying around here. But they should be at your place any minute. If Alex hasn't got it with him call me back."

"I will. He needs it for tomorrow. Bob said he'd take him out on the courts. Anyway, I'll see you in a while."

Kitty hung up, then retraced her steps to the Chevy for her shopping bags, thinking that at least she'd be able to shower in peace now and get dressed without the boys jumping around urging her to hurry. She knew they were excited about the party, so it was just as well they were already on their way.

Before heading for the shower she checked her phone messages to find one from Frank. It was brief. He was back in Palm Beach but something had come up and he wasn't sure he'd make the party. The next one was Angela's, interrupted by Jeff picking up the phone.

She cleared the machine and headed for the shower. She paused. . . . What the hell, she had time to herself. She could run the Jacuzzi and relax a little. She'd been running around all day and it wasn't as if she had to be at the party the minute it started.

She filled the tub and poured a generous dollop of bath oil into the water before sliding into it and turning on the jets. Lying back, relaxing in the soft foam, she wondered how Frank had made out in New York. She wondered if he would have time tomorrow for brunch. He would be relieved she'd handled Jeff. She made a mental note to call Tillie, first thing Monday, to thank her for the excellent advice.

The phone was ringing again when she stepped out of the bathroom shower. Wrapping a towel around herself she ran into her bedroom, noticing that it was almost six o'clock. No doubt Angela was about to get on her case.

"Okay, okay, Ange." She laughed into the receiver. "I'm on my way. I just took advantage of—"

"Kitty, the boys haven't arrived," Angela cut in abruptly.

"What?" Kitty double checked the time. Jeff and the boys had left more than an hour ago to make the fifteen-minute drive.

"He can't be lost, can he?" Angela sounded uncertain.

"No!" Kitty felt a surge of annoyance. "He dropped Alex off the afternoon he took the boys to Discovery Zone, remember?"

"Yes." Angela sounded concerned.

"Well, let me get off the phone and try to find him. I hope he didn't decide to stop somewhere with them. I'll try his car phone."

She dialed it. There was no reply. Then she dialed his number at the house. No reply there, either. Of course not. And he was not in the car. So he must have stopped somewhere with the boys.

She waited a couple of minutes, willing the phone to ring, willing it to be Angela telling her the boys had finally arrived. And as she waited she tried to quell the horrid niggling little thought that something had gone wrong. She tried not to think about Slades. She tried not to think about the run-in Jeff had described to her in the parking lot. No. She pushed the thought out of her mind. It could not be. The creep would not try anything with two boys in the car, surely. Not on Palmetto Park Road. It was too wide and busy.

She redialed the car phone again. And then the house. And then tried each of the numbers again, flinging down the receiver when there was no reply. Almost instantly, she grabbed the receiver and started dialing again.

Her thoughts were beginning to run wild when suddenly she heard Jeff's voice. She had redialed both numbers so many times she had lost track of where she was calling, and her relief at hearing Jeff's voice exploded into a barely controlled anger. "Where the hell are you, Jeff? Angela's waiting for the boys."

There was an ominous silence at the end of the line. "Kitty, I'm home. That's the number you just called, didn't you? And the boys are at Angela's."

"Jeff, they're not!" Her voice rose a pitch.

For a second she wondered if maybe Angela had had one preparty cocktail too many.

"Jeff, did you speak to Angela when you dropped them off? Was she in the apartment or at the pool?"

She heard Jeff clear his throat. "Kitty, don't panic. I didn't see Angela. The thing is, I dropped them off in front of the building and I watched them walk inside."

"You didn't take them up to the apartment?" Kitty felt as if an icy hand had swept across her face. "I don't understand. You let two five-year-olds go into a high-rise alone to get to the fifteenth floor!" She clutched the phone tightly. "Oh my God, how could you?

"Now just a second, Kitty!" She could tell he was rattled now too. "It's a doorman building. The guy was right there. And they promised they would tell him to buzz up to Angela and let her know they were on the way up. I watched them walk across the lobby."

"How did you expect them to know when they got to the fifteenth floor? They could have gotten off anywhere. They could be wandering around on any of the floors. Oh Jeff! That's such a dumb, idiotic thing to do."

"Yeah, okay, Kitty." Jeff's voice was very low. "You've made your point and I'm sorry but Alex told me he'd been up in the elevator, from the pool, hundreds of times by himself. And they begged me to let them go it alone."

Yeah, thought Kitty, and you wanted to be Mr. Nice Guy. "I just don't understand, Jeff. You were so careful with Jamie the other week."

"Come on, Kitty, it's not like anyone could skulk in that lobby. I saw the doorman there. Listen," he added, "I'm leaving right now. I'll be right there to help you look for them."

"Oh don't bother," she snapped, not attempting to hide the disgust in her voice. "You've done enough for one day." She hung up by throwing the receiver onto the hook and immediately picked up the phone to dial Angela's number, hoping that Angela would tell her the boys had already found their way back to the apartment.

But she did not, and Kitty had to tell her what Jeff had done. "I just don't know why he did that, Ange. You know how careful he was with Jamie all last week. Like a shadow."

"Of course, and I wouldn't have asked him to drive them over if I didn't know that. Calm down, Kitty," Angela's voice was more reassuring than Kitty had expected it would be, but then Angela sounded as if she had had a couple gins since their last conversation. "If he saw them walk through the doors, then they're in the building somewhere."

"I'll be right there," Kitty interrupted. "But I'm calling the police first. We're going to need help searching the entire building."

Chapter 47

It was dusk, and Frank's turn again to sit in the chair, when Bill Slades came strolling along the walkway past the window. Frank caught a glimpse of a second pair of skinny legs and held up two fingers, signaling Don even as they heard the door key being inserted into the lock.

Both detectives moved like lightning into the bathroom and waited for Slades to walk in and close the door behind him.

The light in the room snapped on. Frank and Don moved together through the bathroom doorway.

"Bill Slades?"

Frank stared at the big man across the room. Next to him stood the boy, Sam. A skinny, gawky kid with a shock of black hair. It took Slades a second or two to take in the scene. "Who wants to know?"

Frank reached for his badge and flipped open the wallet. "Palm Beach Police, Slades." Then he looked at the boy. "Are you Sam? Move over here, Sam. Come on." Frank beckoned to the kid who seemed to have frozen in the spot.

The boy looked uncertain. He looked at Frank, then at Bill Slades. In that one moment of hesitation Slades suddenly grabbed at the boy, twisting his arm up behind his back till the boy shrieked.

"Tell 'em, Sam. We've done nothing wrong."

The boy shook his head. "That's right." His face had turned pale under the natural sunbronzed color of his skin.

"Don't come any closer," Slades stared defiantly at Frank and his partner. "If you make one move toward me, I'll break his arm." To emphasize the point he twisted the boy's arm again, provoking another shriek of pain from Sam.

Frank didn't move and made no move to reach for his revolver. He wasn't going to brandish any sort of weapon with the kid caught in the middle. He sized up Slades: Six feet tall and about 190 pounds. He wore black shorts and a dark green T-shirt that exposed his thick, muscular arms. Frank figured it would be pretty much an even fight if he tackled Slades, but he didn't want the boy in the middle.

"You may as well let the kid loose, Slades. You've got nowhere to go."

Slades grunted and moved back a step. Frank saw beads of perspiration running down the sides of the big man's face. "Come on, give it up, Slades."

Bill Slades seemed to consider the idea, but then he reached behind to flip open the door, backing out of it and pulling the boy with him. "Stay where you are, the two of you."

Frank moved forward a pace between the bed and dresser. He saw Slades backing in between two cars parked by the walkway. He saw tears of pain welling up in Sam's eyes as Slades forced him to move by yanking on his twisted limb.

Out of the corner of his eye Frank saw the blur of movement across the parking lot where the unmarked car stood. He hoped the officers had their revolvers drawn.

"You break the boy's arm, Slades, and one of those officers behind you is going to blow your head off."

Frank kept moving toward the man and boy.

Suddenly Slades sent the boy sprawling into Frank, then turned, ducking between the cars, and ran for the street.

Frank leaped over the boy. With adrenalin spurring him on, he covered most of the distance between them in seconds until there was just a gap of less than three feet. Frank propelled himself in a tackle that brought Slades crashing to the sidewalk. He felt a knee catch him in the pit of the stomach just a second before gripping Slades's sweaty head in both hands and banging it down into the ground.

Winded and breathing heavily as the two patrol officers and Don surrounded them he looked up at Don. "Cuff him, and read him his rights."

"What are you arresting me for?" Slades screamed, holding his head as three pairs of hands pulled him roughly to his feet.

"Parole violation . . . attempted abduction . . ."

"Hey, the kid told me he was sixteen."

Frank's words came in short, painful gasps. "Attempted abduction of Jamie Fitzgerald, abduction of Timothy Myers."

Don helped him to his feet. As Frank brushed down his jacket, he added, "And resisting arrest. Get him in the car, guys."

Frank took another deep breath and glanced around the parking lot. It was deserted. "Where's the boy?" he asked Don, as they walked back across the asphalt to the open doorway of the motel room.

Don shook his head. "He took off when you went after Slades. I got the patrol officers to radio his description to the other units on standby. He won't get very far."

Frank nodded, sad for the boy. Sam had looked neglected and unkempt. It took him back to Philadelphia and the sight of kids hanging out on street corners in bad neighborhoods, running drugs for the dealers. It was a sight he'd long ago pushed out of his mind. He swore under his breath, cursing the parents who had allowed Sam to roam the streets where perverts like Slades lurked and waited. Then he turned abruptly on his heels and followed Don back to the car.

Chapter 48

*A*ngela, dressed for the party in a long flowing floral skirt and skimpy white silk halter top, was in conversation with a police sergeant when Kitty arrived at the apartment tower less than a half-hour after hanging up with her friend. Three police patrol cars were parked in the driveway, and Kitty could see four uniformed officers in the lobby.

She introduced herself to the sergeant.

"You're the one who called us, ma'am?"

She nodded. "I think we need help, sergeant. They're only five years old and they could be anywhere. All the floors here look the same." She checked her watch. It was coming up to seven o'clock. "They've been missing for almost two hours."

"You told us your friend dropped them off, and he saw them walk into the building?"

"Yes, yes," Kitty nodded. "But that doesn't mean they couldn't have wandered outside again." She paused. "They could have decided to run out to the beach. God knows what goes through their minds, you know. It's going to get dark soon."

The sergeant was kind to her, placing his hand gently on her arm. "Miss Fitzgerald, please stay calm. We know this building and I'm going to have my men search through the outside area first, just on the off chance that they did go running outside. We'll search along the beach and the cabana area around the pool. We've asked for a master key to the cabanas in case the boys got inside one and can't get out, okay?"

He turned to Angela. "You said you're holding a pool party here?"

Her face flushed, Angela nodded, but Kitty thought she sounded coherent enough when she added, "Yes, it's about ready to start. It's not my party. It's for the whole building or at least the residents who are already here. We have one every year at the start of the season."

Even as she spoke an elevator opened and two couples walked off, heading toward the pool area. They glanced curiously at the police milling around but didn't stop.

The police sergeant nodded. "I'm going to make a loud-speaker announcement when more of them get down here. I want them all to go back and check their apartments in case the boys wandered into one by mistake. Then they can help us search the building."

Kitty nodded, feeling a little more reassured. He seemed to know what he was doing.

"We'll check out the stairwells and the basement area and I've asked the doorman to prepare a list of all the apartments that are unoccupied. We're going to have to do an apartment-by-apartment search if they don't turn up in the main areas. What I'm saying is, it may take a while, and it's not going to help anyone, least of all your-selves, if you get overanxious, okay?"

Kitty nodded again. "Can we start now, Sergeant?"

He nodded. "But is there someone in your apartment, Mrs. Baines? In case they turn up."

"My husband is waiting up there," Angela reassured

him. "But I'll ask one of my neighbors to do it. I know Bob wants to get on with a search."

"Very well then, let's start outside. But first, Miss Fitzgerald, give me the name and address of the friend who dropped them off. I'll have an officer run over to get the exact time and details and the exact location where the boys were last seen. Maybe they said something that will give us a clue where they went. You just never know."

Kitty took a notebook out of her tote and ripped out a page to scribble Jeff's name and address on it, together with directions of how to get there. She handed the paper to the sergeant.

"He lives in Palm Beach," she added unnecessarily.

"That's okay. I want to cover all the bases."

She followed Angela and the sergeant back into the building. One of the uniformed officers approached him. "We've spoken to the doorman, Sarge. He says he didn't see the boys come in."

"He didn't?" The sergeant's eyes narrowed. Then he looked over to the reception desk.

"But he says they could have slipped by without him noticing. He says he's not usually looking out for little people."

The sergeant nodded and Kitty looked across in the same direction. The reception desk was about five-feet high. If Jamie and Alex had sneaked in, she told herself, they could have rounded the corner to the elevator banks without being seen.

"Sergeant, maybe Mrs. Baines and I could start on the beach. We'll check around the chaises. They could be hiding in one of those."

The sergeant hesitated for a second, then nodded. "Okay, we'll start with the stairwells and then go floor to floor while the doorman alerts the apartments which have tenants in residence."

Kitty gave the doorman another glance, then followed Angela out of the lobby's back exit into the pool area. About a half-dozen of the Tower residents were standing with drinks already in their hands as the piped music wafted out of the loudspeaker system. Long tables had been set up with bowls of punch, appetizers, and Sterno serving dishes. She knew that Angela, who had been on the organizing committee this year, had worked hard and had been looking forward to the evening, and she was sorry that it was now ruined.

Determinedly, she took the lead running down the wooden steps to the sand. "Jamie! Alex! Can you hear us?"

She stopped at the bottom of the steps, staring for a moment out at the ocean. The waves were whitecapped and angry, crashing into the shore. Kitty shuddered.

"Angela, do you think there's any chance . . ." She didn't have to complete the sentence. Angela put her arm around Kitty's shoulders. "I don't think so, hon. You know they've both been told to stay away from the water if we're not with them."

"Yeah," Kitty laughed sharply. "They've been told . . . but . . ."

"Anyway," Angela suddenly brightened. "I was out on the terrace when I was waiting for them. And Babs Mott was down here, helping to set up. She would have seen them go down to the beach. Come on, let's check out the chaises. If they're hiding in one of those I'm going to skin both of them alive."

A half-hour later Kitty agreed with Angela that the boys were not on the beach. They had checked out the area and all the chaises that still had their awnings up. Then they had walked all the way to where the beach stopped on the south side of the Boca Inlet, Kitty cursing Jeff silently as they walked.

Returning to the apartment tower, Kitty saw the sergeant walking toward them.

"Miss Fitzgerald," he looked serious, solemn, and Kitty felt her knees buckle. "Can I have a word in private?"

"What is it?" Angela cried out, the anguish in her voice apparent now. "Tell us, Sergeant! Now."

He shook his head quickly. "No, take it easy, Mrs. Baines, we haven't found anything yet. I just want to talk to Miss Fitzgerald about Mr. Haley."

Kitty, with Angela in tow, followed him uncertainly across the pool area until they were back inside the lobby. The sergeant beckoned her to a couch by the elevators and then summoned a uniformed officer from across the lobby. "Officer Palmer's the one who went to speak to Mr. Haley."

"Yes?" Kitty looked at him, puzzled.

The sergeant continued. "Mr. Haley told us that he let the boys go up by themselves after they promised to tell the doorman to buzz up to Mrs. Baines to alert her on the intercom. He says he saw them stop in the lobby, although he couldn't see the reception desk from where he was parked.

"Now, let me ask you, since Mrs. Baines says she didn't get any such call and the doorman says he didn't see the boys: Is it possible that they could have forgotten or just ignored what they were told to do and run through to the elevators?"

"Of course it's possible," Kitty burst out. "They're five-year-olds, Sergeant. But generally they . . . both of them . . . do as they're told, especially if they made a promise."

"Well, is it possible that Mr. Haley isn't being totally truthful about this?"

Kitty shrugged. "I guess. Maybe he didn't ask them to speak to the doorman. Maybe he just thought of that when I called him to say they were missing. It was a pretty stupid thing for him to do, after all."

"Okay." The sergeant nodded. "Let me ask you one more question: Can you think of any reason for Mr. Haley to take them somewhere else?"

"No. Like where?" Kitty stared blankly at the police sergeant.

The sergeant shrugged. "Well, let's keep looking. We've still a few areas to check."

He turned his attention back to a couple of patrol officers who'd entered the building, leaving Kitty to sink down on the couch in the center of the lobby, her thoughts suddenly running amok while an iron fist seemed to grip and squeeze her heart.

Can you think of any reason for Mr. Haley to take them somewhere else?

"No," she'd said. But now . . . She blinked and stared at Angela.

"What's the matter?" The other woman was staring back at her.

"Maybe Jeff did take them someplace," Kitty said softly.

"Like where? Wouldn't he tell us? Wouldn't he call? I thought you said he was—"

"That was back then," Kitty snapped. "I had a big bust-up with him, Ange. Then today we seemed to sort everything out, but . . ."

"What? But what?"

Kitty shook her head. This was not the time to go into detailed explanations for Angela. Not now when all she could remember was the way she'd tapped on the table at lunch, hammering her points home—pushing Frank into Jeff's face at every turn.

She put her arm around her friend. "Listen Ange, I'm going to drive to Jeff's. This could be another silly game he's playing." She hesitated. Silly wasn't the right word, but she didn't want to alarm Angela. "What I mean is . . . if he has them they're not in any serious danger. Trust me on that. He's just putting *me* through the wringer."

"What do I tell the cops?"

"Don't say a word to them. Just carry on searching here. You never know, I may be totally off-base."

"Yes," Angela nodded. "They could very well just be hiding, laughing their little heads off."

Kitty patted her friend's hand, not bothering to voice the thought that five-year-olds wouldn't have the patience to stick with a game of hide-and-seek for this long. She got to her feet and walked across the lobby.

She heard her heels clicking on the driveway as she hurried to her car. Jumping in she checked that her tote was still behind the seat, and snaking her hand into the bag she felt for the .38 revolver. One way or another she was going to get the truth from Jeff.

🦋 Chapter 49 🦋

rank and Don stood outside the interrogation room with Chris Roberts and Al Parkins. Through the two-way mirror, the four of them stared at Bill Slades. Frank studied the round, jowly face and noticed the thick black hair that curled along his bare forearms. The dark green T-shirt Slades had been wearing when they'd arrested him had deep dark stains of perspiration down the front and around the armpits. But that was the only clue they could see to any anxiety he might be feeling.

He sat still and impassive at the long, narrow table, staring directly ahead of him as if he knew he was being surveyed through the mirror. Frank noticed his eyes. Narrow, mean, and a bright cold blue. But nevertheless intelligent.

Frank turned to his partner. "Did you call the lab guys? Did they get Slades's blood samples and hair combings?"

Don nodded. "But they say we're asking for miracles. There's no way they can make any sort of useful match with hair found at the scene. You knew that, Frank."

"Sure. But they'll be able to tell us if the hairs *don't*

come from Slades. Are the fingerprint guys working on finding a match? And the Caddy? Have we got the technicians going through that?" He paused. "And we need a lineup. Get that young teacher in here."

"Yeah, yeah." Don nodded again. "Are we ready?"

Frank motioned for him to follow as they walked into the room.

Slades didn't move or flinch. Only his eyes followed Frank from the door to the table. Frank took a seat across the table from the child molester. "Are you sure you don't want an attorney, Slades? You've a right to one, you know."

Slades shook his head. "I've done nothing wrong."

"Why did you come to South Florida, Slades?"

"Why does anybody come? The sun, the beaches . . ."

"You're in enough trouble, don't make it worse for yourself. You got sun and beaches in New York at this time of year. Want to start again? Why are you here, Slades?"

Slades blinked once but didn't say anything.

Frank pushed back his chair, paced to the wall and back again, looked at his watch. "In about a half-hour, Slades, we're going to take you down for a lineup. We have a witness who's going to place you at the scene at the time that Timothy Myers was abducted from the playground of the Learning Academy in Boca Raton."

"I didn't commit any crime."

Frank noticed that the dark stain on the green T-shirt had grown deeper and bigger.

"Abduction is a crime."

"I didn't harm the boy. I took him to the hospital."

"You were impersonating a doctor."

Slades smirked. "I didn't think that was a felony."

Frank ignored the comment and pressed on. "Let's talk about the attempted abduction of Jamie Fitzgerald from the Sands Plaza parking lot, also in Boca Raton."

The narrow little eyes widened a fraction. "Who says?"

Frank didn't reply.

"I was in a minor fender bender in that parking lot,

that's it. I suppose you got some witness to ID my mugshot there as well, did you?"

Frank surveyed the other man's face. Interesting, he thought. There had been a discernible reaction to the idea that there was a witness to that event—and it was Jeff Haley who'd been with Jamie in the Sands Plaza. Was it disbelief on Slades's part that Haley would be a witness against·him?

"Why Jamie Fitzgerald, Slades? Tell us about Jamie."

Slades looked away for the first time.

" 'Little boys like playing doctor.' Does that ring any bells?" Frank paused. "Interesting thing, isn't it, since you like playing doctor too. I understand you used to have quite a collection of porn movies. Way back in your other life. I expect most of those are buried in a police property room, and it might take a while to unearth them, but maybe we could compare the techniques and locations with a porn video that surfaced in this area recently."

Frank drummed his fingers on the table and stared at the thick black curls of hair on the other man's forearms. They glistened with sweat. Time to change the subject, thought Frank.

"Tell us about Wallkill, Slades."

Slades shrugged, wiped one cheek with the back of his hand. "Nothing to tell. It was a quiet place."

"Make any friends there?"

"Didn't meet anybody there." He looked as if he was about to smirk again but the twitch died on his lips. "I was kept away from the other inmates."

"For your own protection, no doubt."

Slades shrugged.

"Does the name Haley mean anything to you?"

"No."

"You don't watch TV news?"

"No. I've been busy."

"Of course. What about Jeff Haley? You don't recognize that name either?"

Slades shook his head.

They could circle like this all evening, Frank thought. Slades wouldn't admit to contact with Haley if he could help it. Abduction was one thing, but Haley was a link to a murder rap.

Frank grinned. "He remembers you."

Slades's jaw tightened. "Who?"

Frank shook his head and sighed. "Jeff Haley. That's who we were talking about, isn't it, Slades?"

Out of the corner of his eye, Frank caught the movement of the door opening into the room. He was aware of a whispered conversation going on behind him. Then Don was crouching beside him. "Frank, I'm sorry, but this is important. The Morettis are downstairs. They just turned themselves in."

Frank stood slowly, aware of a pounding in his temples. *The Morettis had turned themselves in? Now?!* He stared across the table at Slades, then turned back to his partner. "Okay," he said in what he trusted sounded like a calm, even voice. "I'll be right there."

As he turned to leave, Slades suddenly pushed back on his chair with such screeching force that the uniformed police officer standing by the door leapt toward him and grabbed for his sidearm.

But Slades remained seated on the chair, his arms outstretched as he gripped the table in front of him.

"Hey! I want a lawyer. I want to talk to a lawyer."

Frank paused in the doorway. "Hey!" he echoed. "You can have one. We told you that a couple of hours back. You got anyone particular in mind?"

Slades slumped back in his chair. "Yeah, David Roth."

"David Roth?" Frank shook his head, allowing himself to laugh out loud at the reference to the famous Palm Beach criminal defense lawyer. "Sorry, Slades, you're shit out of luck. You want to try him, be my guest, but last I heard he retired from defending the likes of you."

Frank turned to the police officer at the door. "Get him the Yellow Pages."

Then he walked out of the room.

❧ *Chapter 50* ❧

She had burned rubber reversing out of the driveway of Angela's apartment building but had observed the
speed limit along A1A and on Palmetto Park until she
reached the interstate. It took her just about a half-hour to
get to the Flagler Bridge, and about ten minutes after that
she was pulling into the driveway of the Haley mansion.
She noticed lights on all over the house as she hauled her
tote out of the Blazer and ran to the front door, pounding
on it with both fists until Jeff appeared in the open doorway.

"Kitty! Did you find the boys?" He gripped both her
hands, drawing her into the foyer.

She pulled away as Jeff closed the door behind her.
"Cut the crap, Jeff. Just tell me what's going on. Why did
you lie to me and the cops about the doorman?"

She paced across the foyer, glancing in through the
doors of the den and the living room, and then back at
Jeff, who was leaning against the front doors watching her
with a look of quiet amusement in his eyes.

"Where are the boys?" She took a step toward him.

Jeff remained standing with his back to the heavy mahogany door, eyeing her brazenly. "They're not here, Kitty. You think I have the boys? Here?" He seemed to be laughing at her—and suddenly she knew for certain.

"Cut it out, Jeff." She took another step toward him. "You have them. Why did you have to do that?"

He turned very slowly and slammed a sliding bolt across the top of the door. Then he turned back to face her. "You're right, Kitty. You figured the first part out nicely. Then how come you don't get it?"

Kitty's heart thudded painfully against her ribs as they stood staring at each other. "Why, Jeff? Why did you do it? Do you realize half of the Boca police are searching for them? And Alex's mother is frantic. Come on, Jeff, please, let me have them. Don't use them. They're only little. I know you wouldn't want them harmed or frightened in any way."

"Ah, so you do know that, eh, Kitty? Well, you're right. I would never harm a child. Especially not Jamie. You know you can trust me on that."

"Why did you do it, Jeff?"

He smiled lazily. "I thought you would have figured that out, too. But let's put it this way: You're here, aren't you?"

Kitty realized that Jeff had not yet made a move to approach her physically and her fear abated a little. Jeff did not appear threatening.

"Okay, I'm here. You couldn't wait till tomorrow?"

"For you to slot me in before brunch? How long were you going to give me, Kit? Five minutes? Ten? Or were you just going to leave the motor running and rush in to get all the letters and papers you wanted?" He sighed loudly. "I want you to spend a little time with me."

"I see."

"No," he shook his head. "I don't think you do: I want to talk to you, I want to show you a few things I've done around the house. I want to tell you about some plans I have, and I want to do it all without being afraid that you'll throw me out or walk out on me. I want your undivided attention for a couple of hours."

"How can I give you my undivided attention when all I can think about are Jamie and Alex?"

"The boys are fine, Kitty. You must trust me. They think they're playing a big joke on their moms."

"Where are they, Jeff? Just let me see them and then you can have my attention."

He shook his head slowly. "They're not here, Kitty. They're with friends."

"They're with the Vascos? In their apartment?" Kitty raised her eyes hopefully to the second floor.

Jeff laughed. "Oh dear. Guessing games. No, they're not with the Vascos. The Vascos are gone. Do you think I'd keep on housekeepers who let strangers walk in here and kill my mother?"

He glanced at his watch and shook his head again. "Forget it, Kitty. You're not going to see them until I've had my say. So you may as well just relax."

"And, after you've had my undivided attention Jeff, do I get them back?"

"Of course, Kitty."

"And then what do we tell the police in Boca?"

"I'm so happy you said 'we'." Jeff grinned. "Because we tell them it was all a big giant misunderstanding. Or that it was a joke which went too far, and we'll apologize for causing so much trouble and we'll hand over a nice big fat check for the Police Benevolent Association, and everything will be fine, you'll see."

He came toward her and took her arm. "Let's start in the living room . . . come on."

She followed him mutely into the big room, where she noticed the drapes had been taken off the windows. The carpets had been rolled back, the furniture covered in dropcloths, and a worker's ladder stood against the side wall.

"I had an interior decorator come in, and she suggests

that first of all I open up this room by installing atrium doors which will open up onto the veranda." Jeff paused. Throwing open the doors, he motioned for Kitty to step forward. "And, of course, I'll get rid of this overstuffed furniture. Cheap and chintzy is how Fran described it."

Kitty nodded and scanned the room, feigning interest though her thoughts were lagging behind, still trying to make sense of Jeff's easy dismissal of the Boca police.

His cavalier attitude was disturbing. It was as if he was suddenly in his own little world.

"And you see here, the veranda," he took her hand and led her to the big windows. "I'd leave this part of it open but round the side of the house I'd glass it in, atrium style with access from the den." He turned to her. "What do you think, so far?"

"Good," she nodded. "Very nice."

"Come on," he took her by the hand, and she was dismayed to realize that he was leading her up the stairs. She hung back, looking at the closed doors of the den. Attempting to keep it light, she said, "What, no refurbishing in the den?"

"Later," he smiled. "We'll see the den later. First the master bedroom. I have more to show you."

She followed down the hallway. She realized they were heading for Marina's bedroom. Jeff flung the doors open.

"You like it?"

She stared. He had had the room totally repainted in a bright pastel lemon paint with a striking Laura Ashley border. New carpeting of deep thick-pile ivory covered the wood floor and the heavy drapes and sheers were drawn back for what she guessed, in daylight, would be a stunning view of the ocean. A chaise stood in front of French doors that were open to the upper deck.

Jeff beckoned her onto the deck and walked over to a glass-top rattan table on which stood an ice bucket with a bottle of champagne. Two crystal glasses stood on a little silver tray beside it. He popped the cork and poured, handing her a glass.

She tried to decline. But he insisted.

"Sit down, Kitty."

"Jeff, I think you've done a wonderful job, and I thought we had come to an understanding, too. You should be looking to the future."

"I am, Kitty. That's what I want to talk about. Because I can't see my future any other way except with you sharing it."

She tried to interrupt but he wouldn't let her. "No, let me say my piece first. You've never really listened. All this can be yours, Kitty. I'm offering it to you.

"I want you to consider the life we can have together. We can live here or in New York. You can take over the refurbishing and do whatever you want in this house. If you don't want to do that, leave it to Fran, and we can work together on TV stuff. We can even install our own editing room. You can produce your own documentaries. If you don't want to do that you can sunbathe on the beach or by the pool all day, and when you get tired of the sun we can fly to New York and do the party scene up there. You wouldn't have to worry about money or making ends meet or about Jamie's future."

"Jeff, I appreciate the—"

He wouldn't let her finish. "No, Kitty! Don't give me those trite words." His voice rose a pitch. "You don't appreciate. You can't because you won't give yourself the chance to try it. You know what your problem is, it's the same problem Marina had. You're so alike, Kitty. Both of you so talented and smart when it comes to work but so incompetent when it comes to organizing your personal happiness.

"Look at the way Marina screwed up with that asshole Davenport—and now you want me to sit back and watch as you screw up with some dope of a cop. You don't know what's good for you. Neither did Marina."

She slumped back in the rattan chair and took a deep breath as Jeff went on.

"Kitty believe me, Frank Maguire is not the man for

you. He can't give you what you need. He can't look after you the way I can. Don't you see that? I love you. I love Jamie. I want to make you happy. I would dedicate myself to making you happy. Why can't you give me the chance? You would love me eventually. And one day, you'd suddenly wake up and wonder: Why did I fight this man for so long?"

Kitty bit her lip, trying to control the hysterical giggle that had suddenly sprung to her lips. But even as she did so, Jeff got to his feet and held his hand out to her. "Come on, I have one more thing to show you."

He led the way across the bedroom and into a dressing area, where new Corian countertops with double sinks had been installed. A large theater mirror with light bulbs surrounding it filled one entire wall. Then he opened the door into a huge walk-in closet and snapped on the light.

Kitty gasped. One entire wall of the closet was hung with dresses and outfits. New, with price tags still attached.

"Go on, take a look," Jeff urged her. "They're yours, Kitty. Anything you want to keep, that is."

Kitty stood rooted to the spot, eyeing the shoes and purses.

"Come on. Look here." Jeff took a hanger off the rod and held out a cream-colored chiffony outfit with a soft swing pleat skirt. "Take it."

"No, Jeff. No, this is—" She broke off. She was going to say "insane," but something made her realize it was not a good word to use.

"Try it on, Kitty. It's an original Carolina Herrera. Please, let me see you in it."

She didn't move.

"Try it on, Kitty." She heard the hard edge in his voice, and she felt herself stumbling forward, taking the dress from his hands. "Go, on, I'll wait outside." He paused. "Oh, here are the shoes to go with it." He pulled out a pair of cream satin pumps with high heels and pushed them at her. "Don't take too long," he added, before closing the door behind him.

Kitty stood in the empty closet, looking at her face in the floor-to-ceiling mirror on the back of the door.

Her eyes stared back at her, bewildered. She had to believe that if she went through with this nonsense, she would get the boys back. She had to believe that they were safe . . . somewhere . . . But where?

"How's it going?" Jeff rapped sharply on the door, and she grit her teeth and slipped into the dress, trying to ignore the tightness in her throat as she tied the sash.

Jeff beamed as she walked out of the dressing area and into the bedroom.

"Divine. Just divine, Kitty. I knew it would be, the moment I saw that dress."

Kitty noticed that while she had been changing, Jeff had put on a jacket and tie. There was a single blood-red rose in the buttonhole of his jacket. He looked as if he was about to go out. They both looked as if they were ready for a night out on the town. What the hell was going on? Surely he did not think she was going to join him for dinner?

He led her back into the dressing area and made her stand in front of the mirror. "Handsome devils, aren't we?"

Kitty smiled weakly, but her tone was firm. "You made your point, Jeff. But I'm worried about the boys."

Jeff appeared not to have heard her. He was staring from her reflection in the mirror to the real thing, awe in his eyes. "When I saw the dress I thought it would be perfect as a wedding outfit. I mean, I know you never had a white wedding but I didn't think you'd really want to go for the veil and train and all that juvenile nonsense. This is so much classier."

Kitty blinked. "A wedding outfit?" she echoed his words.

Jeff's grin widened. "Of course, you need a wedding outfit for our wedding."

"Our wedding!" she burst out exasperated and angry. "Jeff, this isn't funny anymore. You wanted my attention, you got it. But ...," she hesitated for a moment, "this isn't going anywhere. There isn't going to be a wedding, Jeff. Not for you and me. Please stop this now and take me to Alex and Jamie. Please, Jeff."

"No, no, no." Jeff shook his head at their reflections in the mirror. "No, Kitty. You can't make a decision, not yet. You've got to see how it could be. Come." He ignored her stricken expression and entwined his arm through hers, pulling her in to his side, firmly and decisively, making it clear that he was not going to let go.

"Let's get on with it, my love. Everything is ready and waiting in the den. All we need is the bride and groom."

❧ Chapter 51 ❧

$\mathcal{I}$t was approaching 8:30 P.M. when Frank returned to the conference room to deal with the Morettis. He had met with them briefly when Don had brought them up to the second floor, some twenty minutes earlier. They had arrived with two other males in tow. But the round of introductions, during which the Morettis had revealed their true identities, had left him momentarily at a loss for words. He'd had to leave the conference room to reconsider the best way of handling the situation. Taking advantage of the forced break, he'd ordered in a pastrami sandwich.

Now he stood and surveyed the group of four sitting on the other side of the big round table. On one end sat their attorney, who'd introduced himself as Oliver Webb. In the middle sat the Morettis, whose real names were Vincent Moore and Rosie Diamond. He stared at them. He could have passed them in the street the day after their disappearance without having recognized either of them as a Moretti. Moore was gray and balding with a hairless face.

Rosie Diamond was a platinum blonde with a pageboy cut and now wore big, tinted glasses. Sitting beside her was their boss and employer, a big, fat man by the name of Tom Bassett, who, as Frank had been informed earlier, also held the title of deputy executive editor of the *Weekly World Mail*, a tabloid that could be found alongside the *Enquirer, Star,* and *Globe* at most supermarket checkouts.

Frank sat down on the opposite side of the table and addressed the lawyer first. "So, Mr. Webb, do you have a reason why I shouldn't charge your clients with obstruction of justice?"

Webb cleared his throat and started. "For the record, Detective, I'd like it noted that my clients, Mr. Vincent Moore and Miss Rosie Diamond, are appearing here this evening voluntarily."

Frank nodded. "Noted, Mr. Webb, with the addendum that it's almost two weeks since we appealed for them to come forward to help us with our inquiries. Now, let's hear the rest," he said coldly.

Webb cleared his throat again. "At the time of Marina Dee Haley's death both Mr. Moore and Miss Diamond were on assignment for the *Mail*. Aside from not making this clear to you on the morning of August thirty-first, Mr. Moore and Miss Diamond have signed an affidavit stating that all other statements made to you that morning were truthful and accurate."

Frank drummed his fingers on the table. "Aside from not making that little detail clear to me, Mr. Webb, they also told me that they were replacing the Vascos because of a family emergency. That was an outright lie, was it not?"

Oliver Webb held his hand up. "I include that in the deception over their true roles at the house, Detective."

Frank allowed a pause. Then, "Let's start at the beginning, Mr. Webb. Maybe you can first explain the exact nature of the assignment for me."

Tom Bassett jumped in before the attorney finished clearing his throat. "Our interest lay in Marina's son, Jeff

Haley. We'd gotten the word that he was to be paroled to his mother's home, and we, at the *Mail*, felt that it was in the public interest to take a closer look at a case where a convicted felon was to be paroled into the lap of luxury, here in Palm Beach."

Frank laughed out loud both at the words and Tom Bassett's self-satisfied look. Did these people really believe that anything they did was in the public interest?

"Please, Mr. Bassett, don't insult my intelligence with your ideas about public interest. I'm more curious as to what the assignment entailed. Was it your idea that Mr. Moore and Miss Diamond gain access to the Haley mansion under false pretenses?"

Tom Bassett flushed. "It was my idea that we should get pictures of a reunion between Haley and his mother."

Moore interrupted. "Rosie and I brainstormed for a couple of days on the best way to secure the pictures and story we needed. We wanted to gain access without breaking the law."

"But nevertheless under false pretenses, Mr. Moore."

Moore shrugged, leaned back in his chair, and crossed his jean-covered legs. "Not ours, Detective. It was the Vascos who conned Mrs. Haley into accepting us as stand-ins. They were ready to take the money."

"You misrepresented yourselves to the Vascos. No, don't be modest, Mr. Moore," Frank stopped him as Moore opened his mouth. "You duped two people into allowing you access to the Haley household for the purpose of invading the resident's privacy, and for plain and simple snooping, and," Frank stared intently at the group across the table, "for burglary."

He stared first at Moore and then at Rosie Diamond. "I believe you removed a couple of items from the house, including some written work of Mrs. Haley's and a significant amount of cash?"

"Yes," agreed Rosie Diamond.

"No," said Moore.

Frank raised an eyebrow. "Which is it? Yes or no?"

Webb interjected, reaching under the desk for his brief-case. "That's a 'yes' to the written work, specifically a draft chapter from Mrs. Haley's autobiography, and a 'no' to the cash, Detective."

He withdrew a sheaf of crumpled, creased yellow legal pad pages and slid them across the table to Frank. "For the record, my clients retrieved this from the wastebasket. I believe you'll find it contains nothing relevant to your current investigation."

Frank kept his temper in check. "I think, counselor, it would be better if I made the decisions as to what's relevant to my investigation."

"It deals with the identity of Marina's secret lover . . . Jeff Haley's father," offered Rosie Diamond helpfully. "We did truly believe it was more interesting to the readers of the *Mail* than to you."

Frank turned his attention to Bassett. "You intend to publish information from this draft?"

Bassett looked uncertain for the first time. "A story based on information in this draft, yes."

Frank picked up the pages and glanced at the spidery script. There was a series of question marks across the top line. Evidently, Marina had not been entirely sure whether to finally reveal the secret she'd kept for so many years. He stared at the pages. Indeed, if the reporters were to be believed and Marina had discarded them into the waste-basket, she had probably decided against the revelation. He felt a momentary pang of sadness for the woman whose last wish was obviously going to be so blatantly desecrated. But the damage had been done. He picked up the first page.

> *I've often wondered why I've held onto this one secret for so long. In today's world of revelations and exposés it seems there are worse and more lurid secrets to expose. Even my friend Oprah has revealed worse about her own life.*
>
> *The trouble is that at the time when I was growing*

up, when I was just nineteen, what happened to me was a horror I thought only I had experienced.

I was raped by my stepfather, Arnold Foster. It happened a few weeks before I was due to leave home, having found my first job in TV in New York, a low-level job, but a very happy occasion which I've described earlier in the book.

Today I can look back and feel some pity for Arnold. He was a pathetic man who drank and brought no joy to anyone's life. My mother, Betty, on the other hand, was a rock. At least, when I finally confided in her, I was five months pregnant at that time, she did not stick her head in the sand like some mothers today might do. She drove back to Albany from her visit with me in the city, packed her bags and walked out on Arnold.

She found work for herself cleaning houses, and after Jeffie was born, she was enterprising enough to find a job as a live-in, persuading her new employers that she and her new baby had been abandoned, and that she desperately needed the job.

So imagine my horror when eighteen years later Arnold Foster turned up in my life again. . . .

Frank sensed the tension in the room, and he was aware that four pairs of eyes were fixed on him as he read the pages. For a moment he considered setting them aside to continue the meeting, but then he leaned back in his chair, his eyes still on the pages. Screw them, he thought. They can wait.

. . . This was very shortly after I made my big confession on TV about Jeffie being my son. Now, obviously, I have regrets about doing that. It was not the best thing I did for my son. I realize that. Jeff survived however because he is a survivor. But there was another, much worse consequence: It brought Arnold out of the woodwork.

I remember the day in clearest detail still. How could I not? My ratings had taken off and I was pulling in big money, and it was around that time that I had started wintering in Palm Beach and had just closed on this very house where I'm penning my book. Jeffie had flown down with me to meet with contractors who were refurbishing the house and installing all sorts of wonders like a swimming pool and a new wing of guest rooms.

When Arnold walked into my house that day I thought, at first, he was one of the workmen, coming to tell me they were done for the night. He looked so unkempt and rough I had to look twice, and then my heart sank.

It was Arnold. Like some horrible nightmare, grinning and congratulating me. "You've done good, Marnie," he said using a name for me that I've never allowed anyone to use since. "I watch you on TV and I'm proud that you were my girl once." He made my flesh crawl even after all those years. I wanted to get him out of the house.

But then he said he knew Jeff was his son. "I figured it all out, Marnie. When I saw you and Jeff on TV, it started me thinking. Answered a lot of my questions like why your dear mother walked out on me after her trip to see you. Look at me." Then he turned sideways. "Go on, look at this handsome face and tell me Jeff isn't my son."

I was speechless and horrified. But worse was to come. "I'd like us to be a family, Marnie," he said, grinning and moving toward me. "I'd like to make things up to you and my son."

. I wanted to smash that grinning face. I wanted to scream, but somehow I managed to keep my cool. "Get out," I told him. "Get out before I call the police."

At that moment I heard Jeff's voice from the doorway behind me. I whirled around. "What's the trou-

ble, Marina?" I wondered how long he'd been standing there. How much he'd heard. But it didn't matter. I knew I had no chance of keeping any of it from him any longer because just then Arnold stepped forward. "Jeff," he said. "Finally I get to meet my boy."

That's when I screamed and fled up the stairs to my room. About an hour later I heard a car start up in front of the house, and I suspected that Arnold was leaving at last. I wondered what he and Jeffie had found to talk about. I crept out of my room to find Jeff. I felt he would need to talk to me, but he didn't respond when I called his name and I decided maybe he just needed to be alone.

I tried to talk to him again the next morning when I found him sitting on the veranda staring out across the backyard.

"Tell me what happened, Jeffie," I urged him.

My son pretended not to hear. He paced across the veranda, staring hard at the workmen in the yard where they were pouring the concrete for the pool.

"Jeff," I said. "Please look at me. I know you're not that interested in the pool. Don't avoid me. We have to talk. He's a despicable man and I'm afraid he's not going to leave us alone now. I'm sure he wants money."

Jeff finally sat down beside me. "It's okay, Marina. He knows neither of us want anything to do with him. We had a long talk after you ran upstairs and I did point out to him that he should go away quietly if he didn't want you reporting his crime to the police."

I couldn't help smiling at that. Jeff was turning into such a competent, smart young man. "But," I had to point out to him, "reporting the crime [I couldn't get the word rape *out] isn't going to help, Jeff. There's a statute of limitations."*

He silenced me with a dismissive wave. "Don't

*worry about it. Arnold's too stupid to know that."
He took my hand then. "I took care of it, Marina.
Let's never talk about him again. We can just pretend yesterday never happened and you can keep
your secret, forever, if you want."*

*I wasn't entirely convinced by Jeff's words. I kept
looking over my shoulder for Arnold's face to reappear. But he didn't. And then the months went by,
and the years went by, and he never did show again
and I was finally able to sleep at night.*

Frank set aside the pages and exhaled loudly. He noticed a scribble in the margin of the last page. "Discuss
with Jeff when he arrives next week."

Discuss with Jeff? What? The inclusion of this story in
the book? Frank shook his head and looked across at Don,
who was a page or two behind him. Neither man said anything when Don caught up on the pages. But Frank knew
when his partner looked at him, shaking his head, that Don
was entirely on the same wavelength. Even Don with his
open objective mind couldn't miss the implication in this
maternal indictment.

Haley, it seemed, had started his murderous career a
long time ago. Frank wondered if a judge would grant
them a search warrant to excavate the Haley swimming
pool on the basis of Marina's draft chapter.

A shiver of excitement and satisfaction surged through
him, and he had to force his attention back to the group at
the table.

"When exactly will this story appear?" He put the question to the editor.

The editor looked uncomfortable. "In the edition which
comes out on the stands Monday."

"You've waited a while."

"Our lead times are very long, Detective. We go to
press almost two weeks before we go on sale."

"Is that so?" Frank said, and then suddenly he understood what had happened. Moore and Diamond had disappeared and played for time to get the story in the paper.

Frank's anger simmered as he considered this. "Okay," he said finally. "Mr. Webb, let me tell you the consequences of your clients' deception: It tied up a homicide investigation with hours of unnecessary work and energy. It tied up manpower and resources. Your clients also tampered with evidence, and willfully misled myself and other investigations officers with deliberate lies."

Frank got to his feet. "I do intend for charges of obstruction of justice to be brought against Mr. Moore and Miss Diamond and possibly against Mr. Bassett."

"Oh shit!" Rosie Diamond leapt to her feet. "Come on, Detective! We were just trying to do our job. It's not like we can all get our information by sleeping with the officer in charge of the investigation."

Frank stopped midway across the floor and turned around. Rosie Diamond stood glaring at him as Vincent Moore glowered at her with a dismayed look on his face.

"What's that supposed to mean?" Frank asked curtly.

Rosie Diamond stared defiantly at him. "You know what it means, Detective. I'm talking about that *Inside Copy* reporter, Kitty Fitzgerald. And I only mention it because along with Marina's last chapter we picked up an interesting document from Jeff Haley's luggage."

Frank took a couple of steps back to the table.

"And that's not evidence we tampered with, either," she blazed. "That came with Haley, two days after the murder. So—"

"So?" Frank interrupted her coldly. "What document?"

"A private detective's report. Haley had you and Kitty Fitzgerald under surveillance for about a month, way back in July . . . beginning of August. Now, that would have made a great story for the *Mail* but we haven't used it."

There was a long, unsettling silence in the room before Rosie Diamond reached into her own briefcase and brought out a big yellow envelope.

"It's all here . . . times, dates, photographs."

Frank stretched out his hand for the envelope that Rosie Diamond passed to him without protest. He emptied the contents onto the tabletop and stared at the pictures. Big eight by tens of him and Kitty sitting together at Testa's, brunching at Chuck and Harold's, walking down Royal Poinciana—this one shot from the back showing Frank's hand resting on Kitty's behind—and one of Kitty leaving his townhouse in the dark.

Then he looked at the next half-dozen shots, all of them apparently taken with a telephoto lens through Kitty's courtyard gates, showing him and Kitty in various semi-intimate poses as they necked and hugged and generally played around on the pool deck.

He turned the photos over. One of them had his name printed on the back: Detective Frank Maguire, Palm Beach PD. The others all had various dates in July stamped on the back. He wondered how the photographer had taken all those pictures without him or Kitty ever noticing. He tried to picture the angle, figuring the photographer would have had to sit somewhere across the cul-de-sac. In a parked car?

Rosie Diamond slid a folded piece of paper that had fallen out of the envelope toward him. "Take a look, that's the bill for Haley from the private detective agency. It's ten thousand dollars!"

Frank glanced at it, noted that the invoice had been stamped Paid by Gates and Welles.

"Haley has quite a thing for Miz Fitzgerald," Rosie Diamond stated the obvious. "We found a couple of other pictures of her in his bag but left them."

Frank raised an eyebrow.

"He had one of Kitty Fitzgerald when she was pregnant. A Polaroid which she must have taken herself. She was naked in the picture."

Frank's throat tightened. Haley had stolen that photo from Kitty. He remembered her mentioning it when she'd told the story of finding Haley at her desk, just before their big argument. He felt sickened. Haley had taken the picture with him into jail. How many low-lifes had seen it and stared at it?

Rosie Diamond's voice broke into his thoughts. "You know Haley tried to kill himself about a week after he got the private detective's report."

"What?"

She nodded. "He drank some kind of toxic cleaning fluid. Gave himself severe stomach cramps."

"How could you possibly know that?"

"We have sources all over the place." She paused. "Quite a startling love triangle story, isn't it, Detective."

"Shut the fuck up, Rosie," Tom Bassett suddenly burst out. Then he turned to Frank. "Rest assured Detective we have no intention of using any of this. Here . . ." He slid all the pictures back into the envelope and handed it to Frank. "Take it."

Frank stood up. He figured they'd brought the pictures and the report to hand over to him as a quid pro quo. They wouldn't run the story if he didn't charge them.

He stared at the foursome seated opposite him. "The charges of obstruction stand," he told them. "And should you change your mind about running the story, I have to warn you that I would seek legal redress and so would Miss Fitzgerald." He paused, trying not to let his impatience show. His thoughts were racing in a totally different direction now and he wanted to wind up the meeting. He turned to Oliver Webb. "Your clients may leave now but we will be in touch."

He watched the miserable little group troop out of the room, but he stayed seated at the long conference table with Don. Without saying anything he spread the photos of himself and Kitty out along the table. Then he placed the yellow pages of Marina's last chapter next to the photos. Lastly, he reached into his pocket and brought out the note Don had handed him in the car, and placed that next to the draft pages.

"You know what we have here, pal?" Without waiting

for an answer he answered his own question. "A psycho-path. The genuine article, Donny-boy."

"You'll get no argument from me." Don shook his head.

"Look at this." Frank waved his hand over the table.

"It all fits like you said," Don said quietly. "He gets the photos and the private detective's report, drinks the cleaning fluid and ends up in the infirmary where he meets up with Slades."

Frank nodded. "And that's where he wakes up and decides he's not going to take it anymore. He's going to punish the women who have made his life so miserable. He's going to do what he's always done in the past when someone comes along to upset his cozy little world. Like he did to his father and his stepfather."

Frank got to his feet. "And there's not a thing we have on him—unless Slades sings." He paced to the door and then back to the table, suddenly grinning as he picked up the note Haley had brought in with him for his interview with Don that morning. "But you know, I think we can help Slades. All he needs is the right note to start on."

❦ *Chapter* 52 ❦

She heard the grandfather clock chime the half-hour in the foyer. But Kitty had no idea which half-hour. It could have been half past eight or nine. All she knew was that since she had come into the den with Jeff it had gotten dark outside.

She stood in the window, looking out over the front driveway, her back to Jeff and the room that he had rearranged so grotesquely.

She had not known whether to laugh or cry when he had flung open the doors to the den. He had strung up hundreds of tiny little fairy lights across the ceiling to give the impression of a canopy of twinkling lights.

The couch and chairs had been moved from the center of the room and replaced with six rows of white folding chairs on each side of a center aisleway. At the end of each row stood silver urns with towering white lilies. The chairs faced the giant-screen TV—except it did not look like a TV anymore. A white lace cloth had been draped over it to hide the screen and to serve as a backdrop for the two velvet-cushioned footstools. Between the footstools and the TV stood a camcorder on a tripod.

"Imagine the camcorder as the minister," Jeff had told her, leading her by the elbow to the footstools. "We'll be married by camera, on camera. Very fitting, don't you agree?"

She had yanked her elbow out of his grip and backed away toward the window where she now stood. Had she been there for more than fifteen minutes? Or was it an hour and fifteen minutes?

Jeff had made no move to come after her. He had sat on a folding chair, the last one in the last row, one leg crossed over the other, an arm draped casually over the back of the chair.

They had looked as if they were waiting for their guests to arrive. When she finally turned around, he was still sitting in the same spot, same position.

"Jeff?"

"Yes, my dear?"

"This is . . ." She waved her hand feebly toward the camcorder and footstools. "I don't know what's going on. This is not for real."

"Of course it's not for real, Kitty. I realize that. I'm not crazy, you know. I just wanted you to get a good idea, a feel for how it could be. I mean, imagine our friends and acquaintances filling these rows here—and the music. Wait, let me switch on the stereo."

"Jeff!" The name came out in a scream. "Stop it! Do you understand that people know where I am? They're going to come looking for me. If you don't take me to Jamie and Alex . . . if you don't tell me where they are, there's going to be big trouble."

He sat down again on the folding chair. "I don't think so, Kitty. There might be a little bit of trouble but not big trouble. I mean, what exactly are you going to say to all these people who come looking for you? That I took the boys? That I have the boys?

"I'll deny it. And what are the police going to do?

They'll search the house from top to bottom. And they'll find nothing. No boys. No trace of boys." Jeff paused and got to his feet.

"All it will do is waste a lot more time. And, while the time is wasting, the boys will still be missing, and you won't be any closer to knowing where they are. The cops can't beat the information out of me, you know. Think about it."

He didn't have to say it. That's all she could think about. How long would it take to find the boys? Every hour that passed made her feel more desperate. Suppose they were alone? They had to be alone. The story about a friend's house was bullshit. Jeff didn't have any friends in Palm Beach. Suppose they were in the dark? Scared? Terrified? Calling out for her, and for Angela?

Jeff had crossed some kind of line, and she could no longer be sure of the outcome here. Except that the longer she refused to play along with whatever game he was playing, the longer the boys would suffer.

"What is it exactly that you want, Jeff?"

He got to his feet again, smiling. "Good girl." He came up to her and took her hand. "I'll explain it again: I want you to marry me, Kitty. I want to celebrate our love and our marriage the way normal people celebrate. I want to love you, Kitty. With my body, I want to worship you. I want you to know and see how I can love you."

Kitty felt her throat tighten painfully as bile rose in her stomach.

"And, after that?"

"Oh, Kitty." He slipped his arm around her waist and hugged her to his side. "After that we'll go pick up the boys. Well, we'll pick up Jamie. Angela can come and take Alex. And then you and I and Jamie will go on our honeymoon, together."

She said nothing.

"Don't you want to know where we're going?"

"I guess."

"We're going to sail to the Bahamas. I've got the boat ready."

"The boat?"

"Sure. You know about the boat. The one Marina bought for Larry when they got married. The *MaraLar*. It's docked in the Sailfish Marina." He hugged her to his side again. "Isn't it great being rich? Being able to take off, go anywhere you want to go?" He paused as they reached the footstools. "Anyway, first things first. Let's make it legal."

He let go of her waist and took a step forward to switch on the camcorder. Then he returned to her side and took her hand in his.

"So," he began. "We know why we're gathered here. Now Kitty, I want you to repeat after me . . . I, Kitty Fitzgerald."

She closed her eyes and felt a tear rolling down her cheek as the words came out in a hoarse, choked whisper, "I . . . Kitty . . . Fitzgerald."

She kept her eyes closed, repeating the rest of the phrases mechanically and woodenly, not thinking of what she was saying, just willing the whole insane charade to be over.

She had never heard about the boat before, but if there was a boat, if the stupid goddamn boat was part of the charade, maybe Jamie would be part of it, too. At least she would have Jamie with her.

"I think I'm allowed to kiss the bride now." Jeff's voice broke harshly into her thoughts. She turned her face up to his and allowed him to brush her lips before pulling away.

"Let's go do it, Jeff," she said coldly.

But he seemed not to notice the hostility in her voice or her body language, and as they entered the master bedroom she glanced at his face to see a broad grin pasted all over it.

"Wow!" he sighed. "I'm glad all that formal stuff is over and we can relax. Come on, love, let me show you a little surprise."

He led her to the walk-in closet. Reaching for a hanger, he brought out a long, satiny white nightgown with a scalloped neckline and spaghetti-thin straps.

"Would you wear this for me tonight? Go on." He thrust the nightgown at her and gave her behind a pat, easing her toward the bathroom door. "Go on, have a nice shower, relax a little. I'll be waiting right here."

She stood hesitantly by the door until he took off his jacket. Then he started to unzipper his pants.

She disappeared into the bathroom, slamming the door behind her. For a moment she stood, her back against the the door, her knees shaking so violently she didn't know if she was going to be able to walk out again.

I can't, she thought, squeezing her eyes shut. I can't do this. I'd rather shoot myself. No, I'd rather shoot him. Why the hell did I leave my tote downstairs?

"Kitty!" The knock on the door was gentle. "Kitty, sweetheart, are you okay?"

She took a deep breath. "I'm fine. I'm just fine." She tore at the buttons on the dress and pulled it off over her head. Then she unhooked her bra and slipped out of her panties before sliding into the satiny nightgown.

Another deep breath as she raised her hands to her breasts and pinched her nipples hard to make them stand out against the soft folds of the nightgown. She flung open the door.

"What do you think, Jeff?"

The question was unnecessary. She could tell what he thought as he stood gawping at her in his skimpy little briefs. "Oh, Kitty, oh, princess . . ."

"Jeff, I have to go and get my purse, my tote. I need . . ."

He shook his head. "Look in the cabinets, Kitty. Anything you need is right here. Hairbrush, toothbrush, toothpaste . . . your brand . . . it's all new."

She took a step toward him. "Jeff, what I need isn't here." She lowered her voice and cleared her throat. "I

need my own personal things. What I mean is . . . I don't
want to worry about getting pregnant tonight."

He seemed to hesitate.

And don't fucking say you want me to have a baby!

"Please, that would really upset me."

He spun around. "I'll go get your tote," he said curtly.

He returned very quickly with the bag, and she took it
from him, hoping he wouldn't notice her trembling hands.
She walked back into the bathroom, her hand immediately
diving into the bag.

Her fingers closed around the gun buried under all her
things, and she offered up a silent prayer. He hadn't
looked. He hadn't found it. *Oh God, please don't let me
screw it up now.*

She brought the gun out of the bag and let her arm drop
to her side, glancing at her reflection in the mirror. The
gray revolver wasn't visible behind the folds of the nightgown, though it really didn't matter one way or the other.
Jeff would see it soon enough.

She opened the bathroom door slowly, feeling her heart
pounding and thudding in some crazy dance against her
ribs. Jeff was no longer standing outside the bathroom
door. He was all the way across the room, turning down
the covers on the big bed.

He looked up and smiled, holding a hand out to her.

She took a step into the bedroom and then brought
her arm up, holding the revolver stretched out in front of
her.

He seemed to freeze, one hand still in midair, the other
clenched at his side.

"Now, Jeff," she said very softly. "Tell me where the
boys are."

He took a step toward her.

"No, don't come any closer. Just tell me where they
are."

He stopped, now with both fists clenched at his side.
Then he took a smaller step.

"I mean it, Jeff."

"If you kill me, you won't know where to look for the boys." She noticed he was still smiling.

"I don't intend to kill you. But I will maim you." She cocked the trigger, the way Frank had shown her, and aimed at Jeff's groin.

"Either way, Kitty," he shrugged, starting to walk toward her. "Kill or maim—I think you'll need these first." He brought his hand up and opened one clenched fist.

Kitty stared in disbelief, a numb horror seizing her at the sight of the six bright round little bullets lying on his open palm.

She stared, rooted to the spot, watching the palm moving closer to her. His other hand took the empty gun from her fingers. He started to laugh . . . softly at first, and then more loudly until the manic echo seemed to be bouncing off all the walls in the house.

❧ Chapter 53 ❧

I need a smoke."

Bill Slades drummed his fingers nervously on the table-top as his eyes darted to his lawyer, a sallow-looking man in gray slacks and an open-necked pink shirt. Then he looked at Frank; then at Don West and lastly his eyes rested on Guy Lewis, who had arrived from the state attorney's office.

One by one, each man shrugged. "Sorry Slades, you're out of luck," Frank told him. "Even if we had one you'd have to go outside to smoke, and you're not going anywhere for the moment. Now let's cut through the bullshit and get down to it. We were talking about Jeff Haley."

Frank leaned back in his chair. "As I was saying before: Haley remembers you. To jog your memory: You were together in the prison infirmary. Ring any bells yet? He was brought in after trying to kill himself."

Frank took the note that Jeff Haley had given Don and held it in his hand. "Okay, let's give you a couple more clues: He drank cleaning fluid. He was the only other inmate in the infirmary at the time."

Slades's clear blue eyes flickered as he glanced at his lawyer.

"How about this?" Frank held up the note. "Remember this note, Slades?" He handed it to Slades. "Look at it carefully. Haley found this on his towel when he stepped out of the shower, next door down from the isolation unit."

Slades's eyes widened in horror. "Haley gave you that?"

Frank stared at him in silence. This was more like it. He held his breath a second.

The silence filled the room. Then Slades turned to his attorney who gave a short, sharp nod. Slades's voice cracked when he spoke, but his attorney's nod seemed to unleash something inside him. "I didn't write that. I never threatened him! Me? Threaten that crazy motherfucker? No way!"

"Crazy?" Frank spoke softly, keeping his eyes directly on Slades.

"Yeah. Crazy. First of all he tries to off himself over a piece of ass. Then, when I offered to take care of his problem, he punched me out."

"What was his problem, Slades?"

"He found out that she was knocking around with some other guy. I didn't ask about the other guy but I offered to take care of the woman."

"Meaning?"

Slades hesitated, then shrugged. "I told him I'd teach her a lesson, so to speak."

Frank felt his gut turning. "So he punched you out. Then what?" Frank waited. Several seconds passed before Slades spoke again.

"Then he came to me with the idea."

"To kill his mother?"

"No. To snatch the kid."

Frank nodded. "He wanted to punish her?"

"No. He wanted to get back with her."

Frank laughed out loud. "That's a novel way to go

about it. You want to get back with a girlfriend so you have her son kidnapped by a pedophile. You're going to have to do better than that."

Slades pursed his lips and glanced across at his attorney, who sat up straighter in his chair as if he had suddenly remembered that he had a role to play in the interrogation. "What's in this for Mr. Slades, Detective?"

"That depends on what he has to tell us." Frank drummed his fingers on the table. "But specifically, can he give us Jeff Haley as the instigator of the plot to kill his mother?"

"No," Slades interrupted. "I can't."

Frank leaned across the table. "Listen Slades, you dumb fuck. You can't have one without the other. We've got enough to nail you on the abductions and you're going away for those—with or without Haley."

But Frank wanted Haley. He got to his feet and paced around the table, loosening the collar of his shirt.

"Now, if you're telling me that killing his mother was not part of the deal then you'd better start praying that the crime scene guys going through your car, right now, don't find a single hair or fiber or fingerprint or soil sample, leaf, or twig." He paused. "Nor a single dollar bill that can be traced back to Marina Dee Haley's property or person."

Slades shifted in his chair as Frank continued.

"Because if there is, you're also going down for murder, and you know what that means in this state? The death penalty.

"As for Haley, he'll be sitting back, laughing and sipping cocktails on the terrace of his multimillion dollar oceanfront estate."

Slades's attorney cleared his throat. "Do you actually have any evidence placing my client at the murder scene, Detective?"

Frank shook his head. "I can't answer that." He walked to the window. He had taken a gamble on mentioning the dollar bill. If Moore and Diamond hadn't taken Marina's hurricane money, then that left only Marina's killer.

He stared at Slades and saw his mean little eyes darting furiously round the room. He wished he could read his mind. What could be going through it? He had to be weighing up the probability of at least a tell-tale hair or fiber turning up in his Cadillac. Was he going to take a chance on it? Or would he take a deal? He saw Slades lean over and whisper into his attorney's ear. He hoped Slades was going to be smart about this.

The attorney cleared his throat again. "If my client tells you what went down between him and Haley, and you don't have enough to charge and convict Haley, what's the deal then?"

Frank smiled pleasantly. "What would you like it to be?"

It was Slades who broke the silence following Frank's question. "I'll tell you what happened but no death penalty. I didn't go there with the intention of killing her."

Frank sat down at the table and looked across at Guy Lewis who stared back impassively.

"I'm listening," Frank said.

Slades wiped his face with the bottom of his T-shirt. "Like I said he came to me, after he punched me out, and said: 'Why would you do that for me?' And I told him: 'Not for you. For me. I need money when I get out of here.' I also wanted to stick it to her sister who did me a bad turn, but I didn't tell him that." Slades paused. "Next thing I know he's laying it all out for me, telling me to abduct the kid."

Slades shrugged. "That was the deal. He told me he didn't want to hurt her or punish her. But he did want her back. He wanted to be together with her when he got out—and this was the only way he could be sure she'd come back to him.

"He was going to fly down to Palm Beach after I abducted the kid and he was going to step in and negotiate with me. Then he would put up the money, pay me the ransom, and get the kid back for her . . . show her he was smarter than the cops."

"And be her hero," Frank interjected, nodding to himself.

"I think you've got it." Slades sat back in his chair, picking at a tooth with his fingernail.

"Not yet," Frank responded. "How was this supposed to work, Slades? How did he think he was going to get away with it?"

"He said he had it all figured out. He said the dumb cops would be no problem. All I had to do was hold the boy and make the calls. The first day I was supposed to demand fifty thousand dollars. Then I had to call again the next day and ask for a hundred, and then . . ."

"Come on, come on, Slades."

"Hundred was it. Then he said he would be there and he'd negotiate with me and he'd give me a couple of different phone numbers where to reach him, so that the cops couldn't bug all the phones. Then he planned on losing the cops and making the switch. I would hand over the kid. And he was going to hand over the money."

"Why did you send the pornographic video and the note? Was that Haley's idea?"

"That was mine. I thought it would drive her loony . . . and confuse the cops. They wouldn't know who they were looking for. A kidnapper or a . . . a . . ."

"Or a filthy, dirty pedophile." Frank supplied the description and then got to his feet again. "So, how did Marina Dee Haley figure in all this, Slades?"

Frank noticed Slades running his tongue round his mouth—and the beads of sweat forming on his forehead.

There was an anticipatory silence in the room.

"Are you sure you can't find me a smoke?"

"Just get on with it," Frank told him.

He ran his tongue around his lips again. "I told Haley I needed money up front. I knew he was good for it. He said he couldn't do that. He laughed at me. He said: What do you want me to do? Call my attorney and ask him to write you a check?

"He was very careful about the whole thing. He said he

was going to make sure that there wasn't one bit of evidence linking him to me. He didn't even give me Fitzgerald's address. He said: 'You're on your own. I've given you the names and the area.' He meant Florida. That's it."

Frank shook his head. "Marina Dee Haley, Slades? What happened with her?"

Droplets of sweat trickled down the side of Slades's face and fell onto the table. "Okay, I'm coming to it. When I told Haley that there was no way I could do the job without some cash up front, he finally agreed there was one way he could get me five grand."

"Five?" Frank's eyes narrowed, and he felt his pulse pounding.

"Five." Slades nodded. "He said his mother had always kept some heavy bread in the house. He said I should get into the house and take the cash and keep my thieving hands off everything else. He said it would be easy getting into the house, and that his mother kept a large sum of cash stashed away in her den, hidden in the same place for as long as he could remember. He even drew me a little diagram of the place, and which doors were likely to be open, and where the cash was, on exactly which shelf."

"You have that diagram, Slades?" Guy Lewis asked the question.

Slades shook his head, causing more drops of sweat to fall to the table. "No, he took it back after I'd looked at it. Like I said, he wasn't going to leave any paper trail."

"Go on."

"Well, that's how it happened." Slades shrugged. "I got it all sussed out. I waited for the staff to leave the house for the evening. I watched for the lights to go out in the den, and then I watched Haley's mother go to the pool, which was perfect because the back door was unlocked and all I needed was like three minutes to get in, get the money, and get out."

Another droplet of sweat fell on the table. "I should have just left by the front door after I got the money, but I couldn't be sure that I wouldn't be seen, and I didn't know if the front door was on an alarm. So I just got ready to sneak out the back again. And she must have forgotten something or . . . maybe she just needed to piss." He paused and shrugged, wiping his forehead with the back of his hand. "Anyway, I walked out of the back door and there she was coming back up the pathway, she hadn't even been in the pool."

"So you just struck her down?" Guy Lewis put the question simply.

Slades was shaking his head, the droplets of sweat pooling rapidly in front of him. "She wouldn't let go. She grabbed me, and I pushed her back . . . I just wanted her to let go of me . . ."

Frank paced across the room and back again. He glanced across at Guy Lewis. The prosecutor didn't look happy. Evidently he was sizing up Slades's credibility. How would he look on a witness stand up against Jeff Haley if there was no tangible evidence to link the two men?

But Frank was not about to let go. He believed the story. The abduction plot had Haley's perversity written all over it. Sure, he'd wanted to show Kitty how dumb the cops were. How dumb Detective Frank Maguire was, in particular.

"Haley told you where to find the money. You wouldn't have known where to look otherwise, would you, Slades? Haley told you to break in and steal the money and Marina's murder was an accident as a result of his incitement. That's what you're saying, isn't it?"

"I guess," Slades mumbled.

Frank glanced across at Guy Lewis, raising an eyebrow. Then he turned back to Slades. "Did you have any contact with Haley in Palm Beach after you failed to snatch Jamie Fitzgerald?"

"Just once. There was a bar near the airport where I met him when he arrived in Palm Beach. But when he found out about the screw-up he told me to get lost. I said I could still do the job and that I was right on it. I followed

Fitzgerald that night even though he called me a fuck-up and said I'd done enough damage. He wouldn't give me another cent, either."

"What did he say about his mother? Didn't he call you a fuck-up for killing his mother?"

Slades shook his head. "He asked me if she put up a fight. And I told him, yes. Then he laughed and said: 'I was going to warn you about her but you took care of it just fine.'"

"You took care of it? As if he had expected it?"

Slades shrugged. "He wasn't grieved, anyways. He said he'd just lost five years of his own life because of the bitch."

Frank nodded. "Did he say what he meant by that?"

"No."

"Did you see or hear from him again?"

Slades nodded. "He called me the following night and said if I wanted to earn a few bucks he needed me to break in to Fitzgerald's house and clear out everything I could find which belonged to the boy. Which I did. He gave me a couple of hundred for that. And then again, a couple of days later, he told me to stage a fender-bender at that Sands shopping plaza."

Frank stared hard at Slades. "What did you do with Jamie Fitzgerald's things? Did you hand them over to Haley?"

"No. He told me to put them in a couple of black trash bags and carry them across the street to a house, which he said was empty. He said to just dump them in the shrubbery. He would take care of the bags later."

The house, Frank thought. The house across the cul-de-sac. Good angle for the pictures he'd seen. He felt his heart thudding, and he beckoned for Guy Lewis to follow him outside the room.

"I bet you we can link that house to Haley. There'll be a paper trail on that, all right."

Lewis looked uncertain.

Frank nodded firmly. "If Slades was acting alone, how

would he know about the house?" Frank paused and pushed the envelope from the *Mail* into Lewis's hands. "Take a look at these. Haley had private detectives taking photos from this house. Who do you think paid for the rental?" He paused. "Either way, whether he or the agency paid, we can link it back to Haley. And maybe if we find the bags there we'll get his prints off them. Guy, it's all there. You heard him yourself. He sent Slades into that house knowing Marina was there, hoping she'd get in the way. He wanted her dead."

Guy Lewis cracked a smile for the first time that evening. First time that year, maybe, thought Frank. "Detective, you can't charge a man with wishful thinking."

Frank pursed his lips as the assistant state's attorney surveyed the contents of the envelope. Then Guy Lewis nodded curtly. "Okay. Bring in Haley."

❧ *Chapter* 54 ❧

*H*e said nothing as he sped down North Ocean Boulevard, but he allowed himself to savor the moment that lay ahead of him. It was over. Haley would be in custody before the night was over. Then Frank would get a court order to dig up Marina's pool.

His pulse raced as he walked across the gravel to the front door. Getting no answer to the doorbell, he walked around to the side of the house. Haley was in, he was sure. He could see the garage doors open and Haley's red Mustang standing inside the garage. All the lights were on in the house. Boldly, Frank walked through the garage and opened the door leading into the house.

"Haley!" he shouted, stepping down the narrow hallway leading to the entrance foyer.

He glanced upward at the staircase. "Haley! Come on down! It's Frank Maguire. We need to talk."

The house seemed quiet, with an empty feel to it. Frank sighed and beckoned the uniformed officers, who had followed him, to start looking through the house.

He followed at a slower pace, glancing into the living room, then into the den.

He stopped in the den doorway. What the hell was this? he wondered. The room was set up for some kind of service. Maybe a quiet memorial service for Marina. Too late, pal, he thought, walking to the stairs.

He followed the second-floor hallway to what he remembered had been the master bedroom. No doubt Haley had already moved in there.

A uniformed officer was opening closet doors. "Think he's hiding in the closet, Sommers?" Frank asked, only half-joking.

"No sir," the patrolman replied stiffly. "It doesn't look like he's here but if this is his bedroom he sure has a weird taste in clothes."

Frank strode across the room and peered into the closet, raising his eyebrow at the sight of the dresses and outfits that hung on the rail. He noticed the price tags. Then glancing at the floor he spotted the bag.

He stared at the tote that looked so much like the one Kitty carried everywhere, and for one heart-stopping moment he thought it was hers. He nudged the bag with his toe and then crouched down to look inside.

It *was* Kitty's tote. He recognized some of the junk she insisted on carrying with her—legal pads, her makeup case, her hairbrush, cellular phone—and the small blue yo-yo he had fixed for Jamie.

His heart slammed against his rib cage. Kitty never went anywhere without the tote.

"Sommers, check every room up here, okay?" he directed the patrolman, then took the cellular out of the bag and dialed information, asking for Angela Baines's phone number. He stared at the tote lying at his feet as he made a note of the number. Kitty was supposed to be at a party. *What happened here, Kitty?*

But he knew. We tipped the bastard off, he thought. We asked him about Slades. The psychopath had been tipped off and now he had Kitty.

He stared blankly at Kitty's cellular as he punched out
Angela's number.

Don, accompanied by two uniformed officers, stood at
the door of the Palm Glades house across the street from
Kitty Fitzgerald's home. He had rung the doorbell twice.
There was no answer and he didn't really expect one.
There were no lights on in the house and no sounds from
inside. He had checked the door that led into the garage
from the courtyard and it had opened easily. There had
been no vehicles in the garage, either.

"Okay, let's move in." He beckoned to one of the uniformed police officers to get the door just as the patrolman's walkie-talkie crackled in the quiet courtyard.

Don heard the instructions to call his partner and,
cursing under his breath and hoping there was no last-
minute hitch, retraced his steps to the car. He picked up
his cellular and dialed the number he'd been given.

"Don?" He heard Frank's voice answer on the first ring.
"Did you get to the house yet?"

"Sure did and we've just gained entry. Or we're about
to. . . . It's the one, for sure. Place is in total darkness."

There was a strange silence on the other end. "There's
no one there?"

Don walked back up the path and saw the door standing
open. "No. I didn't think there was supposed to be. What's
going on, Frank?"

"Listen to this," Frank cut in sharply. "Haley has gone
and it looks like he took Kitty with him. I just got off the
phone with her friend. Jamie and the friend's son, Alex
Baines, are missing, too." Don heard the strain in his partner's voice. "Haley was with the boys this afternoon.
We've got a very bad situation on our hands here, and I'm
going to stay on the line while you go through that house."

Don didn't have to ask for any further explanation as he
moved to the open doorway.

"Okay," he spoke into the phone. "I'm inside the house
now . . . moving through the foyer . . . into the master bed-

room. Like I said, Frank, there doesn't appear to be a single soul in here," he added, then grimaced at his choice of words.

There was no response at the other end. He stepped into the bedroom, casting his flashlight over the room.

He walked across the wood floor to the bathroom and switched on the light over the sinks. It cast an eerie glow into the empty bedroom. "There isn't even any furniture in here." He spoke again to his partner as he looked around.

"Check the closets, Don." Frank's voice sounded hoarse.

Don swung the flashlight over the room, spotted the closet door next to the bathroom. He walked over to it and flung it open, staring into the blackness of what appeared to be a walk-in.

He stared for a few moments longer. It was empty except for something lying on the floor. It looked like a heap of clothing covered by a quilt or bedcover of some kind. "Uh ... I think I've found the stuff stolen from Kitty's son." He crouched in the closet doorway. "Yep, this is it. I can see a pair of shoes ..."

Don pulled at the quilt and uncovered the mound. He stared hard at the weird shape that lay on the floor, and then realized what he was looking at. They were lying back to back. Two small bodies, their heads and backs touching. . . . He leaned forward and over them.

"Frank!" He heard the hoarseness in his own voice. "I've found the two boys."

Chapter 55

*F*or the first time that evening Kitty felt afraid for herself. Jeff had not said more than a half-dozen words to her since taking away her gun in his bedroom. He had stopped laughing while he had replaced the bullets in the .38. Then, pointing the gun at her, he had told her to walk downstairs to her car.

She had wanted to put on her clothes, but he'd refused to let her do it. He'd forced her instead to get into the passenger seat of the Blazer while he took the wheel, driving with one hand, holding the gun to her head with the other.

It had been a very short drive, no more than a few blocks across the North End to the Sailfish Club on North Lake Way. He had gripped her arm painfully, forcing her along the piers until they reached the *MaraLar*. She had stumbled and bruised her ankle in the darkness and she was soaked from the rain by the time they reached the boat. But Jeff didn't notice her discomfort.

"Magnificent, isn't she?" Jeff had said, looking at the cutter-rigged vessel in the water. "I had her taken out of dry dock and spruced up to be all ready for our trip. I think you'll love this boat, Kitty. It was custom-built and rigged for single-handing."

It was a big boat, maybe some fifty or so feet. Kitty had stepped aboard eagerly, believing that she would find Jamie and Alex.

Now she realized she was wrong. There was no one else on the boat. Just herself and Jeff, staring at each other in silence across the main salon, Jeff still pointing the gun at her. One soft light illuminated the cabin. Jeff stood near the companionway, adjacent to the galley. She sat on the edge of the settee bunk, listening to the lapping of the water against the side of the boat. It was the only sound that broke the eerie midnight silence. She measured the distance between them. She glanced at her car keys lying on the galley counter where Jeff had thrown them. But there was no way she could get past him. ...

She did not have a single clue as to what was going on in Jeff's head. She did not even know if she could get through to him. But she knew she had to try.

"Jeff, why don't you put down the gun? I know you're not going to use it on me."

"Really?" He laughed out loud. "You were going to use it on me."

She shook her head. "I was angry. You've got Jamie and Alex. Can you imagine what that's doing to me? How that hurts?"

He nodded. "Of course I can imagine. I know what hurt is. God do I!"

He leaned back and Kitty could see he looked tired—and sad.

"You don't want to kill me, Jeff. I know that."

"You're right, Kitty. The only good thing about killing you would be getting custody of Jamie. I'd have no problem with that, I'm sure. But Godammit!" He broke off and slammed the gun against a cabinet in the galley. "Godammit! I want you, too."

He straightened up and brought the gun back to point in

her direction. "I'm not a quitter. You know that, Kitty. I didn't quit on Marina. I could have walked out on her, years ago. I should have left after she humiliated me in front of so many people. Telling me on network TV that I was a bastard. I was going to run away but I stuck it out, and I made her happy, in the end.

"Same with you, Kitty. I knew from the first time I saw you that you'd be hard work, but I was ready. I knew I could please you. I knew I could make you happy. But then every time I got close, you'd slap me back. Both you and Marina let me down so badly in the end."

"Why did Marina let you down, Jeff?" Kitty asked, hoping he would keep talking. Maybe she could divert his attention. But she wasn't sure if Jeff had heard her question. He was going back to the night of the shooting.

"Remember the night you threw me out of the apartment for sorting out the mess on your desk . . . the night I went back and shot Larry Davenport? Do you know what I thought in the second just before I pulled the trigger? I thought to myself: 'Jeff, if you kill this drunken pig, and get into trouble, Kitty will feel guilty, and she'll take you back.' I thought I'd worked it all out in that second, Kitty. I thought Marina would be grateful, too.

"But no." He laughed shrilly. "No, she wasn't grateful. Not when she ran down here to hide and I ran down to see her. She was so mad at me. I said, 'But, Marina, it was an accident. That's all you have to tell them. Remember Larry attacked me and threw that heavy crystal glass into my face and then he came at me with that big chunk of broken glass? He was going to kill me. What else could I do? That's all you've got to tell the grand jury.' " Jeff hung his head. "That's all she had to do, Kitty. That's all. The cops saw the broken glass. All she had to do was tell them my story."

Kitty swallowed nervously. "Your story? Why wouldn't she tell it, Jeff?"

He started to laugh. "She wouldn't lie, Kitty. Can you believe it? This woman who lived a lie most of her life said to me, 'Jeffie, I'm not going to lie again.' Then she laughed at me. 'Don't be silly, Jeff. Who would believe that? Larry was stone blind drunk. I don't think he even saw you. He stumbled and tripped and smashed the glass when he fell. And I'm not going to cover for you again, no matter how grateful I am that he's out of my life'—" Jeff broke off, his eyes glazed as if they were reading Marina's words off the wall behind her.

Kitty stared at him, horrified, as he slumped momentarily against the galley counter. Jeff had killed his stepfather in cold blood. She remembered Frank's observation—it seemed years ago—at Marina's house. "What did she mean, 'I'm not going to cover for you again'?"

Jeff's eyes focused on her as he waved the gun above his head in a dismissive gesture. "That's another story, Kitty." She bit the inside of her lip as he took a step toward her. "All I know is that everything is such a struggle for me. I'm so God damn tired of chasing dreams, Kitty. I killed Davenport and you took me back, and I made everything all right for you, didn't I, Kitty? And then you did it again. You turned your back on me. You moved twelve hundred miles away and met some dumb cop. And I tried to kill myself over you and that dumb cop."

Kitty stared in disbelief. "You knew about Frank when you were in jail? How?"

She saw the flicker of a smile on Jeff's lips. "Smart, aren't I, Kitty?" The flicker died. "How do you think I knew? I made it my business to find out. I knew you had to be screwing around with someone. So I got Gates to hire a private dick." He paused and laughed. "Oh, yes. I knew what you were doing every night. It cost me ten thousand dollars Kitty. That was the rental for the house across the cul-de-sac. The landlord wouldn't rent it for less than six months but I got my money's worth."

Kitty felt her heart thudding hard against her chest and hoped that Jeff couldn't see the emotion reflected in her face. He'd rented the house across the street. For six months. When? Was it possible he still had access to it? Was it possible that's where he'd taken the boys?

"It's a painful story, isn't it, Kitty?" Jeff's words interrupted her racing thoughts, evidently misunderstanding the look on her face.

She nodded unhappily. "So now you're punishing me, aren't you? Jeff, tell me what I can do. Just don't hurt the boys."

"I don't know anymore. I know I can't make you love me but I can't let you go back to him. I want you too much, Kitty, and I've wanted you too long. I just can't let go." His voice rose to a painful pitch.

"You have to let go, Jeff," she said, her throat tightening as she reached for one of the thin silky straps of her nightgown, slipping it off her shoulder. She closed her eyes for a second, focusing on her only thought: She had to get off the boat. She had to find the boys.

She sensed Jeff moving toward her. "Don't make fun of me, Kitty," he said coldly. When she looked again, he was no more than a foot away from her, the gun still aimed at her.

"I'm not doing that." The coldness in her voice matched his. "You keep telling me you want me. That you must have me. I want you to tell me why. Think about it." She reached for the other strap, slipped it off and let the nightgown fall to the floor. "Look at me, I'm not the most beautiful woman in the world. Think about it, Jeff. There're a million women out there and I'm not the pick of the litter."

She watched his eyes sweeping over her nakedness and heard his shallow breathing. "You *think* you want me, that's all. And you want to know why? Because it's never happened for us, that's why. You always want what you can't have. Don't you know that?" Her voice dropped to a calm whisper. "Jeff . . . maybe you've held onto the dream too long. Come on, I think it's time to put that dream to rest."

She watched as he moved to her with a bemused look on his face. Then he reached for her hand.

She saw the half-smile appear on his lips. "Kitty, you're nervous. Your palms are sweating."

Of course I'm nervous, she thought. I'm going to get one shot at this and I've never tried it before. Aloud, she laughed softly. "Of course I'm nervous. You've still got the gun in your hand."

He inched closer. "How can you say you're not the pick of the litter? You're beautiful, Kitty. Come here." He tugged at her hand, drawing her against his chest. She eased her body into his, gritting her teeth as his mouth nuzzled her neck. Then she brought her lips closer to his ear.

"Put the gun down, Jeff," she said spitting each word out so harshly and forcefully that she felt his momentary recoil, but the split second of confusion was all the time she needed to bring her knee up into his groin with all the force and anger she could muster.

She saw the stunned expression on his face, and heard the shriek of pain as he bent over double. She brought her knee up again, catching him under the jaw before pushing him back, away from her, to send him writhing on the floor. She saw the gun fly out of his hand. She thought it had landed on the bunk—but she couldn't stop to look for it. In one swift movement she snatched up her nightgown and propelled herself through the air, leaping over him, tearing for the stairs, scooping up her car keys from the counter where he'd dropped them. Then she took the stairs two at a time and ran across the deck, stumbling in the dark as she jumped and landed on the dock. She looked back momentarily but saw no movement on the boat. Slipping the nightgown over her head, she ran toward the Blazer.

Chapter 56

*T*he rain started again as she passed the Boynton Beach exit on the interstate but she did not slow down. She kept her foot on the gas, at a steady eighty, praying for a patrol car to come up behind her, lights flashing. The clock on the dashboard told her it was coming up to one o'clock in the morning, and she saw nothing in her rearview mirror. She wished she had her cellular phone with her. She wouldn't be wasting precious minutes now if she could alert someone to go to the empty house.

The rain had turned into a torrent when she made her final turn toward the gatehouse, just in time to see the back of an EMS vehicle shoot through in front of her. An instinctive dread seized her. And instead of stopping at the gatehouse to speak to the security guard she shot through, chasing after the ambulance, knowing that it was heading for her cul-de-sac.

As she turned into her street, her heart lurched in her chest. Outside the house, which Jeff had described to her, she saw a half-dozen vehicles: police patrol cars with their lights flashing silently, a couple of station wagons, and Frank's Thunderbird.

She slammed the gear into Park and stumbled out of the Blazer into the rain. Oblivious to her bare feet and flimsy nightgown she raced through the courtyard gates.

The front door stood ajar and she saw a group of people milling inside the house. She pushed her way in, ignoring a uniformed cop who tried to stop her.

"Frank!" Her scream echoed through the house.

She ran to the master bedroom and stopped in the doorway when she finally caught sight of him. He was kneeling in the middle of the floor beside a coverlet that looked like the one that had been stolen from Jamie's bed. Then she saw her son's little blonde head, with a darker head nestling beside it. The boys were lying side by side, their eyes closed.

Her scream echoed through the house. Instantly Frank was beside her, holding her in his arms. "It's okay, Kitty. It's okay. The boys are okay. But you? Kitty . . ."

She heard the words "okay. The boys are okay," and she slumped against Frank's chest, her body rattling with cold and pain, her hair plastered to her head.

"Jeff did this," she whispered hoarsely. "He's on his boat, Frank. You have to pick him up. It's the *MaraLar* at the Sailfish Club."

Frank Maguire stepped into the foyer but returned within a moment to take off his jacket and throw it around her shoulders. She flung herself to where the two little bodies lay on the floor, gripping each boy's hand tightly in hers.

The hands felt warm. She held Jamie's fingers to her lips.

Frank knelt down beside her. "They're sleeping. Soundly."

"Did you call Angela?"

"Of course. She should be here any minute."

Kitty caressed Jamie's fingers in her hand and leaned over to feel the warmth of his face against hers.

"Are they going to be okay?"

Frank nodded. "The EMS guys checked them out. All the vital signs are good. There was probably a mild sedative in their juice. But there's nothing else wrong with them that we can see, although I know the paramedics would like to get them to the hospital."

Kitty gripped her son's fingers. "Come on, Jamie, come on, sweets," she whispered. "Wake up. Open your eyes." She caressed her son's cheek and shook him lightly by the shoulder. He stirred, but his eyes remained closed.

She looked up at Frank. "I don't want him in the hospital. I want him with me. I want him to wake up at home. If there's nothing wrong with him, he's staying with me." She paused, her eyes filling with tears. "And with you, Frank, okay?"

She turned her attention back to her son until, aware of movement behind her, she looked up to see that Angela had arrived. She hugged her friend as Angela dropped down on the floor beside her. They held onto each other.

"They're going to be okay, Ange," Kitty whispered. She looked for Frank. "If you get someone to help Angela with Alex, maybe then you can help me carry Jamie across the street to bed. I'm going to take him home now."

She kissed Frank lightly on the lips. "How did you get here, anyway? How did you know?"

"Long story," Frank grinned. "But Slades confessed."

Kitty gasped. "You got Slades?"

Frank nodded. "And he gave us Haley. They were involved together in everything, Kit. Oh, you don't know the half of it. We got a warrant for Haley's arrest and I went to the house." He paused. "And Don came here."

Kitty gestured impatiently at Jamie. Later there would be time to hear the rest. For now she wanted her son tucked safely into her bed. "Come on, let's get him home."

She straightened up as Frank lifted Jamie gently but firmly. Together, they walked across the cul-de-sac to Kitty's house. She led the way, opened the door, switched on lights, and finally tucked her son into her bed. She put her arms around him and hugged him, kissing his face and his eyes. She thought she saw his eyelids flicker. But still they didn't open.

When she looked up she saw that Don had followed Frank into the house, and the two men were standing in the doorway together.

Frank looked grim. "The word from Palm Beach is that Haley's not on the boat."

"Not on the *MaraLar*?" Kitty stared at both men, puzzled. "Did anyone check the house? He could have gotten back to the house. It's not so far. He could have walked to it in a matter of minutes."

"No," Frank shook his head. "They haven't checked the house yet but they're on their way over." He frowned. "I'm sure they'll get him. . . ." He hesitated, and Kitty felt he was torn between going back to Palm Beach and staying with her.

She followed the two detectives out of the house and into the cul-de-sac. Frank stopped beside Don's car.

"If you feel you should go—" she began, but Frank stopped her, shaking his head.

"Haley's not going anywhere," he said grimly. "I'd like to be there but it's not necessary. They'll probably have him by the time I get there, anyway." He motioned for Don to move. "Go on, call me when you've got the bastard."

Then he turned back to her, rumpling her wet hair. "Come on, let's move the Blazer out of the street. Where are the keys?"

For a moment, she couldn't think where she'd put them, but opening the car door she realized they were still in the ignition. She slid into the driver's seat, waving off Frank's offer to drive into the garage. "I think I can manage this," she smiled, waiting for him to jump in next to her just as a fresh torrent of rain hit the windshield.

She pulled slowly into the garage and slammed the gear into Park. As she did so she heard the garage door closing behind her.

For a moment, she thought Frank had hit the remote. Then she saw the flurry of movement. In the next second both she and Frank saw Jeff emerge from the shadows behind a stack of boxes she had stored beside the hot water tank.

She felt the prickle of the hairs on the back of her neck and head as her whole body stiffened.

"Sunuvabitch," she heard Frank mutter under his breath, and she realized that, like her, Frank had seen the gun in Jeff's hand. She was rooted in her seat, unable to move as Jeff took a step toward Frank's side of the car, motioning for him to raise his hands.

Jeff said nothing for a moment, but stood staring at them through the open passenger-side window. Then he raised the gun to Frank's head.

"Come on, Kitty. Switch off the engine and tell your boyfriend to get out of the car."

"Listen, Haley, there's no way you can get out of this. Don't be stupid about it." Incredibly, to her ears, Frank's voice sounded firm and calm.

"Stupid!" Jeff laughed shrilly. "No, I'm not the stupid one." He looked over at Kitty, beckoning to her with the gun. "Come on, Kitty, be a good girl, tell this dumb cop to get out of the car or I'll put the bullet through his head right now."

She couldn't move. She couldn't speak. All she could do was stare in horror.

"You heard me, Kitty. It's really me. You're not imagining this—or dreaming it. You don't have much of a punch in those sweet, delicate knees. How long did you think it would take me to get back to my car? Now please, Kitty, switch that damn engine off."

She sat, still unable to move, his laugh chilling her.

"Very clever, Haley." Frank's words cut through the laughter. "But why don't you hand that gun over to me? There's a police patrol car in the cul-de-sac. There's an APB out on your red Mustang. You don't have a prayer."

Jeff smirked. "My Mustang is parked two streets away.

You think the stupid cops are going to think of looking there?" He paused, and his eyes narrowed. "Okay, enough chit-chat. Maguire, get out of this fucking car, and get up against the wall, over there, in front of the headlights. I want Kitty to have a ringside view."

Kitty could hardly breathe, horror-struck that Frank was opening the door and getting out of the Blazer. He had to be hoping that she would help in some way. She had to do something. She tried to think of what she could do to divert Jeff's attention ... to give Frank a chance.

She wanted to reach forward, switch off the car lights, and plunge the garage into darkness as Jeff nudged Frank to step in front of the Blazer. But her fingers wouldn't move and there was a strange haze in front of her eyes.

In the next second, the haze cleared as she saw another movement to her left. She blinked back the wetness in her eyes as the garage door from the house opened wider and she saw Jamie standing, hovering uncertainly and drowsily, in the doorway. She saw him stepping forward, into the garage.

"Noooooo! Jamie!" The scream sprang to her lips in the same moment that Frank threw himself at her son, covering him with his body, using the force of his movement to push them both back across the threshold.

She took in the scene as if she was a spectator in a theater: She looked from the doorway to Jeff, who was pointing the gun at the tangle of the two bodies. She saw the momentary hesitation in his eyes and the confusion and uncertainty on his face as he looked back at her, his expression caught in perfect focus by the glare of the headlights.

And then, her hands finally moved; jerking upward, as if in a spasm, she grabbed the gear lever, threw it into Drive, and floored the gas pedal. She saw the confused look in Jeff's eyes change to one of horror in the split second before she hit him.

She closed her eyes as the car jolted forward and slammed him into the wall.

❧ *Chapter 57* ❧

Sunday, September 17

*K*itty woke out of a deep sleep to hear the phone ringing. Reaching for it, she glanced at the bedside alarm clock. It was 12:52. But the sun was streaming in through the half-drawn drapes.

12:52! Almost one o'clock in the afternoon!

She sat up abruptly, hearing Todd's gravelly voice on the other end. "Hey, Fitzgerald, what's going on down there? We just got word that Jeff Haley is dead. Killed in some sort of car accident. Do you know what's happening?"

"Give me a minute, Todd. You woke me." Kitty looked across the bed to check on the little head burrowed under the sheets. She leaned over and reassured by her son's even, steady breathing slid out from under the covers with the remote in her hand.

"So, what do you know about it, Fitzgerald? Nothing, I suppose, since you're still in bed."

Todd sounded impatient and irritable. As if he'd been awakened himself.

She blinked to clear the nightmare images that flooded into her head: Jumping out of the Blazer as the engine died, she had not looked to the spot where Jeff had been standing. All she had cared about was getting to Jamie, to get him out of the way without frightening him. It had been difficult to control her trembling limbs and body.

Later, when the police and the EMS staff had gone, Frank had come to tell her that Jeff was dead.

"It was instant, Kitty," he'd told her, and she had not questioned him on it.

Now, through the half-drawn drapes, she saw Frank, already outside, standing by the edge of the pool, pushing the vacuum hose across the bottom. The pool didn't need cleaning. She could tell his thoughts were elsewhere.

"Hey, are you there?"

She cleared her throat. "I'll check it out, Todd."

"Yeah, you get on it, Fitzgerald. If there's something in it, I'm going to need it for tomorrow's show. I've got holes to plug all over the place. You wouldn't believe the things that have gone wrong this week."

For me too, she wanted to say, and stifled a sudden urge to laugh out loud.

"Oh, and talking of plugging holes, where the hell is that story on the bisexual attorney who got slashed?"

"That story isn't going to work, Todd."

"I'll take it the way it is, Kitty. I'm desperate. What's not going to work about it?"

She took a deep breath. "I'm not going to send it."

There was a silence on the line and she jumped in, taking another deep breath. "I'm not going to send it because there're two little boys involved. The attorney's kids. Two little kids whose hearts are going to break if we air that story. I don't think—"

"You don't think! That's obvious." Todd exploded, cutting her off in midsentence. "What the hell are you talking about, Fitzgerald? I . . ." His words trailed away.

It was the first time she'd ever heard Todd at a loss for words and it lasted only a couple of seconds. Then he came back at her. "I've never heard anything like it. Jesus! There's always effing someone, kids, mothers, brothers, sisters. If you take that attitude you may as well quit."

She stared into the phone, shaking her head. "Oh, chill out, Todd. This is not brain surgery, you know." She hung up on him, but carried the remote with her when she stepped outside through the sliding glass doors.

Frank's face lit up when he saw her. "Is Jamie awake, too?" he called from the other side of the pool, laying aside the pool vacuum and coming around to hug her. "I found some baby frogs in the pool. I put them in a bucket for him."

"I think he's going to sleep all day. I would have, too, if Todd hadn't woken me."

Frank shook his head. "What did he want?"

"Oh, the usual," she laughed, sinking down on the chaise and placing the phone on the table beside her. Todd would certainly call back within the half-hour. "The news about Jeff is out already," she added.

Frank nodded. "Don't tell me. He wants the story with reenactment."

"Don't." Kitty shivered, and suddenly her eyes were brimming with tears. She turned away but Frank cupped her chin and forced her to look at him.

"Kitty, there was no other way out."

The tears rolled down her cheeks and spilled onto the seat. "I killed him, Frank."

"He was going to kill you and me."

"But not Jamie. He hesistated, Frank. I saw the hesitation in his eyes and then he turned to look at me, and I knew he was going to shoot me. He didn't want to but I knew. . . . I realize it's idiotic but I feel sorry for him. His mother was—"

Frank shook his head. "Stop right there, Kitty. Don't bring his mother into it. I know it's fashionable to blame mother, father . . . whomever the shoe fits. But I don't want to hear that. Jeff Haley was a bad person."

Kitty wiped her face with the back of her hand. "He was sick. He was mixed up."

Frank shook his head again. "He was definitely sick. But mixed up? I don't know about that. He planned Jamie's abduction. He was going to put you through days of hell." He broke off for a moment to walk through into the kitchen. Whe he returned he was holding two mugs of coffee. He handed one to Kitty and sat down on the chaise beside her.

"He planned it and plotted it all, Kitty. Very thoroughly and meticulously. He took Jamie and Alex and left them in a goddamn closet! I don't care how his mother treated him. He knew exactly what he was doing. He killed his father, too."

"I know." Kitty picked up her mug of coffee and sipped the hot liquid. "He told me it wasn't accidental. He said his mother wouldn't testify. You were right about him."

Frank nodded and grinned. "Of course I was. But I meant . . . he killed his real father."

Kitty sighed, leaned back in the chaise, and closed her eyes. She didn't want to hear any more about Jeff Haley for the moment. But Frank hadn't finished.

"What are you going to do about the money?"

"The money?" She paused, then brought her hands to her mouth. "Oh, my God. The Haley estate! And Jamie's the beneficiary!"

She glanced at Frank and shook her head. "I don't know what I can do."

She saw a smile playing on his lips. "I don't know, either. Jamie's the beneficiary, and if you're mentioned at all in the will it'll be as a property guardian. If you're not then a court will have to appoint one. But I'm willing to bet there's no way you'll be allowed to just give away your son's inheritance."

"You mean we're stuck with the money?"

They looked at each other, and Kitty wondered if her expression looked as ridiculous as the expression on Frank's face.

The ringing of the phone cut through the silence in the courtyard.

It was Todd. Of course. "Hey, Fitzgerald, I take all that back. You're not going to quit, are you?"

She winked at Frank and slipped her hand under his T-shirt to caress his bare chest. "I don't know, Todd. I'm just working out my finances."

There was no response at the other end, as if Todd was trying to figure out if she was serious, and she bit the inside of her lip to stop herself from laughing.

Then she heard him chortle on the other end. "Yeah, very funny, Fitzgerald. Take thirty seconds and call me back."

She felt Frank's arm around her shoulder and his fingers caressing the hollow of her neck. His lips nuzzled her left ear. She snuggled down, laying her head on Frank's chest. "No, Todd. After that I'm going to take care of some overdue personal business. I've had a very busy couple of weeks."

"Hey, Fitzgerald—"

"Bye, Todd, and don't bother calling back . . . I'm taking the phone off the hook," she added, breaking the connection.

Frank laughed beside her. "Nice idea, but that's not going to discourage him. Here, give me that damn thing. I want to take my time on this personal business."

He took the phone gently from her hand and then flung it into the pool.

THE BEST OF FORGE

☐ 53441-7   CAT ON A BLUE MONDAY $4.99
Carole Nelson Douglas   Canada $5.99

☐ 53538-3   CITY OF WIDOWS $4.99
Loren Estleman   Canada $5.99

☐ 51092-5   THE CUTTING HOURS $4.99
Julia Grice   Canada $5.99

☐ 55043-9   FALSE PROMISES $5.99
Ralph Arnote   Canada $6.99

☐ 52074-2   GRASS KINGDOM $5.99
Jory Sherman   Canada $6.99

☐ 51703-2   IRENE'S LAST WALTZ $4.99
Carole Nelson Douglas   Canada $6.99

Buy them at your local bookstore or use this handy coupon:
Clip and mail this page with your order.

Publishers Book and Audio Mailing Service
P.O. Box 120159, Staten Island, NY 10312-0004

Please send me the book(s) I have checked above. I am enclosing $_____
(Please add $1.50 for the first book, and $.50 for each additional book to cover
postage and handling. Send check or money order only—no CODs.)

Name_____

Address _____

City _____ State / Zip _____

Please allow six weeks for delivery. Prices subject to change without notice.

THE BEST OF FORGE

☐ 55052-8   LITERARY REFLECTIONS $5.99
          James Michener   Canada $6.99

☐ 52046-7   A MEMBER OF THE FAMILY $5.99
          Nick Vasile   Canada $6.99

☐ 52288-5   WINNER TAKE ALL $5.99
          Sean Flannery   Canada $6.99

☐ 58193-8   PATH OF THE SUN $4.99
          Al Dempsey   Canada $5.99

☐ 51380-0   WHEN SHE WAS BAD $5.99
          Ron Faust   Canada $6.99

☐ 52145-5   ZERO COUPON $5.99
          Paul Erdman   Canada $6.99

Buy them at your local bookstore or use this handy coupon:
Clip and mail this page with your order.

Publishers Book and Audio Mailing Service
P.O. Box 120159, Staten Island, NY 10312-0004

Please send me the book(s) I have checked above. I am enclosing $ _____
(Please add $1.50 for the first book, and $.50 for each additional book to cover
postage and handling. Send check or money order only— no CODs.)

Name _____
Address _____
City _____ State / Zip _____
Please allow six weeks for delivery. Prices subject to change without notice.